Craig W Thomas

Big School

Inside Corner Books

First published by Inside Corner Books Ltd 2005
Inside Corner Books Ltd
19 The Hollins
Holloway
Derbyshire
DE4 5BA
Email: insidecorner@tiscali.co.uk
Webpage: www.insidecornerbooks.com

© C.W.Thomas 2005

All rights reserved. No part of this publication may be reproduced, stored in a retrieval system, or transmitted, in any form or by any means, mechanical, photocopying, recording or otherwise, without the prior permission of the copyright holder.

ISBN 0-9549672-1-6

Printed by Juma, Trafalgar Works, Wellington Street, Sheffield, S1 4HD

The Author

This is Craig W Thomas's third book. The first, Losing My Religion, an autobiographical football fan addiction story, was published by Juma in 2002; his second, Roads to Redemption – A Guide to Major League Baseball, was published in the spring of 2005. Craig spent twenty-four years teaching in various secondary schools in the London Borough of Bromley and Derbyshire, and is now recovering. He lives in Derbyshire.

All the characters in Big School are fictitious.

Peregrine Lane Grammar School, Yarrow Staff List 2002-3

Peter Precision - Chair of Governors
Michael Peniston - Headteacher
Elaine Checkman - Deputy Head Pastoral Care/Biology
Malcolm Went - Deputy Head Curriculum/DT
Molly Factor - Senior Teacher/Maths
Susan Climer - acting dep head/head of English

Maurice Butter - Head of Maths
Will Tick - Maths/Head of Y10
Jack Rush - Maths
Carol-Anne Angel - Maths
Annalie Towers - Maths
Bob Whizzby - Maths
Charles Dejong - Maths

Susan Climes - Head of English
Sefton Demmler - English
Narida Harrington - English
Alex Carfman - English
Fiona Twyford-Sounding - English
Liam O'Neil-Neil - English
Jezebel Treat - English
Dr Tim Weaver - English

Colin Mouse - Head of IT
Derek Presario - IT
Callum D. Writer - IT

Angela King - Head of History
Andy Crucial - History
Nathan Byas - History
Mahandra Bharakangford - History

Simon Cupboard - Head of Geography
Glynis Mapp - Geography
Emma Lake - Geography, Head of Lower School
Misty Wellbrowser - Geography

Trevor Money - Business Studies
William Banks - Business Studies
Colin Nostrum - Sociology
Milton Davis - Sociology

Sid Lemon - Head of Design Technology
Les Person - DT
Rob Rodder - DT
Linty Marbsford - Food Technology
Sandy McDiver - Food Technology
Daphne Cloth - Textiles
Worth Reynolds - Textiles

Joanna Singer - Head of Music
Jamie Nice - Music
Alana Lush - Music/Head of Year 9

Hetty Kiss - i/c Drama
Livvy Lovejohn - Drama
Boris Fairbanks - Drama/Head of 6th Form

Lulu Panton - Head of Art
Angelica Burgoigne - Art
Mura Fleece-Ravings - Art

Alice Vashnikov - Head of German
Andrew Millibandon - German
Jolyon Preefer - German

Pierre Legume - Head of French
Chris Lampeter - French
Safety Harmiss - French

Jack Bracksher - Head of Spanish
Dainty McFormage - Spanish
Mariana Spooley - Spanish

Andy Chap - Head of Boys PE
Bobby Coulson - PE
Pete Tracker - PE
Mick Trance - PE
Maggie Tripper - Head of Girls PE
Sally Foam - PE (girlfriend of Liam)
Angela Bellingham - PE/Head of Y7

Dr James James-James - Head of Science
Jeff Bunsen - Chemistry
Lionel Waft - Chemistry/Head of Y11
Jeff Loin - Biology
Tamsin Cell - Biology
Alice Sinclair - Biology
Chris Craft - Physics
Chris Barton-Jones - Physics
John Speckle - Physics/Head of Y8

Alun Christian-Grieves - Head of RE
Abdul Raza - RE
Jane Fairey - RE

Jesse Frump - School Secretary
Maisey Rankster - Secretarial
Pearl Driss - Secretarial
Merton Alibhati - Reprographics
Tom Reaks - Caretaker
Alf Stretchley - Assistant Caretaker
Doris Manicure - Tea lady

Thelma Heffley - Head of Special Needs
Suzanna Smith – Special Needs
Barbara Lint - School Nurse
Crief Caniacincth - Nurse's assistant
Dorothy Dancer - Chief Hygiene Officer

1
The Gatekeepers of Knowledge
Autumn Term - Week 1 Day 1
Monday, September 2nd, 2002
The Peregrine Lane Grammar School, Yarrow, Staff room - Morning

Even now my stomach turns to a fast stream surging down my colon when I think back to my first day at Peggy Lane. It was predictably a Monday, but the ground zero of standing before my first class of school children was mercifully 24 hours away. Meanwhile, a day of introductions and meetings waited for me. A single reflection on the whole enterprise produced a cold, clammy ghost trying to climb into my shirt, then a monster in the shadows waiting to stalk me endlessly down dark corridors and musty classrooms, torturing me until I could take no more.

I'm an English teacher. How could you tell.

At 8.18.am on Day One I pulled my front door shut behind me and crossed the street to the bus stop in front of the The Flying Bucket. A minute later and I would have missed the 419 that began its valley descent high up in the village of Holmes Farne bound inexorably for Yarrow, but there it was, just 400 yards away from easing to a stop in response to my outstretched arm. When it came I paid my money and found a seat near the front. It was nearly empty this morning. Before I began to feel my stomach aching with adrenalin and hunger we stopped again by a farm. An old man with a flat cap and a bursting girth cheerily boarded.

"'ey oop, Fred," said the driver.

"'Frank," he replied, nodding as he watched the driver bang the buttons which swiftly coughed up a curly white ticket. "Quiet, this mornin'."

"Won't be tomorrer, it'll be full o' kids again."

"Oh, bloody 'ell," replied Fred. He was a shouter. You could have heard him on the back seat through a Walkperson. He was still chortling as he half-walked, half-shuffled down the bus a few feet and dumped his bulk into the seat one row in front of mine across the aisle. I watched him and briefly compared his life to mine. Poor bastard. He looked, if his personal hygiene and his clothes were any guide, as though he had no money, no family and no friends. Not in the modern sense anyway. His most important possessions would be rheumatism, diabetes and the nagging threat of Parkinson's and Alzheimer's. Mind you, he wasn't facing my death sentence, I'd give him that.

Outside the window, green fields soaked and shining in silver dew, drifted up to a skyline of sweet-looking hills as we rattled down some of the prettiest country lanes anyone like you or me can imagine. All very restful and lovely when you haven't got a feeling of looming dread upon you. I hadn't slept well overnight. Every two minutes, so it seemed to me, my subconscious would douse my unconscious awake with a measure of iced water, causing me to writhe helplessly in fragments of miserable thought: 'what on earth are you doing, thinking you could be a teacher?...a role model, a life enhancer, a...' God, what did the advert say? - 'a window-opener?'

I was already showered, dressed and pacing up and down the living room by the time I heard my radio alarm kick in upstairs. And now the bus took me unstoppably to destiny. Teacher? I'd take 'survivor' to start with and move on from there. To avoid getting battered and humiliated by the youth of Great Britain was all I asked.

And to fit in.

Too soon we rumbled across the tiny suspension bridge over the river Whardle that meandered along feeling pretty pleased with itself each day, and slowly negotiated town streets clogged up with getting-to-work traffic. As we pulled up at the bus terminal beside the railway station, I let the fat man hoist himself to his swollen feet so he could get out in front of me. It was the least I could do.

"Thank-yer very mooch, yoong mun," he said, smiling at me kindly. I sort of winced back and followed him at a half a mile an hour to the door and waited for him to plop down the bus steps, holding on to the rail for dear life as he shambled his way on to the street. But an arm came out to help him from the pavement.

"Coom on, Dad, ye'er alright."

"Thanks, loov."

"Grandad!"

"'ello, me darlin' 'ow are you this lovely day?"

"Fine, Grandad."

"No school today, eh?"

"Not 'til tomorrer - 'ooray!"

"Oh, bloody 'ell," said Grandad, and they all laughed.

"Coom on, you lot: antie Jean'll have the bacon on by now. It'll be burnt if we don't gerra move on."

On the West Yorkshire Council application form I was 'Dr. Timothy Weaver, PhD' but what did I really know about anything?

Looking both ways carefully so I didn't actually die or put myself in a wheelchair for the rest of my life on my very first day, I skipped across the road now worried about being late. At the hairdresser's on the corner I turned into the school road. Before you made the short tramp up to the gate you had no choice, if you were new to the journey, to look up at the high horizon and the outcrop of huge boulders there. The moor was the only factor in the town's small fame - until the events of autumn 2002 at Peggy Lane drew the media up here like a kid sucking melted ice cream up a straw that is - and I duly elevated my gaze. The game September sun was gently warming the rocks and heather already turned purple. So it was official now: I'd arrived in the north.

The fast-approaching red and gold signboard at the school entrance announces *The Peregrine Lane Grammar School (est. 1847)* to the visitor, but it's 'Pegs' or 'Peggeh Lairn' to the locals in an accent you could bottle and sell at a craft fair. It proudly resides in the town of Yarrow in Yorkshire - to you? somewhere above Leeds. You probably won't know Yorkshire: the biggest county in England but practically unknown to the English. It's a pretty cool place to those in the know. There are prettier market towns in the area, especially if you venture further into the wild and woolly northlands of the kingdom, that sit among steeper green hills that rest above them like piles of green rumpled duvets. And sure, they have prouder little market squares too, boasting snug little buildings of rustic stone and hanging baskets of cheering flowers singing in the breeze. But all of them have fine Yorkshire beer and the best fish and chips England can offer, and that, as everyone should know, means the whole world. All-in-all, fair the town of Yarrow is, nestling and until this juncture in the space-time continuum, dozing in peace in its allotted hollow in the landscape. And right now here it was with me in it.

It would have been doing just that the day, months earlier, I, miles off in a far southern distance, saw an advert for an English job at 'a traditional, highly successful 11-18 comprehensive with a strong commitment to academic standards' in the *Times Educational Supplement* (teachers job Bible, out every Friday, £1.20). I'd done a little research and had it confirmed that the title 'Grammar School' was just a smokescreen: a desperate clutching to the past and proven attractor to local middle class parents in Guiseley, Keighley and sundry other outlying districts. The school was over-subscribed every year without fail.

This was exactly what I wanted to hear. I wanted a place where the kids knew how to behave and weren't likely to treat me to a Christmas nervous breakdown. Look, I'll admit it: I wasn't brave and I wasn't a crusader. I just wanted a safe job in teaching, and 'Grammar School' said all I needed to know in that respect. The imperious-sounding 'Peregrine' and haughty 'Grammar' probably conjured frightening images of Oxbridge entry and the cane for the others out there like me scouring the country for work. But I'd seen all that as a braided-blazered schoolboy so I wasn't put off. And besides, we'd had a motivation specialist come and talk to us one slow college afternoon, so I knew not to be scared by the intimidating propaganda of schools desperate to attract the best unused material out there in the land of the greenhorn trainee. So what was there to lose? I applied, and shock, I damn well got me the position.

The nervous ache was still goose-stepping on my stomach lining as I crossed Moor Lane at pace now, almost losing one side of my body to one of those dreadful 4x4 four cow-crushers in the process but finally, I made it. Peggy Lane's faux-gothic tower of blackened stone stood defiantly in the climbing sun looking down at me. 'Weaver,' it said, 'come in here if you must, but mind yourself and no lip!'

Accepting that, I crossed the threshold.

I followed a number of fellows and females through the entrance hall and we all made a right turn to see a whole bunch of staff just twenty feet away up some steps milling around the staff room door looking relaxed, the long summer holiday still clinging to them. They looked as though they all belonged properly and thoroughly to the old place, and the image made something inside tug at me hard. If I could only just be a part of this. The thought quickly had company though, a sibling that crept out of a black hole in the mind, talking to the outsider again: 'what on earth are *you* doing here?' it said.

"Ah, Tim: Hi."

Susan, my head of English – my head of faculty, in fact, had spotted and remembered me. Rescued me.

"Come through..." she said, smiling.

And from that moment, I think, I was a member of staff at Peggy Lane.

The staff room was more cramped than I remembered it from my interview. It had seemed enormous then, but it was almost empty when they traipsed us through as part of the traditional interviewee tour. The odd head turned to peer at a bunch of callow, stupid-looking hopefuls, four of the five of us predestined to be cast out as failures, and then quickly went back to conversations, marking and photocopiers. Now it was crammed to bursting with The Staff, almost all in mufti and making a racket. The walls were a sickly light green, but at least there were notice boards everywhere to minimize the damage that might have otherwise been inflicted on everyone. In one corner those bulletins and notes not pinned properly, flapped in the 8.40.am breeze from a fan that whizzed round on a nearby table. It was going to be warm later on. As if reading my mind, a woman who looked old enough to be my grandmother, but who was clearly still teaching, began opening a window down the far end as I looked for a place to put myself.

Susan ushered me to an orange ten quid sofa - more a padded bench actually - just to the left inside the door, where five of us had to cram ten buttocks into a space meant for six. This was our domain - the English Faculty - for meetings such as these; we and one or two refugees from other faculties who sat here every morning break and lunchtime, and couldn't bring themselves to depart from habit, not even once a year.

Snatches of conversation surrounded but didn't include me, concerning just-taken vacations and school stuff that sailed way over my head like the balls Babe Ruth used to smash out of baseball stadiums:

"...I thought Palm Springs was in Florida!"

"...have you seen the new school PANDA?"

"...you should see the baseline data for my Year 10s, Christ!"

"...that new Head of Year: gorgeous, I'm telling you,"

"...and we saw Rupert Castle Donington-Thali mime a one-man version of *Macbeth* at the Fringe - it was fabulous!"

"He can go and f-fuck himself with a b-bat handle for all I care," said a man with an accent that immediately took you to the bars and backstreets of some southern Irish town. He saw me looking as well as listening and inspected me as if I might be a patch of mould on an old piece of cheese before changing it to a short grin without an agenda. I nodded and smiled back. There was some hope of conversation here at least, but not yet, for the crowd noise had already fallen away. I followed the swiveling bodies and bug-eyed expressions that were now fixing themselves on a man in a sharp navy suit standing by the coffee hatch flanked by a couple of minders also in formal attire. Even I knew who this was: the headmaster, a man with whom I had at least one point of common connection: he was a new boy just like me.

He surveyed the crowd with an expectancy that was mutual. The air was so taut you could have cut it with foam rubber. He waited for the last buzz of conversation to die away with a smile that was open and hopeful, but one that had a back note of concern about the possibility of his inadvertently depositing a brown brick into the seat of his expensive trousers. This gave us all the chance to give him a good once-over even before he started to speak.

He wasn't that tall and he wasn't that slim. His light, finger-combed hair that had been blatantly cut for the occasion came forward with every sign of continuing thickness.

"Hello, everyone," he said, "I'm Michael Peniston..."

He took a time-out to give the whole room a good appraisal again, as if he'd been well-trained for this specific occasion.

"...and I want to welcome you to the start of another new year at Peggy...I mean..."

He had to wait while half a dozen people laughed, some surprisingly enthusiastically.

"...The *Peregrine Lane* Grammar School."

And then he grinned and took in some giggling from a colleague-cum-minion in the front row just in front of him, before being forced to keep us waiting even longer: he was distracted by the woman at the hatch in a lemon housecoat putting out a row of cups and saucers and making too much of a rattle as she made her line. She looked up to see that the whole room was suspended on a wave of frustrated anticipation on her account and looked completely put out. She didn't '*tut*' but instead fixed her new boss with a beady eye and stopped work.

"Thank you very much, Mrs. Manicure," said Michael, and cast his eyes to the heavens this time, as if to say, 'too much like hard work this headmastering lark.' This got another laugh. Then at last he leveled his gaze on us again, and set off for real.

"It's a wonderful thing to be given this opportunity. To be placed in charge of such a fine school is a great honour - a scenario I am looking forward to tremendously."

This was not the impression I'd got from the local rag, where he had openly expressed his displeasure with the school's current situation. I can't recall the exact words, but it went something like this: 'we're in the crap house, we're falling behind most of the rest of the schools in the county and I'm going to kick some butt to put it right.' We were probably going to get the same thing here, only the long version.

"However, those of you who have read last week's *Yarrow and Oatley Examiner*..."

Another pause.

"...will know that we have a lot of serious work to do to turn the school around."

No laughter this time.

He began to unreel the big speech, one he'd probably fretted and fussed over for weeks, and I tried to set my concentration level on full so I could begin to bed into the place. But the controls didn't want to function. There was just too much competition for too little oxygen in my blood. My new colleagues were spread out all around me for silent perusal and sly analysis, and I still wanted to question the whole point of me being right here in this room, at this time. I could still skip the country if that's what I really wanted.

I tried closing my eyes to see what that would do and heard the hum of my internal mechanism, the machine that could never be switched off, churning out the same old slop. I was getting a lecture. 'Uh-uh, not this time you don't, buster: you're going through with this so accept it, sit there and *listen!*' I opened my eyes again and came back into the room.

"Having spent much of the summer looking at the full range of cohort data," Michael was saying gravely, when I suddenly noticed the Irishman smiling at my lack of attention. He gave me a wink before turning towards Michael again.

"...the figures from the past five years are eating holes in our key stage 2 performance levels, pouring custard into our values in Y9 SATS on top of GCSE sauce..."

The rest of the assembled multitude may have been reveling in Michael's fluent educationese, but for all I knew he might have been trying to sell me a bag of carrots. Fuzzy buzzwords were flying around the room like a squadron of angry war planes. I listened harder, hoping that things would straighten out but new phrases were trying to choke me in a jargon blanket. I yawned to find I was dog tired even though it wasn't even nine o'clock. I started drifting away again into a fog.

'Face it, Weaver, you've always hated headmasters.'

Baldy Haldey was my first of several. Back then I was in England still. Haldey was as tall as a building, essentially an alien from a weird planet in a far distant solar system and armed with the power to kill. When you'd done something wrong he stared at you with a raised eyebrow over a beady right eye that made him look like a demented crow. No wonder I was frightened of him. I was eleven years of age when he changed my life for good. It began when in one of Ernie Veal's boring Geography lessons I decided to amuse my ego. I wiggled my forefinger through my open trouser-fly at as many of my neighbours as would pay due court to this magnificent display of high comedy. It got a lot of laughs. Ernie, short-sighted and comically old, thought they were for him and smiled with his narrow eyes at the wall at the back of the room. He then paced way past me up the centre aisle, so unless he had eyes in the back of his grey head, I had free reign. My counterfeit wizzer wiggled again and I pushed my little groin in and out this time, causing the laughter to increase. Ernie had sensed that something was amiss.

"Stop that talking!" he barked.

In the quiet I carried on, keen to put in one encore at the very least, when something made me check the large pane of glass in the door. The Face of Doom was staring in at me as if I'd committed murder - which I probably had in his malevolent eyes. My insides melted and my forehead burst into a shower of sweat while I sat ramrod straight in my chair, now trying to do an impression of the best behaved student in history. I looked over at the window when I dared to - about three minutes later: the face had gone. There then followed fifteen minutes of shocking inner turmoil as I waited for the bell. Would stopping me in my tracks have been enough for him? A few moments after the infernal *drrri-innng!* ceased, Veal let us go and I shuffled out to the doorway hoping with all my might for a complete absence of headmasters. But there he was. He drew me aside as a mob of blazers poured through the corridor heading for their next lesson.

"Name?"

"T-Tim, sir." I felt my knees banging together like two parts of a foundry steam hammer. Brave I never have been and never was.

"Tim, what?"

"Eh, er, W-W-Weaver, sir."

"So, Mr. Weaver, what were you doing in there, exactly?"

That was enough. My lip wobbled and my eyes bubbled up with salty liquid. I couldn't answer. I just looked up at my headmaster and shook my head, lost and humiliated in front of about twenty young herberts who'd stayed on in the corridor to see what Haldey would do to his latest victim. He stared at me long enough to know he'd done sufficient damage to my psyche, before turning for the stairs, gown flapping, calling over his shoulder as he departed,

"School detention. See Mr. Challenger at the end of the day."

And that was my showbiz career up the chimney. Strange how we used to do impressions of his manic stare and laugh at the old git, but he bestrode our puny lives like a colossus. He was a God controlling our destinies with the twitch of a few facial muscles. I don't think I ever really recovered from the finger wiggling incident. Something I should have taken through my teenage years, something good, was robbed from me in that corridor.

'Was Michael Peniston going to be a God to Peggy Lane kids?' I wondered, as a late wasp hovered twitchily by an open window having saluted a strand or two of ivy. He certainly didn't look frightening, just smooth and professional, streaming on effortlessly in this foreign language.

"...be accessing to the full, the new streams of government fundament now flowing into schools with arses this size."

He actually was like Haldey in one way: he made me feel like an inferior being. It could never be me up there. I almost guffawed out loud at the very idea: Dr. Timothy Vespasian Weaver, headmaster of a secondary school. If I ever made it to Michael's age I wouldn't look like this: fresh, forty and fucking ready for anything. I couldn't see myself dressing like that either. Whoever made his pristine, glossy outer covering had clothed someone to look more like a barrister than a teacher. And the tie was of a deep crimson depth that would have sat well upon an up-and-coming junior minister's shirt. I liked to watch *Newsday* with the sound down late at night so I knew what those dudes looked like. And even if Michael spent more time in front of a mirror than was good for him, he had to be a better bet than old Baldy Haldey, who even ten years ago was an embarrassing throwback with his bad brown shoes and two pound-fifty comb-over.

Mr. P. was smoothing his way through his oration now, words flowing into the air like miraculous jelly. I summoned up every ounce of waking energy I had; this stuff had to be good for me so I'd better start trying to catch on...

"..Key Stage 3 Average of 5.5 is not sufficient for a school with our socio-economic profile, especially in the current nudist. With the government breathing down our necks I want us to be pushing the envelope wherever we can....."

"Which reminds me: I've got a couple of letters to post, f-huh-huh."

We were packed in so close together I couldn't help but hear that. The comedian was sitting to my left in a rickety armchair behind the door: a guy, late-thirties maybe, with wiry, russet hair and an unkempt moustache that went out of fashion in the 60s and wasn't coming back. His laugh sounded like someone trying to turn over a rusty engine. He looked at me looking at him and raised his eyebrows in a 'hello' that said, 'it's okay mate, we're both on the same side - trust me.' I wasn't sure whether to disapprove of his cheek or not. Then before Michael had finished another paragraph, another aside wrecked what was left of my concentration. This time it was my new Irish colleague.

"Sef, you're m-missing 21st century m-man."

He was whispering to a very late arrival who'd just squeezed through the crowd and sat down on the bench to my right where a space had magically opened up for him. He was in the wrong place. He was too stylish to be a teacher, with his expensive black t-shirt, perfectly faded Levi's and an ancient denim jacket Elvis himself might have owned. The cropped hair on a balding head looked so good I almost wanted to start pulling my own out in lumps, while the tan and overwhelming sense of quiet assurance said 'Italian film director'. He was me at 55 in my dreams.

Damn! Strike three. He caught me staring and returned it with a rapid flash of mesmeric steely blue. He then swiveled his gaze elsewhere as if I wasn't worth the bother. Or maybe he was just ticking me off for gawping at him like he was some kind of zoo creature. Or maybe my nerves were making me paranoid. I rejoined my new boss.

"...and of course, the A level results this year mean that those challenges are to be made into a warm, crusty bedpan in time for October half term."

As the clock moved past nine and the sun moved past the limbering up stage, the air really began to close in. I loosened another shirt button. Some of those around me looked less and less engaged as the minutes containing Michael's big opening performance slipped by. A dapper man in a bow-tie to my left who looked like a local art critic yawned with great care, while an asparagus-thin middle aged fellow opposite looked ready to give his right nostril a really good rake with his left index finger but, it seemed to me, remembering where he was, decided to defer the pleasure. In front of me a woman with a distracting figure reached up to open one of the higher windows. The sound of birdsong drifted in to us and a car changed down a gear in the distance to climb a hill. I tried not to look as a pair of bare brown legs lengthened with the long stretch upwards to get the catch, but if I'm honest, I deliberately didn't put in enough effort. The resulting look the film director shot me tore into my soul and almost caused me to lose the will to carry on right there and then. Suddenly, hitching a ride on Michael's drone became a very comforting alternative.

"...So we need to initiate a more organized flatulence procedure. I have asked Susan Climer to take on a new role, as head of Assessment, Recording and Peanut Stamps in addition to her responsibilities as head of the English faculty..."

Whoah! Susan moving up in the world, good for her. She was sitting directly across from me under a window and had coloured slightly at the mention of her advancement. She was immaculately dressed today, where almost everyone else was in casuals, in a classic power ensemble: black suit, black tights and black shoes with a big heel. The jacket was slightly too big for her, but still. She would probably divest herself of the costume and shove her body into a pair of jeans and a loose sweater within three seconds of shutting the front door, but she still got my vote for professional effort. 'Something you could learn from, Weaver,' I mused.

Michael had that 'I'm coming to the end of my speech' tone in his voice now. *Come on, Tim, concentrate now or you'll miss something really important and regret it later...*

"So it's become clear to me," he said, pausing for big effect, "that what the school badly needs is..."

He stopped, hoping the build up of tension and subsequent release would leave his big message of the morning imprinted on our minds for all time.

"...a vision!"

The response was probably not what Michael had intended. Had the school employed an artist-in-residence at that point in time, they might have drawn a blank face on a big white piece of paper. The boss carried on anyway.

"What that 'vision' should be for Peggy Lane I'm not exactly sure, but I want to build that vision with you in the coming term, so that by Christmas..." Another stage pause: "...we know clearly and precisely where it is we're going as a school."

"Well, I didn't think you meant as a tractor, f-huh-huh," said the ginger moustache, grinning. He seemed so pleased with himself, but so vulnerable at the same time that I decided I couldn't dislike him.

"An integrated part of the plan..."

Now there came a '*tut*' from the direction of the faded Levi's. This was fair enough; Michael meant 'integral,' that was certain. Even I noticed that.

"...naturally, is the word, 'targets.' No longer can an organization like this get by without clear-sighted goals..."

"I'd go back to using wingers, meself, f-huh-huh," said the chuckling moustache.

"The scenario, then, is that the school *has* to look forward and outward to move onward."

"Poetry," said ginger, looking right at me now. I almost burst into laughter but held on. I looked back at Michael and it was clear that fortunately, he hadn't heard. He was much too deeply immersed in his own world, though he could hardly be blamed for that.

"I want to leave you with this: something I'd really like you to remember as you go through the term: we are all gatekeepers of knowledge. Let us open that gate to the best of our ability at all times."

And there he stopped for the last time but one, to see what effect his grandstand finish had had on his staff. There was a cough behind me that was neither polite nor redolent of illness, while a white butterfly flapped its gentle way into the room before deciding it didn't contain a large flowering bush and flitting out again into the mellow morning. Apart from that and someone sniffing, there was nothing to report. Maybe there was a certain density in the silence - maybe I imagined it.

"Okay. Thank you. Thank you for listening."

He strode back down the room and out through the door like visiting royalty. A crumpled looking managerial type I would later come to know as Malcolm then took us through the itinerary for the rest of Monday above a very low, murmuring chatter.

So that was the first part of my first day done. I was beginning to feel okay sitting there amongst my new colleagues, with my new boss having set out on the road to taking the school forward or skyward or whatever it was. But it could hardly be Michael's fault that I wasn't connected up yet to the new education practices sweeping the country; it was probably mine for being a 28 year old spoiled pseudo-American twerp with a bogus doctorate. But something there sparked me into life making me think, 'hey, maybe I can actually play a part in this.' If the kids don't take to me like undernourished lions falling on a side of warm meat, that is. And as long as someone sat me down pretty quickly and translated what Michael had said into English.

I was just trying to retrace the big end to his speech, something about Goalkeepers of the Flame, when I stood up with everyone else to stretch and maybe find someone to talk to when suddenly I saw her.

A real vision.

She'd been five feet away from me the whole time, two scrunched bodies to the right. She was small and young, with short dark spiky hair and eyes like big dabs of shiny chocolate. She was talking to Susan when suddenly her face became a smile. Inside my head whole cities collapsed in ruins and rivers of blood poured through huge clouds of angry dust. Almighty screaming broke out as a million coloured rockets crashed into the soft open sky. I was suddenly wide awake. I'd just seen Jez for the first time.

2
AWOL
Autumn Term - Week 1 Day 1
Monday, September 2nd, 2002
Yarrow Town Centre - Lunchtime

I felt an arm around my shoulder - a firm, bony one.

"What you need, dear boy, is a drink."

Now several things were odd about this. Firstly, no one - I don't think - had ever addressed me as 'dear boy' before, my appearance at large country houses having been limited by a high school baseball injury and several hundred other factors. Secondly, I hadn't imagined lunchtime drinking was something teachers went in for; I didn't fancy my chances of unraveling the deep mysteries of Billy the Shake's iambic pentameter to a GCSE class after a couple of pints any more than the Bard had written his stuff on absolute skinfuls, though knowing him...Thirdly, from what I'd seen of Sefton Demmler that morning, there seemed to be more chance of his slipping out of a hedge on Moor Lane and slitting my throat on my way back down to the bus station than his suggesting that we go socializing together.

'Dear Boy.' I liked that though, because I already liked Sefton. Wait: I lie. I was ready to like him if he gave me the opportunity. In the faculty meeting earlier he'd given the impression of being about as approachable as Prince Charles or Michael Jackson. He sat there beside Susan like someone sent down from the mountain of the Gods to observe human behaviour, knowing that his kind normally got much better assignments than this.

If his disdain was unforgivably disrespectful to the team - and it was, I guess - my inner workings were already making excuses for him. The principal one was the fact that after about a quarter of an hour, it was clear that the meeting was going to be about as interesting as televised chess. That was a precocious, or even plain stupid reaction though, for who was I to comment on what we should have been doing in a first-day meeting? This was my first work meeting of any kind. I hadn't done 'meetings' jobs before. They didn't go in for them at the jam factory, or if they did, I hadn't been significant enough to be included.

So I sat and tried to listen to Susan talking sensibly about 'development plans' and 'whole school policies,' but was more intent on sniffing the air and wondering how the room got to smell like a floor polish museum. Then I started to suss out my colleagues, hoping all the while that Susan wouldn't ask me anything. Seeing as I didn't know anything, however, I felt I was on pretty safe ground.

There were only eight of us around four desks pushed together; Peggy Lane wasn't that big a school. Susan at the head of the table and Sefton, who sat immediately to her right taken care of, sitting opposite me was the girl who likely as not would launch a thousand pointless daydreams into the air before the week was done. I was already falling for her completely; I'm not ashamed to admit it. Her name was Jezebel. 'Typical bloody English student's name,' I said to myself, but she looked so good I forgave her parents without a thought. She could be Jezebel for just as long as she damn well pleased, especially if I could get her to take some interest in me. She sat there so neatly, trying not to steal a look at her in her perfect biscuit-coloured sweat and silver earrings dangling down and dancing was like not looking at a bad road accident while driving through Nebraska.

I was careful not to overdo it though, and kept focusing some attention on the others. Next to Jez was the art dealer from the staff meeting, a smooth looking man with greying temples who actually appeared to be deadly serious about his dickie-bow and double-breasted blazer. This was Alex Carfman. His *Morning Telegraph* was probably an amulet to ward off the modern world. There was an outside chance that I'd see him with it later on in the staff room, hunched over the racing page wearing a look of haunted intensity on his face, but somehow I doubted it.

Next to Alex was the extravagantly arty-farty Narida Harrington. She must have been about 50 but she was decently preserved. In a loose purple top that spilled down over a long black skirt like boiling lava, and a whole market stall of bangles on her arms, she was only a headscarf shy of looking like your archetypal Brighton pier palm reader. 'Prone to exaggeratedly noisy orgasms, Watson,' I mused, not remotely trying to get sex off my mind.

Talking of which, bang opposite Susan was Fiona Twyford-Sounding - way out of my league as a person all round. She looked and sounded like the spelling should have been 'Pfyona' and can only have washed up in teaching because she'd wanted to be a model but Daddy, wanting her married off to the Liechtenstein royal family, hadn't allowed it. So she'd lowered herself to this profession as a form of revenge. Or maybe I'd just read too many cheap books. Her hair was the colour of hazelnut ice cream and it flowed down to her shoulders in casually perfect, sensuous waves. Yet she looked like one observation about Keats would wipe you under the table. Altogether I was about fit to fetch coffee and lunch for her, or carry her pencils, and absolutely nothing else.

Finally there was the Irishman, desperate to make any discussion point he could, the rangy, four-eyed, Liam O'Neil-Neil. I liked this guy straightaway. His eyes were like dancing leprechauns, I would tell you, if it didn't sound so patronizing. He was a mixture of academic and wasted heroin addict. Just something about his eyes told me he obviously knew how bad a hangover tasted in the mouth. Having spent most of my life as an in-and-out member of the Introverts Club, I was always drawn to people like Liam.

So that was it: add me and there you have The Peregrine Lane Grammar School Faculty of English for the academic year 2002-3.

"They sound like a right bunch of fuckin' dropouts," said my pal Muff at a later date and he was about right in a way. Throw me in as the latest addition and we were a *raight* collection of disparate individuals. What the team spirit was like I dreaded to think. I just hoped there were people in the room who would come to my aid if, or rather, when I required it. The last thing I needed was to land in a department full of turmoil. I'd seen one of those on my first practice and teaching properly there had been like trying to get a quiet shave at the battle of Stalingrad. However, having been around English students at University for seven years and knowing them, us, mostly to be groups of highly-strung luvvies, neo-toffs and badly wired-up weirdos, my hopes, for the time being anyway, had already begun to sink into the west. I consoled myself by sneaking furtive looks at Jezebel or Jez, as Susan was already calling her, and idly wondering what Fiona might be thinking about. Whatever it was, it couldn't be the content of this meeting, a dead loss for me particularly, consisting as it did mostly of evaluating the exam results of students I hadn't taught, discussing proposed new syllabuses I hadn't read and sorting out who was going to put up display work this term. It was hardly the stuff of dreams.

And so the long morning wore on.

It's funny how I was swept along with the day like a biscuit on a factory conveyor belt. Cover half of me with vanilla icing: English Faculty Meeting. Three chocolate buttons evenly spaced down the middle: Year Meeting in preparation for life as a Y9 form tutor. Final dusting of sugar: short meeting for Newly Qualified Teachers. Spewed out of room B6 into the corridor leading towards the school entrance at one o'clock I already felt part of the machine, so yeah, you could say I was ready for a drink.

Not that this would have remotely occurred to me without the impetus of the almighty Sefton. I was just pondering how I was going to make modern English poetry come alive for the Year 11 class I was inheriting next day when the aforementioned late-arriving, 30 carat misery bag, now beaming like a light bulb, began walking me out past the staff room towards the main entrance.

"Come on, let's get out of this fucking place," he said.

Emerging into determinedly bright sunshine, my stomach lurched downward like a bagged pheasant dropping out of the sky. Jez was right there, grinning a welcome to at least one of us, and looking as pleased as ninepence. Sef had already scooped her up.

"Sure, okay, yeah," I said.

"Liam's coming along too in a bit but he's got to go to the bank. We'll go in mine."

In a couple of minutes we were in downtown Yarrow, easing along the main street past a blaze of flower beds having a civic snooze amid the early lunchtime bustle. Soon we squeezed ourselves out of Sef's ancient blue MG Midget and into the long bar of a pub called The Bastard Farmer. I didn't need to get my wallet out of my pocket. The man from on high was already ordering from a familiar barman waving a big note while I was taking in the wooden beams and horse brasses soused in the aroma of about three hundred and fifty years of typically determined and reflective Yorkshire boozing.

"Well it is nice to have some young blood in the faculty," said Sef stripping the top off a tall glass of Guinness at a table by the door. The transformation from mystery to bonhomie was bewildering. He'd bought me a drink and insisted on it being a pint of the local bitter brew. I said I didn't really drink beer but he wasn't listening. I sipped politely and got a fine surprise - shit, that tasted good - and wondered whether he was winding me up with his use of 'young.' Screaming towards the near horizon of 30, I'd already got used to feeling like my youth was receding like the evening tide.

"We were tauld at college...."

"Stuff what they told you at, where was it..?"

"Sheffield."

"Sheff; I see; my dear girl, it's all ratatouille and bullshit. You've all been got at by the new Puritanism. 'You will have targets, you will give your students targets and you will keep them monitored at all times.' Actually, fascism is what it is."

"But at collidge..."

"Pray tell, my dear, have you any A levels?"

"Three, yeah." I was trying to suss out where she was from. Lancashire, I reckoned. The 'told' coming out as 'tauld' was the giveaway.

"Grades?"

"A's." 'Aires.' Bolton. I had a mate at University who came from Bolton called Sunny and it was the same voice only female.

"And elucidate further for us....ah, Christopher..." - a tall, dark-haired guy had joined us with a glass of what looked like cider - "...how did you come upon these precious awards?"

"'ard work for a start. And I loov'd English, o' course."

"Naturally; and did you require any...*targets* to reach the required standards?" He'd somehow extracted the word 'targets' from his mouth as if it had just enveloped a large turd instead of stout.

"Noah, I 'ad Mr. De Large and he joost inspired us in English and I 'ad reeyalleh good teachers for 'istreh and L*orr*." I just loved the sound that accent made.

"Exactly. The point is, you and Tim must do all you can to avoid all this tedious crap, or you'll end up sounding like a training film about the Inland Revenue, rather than an English teacher. Ay, Lamps?"

"Hi, Chris Lampeter," said the northern newcomer, shaking hands with Jez and me, shyly, almost reluctantly. He had a very friendly smile though.

God! To be sitting in a pub making new friends. This was nice. I didn't know about Jez: she seemed to lack confidence like Pavarotti lacked a square meal, but I needed people like Sef and Chris to look after me. The man they simply called 'Sef' - this to me was like calling Nelson Mandela, 'Oy Mandy!' - was completely mesmerizing, holding court with almost criminal ease. His voice hung on the air crushing the odour of faded fag smoke and the stale beer of ages. It was made of a sort of refined gravel, or barbed wire soaked for a very long time in Scotch whisky. Rich and penetrating it was, without being loud. Unlike the rest of us he was a southerner, some kind of Londoner to start with, possibly, but not a toff like Gielgud, more a working class guy, a Berkoff - one of those guys who within the screwed up British system have to forcibly morph their voice into a decent impersonation of the Queen to get on. I wondered whether this counted as rank hypocrisy, whilst noticing that Jez seemed to be coming under his spell too.

"But lewk, Sef…" she said, sipping lager neatly but still wiping her lips with the back of a slim, purple nail-polished hand. She was dazzlingly self-assured. If I'd known Sef's surname I'd have used that, not his first name and prefixed it with 'Mr.'

"…Yer might be right, but you doan't seem to realize what's goin' on in the reeyal world…" I nearly spat half my pint across the table, but held it back while hoping it didn't jet out of my nose. This was a sound tactic: I felt that Sef might have casually flicked me over his shoulder into the long line of liqueur bottles behind the bar if I spilled so much as one stray droplet of liquid on those clothes of his.

He noticed my discomfort and raised an inquisitive eyebrow in my direction.

"You okay?" he said, looking none too impressed. I nodded vigorously as if this happened to me all the time, a hereditary family affliction I nobly endured. Jez looked at me too with an expression of tepid amusement. There's nothing like appearing as though you'd come so far out of the back woods you'd never tasted alcohol before for impressing the woman of your dreams, I always think.

"'ow long is it since yew were at collidge?" Jez clearly didn't need me to be around to enjoy a good time; she was loving the cut and thrust of the argument.

"Seventy years," said Chris Lampeter, leaning over me to open a window.

Sef gave Chris a seriously 'fuck off' look that I didn't ever want to be on the end of - and now looked as if he might sink into a serious sulk. Outside, the sun was still trying to poke its way into the conversation and glinted off the chrome in the car park. Another late wasp hovered in through the window and body swerved past my glass in search of food.

Meanwhile, Jez moved up into brazen overdrive.

"We 'ave to mek our wair in a different world compared t' the one you were obviousleh brought oop in, me and Tim."

This was recognition I didn't expect. I was doing as much for this debate as Winston Churchill did for the first Beatles album.

"We need to know about student monitorin' and performance indicators and we need mentorin' properleh." Wow, Michael P. is going to love this girl.

"I suppose you kept an immaculate mark book on your teaching practices?" said Sef, taking another hefty draught of his beer and smacking his lips with pleasure.

"We doan't call 'em 'mark bewks' any more. Where 'ave you been? They're called 'teachin' files.'"

He threw back a contemptuous look which could have pulled an enemy fighter out of the sky, and looked ready next to unleash some machine gun fire in her direction, or at least tell her she'd be walking back to school and lucky to avoid being run over by a powder blue sports car on the way, but he sprang forward to the edge of his seat and let forth a volley of laughter so enthusiastic I had nearly five minutes to count his fillings.

"Now I don't know about the Trappist Timothy here, who'd better find his voice tonight if he doesn't want to be limp dog meat by 3.30 tomorrow afternoon, but you, young lady: *you* we might be able to make a teacher out of, ay, Lamps ?"

But Chris was looking over in the direction of the recently opened door and was already making ready to greet another newcomer and it wasn't Liam.

"Malcolm!" he said with some surprise and began to stand up. "Hi, I'll get you a drink."

"No, you won't." said Malcolm, the Deputy Head Pastoral of Peggy Lane. "You'll all go back into school now. I'm afraid the head wants to see you in his office."

I immediately looked down from Malcolm's sour, crumpled expression to the faces around our sunny table and noticed the dust motes drifting through the soft lunchtime air like tiny, lazy planets. They all looked troubled, with the exception of Sefton Demmler, whose eyes and mouth were homing in on the last splash of beer in the bottom of his straight glass. Though I couldn't know it then, there went the last drop of summer down the hatch, disappearing into the lonely God-knows-where of another English autumn. I wasn't to see Sefton Demmler laughing again like that for a very long time.

3
Bang to Rights
Autumn Term - Week 1 Day 1
Monday, September 2nd, 2002
Peggy Lane Headteacher's study - Early Afternoon

There's a saying my grandma often used when she was alive - I never heard her say it after she died, anyway - why eat broccoli when there's a shepherd's pie in the oven? Christ knows why I thought of it now, waiting on the corridor with the others to go into Michael's room, but I did. How could I transpose it? Why get caught down the pub on your first day when you could be sucking up to your boss as she shows you round the Audio-Visual resources cupboard?

Not clever. A severe-looking secretary who wouldn't see 50 again threw a disapproving look in our direction as she rustled past us in the doorway while we waited for the nod to troop into Michael's office. And before we knew what we were doing, we'd shuffled ourselves into a line of the lower ranks, waiting like kids for a shellacking. This would be the New Man sweeping clean. Had to be. Sef mind you, wasn't with us. He was leaning nonchalantly on the door frame as if he were posing for an album cover. 'Surely you'll be our leader under these circumstances,' I thought, and waited, ready to play the wide-eyed innocent for all it was worth.

Michael's office was a broad tube in shape and institutionally dingy. Up at the far end by his desk, a distance from the door, he finished a conversation with a man in a suit with an extravagantly long beard and came over to us. *Click-clack* went a guy in overalls outside the window hacking at some overgrown greenery. The suit and beard walked past us out of the room blanking all of us as he left apart from one.

"Sefton," he said, nodding. Sef, standing aside, gave him a cheerful look in response and returned the compliment.

"Dr. James-James," he replied, suddenly making an immensely grave face as he did so. He still didn't look remotely perturbed by any of this.

I looked around me as Michael collected his thoughts. A framed slogan on the wall said,

>"'Fail to Prepare, Prepare to Fail'
>Roy Keane'"

A football fan. Even I knew who Roy Keane was. Well then, this wasn't going to be so bad, was it? You couldn't follow football and not be reasonable about a bit of rule-breaking. The game was practically all about rule-breaking. Sef decided suddenly to be a good boy and came and stood with us.

Michael saw to it that his door was closed, then turned and surveyed us. A look of pain passed across his features - baby features, I noticed for the first time. His slightly plump, smooth cheeks were like rather tempting apples. Unless I was mistaken, and I easily could have been, he wanted to avoid the sergeant-major act, and was now scanning his mind for a more modern option.

We waited.

He looked at the carpet, a meager affair in prison grey with nasty red flecks, and plunged his hands down deep into his trouser pockets, ruining the line of that suit. There was a faint jingle of change, car parking cash, as he raised his head to our faces, still looking disturbed and doubtful. His eyes drifted warily to Sef's and rested there.

"There's a saying in my family," he began.

By Gumbo, it was going to be shepherd's pie!

"Don't eat the trifle if you can't whip the cream."

"W.H. Auden, headmaster?" said Sef, raising a pair of eyebrows at the speaker. The Demmler eyes were twinkling like angels dancing a can-can on the head of a pin; what front you could display if you were that old. Or if you just didn't care. If only I could deal with my mother like this.

"The scenario is simple: this is 2002; this..." he said, holding his right index finger in the air to make a 1, "...is the time."

Oh, okay.

"Time when The Peregrine Lane Grammar School finds its meter."

"Do you mean *métier*, headmaster?"

Michael blushed and his expression was that of a man who'd just sat down on the plane only to realize he'd left the back door open and a couple of dirty magazines on the kitchen table. I felt like we were all sinking steadily into the mire and began to wonder for the first time what subject Michael had his degree in. I tried to look at Jez, but she was right next to me in the line and my prime instincts said 'be as respectful as you can: keep looking at the boss.' But I caught a waft of her: she smelled like the first newly-minted morning of the rest of your life.

"Yes, yes..." Frantic nodding of the head from Michael, eager to seize the initiative again. "Yes of course. The time is now when this school is going to rise like..." Rio Ferdinand? I couldn't help inserting in my head.

"Well perhaps 'rise' is not quite the right image. But we must strive to improve. We must, we have to," he finished, emphatically, like a front door shutting on a Jehovah's Witness.

His face was now burning red, even with the window wide-open. The birdsong was loud and distracting, but wasn't going to stop just because Michael was making the second big speech of his new career at the top. He paced a couple of steps back up the tube towards his desk before turning and coming right back. It was agony to watch him trying to mine the correct words.

"To do that, I am not having my staff drinking at lunchtimes. I'm not having it on training days, I'm not having it on Mondays and I'm not having it on Tuesdays!"

Please, Sef, I've already got the next line right here in my head and I know you have it too: don't say it!

'Are you not going to be having it on Wednesdays as well, headmaster?'

I shut my eyes, cringing in a pool of embarrassment, waiting for the explosion but there was only dead air. The poor man's syntax had fallen apart like a cricket ball hitting a meringue. Perhaps out of sympathy, Sef decided to withdraw his tanks for a moment - unless he was simply waiting for the Boss to dig himself into an even deeper grave. But he knew right there and then - we all did – that he had Michael Peniston stone cold and that nothing he could ever say would alter this simple fact. All he had left were a couple of obvious verbal moves learned from mediocre television and Hollywood, unless he was going to quit while he was behind, which was unlikely if I knew headmasters. They do, don't they, always insist on having the final word.

'As an experienced member of staff, I expect you to set these new young teachers a better example, Mr. Demmler,' was favourite.

"As an experienced member of staff, Sefton, I thought you might have demonstrated better leadership skills." I missed by only a whisker.

The ingratiating use of the familiar first name made my teeth itch. It was a fair bet that the reply would run along the 'Do call me Sef, Michael,' or '*Mr. Demmler*, to you, headmaster' lines but I was getting ideas above my station. Neither did he produce an 'I just thought these young things are under so much pressure these days a small lunchtime libation might be good for their general well-being, Michael.'

Sef looked to be either on the verge of laughter or an explosion of insubordinatory anger which really would have taken the thing to Code Red, but he held it together like a Zen master and delivered a deft response.

"The thing is," he said, as he stroked his chin with a touch of regret, "I see myself as more of an Eric Cantona than a Bobby Charlton..." A pause to let this take effect. An unfortunate-looking hole was beginning to appear between Michael's top and bottom lips.

"...and I believe, Michael, that Cantona - and that's *Cantona* as in 'conundrum,' not *Cantona* as in 'canned meat' - is the possessor of rather more trophy winning medals than Sir Bobby. It was indeed *le francais extraordinaire*, who wrenched the fallen prestige of the great Manchester United from the ashes of mediocrity and launched them into the glorious skies like a soaring..."

Not phoenix, Sef, surely.

"...B-52 bomber."

I know I was only 28, but I had never seen an authority figure so utterly bereft of thunder. An hour or more seemed to pass before the now only nominal boss looked first at Chris, as the next most senior member of staff - a Lampeter who, in contrast, seemed uptight and discomforted by all this flibberdy-doo - then at Jez, then at me.

"Would you leave us, please?" he said, with as much dignity as he could scrape off the carpet.

And being well brought up and British, we dutifully trooped out.

*

Jez and I found ourselves more or less alone in one of the English classrooms in free time towards the end of the day. We were scooping up our handouts: schemes of work; a wad of summer exam results and a departmental handbook the size of an encyclopedia. Not forgetting our fat teaching files, a large hardbacked affair with thick purple covers, full of pages but all empty of information, waiting to be filled with lesson plans, names, scores, grades and ticks.

"Are yer always this quiet?" she said, hitching up a still immaculate sweatshirt sleeve. It was time to show her that my brain could indeed operate my mouth. I made one of those snorting sounds like a stroke from one of those South American percussion instruments, the precursor to a baby laugh,

"No. Not often, but sometimes. It depends."

"What's oop with yer then?"

"A lot to take in isn't there; a whole lot to think about. And I still haven't recovered from the scene in Michael's office."

"Me neither," she said. "*God,* I thought me bra was goin' ter burst!"

I clucked my tongue and tried to look composed. Whilst trying to get my brain into the recovery position, Jez took up the conversation.

"Soah where are you from, then? You talk like an American - but you're not though..."

"My mother's American. My dad was from Hull."

"Fisherman was he?"

"Paper clip salesman."

"Really?"

"No."

She laughed. *Phew.* She had a smile like something from an advert for one of those fake country restaurants. The ones they made to sell family warmth and homeliness. Only hers was the real thing.

"Soah, you can be funny. 'Oo'd ha' thought? Not sooch a dim Tim, are yer," she said, looking at me sideways.

"Oh, thanks. I had you down for a girl who loves a good wet t-shirt competition in Ibiza."

"Cheeky bastard!" She was smiling though and I'd gotten away with it. I didn't even know where the line came from. She was great - so down to earth, so northern. I was drawn to her helplessly, like a gnat to a podgy knee.

I wasn't so adept in these situations that I could be sure I could avoid coming on with all the sex-appeal of a Mormon dwarf with a cleft palette, but hey, this was good; here we were, talking. It was a start. I looked at my watch. It was gone half-past-three. Going home time - it said so on the handout we'd all been given while waiting for that staff meeting to begin. Christ, that seemed days ago now. I had to keep her chatting though if I could.

"You're from Bolton."

"'Ow do you noah that? Bury ackshelleh." It's a struggle to explain in words how she pronounced it, but it was spellbindingly good. Like honey dripping off the back of a spoon. You'd have to start with the B as in "B is for butter" like you'd do for a little kid, then the U was like a short grunt, then finally say "Red" to finish it, only leave off the D-sound. *Boo-reh.*

"I congratulairt yer for gettin' that. Moast people think ah'm from the moon, not Lancashire. And a lorrov 'em think ah'm thick."

"Don't worry about..." But she cut me off.

"What do yer think the Head did wi' Sef? Ah'm worried abowt 'im."

She looked down at her shoes with eyes standing out like Christmas baubles. I was capable of any amount of paranoid and immature responses. So she was going to fall in love with an older man, then. Typical. Unless he was...whoops, better answer...

"I think he's more than capable of handling himself; and what can a headmaster do? You have to do a lot in this job to get sacked. Sleep with a student, sell drugs to Year 7s..."

"Or drive yer car oaver one or soomthin'. Ah know. Job securiteh's one of the reasons ah'm 'ere."

We stepped through the school front door and walked out into sweet sunshine again, the day lengthening into a big, fat, golden Burgundy. I didn't want to let go of her but I had to make like I really was all grown-up and play some relationship poker.

"I think I need to find Susan before I go," I said, going for an unlikely but not impossible look of complete boredom on my features.

"Good idea. I was thinkin' the same. Let's try't staff room."

Oh, okay, then.

So we did and she was there, talking to a guy in a lab coat with bad skin and matching brown hair.

"...and when Jane and I got to Hammerfest we got to meet the mayor, and when we invited him to come and stay, he said he'd love to, so..."

She saw us and cut the fellow off faster than the tide at Morcambe Bay. Either she didn't like him or she still had a lot to do before she too could go home.

"You two, you'd better come and meet Jim - this is Jezebel Treat and Tim Weaver, our new NQTs..."

"Hello, Jim Bunsen...a chemist."

I was tempted to ask him for some sun cream. He meant he taught Chemistry.

"Hi! Nice to meet some more newly-qualifieds. If ever you need..."

"Sorry Jim, but I've got to give them some final instructions before tomorrow." And Susan, perspiring a little, marched us briskly back from whence we came, out into the corridor with a left turn thrown in. A few steps later she abruptly opened a door to an office - and shut said door behind us.

"Boris won't mind us coming in here for a minute. I think we need a chat before you go home. If you've both got time..."

Naturally we nodded like little oysters ready for a skip up the beach with the Walrus. Susan found us all chairs and stuck a very serious look on the pair of us. I tried not to look at her knees, the bone shining white against the material of black stocking legs, and studied her face instead. She scooped a flopping chunk of brown hair away from her right eye and tried to tuck it behind her ear. It had been a long day.

"I didn't want to have to say this, but in the light of what happened at lunchtime, I think I'd better."

I can take life being this interesting. Some people don't like conflict around them. I don't mind, as long as I'm not the one taking a whacking. Fortunately, I had a good idea here that Jez and me were considered too green to be about to get it in the neck.

"I know you're just out of your year's training, but even our teaching practice students know enough about the job not to go drinking at lunchtimes. And on your first day. I'm sorry, but I have to say I'm very disappointed in both of you."

It was my turn to feel the heat of embarrassment, and there it was at the back of my neck spreading up towards my ears like wet jam.

"Sorry, Susan; I just thought that it wouldn't be a bad thing to get to noah some of the English department a bit better. And I wasn't about to goah slinging pints down..."

Jez wasn't going to lose brownie points without a fight and Susan didn't seem at all displeased with Jez's attempt to talk her way out of trouble. Her pale blue eyes flicked quickly across in my direction as if expecting me to put up a defence of my own but I could only think about that lovely white Yorkshire head on my pint earlier. You couldn't get anything as good as that in Boston, great town though it is. I was finishing the day just as I started it: head in a whirl, a mind in there somewhere capable of doing a job if I could only find it. But I might already have blown it with Jez.

"And it's no use blaming Sefton Demmler. Strange as it may sound, I shall be looking to you two to set him a good example. It's one reason why I'm so pleased to have young teachers in the faculty. I really shouldn't be saying this, but I've been stuck with old staff in the department for too long. Set in their ways, men *and* women, same old staff room chairs, same old lessons - always moaning about anything new or different. But we got Liam in last year, and now we have you two, I'm pleased to say. I think Sef hates having young teachers around, but he's got to deal with it.

"And both of you need to get on the right side of the new head. Michael is going to be shaking up this school and taking things forward..."

Not into the 21st century, please, O new leader of mine – not you too.

"...and if you've any sense, you'll want to be a part of it."

She patted Jez on the knee of a still clean pair of beige chinos very quickly and began to rise.

"But don't feel too bad. Tomorrow the kids get here, we'll all be run off our feet and hopefully, this will all be quickly forgotten. But please, for your own sakes remember: you're not students anymore, you're teachers."

She could have patted my knee. I wouldn't have minded. But she didn't.

4
Some Tyrant
Autumn Term - Week 1 Day 1
Monday, September 2nd, 2002
Peggy Lane Headteacher's office - Early Afternoon

Cllork.
"Do....sit down."
"I'd be very gl..."
"I think, with all due respect, that you should listen to me..."
"Of course, headmaster."
"Thank you....What I want to say to you is this: I am going to be trying very hard for this school...I think you know, this is my first appointment...as a head......and I need as many of the staff to be on my side as possible.....I...*we*...have a hard job to do to turn this oil tanker round...."
"Oil tanker?"
"Yes - big comprehensive school - most of the staff have been here a long time - people are used to doing the same things in the same old way. It makes things difficult. An oil tanker is what this school really is."
"Of course. I should have..."
"And the thing is - um, sorry to cut you off - it's experienced staff like you; people who are respected...by...other people...been known here for a very long time, that are the most important."
"'Who,' headmaster."
"You. I mean you; people who know the kids, people who are respected. But...I need you to change a little too. Bend a little."
"What makes you think I won't bend over backwards for you, headmaster?"
"Oh come on now. I may look stupid, but...it's obvious you don't like me."
"Why is it obvious?"
"Oh come on - your attitude just now. It was appalling, you know that - deliberately trying to humiliate me in front of two young new members of staff, and on my first day - I'm not going to accept that."
"You didn't think it was demeaning to Christopher and myself to be marched in here like a couple of 13 year olds with two new young members of staff?"
"Isn't it insulting to me to be drinking beer at lunchtime?"
"So...let me get this straight: you think you own our behaviour during the lunch hour on a training day?"

"I would say so, yes. In a sense I own you during your working hours here at school. What you do outside the school day is obviously your own affair. But this is how we turn the school into an enterprise we can all be proud of."

"An enterprise..."

"Yes, enterprise."

"I see..."

"Other schools out there are doing better than we are; we have to compete with them. I want to make Peggy Lane the best comprehensive school in West Yorkshire. I aim to make this a flagship school, a beacon, a centre of excellence..."

"That is extremely interesting, headmaster; and you have worked out how you're going to accomplish this feat, I assume?"

"I don't think you want to hear yet another speech from me..."

"Try me for size. You might get a pleasant surprise."

"Look, I will share this with you, as it's just us two in here alone: I was so nervous this morning I missed out a part of my prepared speech."

"Well it must be tough, your first staff meeting. Not something I have ever done."

"Yes, thanks, yes it is."

"I did like your balls tho..."

"The thing is - I'm interrupting you again, I'm sorry..."

"Quite alright, headmaster."

"The thing is, there's a framework I was constantly working towards in my last school. Okay? I call it my 'CCS': Continuity...Consistency...Standardization: an overall action plan for the school. Individual action plans for each faculty and within the pastoral system, which mesh wi..."

"Sorry...which..?"

"Mesh..."

"I get you."

"...with the overall plan: everyone with the same goals; everyone pulling together...for the good of the school. If we all pull together, Sef, we can make this a great school."

"I see."

"I want you to play a part."

"Well, thank you that's..."

"I think you can be an inspiration to others."

"...very flattering."

"Well..."

"One thing: there are over seventy members of staff here and you've just arrived; how is it..."

"I know anything about you?"

"Mmm."

"Malcolm and Elaine. We've spoken together about a lot of staff. Part of my job is to find out about people. And you must know you are the sort of person who stands out."

"And you need me..."

"Of course."

"I'm sorry, but I do have a problem with that."

"You do?"

"Yes."

"Why, exactly?"

"You're a wanker."

"Sor..?"

"Wanker. It's a word. One I use rarely; I keep it in reserve for special cases."

"I beg your p...?"

"Here's a speech for you, Michael:"

"I'm...."

"Wait. You grovel your way up your ladder of educational - what shall we call it - 'ecstasy,' with your empty notions of how a school should work, with what constitutes 'success.' Figures, targets, mantras from a bad text book on management you once had recommended to you on a course by some nonentity..."

"...!"

"...who stands there in the suit and spouts meaningless statistics at meetings anyone with half an idea how to live life would find any excuse to avoid attending..."

"You have n..."

"...and now you think you're up there on high armed with all this useless bullshit, you think you can dump it on us."

"Alright, that's enough. I am not going to be spoken to like that in my own office."

"Then where?"

"How dare you. You...you..."

"'You' what? 'Smart-arse?' 'Old smart-arse?' 'Old balding failure?' What are you going to do now: ask me why after twenty-five years in the job I'm not a head of department? A Head of Year? When you're a headteacher, with what, seventy grand a year, a five-bedroom house and a big suit? Or haven't you done your research?"

"I haven't had the time to go delving into the ins and outs of every teacher's career..."

"But you said..."

"I don't care what I..."

"Let me tell you this, my dear young man...you want to be a headmaster: if you can't take criticism from a mouldering fogey like me you won't last ten minutes trying to run a comprehensive school in your 21st century."

"Get out of my..."

"Your office?"

"Yes, get..."

"Yours? Who said it was yours?"

"What?"

"You think you own it? It belongs to West Yorkshire Educational Authority. They employ you to run this school; to serve the children; to serve the staff; to serve me."

"What? You..."

"And that speech this morning: tell me, why did you insist on addressing a room full of human beings as if they read computer manuals for pleasure? I know Colin Mouse does, but he's head of IT. Is that how you spoke to people at your last school?"

"We..yes..."

"And...they let you get away with it?"

"What on earth do you...?"

"No one has spoken to you like this since you became a head of department, have they?"

"No."

"No one's ever come up to you and called you a fucking cocksucker?"

"*What*?"

"A cocksucker. Are you deaf? A fucking dirty cocksucker."

"Okay, that's it ..."

"You've never had anyone waiting for you outside a pub? To come up to you in a dark, lonely car park to sneer in your face? To dribble their saliva down the front of your jacket?"

"*Get*...nn-of course not, no, why..?"

"...with no witnesses to help you, saying 'the next time we find you we'll beat your fucking face to a pulp, you fucking piece of shit-arse scum'?"

"What are you tal..."

"Work it out! After all, you think you're a clever boy, don't you?"

"Y-y...Nn-nn..."

"So I'm sorry, but if you think that anything you have to say to me about teaching, or anything else come to that, is going to interest me, or affect me in the merest, smidgeonist way...."
"...."
"Can I go now?"
"..."
"Thank you, headmaster. And...may I warmly welcome you to Peggy Lane?"

Cllork!!

5
A Little Light Back Story
Autumn Term - Week 1, Day 1
Monday, September 2nd, 2002
Measby - late afternoon and early evening

I tried to imagine what happened in Michael's office after we left and let it worry me a little. Assuming he gave Sef the same sort of speech Susan had just given Jez and me, I was changing my mind about the balance of power in that relationship. Superior intelligence and smarter wit always win out in books, but in real life I was beginning to see how callow my thinking was. Who after all had the power to make or break whose life? Unless Sef was about to detonate himself out of the teaching profession in a blaze of sado-masochistic glory, he might have to re-think his approach to the challenge of his - our - new boss.

We walked out of school just after 3.30.pm into the same car park where I'd looked up at the gabled entrance-building in major league trepidation earlier that day. It might have been a decade ago. I thought my life got a little strange now and then, but Day One was pushing it somewhat.

I didn't need the lift Jez offered me. She was friendly alright. She lived on the edge of Yarrow in an old village called Gwyn Gyll and said she didn't mind going out of her way to take me home but frankly I'd had enough for one day. I needed some time on my own to regroup. In town, a soft sunshine still fell on late afternoon shoppers walking unhurriedly along wide streets laid out in a neat grid. A most un-English state of affairs. I slouched along a commodious pavement then bought a bun from a posh bakery. The woman in front of me had a real plummy voice, as if I'd magically been transported to Henley-On-Thames. I knew Yorkshire towns weren't all as I imagined places like Halifax and Barnsley to be - working class down to the clog scuffs on their ancient doorsteps - but I never thought I'd find one with middle aged women in £700 jackets.

Walking along in my new town. It was different to all the other places I'd ever spent an amount of time in and it felt good, it felt right. I liked the fact that for once in my life I'd done something a little unexpected. It wasn't rowing across the Atlantic blindfold but to me it was something. So I was feeling fairly pleased with myself ambling along to my bus munching my bun. I'd have started to whistle too but I didn't think the passing locals had done anything to deserve being sprayed with saliva-laden crumbs.

My liking for buses was one of the reasons I didn't own a car. It may be a cliché but it's hard to beat the London red. When I was down there doing my first degree

I sometimes used to ride them all afternoon on a day pass. It used to relax the hell out of me. I'd even sit up on the top deck and read if I got bored with watching and dreaming. If they hadn't jerked around so much I would even have written my essays up there. My friend Muff used to have panic attacks whenever he tried to ride the underground so he'd be with me sometimes.

But I'd just spent the last year in Nottingham where buses slowed up the traffic there too, though it wasn't the same. In London all sorts of people used them but in the town of the old Sheriff of legend you felt like one of the underclass riding these green and white beauties. They were full of poor fuckers who hardly had two 50p coins to scratch their ears with. Old dears having to lug heavy shopping bags on and off because they couldn't get to an out of town Tesco's. It would depress the hell out of me, and Muff wasn't around any longer to keep me cheerful. So I started to walk everywhere, which isn't as alarming as it might sound, because Nottingham is not a big town. I was there to do my teacher training course after deciding that I wanted a change from the metropolis for a spell. London was the only English place I'd known and at 27 it was time for a look around. I didn't think I'd be able to entice many of my friends up for a visit and I was more or less right. Muff was too tied up at his hospital to make his way north but a couple of others did. I was surprised Frenchie came, because for him everyone north of the Holloway Road was a drug-sucking car thief who thinks cappuccino is an opera singer. And Sid was just Sid.

"They have gigs in Nottingham?"

"Yes, Sid, bands and people you've actually heard of. Foreplay played the hockey arena two weeks ago."

"Steady on: you'll be telling me my mobile phone'll work up there next."

And so on.

And a guy I met on my course, Stephan, who was here because it was the only university that'd had a last minute drop-out due to illness, expected to hate it but found to his shock that despite it not actually being Scotland, he could drink, laugh and get laid just as he did at home in Glasgow. It just didn't have Celtic.

It didn't vibrate with the luscious excitement of the big city either but it had its own special atmosphere that you can't quite describe. I've been to Leeds and it has the same thing. The people there have a sense of belonging to their home city that I never felt in London or Boston. It's small enough for you to feel as though it – I'm guessing here – protects you somehow, or maybe it's not that but rather a sense of ownership because it wasn't so full of people it made you feel totally anonymous. But it was big enough to have plenty for you: a great second hand CD shop; some cool new bars and a few half-decent restaurants. It was compact, walkable and pleasantly bustling; unlike The Smoke where the streets of the West End were forever choked with swarms of tourists and day trippers. And you didn't have to be culture-starved. I took my pals to galleries, the castle and the arts cinema and we had a great time until they had to split for the south again.

Of course, at night time on the weekend the place was like Laredo in the 1890s. You walked the streets after 11.30.pm and took your life in your hands. As midnight crossed into the wee, wee hours of the morning the pavements would be awash with young boys - I hesitate to use the word 'men' - honking their guts into the gutter and looking for fights like the ghosts of the wronged dead. And the chicks were as bad. Swarms of them in shocking clothes, cackling like banshees with crotch disease, marauding from bar to bar, wasted and dangerous-looking. Their strategy for a good time – or sacred duty - to get lashed out of their faces whilst making as much mayhem as possible along the way - was a complete mystery to me. Perhaps the time I'd spent in a country where you still couldn't get a drink under the age of 21 had turned me into a prude. But some of my pure blood Anglo-Saxon buddies had the same idea as me: that there were better ways of ending a night out than falling out of a taxi with empty pockets, puke on your clothes and a good chance of having taken part in the creation of an unwanted pregnancy. Maybe we were just getting old.

Another human being of some significance took a firm position on all of my movements and liked to think she influenced them: Ma Weaver. Amused by her dumbfoundment that there could actually be real life to be had out of the Great Metrop' – which was rich for reasons I shall tell you later - and knowing that she wanted me to finally come back to the States, I came further north to piss her off. Was it a belated cry for attention? I'd hate to think so. I prefer the idea that I just enjoyed annoying her.

Yarrow would never have the burgeoning civic dynamism of the city of Leeds, despite *Avanti!* being ready with its faux-Moonbuck's comfort and fancy coffee seven days a week, but it didn't seem to care. It obviously had its own ways and its own cosy style. It had absorbed change down the past couple of centuries, naturally, but whether we're talking about the *Harold Norris Shopping Centre* that disgraced one side of the market square or the new little shops being built into the old station complex it was inexorably moving forward also. England was changing; you couldn't mistake the fact.

Despite the best efforts of the bunch of morons on the council who'd decided a short time earlier to honour the Nozzers, Yarrow won my heart on my first day there, not least because something happened to me to make me think I was now among some of the finest people in the land.

Within minutes of clapping eyes on the place for the very first time, and having arrived way early for a 10.30.am interview at Peggy Lane, I went looking for java and saw a likely looking café with the name '*Avanti!*' on its smart sign and went in. There was a Conranesque sofa and a couple of easy chairs by a huge picture window overlooking the better side of the market square, and a handy counter by more windows next to an atmospheric old alleyway. It was here I sipped a large and actually decent cap of chino. I'd bought a couple of 10p biscuits from a jar standing invitingly next to the till and was in the process of biting eagerly into the first - I hadn't eaten since the night before - when in my enthusiasm for the sweet crunchiness I inadvertently sucked in a mouthful of air and rogue crumb. Choke? I was practically a First World War gas victim. Then this chap next to me, about 50-odd said,

"Coom 'ere, lad," and carefully banged me on the back like a doting father until I'd come back to life. Now how many towns do you know where this sort of thing could happen?

Such things are not to be underestimated. I decided right there and then I was going to interview like a cross between Stephen Fry and Batman and smash all-comers into oblivion. I didn't disappoint myself as I normally did and the chair of governors, a local politician called Precision, offered me the ticket. On a day that went down in my personal history as indisputably great, it felt as though I hadn't chosen Yarrow but that Yarrow had chosen me.

I now needed a place to live. Yarrow being too expensive even for the pocket of my indulgent parents, I looked outside the town. In the nearby village of Measby I bought a nice small stone house - cottage, actually - just across from one of the two pubs on the street. In Measby, rocket was still - you guessed it - what Neil Armstrong went to the moon in. That much was obvious from talking to my neighbour, Barney Plough - pronounced 'Pluff', an old Yorkshire piece of reckoning - a day or so after I moved in. Though 'Barnie Plough' sounds like a 90 year-old geezer leaning over a farm gate with a flat cap and a face like Grimsby, he was - and still is - a thirty-something painter and decorator. He lived in the stone terrace next door to mine and was kind enough to let me know his feelings about my chosen profession during our very first conversation.

'Fookin' teachers, I'd feed 'em to me dogs; do 'em the world o' good,' he said, not making it clear whether it was people like me or his dogs who would get the benefit. I wasn't yet convinced I had a true friend in the making here. If you asked him about shaved parmesan he'd doubtless tell you he'd had money on it when it came in third in the 3.20 at Doncaster the other day.

However, getting home off the 419 to Holmes Farne that first school evening, he wasn't quite at the forefront of my mind. I was in a state Muff often described as 'bollocksed' and I hadn't even taught a lesson yet. I stood in the little living room in my new house, still crying out for furniture and warm home comforts, and felt strange. I hadn't taken in more than a token amount of food all day, so I set about putting that right. I made me some strong coffee and constructed a sizeable sandwich of cheese and a few pieces of crap from the green part of the fridge. I put the television on with the sound low, ate and drank some latent energy back into my system, and lay back on my new sofa with my teacher's copy of *New English Poets*. I let myself think about Jez and her bright softness a little bit. By 5.15 I was dead to the world.

When I woke up darkness was coming on outside the window. With my front door opening straight off the main street into my living room I could hear the occasional footfall and snatch of conversation. I made some more coffee in my top-stove Italian pot and tried to pretend I was Marlowe from Chandler's *The Long Goodbye*, who always made melancholy read like a five-star feeling. I still felt one-star ten minutes later. A planet away from southern California in a small village halfway up a hill in Yorkshire, Great Britain, I still didn't feel mature enough to do what every other bastard of my age had done years ago to earn the right to be considered a fully-fledged adult.

I only had myself to blame, though I liked to bring in my parents here as a rule. It was they who let me spend most of my twenties studying and hiding away from the real world, if there is such a thing. They financed me. Feeling sorry for me I suppose, a child of a couple who didn't love each other any more. If my mother couldn't pay me in feelings, she paid me in dollars and pounds, in no-interest loans for mortgages and any thing else I wanted. Thinking that as long as I needed her money I still needed her. And many times I thought that my ma once did something bad to a gypsy back in the days when she pushed me around in a stroller. Who cursed the little kid to be lazy for the rest of his life. After the British government let me spend three years reading books and writing about them, I'd got so used to the cushy good life I wanted to prolong it for as long as I could. A career? The hell with that. That wasn't the artistic life I wanted to live out. Only I was too young to write novels. I could have gone into journalism but my God, that was impossible. To do that I'd have had to go out and meet strange people. Take notes and talk to them sometimes when they wouldn't want to talk to me. Someone's ideas of a jest, surely. Me? Put myself in harm's way? You're kidding, right?

So, the alternative career plan: a two year Masters? Where do I sign? Another three for a PhD? Thank you very much, sir. Do I have to bend over for that? That won't be a problem. I was 26 when I walked out of the University of London as Dr. Tim. What a joke. I may be stupid but not so dumb as to think that this letters-after-the-name business was anything more than a pantomime. If I were really a doctor I'd be getting up each day and removing a couple of spleens before midmorning coffee. Or be in some lab in Illinois curing lung cancer.

But there I was, good to go with my big degree by my side, earned by writing twenty-thousand words on a theme essential to the health and future prosperity of the nation: *'Darkness of Tone in the 20th century American Crime Novel 1920-61.'* But look - life's tough right? - so if the silly world I inhabited wanted to confer prestige and kudos upon me because I liked reading, why the fuck should I care?

But I did. In the end reality catches up with you. Most of the time the fact that I was a pampered, privileged social non-entity contributing the precise sum of nothing to the Gross Domestic Product and cultural life on not one, but two sides of the Atlantic Ocean gnawed away at me like a rat chewing a corpse.

Two years ago I tried to deal with the issue: I started sucking up the same shit everyone else had to. A friend of the family wangled me a job in the Human Resources department of a jam factory in north London. You can laugh, but it was a first step. Look, don't tell anyone but I read novels there in the afternoons and got away with it. The treadmill? I don't think so: I took sick days when I felt like it; came in late when it pleased me. And got away with it - why? Because I wrote letters of application for an overfed and under-educated HR director and re-wrote his presentations, his reports and *Honey I Want to Jump You* and *Dear John* letters to the women he did, then didn't want to fuck. Wrote letters of complaint to people like Bitch and Thorson so his wife could get a new washing machine and a free fortnight in Florida. It didn't kill the tapeworm but it put me sufficiently back into the mainstream to think, 'screw it, I'll become a teacher'. Of English. Talk about books and teach kids to right. That's a joke. And be useful to society at last. Sort of.

Is that enough back-story for you? It'll have to do.

That first Peggy Lane day had been enough to last me weeks. College life it most certainly was not. Trent University wasn't quite the heaving Megalopolis but even there I could disappear for a couple of days at a time and not have the fact of it register the merest glitch of disorder in the hot, pulsing interior of the bureaucratic machine. I even skipped a few days of teaching practice without anyone seeming to care that much. But just one day at Pegs told me that I couldn't play rat boy and cope with a dirt-stained conscience any longer. The walls had begun to close in. Right there in my new sitting room I could feel all of my past slipping away with each minute of the fading September dusk. That ease, that freedom. That evasion of responsibility. That complete denial of the inevitable. It was all disappearing for good. I'd put up a gallant fight, the fight of a Gambino alley cat in fact, but at one score and the legs of an octopus I hadn't the will to resist any longer. I was solid gone.

The unholy world of work was finally about to swallow me up.

6

Big Game Hunters
Autumn Term, Week 1, Day 2
Tuesday, 3rd September, 2002
Peggy Lane Headteacher's Office – 10.05am

"Ah, Susan, come in."

Michael sheathes his delightful and expensive black Chomski fountain pen and slips it into his suit breast pocket, being careful to push the clip right down on the material. This new working day he sports a fetching charcoal-grey number, possibly his favourite. Three months ago, revelling in his Peggy Lane interview victory, he launched his platinum super-credit facility at a clutch of Dharmani weapons. He'd never been a one for high fashion whilst riding the career elevator, but he wasn't stupid; he'd seen the England team wearing the brand at the World Cup. The move cost him a big penny but he thought of it as more of an investment. He was determined then to make the best of impressions, and of course, still is. He knew that if he was going to expect the staff to smarten themselves up, he had to lead the way.

Before Susan's arrival he has been sitting in his high-backed Richano swivel chair - brought in from home to replace the West Yorkshire Educational Authority standard issue for headteachers - and feels a degree of comfort around his comfortable body; the sense of well-being that only comes to a man from the cut of a great piece of tailoring and his ass on a good chair. 'And I'm going to get myself in training for one of these half-marathons,' he says to himself, but not quite yet. He is going to put the trauma of the Demmler Outburst emphatically behind him first - clear and heal his mind of it - then he is going to pound the streets of four- and five-bedroom houses in Otwood which have eaten up the green belt like obsessive vegetarians working their way through a big bowl of salad, and make himself ready.

His first day for the most part pleased him very much. There was the crisis of the early afternoon, obviously, but he'd been able to shake it off for the most part. The rest of the staff have been great so far. *His* staff - Michael Peniston's staff. A sizeable number of them have already popped in to see him, most of them yesterday, but a few have called already this morning. Teachers from across the eight faculties, knocking respectfully at his door with its simple, understated wooden plaque saying "Michael J. Peniston, Headmaster: Fuck Off, I'm Busy and Too Important to Waste Time on the Likes of You."

It didn't, of course. It said simply, "M.J. Peniston," in black, with the word

"Headteacher" in the same lettering underneath. Michael crossed his threshold perhaps twenty times yesterday and has already done the same three times this morning, and each time he sees the plaque, something deep inside his mind automatically calls out, 'I've done it!' This is felt with more excitement than relief, for he is still young for a head of school.

'Can the English be right, here?' he ponders enjoyably looking up from a piece of paperwork (a government document) and out through his big window towards the craft block.

He has wanted to be a head since his sixth form days and as his fifteen teaching years, er, developed, no vessels of opposition or difficulty ever appeared on his horizon to stop him. *Nichts, nada, niente* came out of left field or up from the depths of the seas of ambition to disturb his progress to happy home port. His career thus far has been an easy dream, a model, in fact, of how to progress through the modern institution: seeking out more senior role models for advice; writing amply competent letters of application in the correct tone; practicing and refining the art of the presentation; putting up for inspection the required image of the deeply aspirational professional on interview days. In short, relentlessly pressing the right buttons at the right time. When you thought about it, it was simple. Almost anyone could do it. Well, perhaps that was an exaggeration. And already the benefits were beginning to accrue. Physics teachers, History teachers, French teachers, whatever teachers have come knocking on his constantly half-open door to pay their respects - homage really - to their leader, to the Peggy Lane Supremo.

"You have got to stop thinking like this," he says, actually out loud, admonishing himself with great seriousness, "or you are going to make a bloody fool of yourself. Calm down. Think straight. Focus."

But he is not wrong. This is exactly what they are doing. They respond to his welcomingly-modulated 'Come in's' with a reserved but smiling entrance and mouth respectful greetings.

"Hi, I thought I'd just say 'hello' - Daphne Cloth, Textiles..."

Michael is, naturally, very keen to meet and greet, basking in this special attention (can you blame him?).

Being new to the job however, it is a moot question whether he is hip to the true social meaning of these micro-events. Has it slipped under the neophyte radar that some of the smiles and 'I just wanted to say's may have been, in just a few cases, a touch less than sincere? Jack Rush (Design Technology) comes by and shakes hands firmly, and smiles as best he can while he takes his first shufti in close-up at the new gaffer.

'Lord love us, another bloody pen-pushing gimp in a posh suit,' he says to himself, realising suddenly that he needs to scratch one of his bleeding piles. Mariana Spooley (Spanish) comes at the start of her free period to grin girlishly through strands of long, lustrous, Latin hair and wishes Michael "every success in your new job," just beating Tamsin Cell to the punch. Tammy has made a detour from reprographics where she has just picked up twenty-five laminated copies of the structure of the eye, to deliver an opening salvo in her attempt to wiggle her way to any promotional post that might be in the offing this year: Literacy Coordinator; IT Development Officer (for Science); Deputy Head of Year (unpaid if necessary) temporary assistant to the Citizenship Coordinator; part-time Washer of Ancillary Staff Clothing. Anything will do.

Several others call to say "good luck" to try to insulate themselves from the negative fallout from any future mistakes or failings should they occur or become apparent: setting too much homework causing a parent to phone in and complain; producing a departmental budget overspend; forgetting to organise insurance for a day trip to the Bradford Museum of Photography, Film and Art; not setting enough homework so a parent writes a nasty letter to your head of faculty about your not stretching Jessica enough. There are many gaffes out there just waiting to be made.

Mick Trance (PE) and Livvy Lovejohn (Drama) make their appearances because they know they were public enemies nos. 3 and 4 during the previous régime (Andrew Covely BSc [Oxon]) and want to make a fresh start. The next caller is Climer, Susan, expected, but not, strangely, 'Item 5' under the 'Morning Section' on Michael's daily agenda sheet, as she might have been.

"Hi, thanks," says Susan a little breathlessly. It's been a busy morning, with Alex Carfman already ringing in sick; she has had to set his class some work then tear back to teach her own. Gone are the days when staff could amble casually from their own to a colleague's classroom for a quick chat and a laugh or two about this, that or whatever. These days, administrative eyes may be watching.

"Come over, take a seat," says Michael from his desk up the far end of his office. Michael likes Susan. He likes the way she dresses, for one. He isn't one of these perverted men who go berserk for women in black tights and high heels, but he doesn't deny that it's an attractive sight, a woman in smart office garb, clicking along the corridor in front of him, an exposed calf of flesh almost distracting him from the important task at hand.

He is happier - he is married after all - to consider Susan's attitude to the job. She is keen, she is organized, she is efficient and she is dedicated. Her car rarely leaves the car park before 5.10.pm, Fridays not excepted. All this is evident to Michael, naturally, from her management uniform, from her neat, sensible hair, her judiciously applied make up and her earrings - not dangly ones, not drops of any sort in fact, but small, bright, sharp and nearly expensive ones. In short, when Michael first met Susan Climer on the second of the two interview days when he came to Peggy Lane to fight for the post, within ninety seconds he'd said to himself: *she* is one of the people I need beside me to take this school forward. He decided this quite emphatically when Susan, the designated faculty head, took him through the twists, turns and parking spaces of the school's curriculum and its development over the previous five years.

As she spoke, Michael was already thinking of Peggy Lane's future. 'I can see this place needs shaking up from top to bottom and I'm the man to do it,' he declared internally. He felt his brow crease with determination like a pair of cheap trousers. The type he wouldn't ever be wearing in the future.

Even before Michael got the job - by a nose ahead of Margot Dillinger (Acting Head of Chelsfield School for Girls, Kent) - he'd set himself a credible and realistic target. When Michael Peniston saw the local authority league tables on the night of the first interview day, part of a data-pack the candidates were handed at 3.30.pm for the purpose of constructing a presentation next day (entitled 'The Peregrine Lane Grammar School and the 21st Century,'), he saw that the school's recent record was poor. He didn't say 'lamentable' because language - use of - was not his strongest suit. He didn't say 'crap' because he wasn't the sort of guy to whom the word 'crap' came easily. In fact, after he'd applied the skills of his Mathematics degree to the tables of statistics in his pack, he spotted the fact that Peggy Lane's GCSE and A level records were among the worst in the whole of West Yorkshire when the ability of its intake at age eleven was taken into account.

"Crikey! These Key Stage Two stats mean that the school should be hitting 65% five A to Cs, minimum," he said, scratching his scalp at the dining room table after he and Grace had finished a Mimp and Spanker Spicy Cream Haddock Bake For Two.

"Oh, my, these CAT scores are high. High! But look at the SAT results!" he went on, chewing a spare biro (he wasn't the sort of man to be found chewing a Chomski, even at home). Which to the uninitiated means it took bright kids from primary schools and didn't educate them properly. The picture was just as bleak when he studied the GCSE, AS and A level results.

"The Value-Addeds are horrendous all the way along the line, Grace," he told his life-partner as she placed a cup of Grescafé Continental Blend just to the side of him. This really was serious: Peggy Lane was letting down its young people right through from end-stage childhood to emergent adulthood. Fortunately for Grace, or rather Michael, she taught Maths at a highly regarded comprehensive in Leeds, so she understood exactly where he was coming from.

Michael, naturally, was excited by this. Peggy Lane was going to be a challenge and he would enjoy every minute of it. Of course he would. Immediately he set himself that target: from twenty-third out of thirty-six secondary schools in the list (in terms of raw data), to the top ten within five years. Top three, value-added. That would do it. He would hit the interview panel with that tomorrow. 'They'll love it,' he thought. It was only five-past Eastenders. By eleven o'clock he had a more than rudimentary action plan ready to wow them with. He slipped himself under the blue pinstriped duvet just after midnight tired but elated, nervous but expectant. Not only was he going to turn Peregrine Lane around 'like a huge oil tanker,' he thought, he was going to make it the talk of West Yorkshire.

And Susan Climer would help him. By the time she stepped across to the seat he had prepared for her next to his, he felt as though he had known her for quite a while already, even though this was only the second time he'd been close enough to smell her sweet, garlicky breath.

Waiting for her to arrive for this delicate appointment just now though, his thoughts had fallen back into yesterday's disaster. He couldn't afford to let the memory of it climb out of the mental rubbish bin he'd finally managed to dump it in last night, despite the excruciating pain throbbing from it that continually threatened to upend it from the inside.

When Sefton left the scene of yesterday's debacle unbidden, his nominal superior was not so much deflated as lying in buckled pieces on the hard shoulder. Even the Richano swivel chair was no comfort. He slumped in it like a long lump of dough and swiveled away from the window to stare at the wall, bombed. The Matisse print and art work produced by some talented sixth formers from his previous school failed to console. He sat. And sat, and sat. At 2.40.pm Jesse Frump, the indomitable school secretary and PA to the past three headteachers, wondering whether the most important office in the school now contained a body beginning to stiffen with *rigor mortis*, knocked tentatively on the door.

"Erghh." Michael had tried to say 'come in' but found only a gutteral noise exiting his mouth.

"*Cer-hergh*, Come in!" he said, finally rediscovering the ability to pass sound waves over his larynx. He sat up, trying to recompose his body and features up into the shape of Man at the Helm on Top of his Game, but fearing his agitation would reveal an obvious lack of composure, let his body go slack again. An idea had flashed into his clever head. He swiveled round to face the incoming Mrs. Frump.

"Hi, Jesse: sorry, I've just had some bad news. I've just heard on my mobile that my aunt Mary died this morning. I'm a bit shaken."

At such a point down the decades, many a headmaster's secretary has carefully shut the door and offered her boss a considerable measure of consolation. One or two have carefully slithered up close, cradled the coveted head and begun to stroke it tenderly. But much as Jesse wanted to do this, she hardly knew Michael, and anyway accepted the fact that she was much too old for him, so she moved a few sensitive steps towards him and said,

"Can I get you anything? Cup of tea?"

"Thanks. That would be nice. Thanks, Jesse."

Michael didn't get to be headmaster of one of the largest and potentially best schools in Yorkshire without being able to fire off a round or two of self-protecting bullshit.

By the next morning, and after a terrible night pacing the floor and mouthing mild obscenities over and over about Sefton Demmler, both within the hearing of Grace and without, Michael had managed to achieve something of a personal renaissance. After two showers, a dash of Hugo Bosh and a perfect shave, he felt refreshed and renewed. Mantras of positivity now filled his mind: 'To every problem, a solution,' *Carpe diem* - seize the day,' 'Don't get mad, get even.' Personal favourites all. He would see to Sef. Or to be precise, and as he didn't tell Grace, 'that bloody arse-bandit.' And to get Sef, he got Susan.

She now waited for the meat in the sandwich of this meeting. She had been summoned by Jesse, ringing down to Susan's office only minutes ago.

'Come up immediately, Michael wants to see you.'

'Ominous words,' she thought, 'I wonder what this is about.' They'd already discussed her new role the previous morning, confirming its details in a slick and professional manner. Perhaps Michael had belatedly cottoned on to the fact that the English Lit. A level pass rate was down by 1.2% this year and wanted a few words; maybe ask her to produce a Faculty Action Plan within the next week or so. Susan couldn't think of what else it could be. The GCSE results were up slightly on the previous summer, so it probably wasn't that.

"Hi. So. Everything alright?"

"Fine, yes. We're all set and ready to go, I think," and Susan, intelligent, straightforward woman in her early-mid-thirties that she was, with a pleasant, quite good-looking kind of face, smiled a little unnecessarily, as women in her position are wont to do when addressing the male headteacher.

Michael looked into her pale blue, not especially distinctive eyes, took in her mouth and its absence of lipstick, tried not to look down at the place her thighs would be, and went for it, like Baby Face Nelson attacking a sleeping bank,

"Susan, we have to get rid of Sefton Demmler."

Now Susan, who'd read a great number of 19th century novels in her student days, and would have fancied herself to be something of an expert on the early works of Thomas Hardy were she not so self-effacing, thought immediately that if her life were normally a Brontë novel, it had inexplicably moved forward into a bad re-mould of the New York of Damon Runyon. She hadn't heard Michael correctly had she? Her mind fractured into sections, one of them momentarily wondering how they'd dispose of the body, until a dominant strand of thought took control, composing the word 'huh?' in the centre of her conscious mind. Then the ball bearing rolled into the slot and she started to grasp what he meant. Michael: new head, new broom, new methods, New Labour perhaps - she wasn't entirely ignorant of government education policy - pupil attainment targets, chance graphs and smart managerial clothing and of course! Sef didn't fit Michael's mode of thinking - not at all - and he wanted to find a way of sacking him. 'But you can't,' she thought. Her face went through eight or nine contortions, not distracting Michael from the plan he was about to reveal to Susan if she'd let him, because her eyes were, as already hinted, less than large and expressive. It was in the pleasantly full eyebrows and forehead wrinkles that he finally noticed the fully-expected facial signs of doubt and consternation. But not, he quickly perceived, horror. He wasn't the fastest on the draw when it came to shooting down the meaning of human body language but he was competent enough to notice within seconds this faint absence of humanity in his head of English and thought, 'She's in!'

"But..." Susan was frowning now like a dim general trying to sort out a war. She'd never been asked to play a role like this: the scheming Roman; the Machiavellian court figure; the Lady Macbeth - Christ, she was no Lady Macbeth! She was nice, sensible, Labour-voting, Guardian G2-reading Sue Climer and....getting rid of Sef...suddenly appealed to her as a great idea. She felt a shiver of pleasure bolt down the hairs on her back, thrilling and liquefying her spine in one go. A *frisson* is what it was, of electricity. The mega-wattage of power. Here was she, just herself and the headmaster in the inner sanctum, the control room which drove the whole enterprise. An unprecedented situation of rare privilege in her life. Head of Faculty is a fairly lofty plateau but there are still layers of hierarchy above you, several rock shelves still to climb if you want to get your hands on the true levers of power.

'Naked power,' is what she thought to herself, because Susan, you might like to know, is trapped in a very unhappy marriage. Empty evenings with Mark: two diverging lives trying gamely but miserably to inhabit a space made for two. Emptier nights. Trapped? This is only how Susan feels on the surface of her existence. In reality, as she knows from all the fiction she has read down the years, she is only as trapped as she is prepared to allow herself to be.

Inwardly she shook her head and blinked her eyes hard to focus.

"But...how?"

Michael glanced furtively at the door, then leaned towards his head of English.

"It won't be easy, and it probably won't be quick, but it can be done."

Susan's pupils had dilated to the extent that she was as wide-eyed as she was ever going to get, and those eyebrows were practically digging a tunnel into the top of her nose. So Michael continued.

"I need you to help me. I'm going to make Demmler's life here so unpleasant he'll have little alternative but to quit. How old is he?"

"Fif..." and Susan stopped: she wasn't sure exactly how old Sef was. 'When you're Sef, you don't have an age,' she thought, 'he was simply...

"53; I've looked."

...Sef.'

"Well," said Susan resting back suddenly in her chair and blowing out both cheeks with tension, "what exactly are you going to do?"

"Oh, there are plenty of things we can do. But I need to know his weaknesses."

"Weaknesses!" She wasn't sure he had any. "Sefton, you know, is tough. The words 'weakness' and 'Sef' don't...you know..."

"I know, but there's a huge thing in my favour."

"What's that?"

"Essentially, this is now my school. I make the rules."

'Christ, I'm starting to sound like John Wayne,' he thought and wondered whether he'd actually ever seen a John Wayne film all the way through. He kept going.

"I'm going to lay down a set of new rules for staff to follow. I think I know this about him already - correct me if I'm wrong - he'll hate having to follow strict guidelines, like keeping an accurate, up to date teaching file. All the heads of faculty are going to take in the files once a term, maybe once every half term, to examine. I'm going to make spot checks too. And..."

He stopped to scratch his throat. His new shirt was chafing a little.

"...we'll check his marking. Does he do it regularly? I bet he doesn't. I'll watch his lessons. You'll watch his lessons. We'll get under his skin. We'll kill him."

Now Susan did look horrified.

"Not literally, Susan. I didn't mean that literally. Of course I didn't."

"I should hope not."

"Sorry."

"But why? Why do you want to do this?"

'There had to be a reason,' she thought, 'either that or this guy is completely off his head.'

So he told her, about yesterday, the whole scenario.

Susan looked thoughtful and serious. Not surprised because what Michael had just described was Sef all over. As Michael sketched in another couple of bureaucratic details, looking, in fact, like an Elliott Ness after too many cups of over-strong coffee, she just concentrated on soaking up the information while staring at the thin carpet. She didn't worry too much about processing it yet. After the initial excitement was the uncertainty of two feet in a high, high place on the mountain top way up above the crowd.

"He doesn't keep a teaching file," he said wincing, appalled that any teacher should try the impossible: to function without one.

"How do you know that?" said Susan.

"Because Malcolm told me."

"Malcolm?"

There was a knock on the door, right on cue.

"Come!" The supreme confidence Michael had worn as a deputy head was flowing back into his system like scalding hot water into a winter bath. He was beginning to tread down the awful shock of yesterday deep into the safe area of his memory from where it could be recalled but coped with. 'Better than in the rubbish bin,' he thought.

Malcolm Went entered with a touch of characteristic diffidence, typical of the Man Who Made It to Deputy Head Despite Everything: no talent; no obvious management skills; no liking for school children. How he got to a fifty-grand-a-year position in a secondary school was a mystery alright, like Black Holes to a postman, like the rainbow to Prehistoric Man. Some said he'd done it by sucking up to the right people. Some said it was because he was related to the chairman of the local education authority. Some said it was because he used to ride into school with a previous deputy headmaster who used to work Michael's predecessor like a remote-controlled car. Staff room wag Andy Crucial called him 'Malcolm X,' on account of the fact that he didn't seem to have a personality. But none could deny that he was right there near the top of the Peggy Lane pecking order. Susan registered him as she usually did: his mid-forty-ish age; his lack of height; his doggedly miserable, sagging face and his chronic presentation of self.

"They say you can tell a lot about a man from the shoes he wears," said Andy Crucial of the History department one day just after Malcolm had passed by on the way out of the staff room door, "and it may be so; but you can tell even more from his hair."

DT teacher Rob Rodder looked up from the February edition of *Welding Today*.

"What you on abaht?" Rob was young, but he was pure Yorkshire.

"Look at Malcolm Went's: short; shit-brown and sitting on his head like a disease, f-huh-huh."

"So Malcolm looks like a twat. So what?" said Rob, mystified.

"Not looks. *Is* a twat, brother Rob. That's my point. You can tell from his hair."
"Thank you, Professor Idiot."

Malcolm Went, butt of jokes but unarguably the possessor of a navy blue 2001 Mercedes Benz AR90, pulled up a hard chair and looked at Susan with a rather sheepish, forced smile. He knew enough about right and wrong to feel guilty about being in on the plot too, but he hated Sef, and always had. So.

Susan observed Malcolm's proximity and concluded, correctly, that she was in a conspiracy of three. In a way she was surprised that she hadn't immediately backed away from Michael's opening line but she wasn't surprised about Malcolm. 'You're weak, a follower and I've always despised you,' she thought.

"So do we think there's any chance of Sef starting to comply with the new file regulations?"

An adamant, "No," was Susan's answer. Malcolm looked gravely at Michael and followed Susan with a slight shake of the head. Susan noticed, as Malkie leaned forward in his chair, hands clasped loosely together, how bloodshot his eyes were. She'd never noticed before - she'd never been this close. She almost shuddered. Susan often spent her time considering possible lovers, but the thought of Malcolm was revolting.

"I'm also going to set up a number of committees after half term. Here's my proposed list."

It was comprehensive, representing the full fruit of all that Michael had learned in his previous posts and on the numerous training courses for Heads-To-Be he'd attended in the previous three years. There were eight of them. Michael looked down at the list on his lap with pride, as if they were his children: The Pastoral Care Group; The Curriculum Development Strategy Planners; The New Strategies & Developments Team; The New Teaching and Learning Partnership; The Committee for Blended Learning; The Numeracy Group; The Literacy Group and The Vision Building Team.

"I'm looking for teams of about nine, so all the staff will be involved. As a senior member of staff I will not expect Demmler just to serve on one but take a leading role. Do you think he will?" he said, looking eagerly at the two immediate underlings.

"Not a chance," said Susan.

"Not a price," echoed Malcolm.

Susan's mind produced a thought: 'he'd rather kiss your arse, Michael,' but she didn't think the Head would think much of her turning it into speech. She thought hard about the Sef she knew, quite liked and was at first seriously attracted to. 'God, he used to make me virtually collapse at the knees when I first came,' she reflected. 'The way those blue eyes looked at me, so piercingly...' She heard herself beginning to sound like a cheap novel so she re-made the thought: 'Yes, I admit it: if he'd asked me to run away with him to China, I'd have robbed my grandmother to buy the tickets.'

"You think?" said Michael, seeking the warmth of reassurance in Susan's limpid blue eyes. He didn't actually know what 'limpid' meant, but he'd already thought the word anyway, so it would have to do.

"There's every chance he'll refuse," she said, unconsciously batting her lashes back at him. "He has always simply refused to do whatever he doesn't like. And he's always got away with it."

"Why?"

"Why?" repeated Susan, without thinking - everybody knew why.

"Because he's...brilliant. And the kids totally adore him."

The collected trio of top managerial talent fell silent, pondering their difficulties.

"And because no head has been brave enough to take him on."

Michael stared hard at a different wall - the one with his notices and reminders to the left of his desk. Susan continued.

"Michael, you might want to do this but Sef is not just any ordinary jungle animal."

Malcolm liked animals and watched natural history documentaries on satellite TV often. Sefton was an elephant. No, of course he wasn't: elephants don't inhabit the jungle. 'Do they inhabit the jungle?' he thought. Malkie's imagination pictured a huge grey elephant trampling down thick, wet vegetation, parakeets squawking and scarpering for cover into the upper branches of tall trees, whilst nests of poisonous spiders scurried to and fro and a mass of brightly-coloured toads with bulging throats were crushed under foot. A baby elephant came trotting behind its mother, struggling to keep up. The picture turned into a cartoon as he remembered *The Jungle Book* and going to see it with his older sister at the Leamington Spa Odeon as a small child. 'Ooh-ooh-ooh,' he sang to himself, 'I want to be like you-oo-oo.' Did he see it twice or was it only the...

"Malcolm?" said Michael, seeking some Wentian input, "what do you think?"

Malkie shook his head and tried hard to look as though he'd just been considering the problem with the intensity of a leopard waiting for the right moment to leap from tree branch to prey neck.

"So, we get him on that," continued the Boss. "If he refuses to fill in his file and so on, or if he fails to serve on a committee, I can give him a written warning as to his future conduct. Threaten him with a sub-committee of the Governing Body."

"But surely that's not enough to sack him?" said Susan, feeling both giddy and appalled.

"No. But it'll get the ball rolling and it might just get him on the run. And if I can find the least excuse, I'll insist on a lesson plan accounting for every minute he spends in the classroom. And if he doesn't do those, another warning - and his last chance."

"Michael, with respect, I think it'll take more than that," replied the doubtful Susan. "Once you start, Sef will know what you can and can't do to him in a matter of days. That's if he doesn't know already. If I know Sefton, what can't get rid of him won't hurt him in the slightest. He's got the hide of a rhino."

"Then we'll just have to bide our time," said Michael, imagining himself as the evil one who strokes the cat in the Bond movies. He couldn't remember his name. "Bide our time, and wait. We'll grind him into submission. If he's that brilliant he won't want to hang around here with me on his back the whole time."

'You don't know him,' thought Susan, but she didn't want to spoil the meeting for him. His face was fully animated, flushed with colour and his eyes, she thought, were too close to doing a tribal dance of anticipated victory than was healthy. 'Perhaps this is how it starts,' she said to herself. This scared her. This was not normally her. 'But I'm a compassionate person, really,' she went on. She thought of all she gave to charity. Of the times she'd bought a *Big Tissue* in town. And was content again. 'They might never shift Sefton Demmler,' she thought, 'but at least this'll bring some excitement into the job, some intrigue,' and God - she felt a vibration of self-loathing pass right through her - she was more than ready for that. 'And,' she thought guiltily, 'I won't have Sef forever standing behind me making me feel like a girl in a man's job, clutching a measly C-grade in my own subject.'

Malcolm thought of rhinoceroses and their tough skin. Epidermis, wasn't it? Did rhinos love mud baths like hippos? Is it rhinoceroses, or rhinocerii? 'I'll run it through my spell checker tonight,' he said and tucked the task into his memory.

The big game hunters considered their position quietly for a few moments, looked at each other one final time, thinking their own separate, private thoughts, before breaking up and going back to what passed for their daily grind.

7
A Little Local Difficulty
Autumn Term - Week 1 Day 2
Tuesday, September 3rd, 2002
Peggy Lane Staff Room and Corridors - Morning and Early Afternoon

I cannot deny that a pool of excitement about my arrival in Teacherland sat somewhere in the swirling mysteries of my digestive system as well as fear. But my destiny today was to face my first encounter with my Year 11 group. This I was dreading like cancer. Ten minutes after I'd won the interview competition, in the blur of handshakes and backslapping it may have been the old Head who said,

"11 Set 3'll knock the smile off his face..."

I heard it and didn't hear it. Then halfway through the summer holidays I was walking across Boston Common, sweltering like a commis-chef in a tight galley kitchen when I was hit smack! in the back of the brain with the cold realization that I could soon be facing professional humiliation. I knew from teaching practices that if it happened, if I couldn't control a class, it wasn't a one-off disaster: the problem would be mine for the whole school year of thirty-nine bloody weeks: a fear that hung around your mind constantly as you inched miserably through each day. One thing I knew for sure: I had to get off on the right foot with them; if I didn't get my right foot on their collective neck in the first week, they'd be destroying my peace of mind for the next thirty-eight.

The fact that every single would-be classroom chalk-slinger has the same chilling anxiety before they step onto the stage on their first day gave me not one morsel of consolation. I found that I'd stopped dead in my tracks on the footpath. I came to, realized I felt cold in the suffocating heat, then threw this style of thinking in the trash. I composed myself and found a coffee shop and a donut. Later on I laughed at my foolish cowardice - the event was weeks away! I had loads of time to find a strategy to enable me to cope with a year 11 class. I was being needlessly neurotic. But the weeks had sped past.

And now here I was.

The timetable in my hand told me I had 11 set 3 Tuesday p4, Wednesday p2 and Friday p1.. I did the math again, adjusting down the normal load for their early leaving date to take their GCSEs: ninety lessons. Jesus H. Christ. Ninety. I had better be good.

The part of the day that led up to The Lesson is a blur of action and movement in my mind now, but at the time I spent nine eternities getting to it. There was nothing to take my mind off the event; that was the problem. I should have been teaching my Year 7s period one, but the fresh intake of spanking new eleven year olds were spending the first three lessons of their Day One with their form teachers. I should have had my Year 8s down next, but they weren't asked to show up until period three on the first day of the year. Then it was break. Then I had a free period. Then it was lunch. If it hadn't been for my expected showdown in the early afternoon, the day would have been a non-event. But in five hours time, at 1.25.pm precisely, I would have to don my battle gear and rush out of the trench into No Man's Land.

I met Alana Lush at 8.30am to find out about the form I'd been assigned for the year, but the twenty seconds she could spare me she used only to tell me that I didn't have one after all; that I'd be sharing one with a colleague. Maybe. Bummer. I liked the idea of getting a relationship going with my own band of youngsters as soon as possible. Captain Tim and all that.

"So relax," she said, smiling as she walked away from me down a corridor. "Take it easy." I would have had more success trying to teach a horse to drive a lorry.

So there wasn't much for me to do until after lunch apart from deeply considering the possibility of running off to Hammerfest at the earliest opportunity for a permanent career change to professional snow checker or something. Meet people like Jim Bunsen. The chance of releasing myself from this wide-awake nightmare caused the ejaculation of something warm and relaxing from my pituitary gland, but a slosh of over-reaction from an adrenal direction took over and made me feel sick. Five fucking hours. I looked at the reality of my already crumpled personal timetable again saying 'English 11 Set 3. Rm B2' and could hear Tom Waits' rumbling gravel of a voice in my right ear saying, 'and there ain't no way around that.' So I went off to a work area just next to the staff room where I had a big elephant hole to check I had my gear ready for the class, and to start filling in my teaching file registers with names. It was either that or pace up and down like...like...like an expectant father? A condemned man? A test batsman waiting for the next wicket to fall in the middle of a collapse? I practiced the similes to see how sharp I felt mentally. I needed to be smack on the ball for this. I yawned. Time to get on, do something useful. I got a nice black Ponteus V7 fine out of my bag and started to write: 'Avery Leo; Baffle Rich; Balkan Sobrione; Breda Lucky; Calculum Robert....'

The end of the first lesson saw the door swinging to and fro as a succession of teachers rushed in alone or in twos, each swivel of the hinges bringing in a corridor of kids' noise. Each time, the fall of my curried stomach into my intestines. Abbreviated sights of students in maroon blazers and black skirts and trousers.

Different colour ties for each year group. Mostly the new entrants ignored me. The odd nod and half-smile. Fiona dashed in - then rushed off to another class without so much as a nod. Most of the time it was quiet. Just a couple of staff worked at desks, writing and marking, although how they'd got stuff to correct already was confusing. Halfway through lesson two, the door opened and I felt the comfort of a familiar voice.

"I forgot me board roobber..."

Jez swooshed across to her elephant hole and was gone again. I couldn't stand this. I decided to venture out for a walk.

Along the endless B corridor, a boy of about 14 in a white shirt and an ironically short blue tie was being balled-out by a male teacher.

"...times have we been through this, Mr. Prickle?"

"Sir..."

"How many times have I told you to keep your mind on your work and not get involved in messing about?"

"Don't know, sir."

The world turned, governments came and went, the population of Ethiopia carried on starving, but teachers still came out with the same old crap. I winced as I slipped past the scene, observing as I did so my earnest colleague staring exasperatedly at this seemingly forlorn youngster.

His brow was shiny with sweat, his sleeves were rolled up and he was using a board-marker to make his point, stabbing the air in front of Master Prickle for maximum emphasis.

"This is the start of your GCSE course: it's serious business now, James..."

"Sir."

"...can't you see how important..."

I was glad to get out of earshot. At the far end of B I took the stairs. I didn't really know where I was going but to be on the move made me feel better. Each classroom door had a big pane of glass in its top half, wonderful for taking a peek inside to see at least roughly what was going on. Some past headmaster's fine idea, no doubt, but fine for me too now. I couldn't resist making sideways glances as I ambled along, new shoes squeaking with each step. The scene was essentially the same every time. Sunshine streaming in through the windows on orderly rows of desks, blazers and shirts and a member of staff at the front talking,

"What would be the result of a movement along the hypotenuse of forty-five degrees?" said a short woman with long black hair.

"How would we view the evidence if one of William's men had said this?" enquired an energetic goatee beard?

"What subject would you find being taught nearest the craft block?" said a woman in expensive-looking combat pants through yet another window up on C. About twenty hands shot skywards. Year 7s. Marvellously keen. Fresh-faced, new uniforms and a new life opening out for them. Then as I moved on, a voice right in front of me; it was one of the 7s, a halfling. I couldn't help smiling as I looked down.

"Excuse me, sir: we have to find the photocopying room: do you know where it is?"

"Um, I don't."

This little lady looked about 8 and had the whitest shirt I'd ever seen. Her red tie looked as if it was still warm off the factory machine. She clutched a sheet of white paper. Her friend, in glasses, looked keen but frightened.

"But if you go down a flight of stairs at the end of the corridor," I said, pointing, "to B corridor, and head for the front door of the school, you'll find the school office. Ask there, okay?" The white shirt smiled.

"Okay, thank you, sir."

"No problem."

And I smiled too. For the first time, I was a real 'sir.' So different from a student one. I strolled down to the end of C and my face and voice broke into laughter.

*

Eventually, the school day reached break time. It was a relief to go into the staffroom and find civilization and the comfort of colleagues. Jez was there. For school she wore a thin black cardigan and black trousers and looked great.

"How is it going?"

"Ah've just 'ad me Year 8. Bloody 'ell, it were busy. I was roon off me feet. I doan't think they understood wor ah was tryin' to gerrem to do so ah w's roonin' from desk to desk in a right frazzle. Terrible. I've got to gerra coffee."

Mrs. Manicure, looking like she was here doing community service after being given a lenient sentence for mercy-killing a ward full of geriatrics, was busy dispensing the stuff to plenty of willing customers. I'd already got mine. It was practically undrinkable, but I went through with it - I didn't fancy my chances if Mrs. M. caught me bringing a cup back half-full.

"An' ma form..."

She was back.

"A Year 7 group; worra shower."

"At least you've got a form."

"You can 'ave mine – ah'm telling yer."

"Have you seen Sef?"

"Noah - 'ave you?"

But away by the door I suddenly caught his voice and it was a comfort to hear his clear tones cutting through the noise of fifty teachers releasing the relief of getting the first lessons of the year under their belts. Chris was with him, smiling quietly as they moved through the room to the hatch like a couple of grizzled hired guns in a Laramie saloon.

Liam joined us where Jez and I were standing, cups in hand.

"Look at Sef there, n-not a bother on him after yesterday. Did you hear what happened in the head's office?"

"What?"

"The w-word on the streets is Michael's already put Sef in his place. Told him he has t-to toe the line or else. Interesting. Very interesting. And a lot of shouting, apparently. It's not good and I d-don't like it."

"When the water crosses the bridge, the factory whistle blows all the louder."

"Hi, Les. Have you met these two? Jezeb…"

"How are *you*?" said the newcomer in our midst to us, smiling a trifle strangely, it seemed to me.

"Les Person. Everything okay with you two, then? Tom…"

"It's Tim…"

A young male colleague was walking past, stopped as Les was speaking and butted in.

"'e looks like someone just slipped a bag of shit in his grandmother's groceries."

The joker, talking about me, left us as quickly as he'd been bloody rude.

"Rob Rodder - don't worry. He means well, if you don't mind giving Ovaltine to the Pope."

"Beg your pardon?" I said.

"You don't look well though, young man," said Les. "Here, I've got a joke for you."

"Ah, no, Les, the bell's about to go," said Liam, clearly thinking I needed help.

"What do you get when you cross a light bulb with a tennis player?" he said, sidling up closer.

How could I put this to him? 'How the fuck should I know? And by the way, what I don't need is laughter to take my mind off this afternoon. I'll be delighted to scream the tiles off the ceiling with mirth this evening, but not until.'

"I'm sorry, you've got me," I said.

"Me neither! If you work it out, let me know; the PM wants to know the answer by four o'clock."

"Oh, very good, Les, don't s-sell your chisels quite yet, will you. Les thinks he's going to be a stand-up comedian one day," said Liam, turning to me.

"Or a sit-down comedian; I'm not quite sure yet."

Les, who looked like a BBC weatherman, really did think he was funny and laughed along with his last quip. I tried to keep my face contorted in a rictus grin to be polite. Jez had covered her mystification by taking her cup back to Mrs. Manicure, but she was quickly back. Perhaps he was funny, and I just couldn't see it through my nerves.

"So Liam, wor 'appened wi' Sef and the new 'ead yesterday? I came in this mornin' and Susan and Fiorna were yakkin' abowt it but they shurroop when I walked through't door. I felt like a bloodeh sixth former."

"I was just telling Les: word on the streets is that Michael gave Sef an official warning about his behaviour. I...I have t-to say I wouldn't mind seeing him put in his place: it's about time he was brought under some sort of control. And it's n-not fair on Susan."

"Oh, don't be such a wet haddock, laddie," said Les. "If you were a bit more like Sef you might be half as interesting."

I stood and thought that one out for a bit.

"Sefton'll have Peniston dancing the bagpipes to his tune before half term. You see if I'm correct."

"But 'ee's the y'ed," said Jez in a smallish fog of puzzlement. Me, too. As you already know, I thought headmasters were sent down from the clouds to rule over us mere mortals.

"You haven't worked with Sef for ten years like I have," said Mr. Person.

The storm himself kept his distance as we progressed to talking about Stars in the Toilet, the new hit TV show.

He and Chris were fully engaged with cup and saucer, and deep in conversation in a corner, the occasional cannonball of laughter bursting across the room. Whatever happened yesterday, it didn't seem to have left its mark on Sef. Resplendent he was too, in immaculate black shirt unbuttoned at the neck to reveal the top of a bright white t-shirt. No tie for him - and no jacket. But with beige chinos and suede shoes, he was every inch the dude. The bell rang, the cups began to chink and clunk in unison and the room cleared in seeming seconds. A free period for me, so back I went to my desk next door and committed 'Natterjack, Simon' and 'Nonce, Theresa' to immortality.

If I say that September 3rd 2002 was the longest day of anybody's life, I defy anyone to contradict me. I actually fell asleep over my teaching file somewhere between 'Twenty, Dawn' and 'Winsome, Will' for about ten minutes and woke to find a small patch of drool developing on 'Lift, Nicholas' and 'Lofthouse, Matt' from my Year 8s to be. Lunchtime eventually came somehow, though the time moved through the space it had to travel like an aged man shuffling towards a destiny forever out of reach. Or something very close to that. I went to the canteen for lunch with Liam and sat with a bunch of fellow Peggy Laners but I didn't have any conversation. I just fiddled nervously with a prawn sandwich and a banana yoghurt and thought about how I was going to start my lesson. I kept my jacket on. I had sweat patches under my arms so bad I nearly had to head into town to buy a new shirt. I spent the rest of the hour back in the staff room on Liam's table, pretending to read a book about *Macbeth* so no one would talk to me. It wasn't a difficult trick to pull off. Being the first day of teaching, hardly anyone paused for more than five minutes to sit down. The bell went eventually. Registration. Another ten minutes to kill. I was feeling wrung out, like a pair of Margot Fonteyne's knickers. Eventually, the next bell rang.

So enough of being a pussy. I switched on my positive state of mind and marched out of the room and down to room 2 on B trying to look like I'd just come from teaching inmates in the Scrubs for ten years after seeing action in Sierra Leone as a mercenary. As I crossed the classroom threshold about six assorted blazers were already noisily lining up by the door. I glanced at the whiteboard - *black*boards long gone, man - and it was blank. I dumped my bag on the teacher's desk and pulled out a blue marker pen. I wrote on the board trying not to let my hand shake,

'The Poetry of Carol Anne McCreaver'

Noise was pouring in from the corridor but I consoled myself with the thought that it wasn't all mine. Students were still making their way from form room to classroom. Then as I turned towards the door to get my lot inside, a burst of energy in the form of a small, dark-haired kid fell through the door with a loud,

"Ay! Get off, you fat lump of...argh!"

Laddo's mates now formed a laughing crowd at the door, semi-queuing, while Laddo himself performed a one-man stage act in front of me. Even I could see this was all for my benefit.

"Um, what do you think you're doing?" It's funny how the words just tumbled out before I thought I'd given my brain a chance to form some sort of verbal response to this early challenge. I'd only been a teacher for ninety seconds but already I'd begun to pollute the Peggy Lane air with clichés.

"Sir! Sir!" said the boy loudly. There was no one near him, but this didn't inhibit him.

"He's...argh! Gerroff!" he went on, looking over his shoulder. There was no one there. The door crowd was still laughing.

"Get out! Go on! Line up."

Laddo backed out towards the corridor laughing with his audience while I considered what to do. I had to get some order, so I went to command things at the door.

"Back! Right! In a line, please!"

The crowd made a shuffled reverse towards the rest of the class who were backed up like a series of car accidents behind them. In the space, I looked down what was supposed to be a single line - I'm quite tall, about six feet one if found in a proud moment - and to my frank and bleak surprise, no one was paying me the slightest attention. I couldn't help noticing that a studious-looking girl in glasses was happily talking away to her mate as if I'd said nothing and in fact, didn't exist. If the nice ones were going to treat me as if I was nothing...Okay, then. I'll raise my voice.

"Right! You lot! In a line! P-llease!"

The collective mind of twenty-six fifteen year olds decided that some sort of token response was now required. There was a slow shuffling into a single zig-zag line up B corridor and a dying down of about half the noise. The studious one had stopped talking and was now looking at me properly, which was something. I looked down the line again. There was a clump of four lads right in front of me, including Laddo who was deliberately giggling loudly.

"Right! You! Get over there," I said, pointing to the other side of the corridor.

"But sir, I 'an't done *noofin*'!"

"Just get over there."

"Aw, but why, though?..."

Hardly looking, he petulantly threw his bag on the floor. It hit the deck with a *sloosh* and was about to slide towards the far corridor wall. However, its poetic glide was interrupted by the racing feet and ankles of one Malcolm Went, deputy headmaster. These things are always over in a flash but seem to take forever. As my lower lip dropped towards my shoes, his legs tangled like a plastic bag caught up in complex machinery. This caused him to go hurtling forward in a stylish horizontal dive. I remember his mouth coming open and his eyes widening in shock as they shot past me, the rest of him trying desperately to catch up from behind. Why his arms chose not to work at this point I couldn't tell you. They should, by all that is sacred and helpful on the planet, have reached out to break his fall. But something was inhibiting the part of his brain that spotted danger; something that failed to prevent what was about to become a celebrated disaster, characterized at its key moment by the onomatopoeic sound, *thud*! The word 'sickening' is normally prefixed to '*thud*' in stories like this, and here is the reason why (my head is throbbing now as I write).

There wasn't too much blood, but the terrible loudness of his jaw crashing into the wooden parquet floor, shining impressively in the new term afternoon after a good holiday polishing, brought everything in the corridor to a dead halt. Even those at the back of the line, where laughter was still sloshing around like free booze at an Irish wedding, heard it and were immediately hushed. Our Mr. Went (B.A. Leeds, plus many a course in types of school management, various) lay there like a slaughtered father seal.

My first thought was that I'd killed him, that the force of the collision had sent his chin into his teeth which had in turn rocketed up into the soft underpart of his brain. I was now ready to bring my teaching career to a swift conclusion by running out into the traffic with my eyes shut hoping the end would be quick and painless.

"Sir, I'll go to the office!" A youngster left at a dash without my saying anything. However, Fiona Twyford-Sounding had apparently seen the accident from the other direction twenty yards away and was now bent over the body. She looked up at my class and shouted,

"Right! Into the classroom! Now!"

And while I stood there frozen like a hopeless pole, my class trooped dutifully in except for Laddo who stood and stared at Malcolm much as I did, the energy having been sucked right out of his plan for domination of my afternoon. For the time being anyway.

"You! What's your name?" Fiona had managed to carefully manoeuvre Malcolm into the recovery position and was cradling one side of his face.

"Simon Laddo, miss."

"Get into Mr. Weaver's classroom."

"Yes, miss."

He picked up the murder weapon and quickly made himself scarce. I went over to Fiona.

"Is he okay?"

She looked at me as if I was slightly mad or plain stupid.

"I'm not a doctor."

My nerves had disappeared, but the replacement emotion was not a more agreeable one. Malcolm groaned, eyes shut. Fiona had found a clump of tissues and was trying to stem the flow of blood from his nose.

"Will he be alright, do you think?"

In retrospect I couldn't blame Fiona's for sending me a look of withering contempt.

"You'd better just get into your classroom and look after your class."

8
The Lesson
Autumn Term - Week 1 Day 2
Tuesday, September 3rd, 2002
Peggy Lane Room D2, Corridor B - Afternoon

The atmosphere in the corridor had been smashed into quiet pieces by the accident, much like the victim's nose, jaw and fractured eye socket. It swept into my classroom. Absolute hush fell upon the room as soon as I crossed the threshold. Twenty-six faces looked at me in a new light: a worse one than I started with. My mind was now putting up the shutters: it wasn't my fault; I hadn't thrown the bag; it wasn't my fault that I'd been given a set of lunatics to educate. Ten seconds later, a one hundred-and-eighty degree shift. Fuck Malcolm. I'm not going under because of him. Life's a bitch and the Devil has mighty sharp teeth, hundreds of 'em, but he's not sinking any more of 'em into me.

Not yet, anyway.

I stood at the front of the class and looked at the group; they looked back as if I'd shot Malcolm in the head. Which isn't to say they were scared of me as if I was Mafioso; rather that it felt as though twenty-six souls were pointing their fingers at me, saying 'guilty.'

They shouldn't have looked that intimidating. They were just a bunch of fifteen year olds in the next-to-bottom set for English, Maths and running round the gym (though half of them tried to skive it). They'd already spent years of their school lives knowing they were as good as marked out for failure; sat there in uniform, in shirts not quite as white as those you'd find in higher sets. The blazers were a little short in the arm for some, while others had mothers who would no more send their kids to school looking scruffy than they'd turn down a buy-one get-one-free offer of vodka from Safeways. This wasn't the group right down at the bottom; below my new friends here awaiting my instruction was a small Set 4 who were so crushed by the system and so lacking in confidence they couldn't muster the spunk to seriously challenge you. Unlike this lot, who according to received wisdom were disaffected but intelligent enough to be dangerous.

The silence hung there between us like gas ready to ignite. The girls sat there in garishly applied makeup, chewing gum and looking frighteningly fully grown, all new highlights and tight blouses. The boys looked so raw and innocent they almost made me feel like Clint Eastwood, but some of them were already the size of men. Those with spots were cruelly exposed. A few of them quietly grazed on spidge. It was against the school rules but this wasn't the time to take them on. Not while they were looking at me, waiting and licking their lips. My studious one with glasses now seemed to be looking a little scared. Maybe I had a chance. I decided it was time to treat the silence as a welcome gift and use it. I attacked.

"Alright; take out your exercise books. Today we're going to be starting the poetry section of your GCSE English Literature course. Carol Anne McCreaver is our first poet..."

There was a momentary pause, but the machine gun eyes began to turn away from me, and hands began slowly to reach into bags. The room became sound as a few chairs scraped against the wooden floor, followed by the slap characteristic of books hitting desks. Pens appeared. At least I now knew they could be civilized and that they knew they were here to work. I had a pile of poetry anthologies specially written for the course piled high on my desk. I scooped them up and offered them to the two girls at the desk right in front of me.

"Could you give these out for me?"

They both stood up and took the half of the load I offered them. One looked me grudgingly in the eye while the other didn't bother to look at me at all.

"Thanks," I said hopefully. I raised my voice again:

"When you get your anthologies, turn to page 26, 'Poems of Heart and Mind.'"

I was trying to muster some authority but I could hear my nerves betraying my voice box, bouncing back at me from the far wall and down from the bare ceiling. There then came the briefest of sharp raps on the door followed by Susan walking briskly into the room looking faintly flustered. Blue suit today and pale blue blouse, but a few strands of brown hair were breaking loose over her face, spoiling the effect. She tried to tuck them away as she came up to me close but businesslike.

"Do you have Anne-Marie Somers in here?"

I looked down at my register as the noise level in the room began to rise. 'Rangers, Alan; Rumpling, Marsha; Sample, Lenny; Sedgwick, Lana; Somers, Anne-Marie.'

"Yep, there she is," I pointed.

Susan addressed the class.

"Quiet!" The noise fell away. "Anne-Marie Somers? Are you here?"

A voice piped up.

"Yes, miss." The bright looking girl with glasses.

"Right, Ann-Marie, come with me." Susan bent her head again to me conspiratorially.

"She shouldn't be here. Mistake. She's new. She's very clever. She should be with me, in top set."

Susan smiled and waited as my one banker picked up her bag and walked towards the door.

"Sorry 'bout that," she said and gave me a sympathetic little smile.

I could have hit her with one of the anthologies. It was stupid, but I now felt more lonely and isolated. As if somehow Anne-Marie could have been a good enough role model to save me.

Slowly, the lumbering hippopotamus of an English lesson edged forward. Again 'slap...slap,' as poetry texts landed on desks over a rumble of conversation. Someone laughed loudly at the back at an aside from a neighbour, but when I looked up, the boy cut it off. I mustered the sternest look I possibly could and tried to get behind the hippo's arse to give it another push.

"Okay..." It was more or less quiet.

"So. Firstly, I'm going to read out this poem here, *Lost in Chelsea*, to you. I want you to listen carefully...we're then going to di..."

"Aren't you going to take the register?"

Some cocky fucker to my right - a lad. I noticed the lack of "sir" and it flustered me. Damn, the register.

"Em..."

I felt my inexperience showing through like black knickers under white trousers. My throat was tight, and I was spinning back towards my first teaching practice in Arnold, back on the ledge again, terrified of heights.

"I'll...em...I'll do it later. Now: *Lost in Chelsea*."

'Too quick, you're going too quickly. Slow down.' But I couldn't. I started to read, suddenly pulling up a small pail of optimism from the well. They might like this. This was modern stuff, about love and music. Rock and roll. Drug references. If I was lucky, they might get off on this. I started reading,

"'Lost there completely, in cool Cheyne Walk
Sounds of the sixties, the radio plays...'"

I looked up as I read the second line. They'd taught us this at college, or tried to: to sweep the class like a lighthouse beam as often as you can. So I swept. It was quiet, thankfully, though in the back-left corner two boys were laughing at something in apparent silence. Perhaps they had a sign language system. I thought I might say something but when I tried to form words there was only a hopeless dryness that refused to moisten. So I had no choice but to try to keep the first verse on the move.

"'Sounds of my lover, guitars in the night

Jagger in scarlet, the devil's de...'"

There was laughter. I looked up, my red light flashing hysterically, to find most of the class looking at a boy in the window aisle who was making an extravagant wanking motion at an imaginary giant penis just above desk height, attracting the attention of some class mates not yet enraptured by Carol Ann's timeless take on the psychedelic age.

Oh, fucking hell, no. To this I had to react.

"Right. What's your name?"

"Barbara, sir." Half the class was in plastic stitches.

"Very funny. What's your real name?"

"Adam."

Even sitting down he was tall and obviously well-built for his age, and he swayed back and forth on two legs of his chair, taking me on but coolly weighing me up at the same time. He fancied himself alright, with hair short and blonde and a black t-shirt showing clearly through an unbuttoned shirt. His tie must have been somewhere but it wasn't round his neck as it should have been. The little bastard.

"Right. See me afterwards."

"I can't, I've got to go straight to Maths. Mr. Whizzby'll have me arse if I'm late." More laughter.

"Don't use that language in my classroom."

"Why not...*sir*?"

"You know why not..."

"I don't...and anyway, other teachers let us swear in lessons."

So the dread moment had arrived less than five minutes in: a pupil trying to take me for a big fucking ride. I could feel heat rising from the small of my back as I tried to hold on, but the ground under my feet was bucking and rolling. Everyone in the room watching me for a response.

"Okay, Adam." The use of 'Adam' - another mistake. "You can report to me at 3.30.pm."

"No I can't, I have to get me bus. My Dad says I'm not to stay after school, anyway. So I'm not coming."

There is silence now in the classroom, but it's screaming at me, already sensing a kill. The direct challenge is there on the table and it's for me to pick it up and do something with it. Adrenalin is pumping like an emergency fire hose. It sends electricity flashing through my brain trying to scare up a solution to the problem but nothing comes back. What do I say, what do I say? Erm, erm...I didn't know what to say. Any second now I'm going to fall off the ledge into the abyss. Meanwhile, I'm desperately scanning my memory files for a school procedure to deal with this but there's nothing there and I have to carry on; I have to, there is no choice. A stray thought scrambles itself together and I decide to run with it - I've nothing else.

"I'll see you later but I'm going to continue reading and I want you all to *listen!*"

I've raised my voice to a near shout at the end of the sentence and immediately I can hear how stupid I'm making myself look. But there is no more than a rumble of discontent in response as the herd reacts to the ageless sound of a teacher-like command. My hopes rise. Perhaps I can make it after all.

"'Sounds of my lover, guitars in the night
Jagger in scarlet, the devil's delight.'"

I stop and put the book face-down on the desk.

"Okay. We need to look again at this first stanza and..."

"Sir, what's a stanza?" says a gum-chewing female voice who actually smiles at me as she grinds the last shred of chemical flavour from the stick. She is pretty and I find myself noticing this, despite everything.

"Look, don't call out. If you want to speak or answer a question, put your hand up."

I sort of smile back and feel my neck sticky with embarrassment. A couple of people snigger and one says,

"Right, sir," in mock respect at the back. I ignore it. I decide to push on and ignore the challenge, hoping to brazen it out. I suddenly remember a piece of knowledge from my limited experience; I can hear my college tutor, Alan Atlee talking to us in a seminar:

'If all else fails, get them writing, or give them a spelling test. If it's all falling apart, do that. Don't forget!'

I almost had. There was my safety net. If I can get them writing, I might be alright.

"Okay. A stanza is a verse. What I want you to do," I said, above more low mumbling, "is to take a few notes with a pencil as we go. Now, I want you to write actually on the anthology book."

"We're not allowed to write in text books," says a girl with long brown hair and brash red-y lipstick.

"I know you're not normally, but in this case you are."

"Mr. Carfman..."

"I promise you, whatever you've been told before, you are allowed to now."

I tried to sound commanding but it came out as petulance.

"What in all lessons?" said Laddo. I'd almost forgotten about him, but there he was, scratching the inside of his left ear with a pencil (relief: he actually had one) just to my left in the front of the aisle near the door.

"No, probably not." God, this is like trying to explain Shakespeare to a set of penguins.

"Now, have you all got a pencil?"

"No, I 'aven't."

"No."

"Me neither."

So next I'm running round opening a box of lead pencils from out of my case and playing delivery boy up and down the aisles. They seem used to this. Perhaps my kindness will win them over. I flick my eyes to the window in the door. Don't let anyone be watching me in this nightmare. Please. There is nothing to see there but the blank grey wall across the corridor. I arrive back in position at the front. Keep going, Tim. *Come on!* Yet I know this is a battle I've already lost.

"Right. So. I'm going to read the stanza a line at a time and ask you some questions. Okay?"

I sweep the class again. Still there is a hum of conversation in each aisle, a half-dozen faces at least with laughter or smiles across their lips instead of the intense concentration I want. I know that by the book I should take them on and shut them up but I know this is the best I'm going to get and decide I can live with it as long as it doesn't get any worse.

"Okay."

"*Okay,*" someone parrots towards the back of the room. I stare hard in the direction of the voice. More laughter. And louder this time. I make a stare, desperate for it to have some sort of effect. I say,

"Right!" really loudly, which is all I have to try to keep the lesson under control. I see my safety net blowing away in the wind somewhere below me.

I start the poem.

"First verse…"

"You said 'stanza.'"

"Verse or stanza. Shush.

"'Lost there completely, in cool Cheyne Walk

Sounds of the sixties, the radio plays…'

Okay. Who knows where Cheyne Walk is?"

Again a voice calls out without a hand raised.

"China," says the voice, not giving a tuppeny shit about the poem.

Huge laughter. I cut through it, shouting,

"You are here to take a GCSE in English Language whether you like it or not and you will not behave like this in my *classroom!*"

Silence.

I look at them. They look at me. I can feel it's changed nothing. After a gap of about four seconds, someone goes:

"Ooo-oooh!" the voice you make with hands holding an imaginary handbag in front of you when you want to take the piss out of someone losing their temper. Then there is riotous laughter from practically everybody in the room, followed by cheering and I swear I heard someone calling 'wanker!' from the back of the room. I had absolutely nowhere to go. I knew I could scream at the top of my voice at them but that it would make not the slightest difference. They'd just carry on as before. The sweat under my arms was spreading, and a big bead of moisture ran down between my eyebrows as I stood there dying.

Then the door burst open and this huge presence powered through it, sweeping the whole situation off its feet and into yonder. I almost cowered with the class, whose mood had already changed with a speed I would have said, had I not been a witness, was utterly impossible.

It was Sefton.

Blue eyes blazed wide with interstellar intensity and devoured the room. I automatically stepped away, already becoming irrelevant to the new drama. I edged my way silently up the right hand aisle and stopped at the back wall. Then turned so I could see his face. I was as good as no longer there. He'd taken over. Now in the students I could feel something akin to fear. The cocky sloucher was now upright and wary, like an animal hunted, and wasn't moving a muscle. The girls had stopped chewing and had become twelve again. The boys were back in primary school. I gazed at Sef who still hadn't spoken. His eyes still scanned the room spraying silent machine gun fire. It was thrilling, it was wonderful.

Wasn't I supposed to be the teacher? I didn't care; and as if it mattered right at this moment. He kept looking at them. Then looked some more. He gazed into each pair of eyes, into each soul, examining their histories. Some were painful, some miserable and some murderous; others were as normal as toast. He broke the spirits of those he saw in sorrow, and instantly mended them again, gave them hope. In those who'd had mundane upbringings, with their wall-to-wall packet pizzas and reality TV shows, he made them question their humdrum existences even though they weren't yet aware of it happening. Dawning would come later, much later. In the case of the happy, as far as any teenager can be happy, their hearts leapt with joy to see the lightning and the light in their midst.

Sefton then looked down at my desk, saw my copy of the anthology of poems, and slowly, deliberately, picked it up and drew this tiny artifact into his giant hands towards his face, and after looking again at the class, holding them as if they were stars, read aloud:

"Lost there completely, in cool Cheyne Walk
Sounds of the sixties, the radio plays
Sounds of my lover, guitars in the night
Jagger in scarlet, the devil's delight"

His voice was deep and slow and perfectly soft as he reached into the words to pull out every last atom of emotion put there by the jilted poet. In his mouth, 'Cheyne Walk' sounded sexy and elusive and on 'sounds of the sixties' he made me hear Stratocasters wailing in Wardour Street clubs, wands in the hands of tie-dyed geniuses cutting history to pieces. The lover made noises I couldn't discuss with fifteen year olds. I heard every radio in town blaring Sgt Pepper, Honky Tonk Women and Whiter Shade of Pale. Back then I wasn't even a sperm in my father's gonad, but my aunt Millie had been there and brought it all back home for me. As a child this music was mine too. Even if none of the kids knew who Mick was, the harsh little name became opium-scented smoke drifting across the room. In Sefton's mouth, every student knew it meant something mysterious and was laden with dangerous secrets, even though they were a doomed Set 3. Those who understood no words felt and accepted the transformation in the air around them. Something deep and unreal was happening; the stars they were floating.

And so Sef went on through the verses. My own pain healing, I listened entranced and in awe:

"Lost in the music, drowned in the muse
A Jones for the Jones, frugged by the tunes
Sights in the headlights, speeding in fright
Richards is awol, confused by the sight

Of McCartney and Lennon spinning away
in Rolls Royce and Mini, dreaming the dream
Looks like the house band with Hendrix is playing
Cold harbour daylight in Soho is swaying

I tried hard to reach you, but you were all gone
Following leaders, the new gentry thing
Gone for a guru to Rishikesh town
While I'm lost here in Chelsea, waiting to drown."

I swear to God you could hear a throb of empathy in a dozen of these mere pubescents when he hit the word 'drown.' Then there was total stillness as he slowly let the book fall towards his side before languidly but with care, placing it quietly back on the desk. All this time he hadn't once looked my way and he still didn't now. He looked up at the class again, this dreaded Year 11 and spoke.

"Mr....Weaver...is...my...friend." His words were enunciated with exaggerated care, as if made of gold, and he laid them across the room like a loving undertaker covering a body.

"So...you will be...his friend." This was the gentlest order I would ever hear.

"You will behave yourselves when you are with Mr. Weaver. Is that clear?"

About ten young voices immediately whispered "Yes, sir" back in the direction of the speaker, and about ten more nodded. Adam Taylor did both. Laddo gawped into space like a drugged goldfish. Sef looked over at me and smiled with his ancient eyes, then turned to leave. After his exit the peace was fragile, like a tissue paper flag in a high wind, but it held. The children remained like stars, asked questions, listened to explanations, wrote words on their empty pages and learned.

Things, naturally, were never the same again.

9
I Get Up, I Get Down
Autumn Term - Week 1 Day 2
Tuesday, September 3rd, 2002
Peggy Lane Corridor B, Room 2 - Afternoon

So there I was being able to start all over again from the beginning. By all that is sacred in the holy rule book of teaching, Sef's coming in and taking over like that meant that I'd failed my first test chronically and completely, but that's not the way it felt.

My last class of the day was a Year 8, kids of all foibles, tics and abilities mixed in together. Sef's gold dust still clung to my trouser creases and I more than held my own. They came to my classroom, lined up and I let 'em have the meanest of stares in the corridor to make them realize that they had to please me right from the start. I don't think I'd ever worked up such a head of concentration before, even in an exam. I was a demon, organizing, cajoling, smiling and admonishing, eyes as good as a whole crack squad of police. With my sense of anticipation for a sign of anyone not working hard being about as taut as a Norman archer's bowstring, the thing was a cinch. We worked on building simple but well-constructed sentences. It's boring stuff really, but if I'd had to teach them to re-write the first chapter of Ulysses in plain English I think I could have made a decent stab at it. And when a lad named Ben played the goat at the back of the room, distracting the kid in front of him by flicking the back of his hair with his ruler, I barked at him real hard,

"And what do you think you're doing?" I said.

I just imagined I was Sef and tore right in. He looked up at me in surprise and looked ready to fill his pants with chocolate sauce. I was drenched in sweat by 3.30.pm when I said goodbye to what appeared to be a happy second set of customers. So complicated, this teaching game. As if preparing and delivering a lesson wasn't enough, you feel you have to possess the personal hygiene of an It Girl on top. So I'd kept my jacket on all the while to cover up a shirt that felt like a drenched sheet. I wasn't looking forward to releasing the aroma of such a day later on, but it was a minor thought, for I was in a state of demented exhilaration only a bullet or news of a death could have ended. I went out into the corridor and could easily have flung my arms up into the air like an exultant goalscorer and run towards an imaginary crowd, but I could see a cleaner plugging in an appliance in the distance, so I forgot that real quick. And I became aware of a great feeling: that I might just be able to get on top of this thing. If I could somehow learn to deal with those fucking monsters from Y11, then I could certainly tame the younger ones like puppies and kittens. This, after all, was not a difficult school. Suddenly, it was the best I'd felt in months. I could have laid down right there on the hard corridor and gone to sleep, and for once I would have earned my slippage into sweet oblivion fully. I felt as though I'd been locked in a dark cupboard for a long time and that someone had just opened the door and let the light in on me.

I decided I would go to see Sef to thank him. He was in his classroom. Through his window pane I could see him in a black swivel chair behind his desk - where did he get that from? - upon which he'd propped his feet. Sunlight through the window bathed him as if it were laid on for him specially every afternoon. He was reading a book and looked perfectly at ease. Everything was so easy to him. I didn't want to disturb his stillness but I had to speak to him.

I knocked, but then realized he wouldn't have appreciated the deference so I twisted the door handle and went in. The desk and chair were straight ahead of me. He didn't move until I'd walked three good steps towards him. Then he turned his head to the left with a movement that made me feel as though I was interrupting a sacred act. He raised his left eyebrow in recognition of my presence, but not unkindly.

"I..." I slumped at the shoulders and sighed heavily. I didn't know quite how to form the feeling into sensible words. Then in one sudden movement, Sef uncrossed his legs and swung his body around, shut the book emphatically and pointed it towards me.

"Do you cook?"

I don't know how I looked. A bit taken aback, I think.

"You should. You should learn. Be good for you."

I looked at the book cover on the desk. Some foodstuffs and a casserole dish or something on it.

"Bocuse. A master."

"Isn't he a philosopher?"

"Are you taking the piss?" he said raising an eyebrow quizzically.

God forbid that I should ever. That stare was halfway to the one he'd given the monsters. It was like being pinned to your front door by a Godwhacker. Bocuse. I'd have to find out who the merry shit he was.

"Where do you live?"

"Measby."

"Are you staying? Photocopying? Need to find anyone?"

I was shaking my head.

"Right, I'll take you. Let's go."

I wasn't going to argue. I was flattered to think that he found me worthy of his time. Unless he just felt sorry for me. I tried to banish the thought. So I went back to my classroom and somehow manipulated a baffling number of worksheets, handouts and books into fairly neat piles on the desk, excited like a little child. I grabbed some folders and booklets for some preparation work at home later on and practically ran out to the car park. He was reversing his old, but softly purring vehicle towards me as I exited the main door into another fine September afternoon. Sef's wheels must have been forty years old. I opened the passenger door.

"Sling it in the back."

There wasn't much room. The man already had his black, soft canvas sports bag in there and it wasn't more than a quarter full. My leather briefcase looked like it was ready to give birth to a litter of fine little babies.

"Thanks. Great motor you've got."

"So some would say."

"How is it?"

A stupid question by the look of Sef who turned momentarily and gave me a coruscating look.

"It's just a car."

I felt like a kid now alright. It started out sounding like a reasonable question but was pretty dumb now I thought about it. He had music playing already. Jazz. I didn't really like it – it never seemed to make sense to me - my age I suppose - but it was obviously Sef's terrain. And man, I felt pretty cool now, pulling out of the drive with this man. It might only have been a car to Sef but the pupils waiting on the pavement for their lift home turned their heads as if hypnotized by it. Or by the driver. By association, I couldn't lose. It was just a pity there weren't six hundred more uniforms to see me driving away with Mr. Demmler. What did they make of him? Another stupid question: I'd seen.

"Well," said the man, gliding down the hill in third, "your first day: what did you think?"

"I think you got me out of a jam. You saved me; I don't know how to thank you. I was finished in there."

He sort of laughed, looking straight ahead at the station traffic, but it was one of those that come without the laugher feeling amused. It was a tired specimen, dry and worn out. This patently wasn't the Sefton Demmler I'd sat with in the pub yesterday. He seemed to have aged by a hundred years. This wasn't who or what I wanted to see.

"No, you weren't. That lot has made mincemeat of more experienced people than you. Don't define yourself according to what those poor, pathetic kids do to you."

I didn't look at him - he sensed what I was thinking.

"I meant it literally. They're not at all bad kids. In most respect they're victims."

"Well I still have to say 'thank you.' After you left it was incredible. They were practically eating out of my hand. It was just amazing."

I wanted him to know how great he was. What a colossus he was. But he was more concerned with negotiating the main town roundabout.

"Get out of the fucking way..."

He scared me. It was obvious too that me and my tiny beginnings in teaching occupied only a small corner of his mind.

"How do you do what you did in there?"

"How? Oh, take me a long time to tell you." He laughed a small laugh again. "A long time...a long time."

His voice trailed off as we approached another set of lights and eased into the right lane for the turn. There was so much I wanted to ask him while I had him there. This might be my one and only chance. I thought I might be pushing my luck to ask him in for a pot of tea and a two-hour discourse on the fine arts of the classroom, but I had to do it.

Soon we were out of Yarrow and making light work of the long country lanes that coiled around the hill that ascended to Measby. I felt like I was in bad television, with soulful saxophony oozing out of really nice speakers like expensive chocolate, as we smoothed past classic rustic scenes you normally only see in magazines. Ancient farms and cows standing slow and dreamlike in fields of green. And I really believed that the man next to me could teach a Friesian to tap dance. Then it hit me like buckets of iced water poured down my back. Something I'd forgotten.

"Oh Christ, did you hear what happened to Malcolm?"

"Only that he came a cropper outside your classroom; and that an ambulance came calling for him. You tell me what happened - you know, don't you?"

I suppose I had to expect the story traveling that fast around the school. I told him the story. He 'mm-hmm'd' a couple of times, nodded a bit and winced occasionally. Then sucked in his breath thoughtfully as I described the moment of Malcolm's fall into a solid void. The magic of a moment ago had quickly evaporated. I was on my way down again; going way down.

"So you think it was your fault?"

"Well, if I knew how to control a class it wouldn't have happened."

"True. But you don't think Malcolm should have helped you keep some order outside your classroom?"

"I dunno. He's a deputy head; he's obviously a busy man."
"Do you know how much he gets paid?"
"No. How much does he get paid?"
"Ask him."

I considered the idea for some seconds, but then returned to common sense. I couldn't do that. What I had to do was go see him in hospital to apologize. It was still my fault. But I had no car, no way of getting there. I asked Sef where he thought Malcolm was but he didn't know. It depended on how seriously hurt he was. If it was bad, he'd be in Leeds by now, twenty miles away. We hit the Measby village sign and I told Sef where to stop, a bit further along Main Street across from the pub.

"Do you want to...?"
"I have to get going."

If I wasn't careful the day could yet evaporate into something wasted and end in a long torment of worry. I thought Sef might have wanted to take me under his wing after saving my backside in there, but I was being crass and naive. I should have known a bit better at my age; I wasn't a kid any more. Though he'd just been very nice to me, Sef probably felt a certain amount of contempt for me being so green at nearly 30. I felt my head hanging a bit, and then I suddenly thought of Jez. But instead of enjoying the thrill of her image in my mind, I had to beat myself up. She would probably have done better than me. A lot better. And I felt myself weak and unworthy of her.

"Don't give up on Jez just yet."

I looked at Sef as if he was mad. He looked back at me inscrutably. If there was an important signal there for me, I didn't read it.

"Now get out of my fucking car."

*

Two minutes in the house, filling the kettle and trying to eat a biscuit at the same time, the phone rang.

"'ello, Tim? It's Jez."

My heart crashed into my stomach like a broken lift.

"Er, you alright? Ah joost 'eard abowt thee y'accident."

No, of course I'm not alright.

"Um, yeah. Okay. Do you know how Malcolm is? I'm worried about him, obviously."

"Yeah: not good. Ah'm with Susan now, in the staff room, on me mobile. She's joost 'eard from thee y'ead. He's in Leeds Infirmareh. They're operatin' on him as soon as they can find a surgeon. Tim, what did you do to 'im? Woz it bad?"

I was stuck for words. The sound of crunching bone came back like a reverberating nightmare.

"Look, Jez, I can't...well, look maybe I could call you later."

The faculty phone numbers were circulated among us for just such times as these. Except Sef's - Sef's wasn't on the list.

"Ah'm owt later on with Steve."

I went quiet. I think I knew what came next.

"Me boyfriend; 'ee's coomin' over from Booreh."

Thunk! The sound of my hopes falling thirty-three floors into the basement.

"Oh. Well have a good time anyway..."

"We'll talk tomorrer or soomthin'."

"Yeah, sure."

"Come on, now. Everyone 'ere noahs it weren't yewer fault, Tim."

I wasn't consoled that easily. Especially as the adrenalin had all leaked away now; I was crashing and burning like an old, sick Lancaster bomber...

"I'll see you, Jez."

"Oa-kair - keep yer chin oop. 'bye."

She wouldn't have said that if she'd seen Malcolm's chin hit the floor like a china cup being flung into a slab of concrete. I put the phone down and the hugest of yawns overwhelmed me. I had to lie down. My back was aching and I suddenly noticed my feet inside my shoes feeling sore. Day was done alright.

Drinnnggg! Drinnnggg!

The phone again. Damn the bastard thing. What now? Michael? 'We've decided in the light of Malcolm Went's injury to rescind your contract, Mr. Weaver...Yes, normally you'd be right, but there is a clause in all West Yorkshire Education Authority contracts near the printer's name at the bottom of page five which says that in the event of a life-threatening attack on a fellow member of staff, your relationship with the authority can be terminated immediately...'

"Hey, I was down in Cardiff on hospital business yesterday, you know, down in Wales, and I had to deal with some local mafia guys. They made me an offer I couldn't understand."

"Muff! What the fuck? How did you get my number? I haven't given it to anyone yet."

"The Welsh mafia guys got it for me. They can pull strings."

Muff Mugson. We were at university together in London. I think I told you.

"At any other time, Muff, it would be great to talk, but I have had the biggest, steaming motherfuck of a day and I am going to die if I don't get a drink and a sleep. I'll call you later if I haven't been dragged off by the Leeds police."

"What? Listen, have you shot someone again."

I tried to grin, but I just couldn't do it.

"No. Not quite. Look, man. Later. I'll call you."

"Second. What's long and hairy and goes in and out?"

Not now, Muff, please.

"Okay. What's long and hairy and goes in and out?"

"Fucked if I can remember."

"Muff..."

"Think about it."

Clicckkk!

Still shaking my head I somehow made some beans on toast, grating some cheddar cheese and throwing some paprika into the red bean and juice slop. I used to think this was me being sophisticated but Sef had already changed my mind about that. And my obsession with coffee now seemed pathetic. Who was Bocuse? I had to know. My place was still half-empty of furniture and what-not, and what you could see was a mess, but I had a table where I propped up a paper on a pepper grinder. I tried to read some article about the President but I was seeing double words and the photograph of a smiling, waving guy looked like it had been scrambled by a Pollock on acid. I ate what I could and threw the other half in the bin and sat down, my body and head in a heap, and that was it. I thought about Malcolm and for a second I was on the verge of throwing all up over Dubya. 'Stick a fuckin' fork in me,' I said, aloud, for I was indeed done. And this was the end of one of my best days. Was I ready to quit? As Muff never said to me, for he swore he'd always hated Americans, 'go figure.'

10
Janey
Autumn Term - End Of Week 1
Saturday, September 7th, 2002
Measby - Morning

The rest of the first week went flying by. I met new classes, got into a few scrapes with them and made a lot of mistakes but somehow got away with most of them. The Year 11s aside, who continued to be chilly, the youngsters seemed to think I was alright, in a 'you're one of them' sort of way. I got a lot of
"Sir, are you American?"
because my accent was fractionally mid-Atlantic and I tended to say 'no problem' and 'man' rather a lot. Like,
"Sir, it's nearly ten-past, shouldn't we be packing up?"
"Man, is it the end of the lesson already?"
And when the overhead projector wouldn't work with my Year 10s - a really nice group, a Set One - I told them it was 'on the fritz', a phrase which slid out before I remembered that of course, they wouldn't have heard it before. So I had to explain that. I was a novelty for most of the kids and I didn't mind exploiting that if it got me started at the school.

The novelty of my first real job would have been fresh, interesting and in parts, plain funny, but I was dogged by the feeling that it was me who was responsible for ruining, at least temporarily, the life of one of my colleagues and no doubt his family. It can't have been much fun for his kids having to plod along to the hospital at night to see Dad with his head covered in white bandages and unable to demonstrate the gift of speech. Something about Malcolm's haircut and miserable looking kisser told me he wasn't the most fun a father could be, but even so, this did not mean it was alright for me to practically kill him.

I was ticked off by Jez and Liam and even Susan over the next few days for wallowing in self-pity but it seemed a small price to pay for what I'd done. My mother phoned from Boston; well, from a sort of Brookline direction to be precise, one of the chi-chi outer-suburbs, and she gave it to me too for blaming myself.

'You're just like your father,' she said in her usual helpful, encouraging way. Perhaps this is where I got it from, the tendency to kill myself over and over when things went wrong: mistakes I made not keeping friendships ticking over; screw ups with girls that seemed to happen in an endless cycle; bad career choices, or more to the point, non-career choices. At least no one ever called me an asshole. I've never been an arrogant son of a bitch, a big head. No, sir. Never had that problem.

But I think it is time to fess up about my romantic life. I'll try not to bore you because it's nothing much to boast about. I was a bit of a late starter. I'm lying to you again. I *was* a late starter. See, I wasn't exactly a catch for the girls in school. Schools. We moved around a fair bit. London, Boston. So, okay, two cities doesn't sound too interruptive but I think I'm a person who needs to put down roots and when I was young I wasn't given the chance to do that. I was born here but was living in the States by the time I was two. Came back when I was ten, then left again when I was twelve when we upped-sticks from West Hampstead in north London and went back to Massachusetts. So I went to high school in Boston for six years. I could blame my tendency towards painful introversion on my mother who couldn't seem to decide where she wanted to live or with whom, but I think my shyness is something that just grew with puberty. I wasn't always like that. And I can't blame all of it on Haldey either. I was poked into the pigeon hole of being 'the quiet one,' and I've learned enough sociology along the way to know that if you slam someone into a role and force them to play it, they play it. I know women are supposed to like sensitive men but though the world has allegedly moved on, the girls I knew in school all drooled over themselves to find a cowboy or a quarterback. That was me sidelined, then. So the ones who might have wanted to go out with little Tommy in the corner with the braces were the leftovers, either with too much fat or enough acne to be featured in text books on the subject. I was a leftover too - I knew that. I never got depressed though. Fed up? Yeah, of course, but I just wasn't the type back then to grow a real personality disorder. I think I loved books and sports too much. I used up all my spare time and energy that way. Of course, I'm lying. A man needs a woman from the age of fifteen like a fish needs water and like a bicycle needs an ass to sit on it to make it go. When I was fifteen and a half there was a girl with glasses the size of portholes on the Titanic and so thin, people would come up to her in the street with food parcels, but I'm not going to tell you what I did with her and for how long or where. You'll just have to use your disgusting imaginations.

I want to move on.

I didn't have the self-confidence to break out for real until I went to university in London. Boy, did I work hard to make that happen. Killed my mother, practically, especially when it was her original nationality that made it possible. Anyway, there were so many geeks and nerds around the place it turned out that here was my big chance. Plus, it turned out that the passing of years had helped smooth out a few of my natural disadvantages, as I filled out somewhat with some good exercise, grew about a foot taller and lost the train-tracks. Second week at King's, I was at a college bar when a girl who did science called Jane came over to me. She was as drunk as a dead rabbit.

"Did you know you're good looking?" she said.

"Good, looking at what?"

Now, this reply changed my life. It wasn't exactly vintage Oscar Wilde but Janey really laughed at that. I'd never been known for making jokes, obviously, because quiet, shy people would rather sit on a good joke or a pearl of a one-liner until it hatched into a chicken than use it to burst into the middle of the room and take over the conversation. It's also like this: if you do suddenly think of something hilarious, by the time you've plucked up the courage to speak, the room's empty. But the thing was, Janey didn't know I was carrying this monkey on my back. She couldn't have known and the realization of that suddenly hit me in an instant. I'd made her laugh so I figured: well, hey, perhaps I could pretend I'm Muff or somebody with this new girl who actually came over and sat with me. And it occurred to me that what I'd said actually was quite funny. And cheeky. Made me appear like I didn't give a shit. You know, cocky. Which wasn't me at all. I must have drunk more beer that night than I realized. And luck played a part too as it always does on these occasions. Muff had only left me a few minutes before to go to bed 'because he wasn't feeling well.' Had he been there he'd have whisked Janey off into a corner and it would have been me leaving the scene for an early night. He'd have only fallen on his ass a half-hour later as he nearly always did, but the damage would have been done. I'd have lost her.

As it was, Janey chose me, just sitting there quietly finishing my drink trying not to think about Kafka. So there she was laughing and before I knew what was happening, she'd moved in closer. And man, it was liberation time. Incredible. She was good looking, no doubt about it - a little undernourished, but immaculate. Her hair was chestnut-brown and centre-parted, stopping somewhere near her shoulders. Lovely. When she laughed her eyes seemed to grow in her face and kind of sparkle at you - shit, I know this sounds banal but bear with me, it's true - and kind of lit her up. She smelled lovely, too, justifying every one of the millions of dollars big corporations spend on developing soap and hair products. Inside I was already howling at the moon for this girl. So I acted, in both senses of the word. That's essentially what I did. I acted the part of a guy who was used to being around girls all the time and who was used to getting as much tail as Elvis, and she bought it. House, right here!

It was weird. Having made one funny quip, I found I could do it again, and again, and we got on like two houses burning up. It was the most exciting thing that had ever happened to me in my life. And I think my years in America were giving me some sort of pay off - gave me some sort of alien allure. I suddenly discovered what I'd been missing all my teenage years. I practically climbed out of that old skin and flew like a rocket through multiple ceilings and headed off into space. That's how it felt. We went back to her tiny hall of residence room in Pimlico, and *bang*, out went my virginity like a dead star. Right that night. From sitting at the back of the crowd to racing a dragster in one step. So I admit, at 19, I was one heck of a late starter; but when I did start, it was a case of first big romance and first sex in one large biochemically explosive night.

"It must have come out like cheese," said Muff when I gleefully laid the bare bones of the momentous event on him the next day at the Bar Italiano, the place in Soho that was to become our regular coffee haunt for the next three years. He wasn't far wrong.

Janey and I went out for more than a year and it was a gas. Better, actually, it was a totally blissful time. We hung around the West End of the city together virtually every day, seeing and doing everything our pockets would allow. It was Janey's first experience of London so I took her everywhere and it was like seeing it all for the first time, doing the sights with someone for whom it was all foreign, and being in love. Smashed out of my head in love. I was so gone I even enjoyed Madame Tussaud's and made myself believe the Tower of London was almost worth the entrance money.

It ended, of course it did. Underneath the layers of romance and make-believe, we weren't really compatible. She quite liked loud bars and clubs and I liked quiet coffee places and cinemas. She wanted to get on with her life and I didn't care to do anything but enjoy myself and put off working for as long as I could. She couldn't understand my attitude. I'd like to say it was me who had the brains to bring this major league problem to the surface, but needless to say it was Janey. She it was who looked into my eyes one night and said,

"You know, I want to marry you. Or leave you. I can't work out which. What do you think? Can you see us married? Living the rest of our lives together?"

I give you the short version, naturally. In real time it took her about an hour and a half to tell me this. What could I say? The fact she said it proved she was 19 going on 35, and probably ready to be going out with someone older. I was 19 going on 20. No more, no less. I could have carried on with her for much longer just as we were. She'd put on some weight and seemed to get better looking by the month. I wasn't doing so bad myself according to her, so physically, if you know what I mean, the relationship had always been in good shape. The split wasn't that sudden. We slept together a number of times after the night she opened this little envelope of anthrax on the relationship, but come the Christmas holiday of our second year, we knew we were going home to the end of things. Of course, I was more than upset, but I knew she was right, and wise to have administered the humane killer when she did. Better that than have an on-off romance gradually fading into arguments, sullen silences and bitter recriminations later on with a shit-load of wasted time hanging off the wagon.

It wasn't so bad to think of Janey sleeping with another man, which happened pretty quickly, but it killed me to see them laughing together. Still, I couldn't grow to hate her. I owed her everything for coming up to me that night in the bar and saving me from the train wreck I'd lived in up to that point.

And what can I tell you about things since Janey - who I still think about to this day all the time? Well, it's been a scene of sporadic, disorganized and dull elements of relationships rather than the genuine, organic article. One night stands: some. Hardly a one that's worth remembering. Playing at going out as a couple: two. Both lasted no more than a month. Serious relationships (both partners kidding themselves): one. Lasted five months and a week. Serious relationships (no partner kidding themselves): none.

Numbers, shmumbers. The key thing is how happy it all makes you and what it does to your confidence level. I hadn't been happy with anyone since Janey and my self-belief had taken a bit of a battering over the past few years. That's how it goes. Tell you this, though: the night of my first school teaching day, when I slept for twelve hours straight, waking up to another beautiful blue, late Summer morning sky, I was more than ready for something real solid to start happening again. I mean: 28. Twenty-fucking-eight. All this stuff you hear about men not being prepared to commit to relationships? None of my friends have ever been like that. Not even Muff. You know what? I think it's a media-created thing so bored lifestyle hacks can add another topic to their miserable list of God-awful ideas for articles. Either that or the people who write this shit aren't interesting, attractive or kind enough to keep a man. Or they hang out with the wrong class of men. Does that sound misogynistic? Like I particularly give a shit. All my friends want to have great relationships with women. Or men. Me as much as any of them. And almost all of us want to have children of our own.

Which is why in my mind I kind of threw myself at Jez when I met her. I'm being stupid, probably. She was different, she was fresh, she was down to earth and to me, she looked gorgeous. I didn't care how she looked to anyone else. I didn't know a thing about her but when does that ever matter when you're in the first flush of falling for someone? I was incapable of being cool and analytical about this. But what can you do if you have nothing to lose, when you feel like that new person could be everything you need? Eh? Answer me that.

I tried to disguise my instant attraction to her of course, but with Sef carpet bombing me like that in the car, I was in my usual flummox with these things, only more so. It's hard enough to think straight when you go *zonk!* for some new person.

Maybe she already knew I'd have fallen at her feet if she'd so much as crooked a little finger at me. I know we men are often accused of being pathetic creatures, and I'll hold my own hands up to that. Hang on: is that - what's the reverse of misogynistic? Hell, being an English post-post-grad I shouldn't be caught with my trousers down like this. *Malenthropic.* That'll do. Are you happy now I've run down my own gender? Maybe I needed a relationship with a woman so badly the smell of it was leaking out behind me every wherever I went. Now that would have been a nasty development. Who would want a man in that sort of state? Only the lonely and the desperate, and I was not ready to reach that far down again. Am I making sense about how it was? I'm rambling, aren't I. Okay, I'm going to go and do something else right now. Leave me alone, dammit!

11

The September Manifesto
Autumn Term - Week 4 Day 2
Tuesday, September 24th, 2003
Peggy Lane Staff Room / Room B5

"What did the one-eyed cigarette salesman say to the chip shop owner?" The usual gang was sitting around the usual staff room table one lunchtime.

"Okair, Les, just give uz the punchline and a couple of owers and we'll get back to yer."

This was Jez. She'd settled into the department and, by the look of it, the whole school really quickly. She was one of these people who everyone liked, as if she had an endless supply of Make-Friends Juice and took some religiously every morning before setting out for work. I used to hate these people.

"I don't know: but if you find out before I do, let me know."

"What did the gay one-eyed cigarette salesman say to the chip shop owner at the end of a long shift?"

An interjection from Sef. Silence. He delivered the punchline as he got up and left,

"Got a fag?"

There was an embarrassed silence and poor Les looked nonplussed, like a mole who'd just thrust his head into daylight and realized he'd got his head stuck out of the wrong hole.

"Don't worry, Les," said Maurice Butter, Head of Maths, "he's doing that to everybody these days."

"I'm not," said Les, probably unaware of the double meaning. He didn't seem to be quite with the rest of us in the modern world. He was to style as Al Pacino has always been to black ankle socks worn with open-toe sandals. He was about as good looking as a motorway pile-up. I felt sorry for the guy; we all did, I think. Except Fiona, who always measured out an utterly contemptuous look for him if they ever happened to be sharing the same air, as if she was the Queen, or Elizabeth Taylor. Wait, I take that back. Elizabeth Taylor would have taken pity on Les and taken him home to give him a good bath. I wondered a lot why Fiona taught. She looked to me like she should have been running a high class designer clothes outlet in Bond Street. Liam said she had a husband who worked for MI6 "if the looks of her is anything to go by," and you knew what he meant.

"I'd like to blow the feckin' bitch to smithereens," he said minutes later when she got up to leave.

To my shame, I claimed I was about as political as a jam tart; that I didn't hardly know who that John Major was. It was simpler sometimes just to pretend you didn't know things. It could cost you a lecture from a couple of guys to whose company I found myself gravitating each break and lunchtime: Colin Nostrum, a Sociology teacher, and the ginger jokester from that first staff meeting, Andy Crucial. They were the nearest thing I'd found so far to a staff room comedy double act.

"But Tim," Colin chastised me early in the term, "you have to understand, everything is political: the water, your cup of tea, your socks. Absolutely everything. When are you going to wake up to the fact, mate?"

"Socks are the opium of the masses," interposed Les Person. "I've got a joke about a sock. What did the sock say to the pair of crotchless knickers?"

"Les, give it a rest, please," said Maurice in a kindly way. Les had been trying to hit us with jokes relentlessly for a couple of weeks at this point. The dark rumour going around was that he was seriously considering taking a pot-shot at stand up comedy. But only Chris Lampeter was laughing. Never mind me, so-called 'Trappist Tim;' this guy made me look like Graham Norton. Four weeks into the term and I don't think I'd heard him speak yet. But he'd sit there every day chuckling at Les, or whoever was making a game bid to be humorous. Never looked miserable, that guy and I liked him for that.

Apart from Chris, nobody felt much like being cheerful that Tuesday. Two days before the head had dropped his bureaucratic bombshell on us. 'The Peniston September Manifesto,' Andy called it, impressing no one, though in time the name would come to stick like stale rice pudding to an old oven dish. The staff now stalked the corridors and classrooms like sullen victims of a grave miscarriage of justice. Mark book inspections? An insult to the professionalism of a dedicated staff. New Schemes of Work to be completed by heads of department for scrutiny by half term? Pointless addition to work load and mindless interfering of Orwellian proportions. Committees?

"I'm not goin' on no fookin' committee, wasting my precious time after school." said Rob Rodder. His reaction summed up the feelings of many in this one pithy sentence. Other responses were more subtle.

"A committee is essentially a substitute for imaginative and progressive management," said Colin, his long, sour face making him looking like a depressed donkey.

"Good point," nodded Andy Crucial, emptying another coffee cup, leaving the usual micro-droplets of brown liquid on his untended moustache.

"A committee is the classic way for an autocrat to spread his power. Stalin used it to devastating effect in the Soviet Union."

People didn't quite put their cups down and leave when Andy or Colin went off on one of their frequent lectures but eyes would glaze over and Les would normally try to break the deadlock with a joke attempt. But today he was leaning forward in his seat, elbows on knees, face in hands, thinking as Andy continued our education.

"Alas, my noble colleague, this is all too true," he went on. "You head up each one with a supporter and before you know it you've enslaved a hapless group of workers. Setting up this kind of Machiavellian structure is classic divide-and-rule technique."

Silence. They could sometimes be irritatingly smug about their observations on life, the school and everything, but Crucial and Nostrum looked less than delighted with their incisive analysis. For once, the folks round the table thought they might actually have said something worth listening to. It looked like they were right too, though I'd neither served on a committee nor studied History all that carefully. Sef had been in a foul mood all term. Much worse than normal, apparently.

"He's a f-feckin' maniac," said Liam to me making a quiet aside.

"Don't you mean, 'manic'?" I said.

"Both," said Liam.

Some days he came in full of warmth and light, cracking jokes, ripping the scornful piss out of the Central Management Group - this was Michael's chosen name for his new team at the top of the 'hierarchy,' another of Colin and Andy's favourite words - to much of the staff's huge delight. On others he would stare right through people he'd worked with for years. Throughout Monday's staff meeting where Michael announced the 'September Manifesto,' Sefton had leaned impassively against the back wall, arms folded in a sumptuous black leather jacket, chewing gum.

Chewing gum!

"A masterstroke, I h-have to admit" according to Liam.

And since then, on the couple of occasions I'd seen him, he had a face like impending war in the Middle East. Crossing each other in the corridor yesterday he'd blown past me like a dust storm. Chris, his sidekick, seemed as phlegmatic as always, however. According to Liam, he and Sef communicated secretly with one another using a secret code of hand signals and facial tics.

"I tell you, S-Sef and Chris have conversations about where they're going to meet after work by d-drinking their coffee a certain way. I swear to God. And I think I've c-cracked it. If they take two q-quick sips it's the Farmer. A slow deliberate slurp it's the Ringing Cleft. A sip with a raised little finger means six o'clock; back two fingers raised means s-seven and no raised finger means eight. I saw Sef take a sip with no raised finger but scratching his left ear as he drank which I think means he doesn't think he can m-make it but he'll get there later if he can. I'll have it worked out completely by Christmas, you w-watch me."

Liam O'Neil-Neil was totally off his noggin, of course, but Chris and Sef did have a thing between them that was close and maybe a little strange, and I wished I was in on it. Liam had another interesting theory.

"I t-tell you, Tim, Sef's humping Fiona's brains out. Lucky b-bastard."

"I thought you didn't like her?"

"I don't but have you n-noticed the tits on her?"

"Liam..."

I suppose it was possible. Sef always seemed a little restrained around her, and I understood they'd known each other a long time. It was possible that the understanding they seemed to have was based on some horizontal negotiating from some time in the past or its continuance into the present.

But then again...

"I thought you said he was gay?"

"Ah, well, now. Th-there you have me. Could be he likes an each-way bet."

"'Bent as a corkscrew,' you said."

"Ah, well,"

"'Queer as a posy of male ice-skaters...'"

"Will you hush your noise, h-he's comin' through the door now..."

And indeed, this break time the man himself strode to Mrs. Manicure's hatch with a face like Achilles about to go to war, and a word for no one.

The walking cold bomb that was Sefton Demmler aside, it was turning out to be a good department to belong to. Narida was as deliciously nutty as a bar of muesli, very upper class, very 'Tim, darling' but fun. And somewhat outspoken. One Friday night when we had a semi-official departmental 'do' at the Three Morris Minors in Oatley, I actually did spit a mouthful of beer over someone after she told Liam to "fuck off and join the IRA" when, a pint or two of Guinness to the wind, he got into an intense speech about the role of the British Army in an affair he called 'Bloody Market Day' which apparently took place near his home town of Clontarf. There was a mysterious explosion one night back in the 80s in a barn full of cows and he was convinced the Army and a special unit of the CIA had begun a campaign to undermine the whole agricultural system in the south. Liam was less than amused when we laughed uproariously at this, at which point he threatened to get his Uncle O'Neil-Neil to send one of his 'friends in dark places' over to blow "your f-fecking tits off, Narida." And when Narida, about twenty years Liam's senior, jumped on him in order to rub her enormous fun bags into his face, the landlord had to come over and tell us to quieten down or we'd all be asked to leave.

Narida was a hoot and always absolutely charming with me, forever beaming at me and keen to know how I was getting on in the classroom. I warmed to her even more when Maurice, who'd been at Pegs for a long time, told us that when a much, much slimmer version of Narida first came to the school in the early 70s, she earned herself the nickname 'Knickers Narida' because she used to wear ludicrously short skirts and often sat on her desk to teach. It had started with the kids and spread to the staff room. I was laughing so much at this news it drew comments from everyone of the 'oh, I didn't know you were still awake, Trap,' variety; you know, really funny stuff. But actually, I didn't mind. I didn't feel shy with these folk at all; I just liked to listen a lot.

The down side of the term was still Malcolm. Now a month after the B Corridor Disaster, he'd not long since come out of hospital. It took nine hours for the surgeon to rebuild his jaw and another four for an orthodontist to restructure his gums and clear out the mess that used to be his teeth. Clearly Malcolm would now have to give up hope of ever playing the flute for England. But yes, I did still feel bad about it and half-expected to be subpoenaed at any moment.

So the storm clouds would still gather over me intermittently, and there were times when I felt that they may have settled in for the term but it hadn't actually happened yet - even though I was having to come to terms with the fact that Jez would probably never be mine. It was painful when she came out with us and excruciating when she didn't. To make things better, or immeasurably worse, she was more than ordinarily friendly to me at school, and we spoke to each other a lot and there was always some laughing and joking involved too. But for every time I walked down to the bus stop at the crushed butt of another working day thinking I was making big headway, there was another when I sat on the 419 wanting to wrench the steering wheel out of the fat driver's hands and point it at the nearest dry stone wall with my foot burying the accelerator. I'd get in and spend the night exhausted with work and hallucinating wedding scenes and a beamingly pregnant Jez smiling up at her husband completely devoted to spending the rest of time with him. And I saw myself as a figure in rags stumbling around in the rain on some forlorn Yorkshire hilltop like a demented Heathcliffe, only buoyed by the knowledge in the back of my mind that at last Led Zeppelin had put out a great live album.

And yet, she would touch my arm in the staff room sometimes and hope would rise up in me again. Then later I would be lying in bed listening to my favourite records wondering over and again on a never-ending loop whether I was just imagining her attempting to establish some intimacy between us.

The one bright spot in the weather forecast was that having to get my ass in gear every day to teach lessons to real children took my mind off what you might call my, erm, bi-polar emotional chick-state. The job was so damned difficult, it couldn't be otherwise. I steadily improved. I was bound to, I was so raw when I started - "very steak tartare, aren't you, darling" was Narida's way of expressing it one break time.

"No, Narida, kind of *bleu*, I think," added an inscrutable Sefton. He had this way of saying things where there seemed to be a meaning lurking below the surface like some ugly creature that made its home in a sewer; it was hard to know whether he was trying to rip a hole in me or teach me something I didn't know but ought to. I was still under Sef's wizardly protective spell with those demonic Year 11s and we were starting actually to develop some sort of relationship. A few weeks into the term, Adam Taylor, the sloucher who'd treated me like something the cat shat on the carpet that first lesson, nodded at me on the way out of the room and sort of quarter-smiled at me. I suppose that meant I'd passed some kind of test. Like I wasn't the complete turd he thought I was at the start of September. I was pleased about this, but he could still fuck off as far as I was concerned. You were told on the training course never to take what happened to you in the classroom personally, but I would never forgive him for what he tried to do to me, any more than I would ever forget the utterly callous look in his eye as he did it. I was professional with him, and would continue to be, but nothing else.

The younger ones were just great, though. But as I think I said before, this was an ex-grammar school full of middle class kids, so why wouldn't they be? I was getting to be surprised by a lot of things in my life at this point. Like how keen I was becoming to be a better teacher. I would sneak a look through Sef's classroom door-window whenever I had a free period, careful not to be seen but trying to spot some of the things that made him great. The obvious thing was to go ask him if I could sit at the back of the class to observe one of his lessons, but I didn't dare.

*

We had a faculty meeting the next day after school and the main item was the September Manifesto. There was shouting even before we started, Susan screaming at the door when a youngster entered without knocking looking for a detention room. It showed us how tense she was. To begin with – for the first three agenda items anyway - Sef was still the unexploded nuclear weapon in the room, but with only marginally more explosive potential than several of his colleagues. You could have got the foam rubber out and started slicing again.

Susan had flown through the door late as was becoming her custom since the big promotion, and began to whirl around and about us in a flurry of photocopied handouts. More and more she had briefing notices and what-not typed and photocopied for us, 'as if we were mere drones' was Alex Carfman's regular complaint.

"Feckin' trees dying so that we can chuck p-pieces of paper into files we'll never read again," muttered Liam to me under his breath.

"Thanks a million, Susan," he was saying a minute later when she passed him another sheaf of pristine white A4 80G stained with black, a re-jigged Year 9 Scheme of Work. Then the meeting reached 'Item 4 – New Head, New Strategies' - Michael's name for the Manifesto, and things really got going.

An argument developed as Susan tried to explain to us Michael's rationale for the teaching file-checking. Fiona made a sound case against: 'interference;' 'breach of trust;' 'staff already working under a lot of stress;' which seemed reasonable to me. Then the exam result issue was brought up by Liam in his best Captain Sensible mode.

"I...I...If the head really does think our GCSE results are the most disappointing in the whole of W...West Yorkshire...I don't think the September Manifesto is the right way to improve them."

Susan stared at him, her eyes zombie-like.

"The what?" she said.

"O...O...sorry, Susan. I meant the new measures he ann...nnounced on Monday."

Conscious of the fact that he was still classed as a 'young teacher' by the senior members of staff he was a bit shy in meetings, though he always got involved. Alex then fired off a statistic defending our results, to general approval and Susan, defending the headteacher with a robustness that rather took the team aback, began to get it in the neck from all directions. Well almost.

"They're not even proposals," said Knickers Narida, casting her knitting aside for a moment. "The fact that he's made this announcement as a *fait accompli* is quite outrageous."

"New headteachers: little boys playing with big toys, that's all it is." Fiona. Susan fired her off a look of pure hostility as she tried to get her grip back on the department, her face losing its normal structure with the effort. It changed to one of hunted anxiety as the atmosphere degenerated towards opposite positions of really worrying aggression. Meanwhile Sefton sat on her immediate right leaning back in his chair with his eyes closed as if he were listening to a symphony. I looked for a secret headphone contraption but didn't see one. Susan, determined not to be beaten, not yet anyway, pressed on doggedly with her defense. Making one or two decidedly good points, I thought.

"He's only doing what all other schools are doing. What you...what we have to understand is that this is the way things are going. Michael is simply making sure Peggy Lane does not get left behind. And you can say whatever you like; our results are not as good as they were."

Alex snorted and Narida threw her knitting down in despair. I looked over at Sef. My God. He was now reading a newspaper. The *Frankfurter Zeitung*! And doing so as calm as you like. I looked at Susan looking at Sef and she was now a portrait of restrained breakdown. He was being impossible, the bastard, but I still wanted to laugh - doing this in the middle of an argument that blazed around him with more ferocity than anything I'd ever seen without punches being thrown. But you could see how Susan Climer got to be a teacher with a career on the rise. She wouldn't be beaten down.

"Okay, moving on, I want now to organize, sort out who is going to sit on which committee."

She brushed thick strands of hair out of her eyes for about the thirtieth time since we started. There was silence in the room now, but the air was still full of threat. Narida, Fiona and Alex smouldered; I could almost see acrid smoke rising from their shoulders. Sef broke it — by laying his newspaper down with exaggerated deliberation onto the desk, Susan watching the procedure directly, not even out the corner of her eye.

"Okay. 'Pastoral Care Group.'"

"What's that going to do, precisely?" said Alex.

"Well, it's going to discuss things like the role of the form tutor, the Year system; look again at the role of the Counseling Drop-In Centre..."

"Why, exactly?"

"Well, to find ways of improving each of them."

"What, Susan, is the point of examining the role of the form tutor? Don't we all know clearly what that is? I've been a form tutor for fifteen years and I know exactly what I'm for and what I'm supposed to do."

Susan had been flustered for over half an hour now. But for the first time I noticed small sweat patches beginning to form around each armpit. And was embarrassed for her.

"Look," she said sharply, "Fiona, it's what Michael wants us to do; y...it's simply what we have to do: decide who sits on each committee from the English Faculty. We don't have any choice."

"So you can't tell us why we should have a representative on the Pastoral Committee."

"I've just told you, Alex."

"No you haven't. I agree with Fiona. It'll be a complete waste of time."

"And are you telling me, Susan, that if we decide to change a part of the pastoral system, this committee is going to make the decision? It's going to be Michael, and maybe Elaine, not the committee."

"We don't know that," said Susan, weary, though I half-expected her to reach down into her bag, produce a gun and shoot Fiona Twyford-Sounding in the head with it.

"Oh, don't be so naive," said an un-shot Fiona. I cringed again and watched Susan's face look even more like a strained beetroot. The meeting was threatening to turn into a quiet but effective overthrow of established government.

"I'll be on it."

As it turned out, the conversation had been shot, not a member of the English department. At least the old one was.

"I shall be delighted to serve," said Sef.

We all stared at Sefton dumbfounded, not the least Susan. But she saw the breach in the defence of the naysayers for what it was: a disastrous one. She miraculously brightened.

"Thank you, Sef. Now, 'The New Strategies and Developments Team'..."

Alex again raised the question of what this one was for, but his heart suddenly wasn't in it. In twenty minutes we all had a committee to serve on, once every half term, for an hour after school. I volunteered for the 'Blended Learning Group' because I hadn't the remotest idea of what it was. I think I was also attracted by the simplicity of its name. Perhaps the meetings wouldn't last long.

When eventually the drama came to an end, in an exhausted but still moody atmosphere, I couldn't help but watch Sefton. With a self-satisfied look on his face he just got up, folded his paper under his arm, put his seat up on the desk and strode out in his normal way: saying nothing, like a cowboy with a professorial chair, back to whatever town it was he called home.

12
That Chick of Yours
Autumn Term - End of Week 4
Sunday, September 29th, 2002
Measby - Lunchtime

Brrrppp! brrrppp!
"Yeah?"
"How's that chick of yours, Timbo?"
"Hey, Muff, how you doing."
"Okay. Well? Answer me."
"Man, you know she is no such thing. Didn't I tell you? She has a boyfriend."
"No. Ah, well, makes it more of a challenge."
"Listen, I've got a big enough challenge trying to keep my head above water playing at teachers. Kid today trying to give me the runaround. I could have cut his throat with a clear conscience, I tell you."
"You should have called me. I'd have slit his gut wide open and shown him twenty feet of his own intestines while you did it. We could have found a drain somewhere - made it kosher."
"Muff, I was joking."
"I'm not. Listen. I got back to my bike in town today where I'd locked it against a lamp post and this little fucker about eight years old was about to run off with my front wheel."
"Shit, what did you do?"
"I threw a Bigstone's bag at him - hit him between the shoulder blades and he went down like a small sack of wheat."
"Whoah...you want to be careful. You could get sued. Did you get him or did he run?"
"Oh, he ran. But not before I got hold of him."
"You? You couldn't run a bath: how the hell did you catch him?"
"There was a medical dictionary in the bag."
"Oh. Shit, you're in court already. What did you say to the kid?"
"I told him, if he didn't get out of my sight by the time I counted to five, I'd slit his gut wide open and show him twenty feet of his own intestines if I didn't cut his throat for him first."
"....you really did, didn't you."
"Of course. Little bastard was crying for his mother by the time I let go of him."

"You should start a vigilante group, Muff."

"I might; but you know, I'm thinking of giving up this crap waste of time at the hospital."

"Yeah? Why?"

"It's exhausting and I can't do it."

"You're too proud to quit, Muff, you know you are."

"Too scared to quit is more like it."

"But what would you do instead, anyway?"

"I'm thinking of going into teaching."

"Nice joke, fat guy."

"What do you think?"

"Schools and psychopaths don't really mix all that well, Muff. That's what I think."

"What about you wanting to cut a kid's throat with a clear conscience? Did you know that 93.4% of serial killers are quiet guys like you?"

"That was an aberration. I like school kids, you know I do. And earlier in the day I was helping one out who was in tears at the end of my lesson."

"I knew you'd be a boring son of a bastard."

"Funny. No, this lad has bad problems at home."

"So what the fuck was he doing telling you. You obviously didn't bother to tell him about all those dreams you keep having about wanting to fuck your mother. You should give them all a health warning before you give anyone at that school the benefit of your diseased little mind."

"That's rich coming from you. You who once tried to rape an 88 year old woman."

"I've told you enough times: I was drunk."

"Yeah, that would have changed the jury's view of the case completely."

"And anyway, you exaggerate: I didn't try to rape her. One kiss is all I wanted."

"You are one sick fuck, man."

"Nothing wrong with sampling the ripest fruit on the tree, my good man. But enough of this. I've got a date spying through the curtains at this nurse across the street in five: she takes a shower about this time every night. Tell me about your woman."

"There's nothing to tell."

"In a pig's arse there's not."

"I told you: she's got a boyfriend. Been going out forever. Well on the way to the altar."

"Tell me, do they live together?"

"No."

"Ah, right. Fantastic news. You're there, he's not. Another couple of months working your charms on her, you'll be in there, sucking on her flesh like a tarantula."

"You really are disgusting, do you know that? I'm going to report you to the BMA. You'll never practice. I'm going to make sure of it."

"You'd be doing me a favour, mate."

"Then I won't."

"Getting back to the subject, I know you're an ugly nob-end with bad breath and a gold medal in the athlete's foot, but she's an English teacher so she'll have absolutely no taste and if she's from Bury you'll be an exotic fruit she won't be able to resist eventually, so relax. They still eat tripe and onions for breakfast over there. You probably look like an American Hugh Grant from where she's standing."

"Which would explain everything. She's not interested in me."

"Hugh Grant? Sorry. I meant Beckham. Or that baby faced little twat with the chimp chin who sings. Will something."

"Muff, you are so full of shit. And he's gay."

"Whatever."

"If you worked for the Samaritans, the suicide rate would be higher than the World Trade Centre. Whoops, sorry."

"I rest my case. You need my help, son. If I wasn't so busy here I'd come up and straighten the whole thing out for you."

"Somehow I think not, Mugson. For a start, if you saw her you'd be trying to get her pantees off."

"I thought she was a woman!"

"Muff..."

"Well, use the correct word! It's knickers, geezer."

"Muff. Fuck off and give someone else a headache. I don't need this."

"Nice one. Alright - godda go. Hang on in there. I'm serious. Those teenage romances: they never last."

"Later, Muff."

"Indeed."

Clkkkk!

13
Down At the Bottom
Autumn Term - Week 6 Day 2
Tuesday, October 8th, 2002
Pragmatists School. Oatley, Playfields and Changing Rooms - Afternoon

In crisp, bright autumn afternoon sunlight, the referee's whistle blew for half-time. The team wearing red and gold shirts stopped as one, then began to plod towards the touchline across a mulch of grass, mud and fallen leaves where stood a teacher.

Their tread was somewhat more deliberate than that of their opposition because they, the Peggy Lane Under-15 football team, were two-nil down to Pragmatists High School, Oatley. As things stood, their only fortune was to be losing on another team's pit heap. Were this looming disaster occurring on the pitches behind the lofty stone buildings of The Peregrine Lane Grammar School, the embarrassment would have been almost too complete to bear.

The teacher remained standing in the same spot from which he'd observed the unfolding drama of the first period. His hands were buried way down deep in the pockets of his short, black, double-breasted overcoat, and his legs were planted solidly on the wet turf, slightly apart. Thus, immobile he stood, waiting for his eleven charges and the subs to gather round him for the time-honoured ritual of the half-time team talk. Soon they'd drifted together to form a sweaty bunch of muddy adolescents in front of their master. They were quiet and not a little sheepish. Two of them had colds and were sniffing at regular intervals. One, a short but dynamic midfield player by the name of Tyke Triff, wiped his nose on his gold cuff as often as he thought was necessary, which was about once every twenty seconds on average. Another, Scotty Mint, had only a slight cold but had to cope with another problem: twice he had to free his young balls from tight underwear as he walked over to the touchline and was still wrestling with the problem when he arrived at a temporary resting place slightly to one side of the pack.

'If my mum doesn't buy me some new pants soon, I'm going to go into a shop and nick a pair,' he said to himself.

It wasn't long before the teacher began to speak. There was much to sort out.

"Okay, listen." He checked that they were all silent and looking at him. Centre-back and captain Nicky Crimms was quietly trying to tell right back Gareth Cart how he badly needed to get tight on their wide player on the left, anxious to redress the situation as soon as was humanly possible.

"Quiet, Nicky." He paused, then swept his eyes across the faces of the eleven active participants and the three substitutes, all now fully assembled and still.

"How many years have you been together as a team?"

Scotty Mint looked around at his team mates to see who, if any of them, was going to be the first to speak, decided they were all content with their moody silence, and answered.

"Three, sir. And a bit."

"Correct. And how many times have we lost in all that time?"

Sam Tiddler (sub) was first in this time,

"One sir, in't it?"

"Correct. When four of you played with flu. And who was it who beat us that day?"

Scotty again, knowing that his teacher wanted another quick response, answered, pulling at the side of his crotch as he did so.

"Prags, sir, one-nil."

"Correct. Fucking Pragmatists of Oatley, this bloody toilet town."

The team, to a sticky-knickered, spotty Peggy Laner were taken aback by this. Their teacher never swore. At least, not at them. Jamie Spooner, star striker but so far goalless on this golden and gorgeous afternoon, had never heard Sir ejaculate profanely. Ever. At school the staff never used what his Gran called 'language.' Except Mr. Demmler, of course, who was famous for it, when anyone tried to get away with a misdemeanour like not handing homework in on time. The boys' PE staff, thinking about it, had been known to let loose an expletive or two during particularly tight rugby and footer matches, and even sometimes in PE lessons when someone like Bad Midge turned up without kit for the umpteenth time, as in,

"Midge, you are a bloody waste of space. You're as much use as a..." (i) "Fart in a spacesuit" (much used by Mr. Trance who'd long been a fan of Billy Connelly, (ii) "chocolate teapot" (favourite of Mr. Chap, who was always completely helpless when a cliché rolled into his half-empty brain) and (iii) "chocolate fireguard" (beloved of Mr. Coulson, who had a slightly more colourful imagination. Only slightly, mind).

The Keeper of the Flame for this particular Pegs football team produced this most used and useful word in the English Language for one reason alone: to rock his team to their very foundations. In truth, he was worried by their first half performance. His lads were well out of sorts. Were he a skilful mind-reader he would have been aware of the following information: David Doofer, in midfield, was off his game because his mother was a breeder of pedigree bloodhounds, one of which, Sally, had produced a litter of seven at four o'clock that morning, thus causing the team's only left-footed midfielder to suffer a poor night's sleep; Lee Long was tired out from a late night surfing Internet porn; the aforementioned Spooner had missed two chances he would normally have put away without pausing to so much as fart because his mother had just been diagnosed with breast cancer; finally, and most crucially perhaps, goalkeeper Paulo Gofrey had had a tiff at lunchtime with his girlfriend, the lovely Lesley Spank, blonde darling of 10GT, and was definitely below par as a result. Pragmatists' first goal was gifted to them thanks to Paulo uncharacteristically misjudging a corner. Still worrying that Lesley's exchange of pleasantries with Alan Bunkup of 11FA that lunchtime justified his fears that his beloved was on the verge of ending their intense six-month relationship, he completely misread the flight of a cross. It looped over his outstretched hands, which was bad enough for a lad who trained on Monday nights with Barnsley Youth, but the situation then went terminal. Expecting the customary interception from his keeper, defender Lip Dooson hadn't presented his body at the correct angle for a headed clearance. Thus, the pill landed inadvertently on the back of his head and looped over the line for a very soft goal indeed. 0-1.

Paulo was still fretting about this calamity when an admittedly well-struck drive from the edge of the box from Prags' Tom Mullet flew past his outstretched right hand into the net ten minutes before the interval. 0-2. He would, he knew, on a normal day have tipped it round the post for a corner. But today was anything but normal. From there his team, normally so dominant in their fifteen or so matches per season, let their heads drop and were lucky indeed that Prags striker Leigh Mopp-Carpenter was in a state of stress through the nexus of four different subjects wanting coursework in from him by the end of the week. He too had had a troubled night's sleep and, lacking sharpness as a result, missed two golden opportunities to put the game surely beyond Peggy Lane's reach in the dying minutes of the half.

However, the Pegs team coach was privy to no such information. So the teacher-in-charge launched his speech with a technique he'd rarely had to call upon in his three years (and a bit) in charge. It can be loosely described as Churchill With a Twist.

"So: I want you all to ask yourselves: do you want to go through the next few years of your lives, perhaps the whole of your lives, knowing that you lost not once, but *twice!*" - and here he paused for dramatic effect - "to a bunch of gutless, talentless, no-hope teenagers from a rugby playing - a bloody *rugby* playing town, which is a disgrace to the whole of Yorkshire?"

By the time he'd finished this short oration, his lads had begun to stand up straighter in their boots and were feeling taller, tougher and ready to get a grip on the situation. If he had looked closely at Jamie Spooner - he didn't - he would have noticed the West Yorkshire Under-15s striker (some interest from Nottingham Forest's chief scout) gazing at his silver David Beckham *Winners*, imagining his hero staring down at him in disgust from a cloud reserved for footballing Gods, telling him to stop playing like a prat and get his school team out of the shit. Or 'cart,' as the England captain might have said had Jamie been *au fait* with the Essex vernacular. The rest of the team now looked trustfully up at their leader, determination writ steady and large on their young pock-marked faces. Stuart Pitchfork wiped his gold cuff on his nose, as again did Tyke and Scotty, and all decided they were now ready to put right the wrongs of the first half. The Keeper of the Flame was satisfied. Still looking angry though, he nodded and said one final thing:

"*Come on, then!*"

Nicky, bearing his responsibilities as skipper with his usual gravity, echoed his gaffer.

"*Come on!*" he shouted to his team mates as he ran off to take his place for the restart at the heart of the Pegs back four. His colleagues also ran to their starting positions rejuvenated and resolute.

The Pragmatists' referee stood in the centre-circle on the halfway line, ten metres from the centre spot. The unfortunately named Rex Lung was impatient to get the second half moving lest that arrogant bunch of so-and-sos from the local rival school should have time to recompose themselves. He knew they'd been way off their game so far and could hardly believe his luck that his team had strode to a two-nil lead. Also having to tolerate an outbreak of the cold virus, he blew his nose into a spotted blue and white handkerchief and illicitly inspected the contents before tucking it into the right hand pocket of his elasticated sports trousers. He then blew the second half into existence with a toot on his whistle. Thirty seconds later, left back Blue Mole suddenly advanced to dispossess a dozing Prags midfielder and played in Stuart Pitchfork with a masterful pass (for someone of only fourteen). The tall Stuart, teeth clenched, simply ignored the existence of the keeper and thrashed the ball into the net half way up, making it billow seductively. Those Peggy Lane players who'd managed to cross the halfway line while this lightning attack had hurtled to its speedy conclusion fairly skipped like fairies back to their own half for the restart. 1-2. The Prags lads looked stunned and, all too aware of the mighty reputation of last season's West Yorkshire Schools League and Cup double winners - undefeated in all 17 games - were startlingly ready to accept an inevitable fate, sadly for Rex and their parent spectators. Now a yard and a half quicker and metres hungrier than their opponents, Peggy Lane scored four more in the next quarter of an hour. The young Spooner, inspired by Becks, Mum's cancer and all, smashed in a hat trick during this passage of play. The Lane were 5-2 up now and looking almost obscenely rampant. The hopeful expression of Mr. Lung, so evident in the first period when his underdog lads were leading, had left his face and been replaced by one of considerable dismay. His thin, fair moustache, modelled optimistically on the cover of Frank Zappa's *Sheik Yerbouti*, drooped lower than an un-milked cow's udder. The ref, marching yet again to the centre-circle for a restart, now resembled a Mexican undertaker with a bad case of the jalapeño shits.

Alas for poor Rex, the position of his team deteriorated further. Scuffer Mole came off the metaphorical bench to notch twice, the second a glorious twenty-yard volley that met a poor defensive header out of the box from Shane Bobbley. Will Gaffy trotted up for a corner to head in an eighth and Daz Doofer, taking advantage of a totally demoralized opposition defence, magicked his way past four non-challenges before chipping the keeper for a ninth in injury time.

All the while, the Peggy Lane manager ignored the exultant ejaculations of pleasure emanating from the seven Peggy Lane parent-supporters who'd made a special effort to get to the match seeing as it was a local derby, and maintained the poker face. His hands remained entombed in his overcoat pockets, his left hand fingering a stray lump of snooker chalk. Broadly speaking he was a model of continued, almost studied impassivity. Only occasionally did he reveal a sense of repressed pleasure at the proceedings, kicking at the layer of russet-coloured leaves that carpeted much of the touchline floor after the third and eighth goals. But was he pleased? Oh, he was. Tonight he would go home a coach replete with professional satisfaction. He would greet his loving wife with a modest kiss, stroke his son's hair with especial tenderness, pick up his daughter and give her an extra tickle to make her laugh even longer than normal, then briefly relate to them the heroic doings of his boys. Later, after sausages, mash and onion gravy, he would meet a couple of friends for a Quiz Night at his local, The Lost Whippet, and find that his first pint of Thrapston's tasted even sharper and hoppier than it normally did. After all, good as his team was, rarely did they obliterate the opposition as they had done so viciously this afternoon. A nine-goal second half was unprecedented, and marked a new threshold in their level of achievement. Gofrey; Cart, Gaffy, Dooson, Mole, B; Doofer, Triff, Long, Mint; Spooner and Pitchfork (Mole, S. and Tiddler, subs). These were names whose memory he would take to the grave.

One of the said parents, Miff Mole, could contain himself no longer. He strode over to Pegs' coach, face beaming like a lottery winner, to douse the inspirational leader with congratulations.

"Chris, amazing stuff. The lads have never played so well. And thanks for bringing Scuffer on, second half. You don't know what that'll mean to him."

"Don't worry, Miff, I think I do," said Chris Lampeter. He'd known the father of Blue and Scuffer for over three years now, and was more than happy with first-name terms. He allowed himself a momentary grin too, as he marched back towards the changing rooms, kicking more autumn leaves as he went. In the windless late afternoon, they rose just eighteen inches or so, then fluttered gracefully back to terra firma.

Mole Senior was not far wrong. In schoolboy football terms, Pragmatists High were a good side. They'd finish maybe third or fourth again this season. But the Red and Gold Pegs under-15s had mopped them up as if they were just a drop of spilt milk on a kitchen counter top. Müllered them, given them a junior footballing lesson. This season, the National County Champions Cup beckoned, a dusky football siren that already seemed willing to submit. Quarter-finalists last year but crippled with injuries, this year they would surely go all the way to the final at Molyneux - Chris had already allowed himself a peep at the schools FA website - perhaps even...'no,' he thought with characteristic caution: he wouldn't allow it one single thought until the final whistle called time on the very last game of the season, with the Red and Gold victorious at the elegant and sizeable home of the venerable Wolverhampton Wanderers. Thinking too far ahead wasn't the way to win things.

As Chris entered the Prags senior boys changing room, he ignored the all-embracing whiff of schoolboy sweat mixed with cheap deodorant. He concentrated on his job. He fetched the valuables box from the sadder but wiser Rex Lung, after shaking his hand and pointing out for consolation how the game could easily have been much closer had Pegs not missed those first half chances. He may have been lying, but it was important nonetheless to offer Rex some professional courtesy. Then, he marched back to the Pegs area of the changing room. Some of his lads had gone off to shower, so he'd have to wait there for a bit 'til they all returned. He couldn't give up the valuables box until everything was claimed by its rightful owner.

A few were already putting their uniforms back on, soon to stink their way back to Yarrow, and to these he returned their watches, phones and cash. By the time he'd done this, a couple of the boys had already returned to their pegs, dripping wet and covering their privates with their towels.

"Great result, sir, weren't it?" said a lit-up Lip Doosen.

"Yep," came the typically succinct reply, "you did well."

"No thanks to you, sir," said Lip, his grinning face betraying the attempt to wind up his master. Not that this was going to stop his flow. "If you think that was an 'arf-time team talk, you can forgerrit it, sir. We did it all, not you." This got a big laugh and he grinned with pleasure, basking in the warm approbation of his mates. But the supreme concentration of mental effort he'd needed to find the words that might get under his teacher's skin caused him to drop his towel. Chris, far from annoyed, was laughing in his silent way. Now: in the process of retrieving the wet piece of towelling from the muddy floor, Lip's scrawny naked buttocks presented themselves to an admiring public. This consisted of said stinking shower-shirkers, the returning Doofer, Cart and Mole (B), Chris, and three fathers. The teacher, as full of beans as ever he had been after a match, and at the end of a tiring full Thursday, suddenly decided that the situation demanded a mock reprimand to be delivered to the cheeky young Doosen. A fraction of a second later he delivered his centre-back a sharp thwack to the arse with a playful swish of his left hand. Those who witnessed this act of teacher-pupil camaraderie laughed fit to bust. It was all part of the euphoria of an imperious victory. Lip yelped and grabbed his towel from the wet floor while Gareth Cart cheered aloud. The Three Dads, richly enjoying the moment too, laughed along, one Rip Doosen included, father of Lip.

Lip, still laughing, looked for revenge on the mocking crowd. He whipped the wet edge of his towel across the head of Nicky Crimms for the sheer joy of being fourteen years of age. Not that his mind formed these exact words, you understand. Things may, in different circumstances, have developed into a fully-fledged towel fight, but the boys had too much respect for Mr. Lampeter, and anyway, they were weary from their exertions, and wanted to get home to their rest, their TVs and all the other modern gadgets that filled the lives of Year 10 boys. Goalie Paul Gofrey was impatient for the return journey to Yarrow to commence as he'd decided just after the eighth goal went in that he'd ring the lovely Leslie as soon as he got in to sort out his romantic difficulties.

Across the Pragmatists' side of the shared changing room, however, Rex Lung was not laughing. Acutely aware of the apparently increasing incidence of child molestation in his country, and having heard a news segment on Radio 7 Live that morning about a catholic priest due to appear in court this very day on a charge of indecent assault, he was anything but happy to see Chris Lampeter smack the bare bottom of a boy for whose safety and well-being he was responsible. Arguably it was not Rex's fault that he was unaware of the presence of the young lad's father in the room. Indeed, had he been cognisant of the presence of the relevant parent witnessing this disgusting episode, it would only have made matters worse; made them more embarrassing.

As far as he was concerned, Lampeter was guilty of bringing the profession into disrepute, apart from any psychological damage he may have just inflicted on the boy. Perhaps, thought Rex, he made a habit of this sort of thing. Perhaps other more intimate trespasses upon the privacy of these boys took place on a regular basis, after weekly training sessions perhaps. 'There seem to be more and more evil people in the teaching profession in these sinful times,' he thought, sorrowfully. The priest at his church, the Rev. Adrian Shard at Popplewick Evangelical, had preached a sermon on this very subject only two Sundays ago. He frowned and promised himself he would give the matter further thought. At no point did the humiliation he felt stinging his soul from the 9-2 annihilation that had just been meted out to his side by local rivals Peregrine Lane Grammar School, Yarrow, enter his head.

On the other side of the room the Pegs lads were leaving. Chris came over and shook Rex's hand again.

"I know you badly wanted to give my lads a good stuffing, Rex; sorry I couldn't oblige. Maybe next time, eh? Cheerio."

Rex forced a smile and said 'cheerio,' too, but inside he continued to frown.

14
Up Close and Personal
Autumn Term - Week 7 Day 3
Wednesday, October 16th, 2002
Peggy Lane Staffroom and Corridor B

It was the end of another day of hard, constant teaching. I left my classroom with my stuff for taking home and went into the staff room. Liam was there and sundry other members of staff too, seated in clusters of tiredness and relief. Sometimes I would feel a pleasant weariness at having come through the day in one piece and having done something useful with my time. But mostly my new days ended with an audible *phee-yuuww!* as the door closed behind my last pupil and the sharp, sudden awareness of having made it through another day more or less unscathed hit me.

I liked the staff room at the end of the day. When the last bell of the afternoon exploded at half-past-three, within twenty seconds the air just beyond the door would abruptly fill with the sound of exuberant teenage chatter mixed with a raucous shout or two from youngsters who'd held themselves in all day, a noise that quickly swelled to a crescendo. This would last for around three minutes before dying down to soothing corridor echoes; then the October birdsong conversation outside the window would emerge from a seeming nowhere, though it had been there all day. Sometimes if I was sitting alone, a sense of calm would then settle upon me, knowing that the children had gone, barely disturbed by the *oowhup!* of an automatic key unlocking a car door under the window, and the *thunk!* that followed as it closed a few moments later - the sounds of the first teacher going home. In this quiet sat Liam O'Neil-Neil and me on the last Wednesday afternoon of the half term, until he took off to the bank to throw some blarney at his overdraft problem. I was thinking of leaving myself, but I wanted to see Susan about one of my Year 9s who kept monkeying me around. I thought maybe a spell on Faculty Report might take care of the problem but I needed the boss's say-so to put it into effect. It was getting late, nearly ten-past-four, but I knew Susan often worked there until well after five, so I walked back down to the English area at the far end of corridor B to her office.

When I got there, a cleaner was plugging in an electric polisher. I sidestepped the cable so as not to end up like Malcolm, smiled at her and said 'hello.' I always thought of school domestics as old crones with hacking coughs, but this was Mary, who couldn't have been 30, and who carried around a figure most of the single men in Yarrow would have strangled an octogenarian to get their hands on. The West Yorks. Authority uniform tabard didn't do her any favours, mind. She was pretty too, and what she was doing stuck at Pegs on the minimum wage was anybody's guess.

"'ello," she said in the fetching local accent, smiling back. I was just daydreaming about how she might look wearing that bib and nothing else, closing in on the last few metres of my journey across the school, when I heard voices from Susan's office: one hers - the other, unmistakably Sef's.

It's funny how you start to do things sometimes before you've made the decision to act. I slowed down and made sure my shoes made no sound on the shiny parquet floor. I was within six feet of the voices now, when the door was suddenly pushed shut by an unseen hand from inside. Clearly they did not want anyone to hear the contents of their conversation. Well, doesn't that just increase one's interest in what's going on behind the door? I assumed immediately that they weren't discussing the weather, or Christmas, because to that point in the term, I had only heard those utterly distinctive Sef tones in school in terms of combat with an opponent or making a gentle form of mischief. The latter was never anything heavy: maybe Sef pointing out to someone how their lives were in need of total and complete overhaul due to their having accidentally watched ten minutes of Eastenders one night - 'I suppose if you like to be exploited and treated like an imbecile by brain-dead BBC executives, then fine...' - or that they deserved to have their house gutted by fire because they ventured to suggest that Norah Jones was a recording artist of some quality - 'If you want to join the millions of dull mediocrities out there who think that listening to a vapid excuse for soul music is a useful way to burn electricity, I suppose it's up to you.'

Experienced Sef-watchers all agreed that he'd never been in such a rut of unforgiving negativity and none of them knew why.

"I don't know what's wrong wi' that lad at'minute," Rob Rodder had said that very lunchtime, auditioning for the role of senior member of staff even though he was no more than 23. "He's be'aving like a raight wank."

Maurice Butter, nursing a cold, mused upon the subject for a while then made an offering:

"It's probably Michael and these bloody committees. Sefton's got his first meeting tonight. I know that may seem a little obvious, but..."

Andy was next to weigh in, sounding as ever, the expert's expert.

"The thing to remember about Sef is that he's got a life away from school and well, you know, anything could be happening there."

Andy had worked with Sef a long time so I tried to push him further,

"If it's an out of school thing, Andy, what do you think it is?"

"I don't know, Trap; your guess..." The conversation had quickly become moribund. It struck me that the atmosphere Sef had been carrying around with him for the past few weeks had perhaps begun to affect all of us.

"I can't believe Sef has volunteered for a committee," said Maurice pulling a handkerchief from his trouser pocket to mop up his nostrils. "I'd have had a big punt on him refusing point blank."

"Does anyone know what the bloody 'eck he's up to?" said Rob. "I was hoping he'd lead us out on strike over it."

"I hear you showed up for your numeracy meeting last night bang on time," said Andy. "I thought you were refusing to go on any of these things, brother. I didn't think you needed your Uncle Sef to hold your hand before you made your own personal gesture on the matter, f-huh-huh."

"Yeah, well," said Rob, bogged down in thick mud.

"And what are you doing on the Numeracy Group? You haven't got a Maths GCSE," said Colin.

"He's the only one in the DT department who can count to ten," said Maurice.

Liking his own quip, he laughed, through a rattling cough he could keep right away from me.

"You're the special needs adviser, aren't you, Rob," said Andy, "with a lot of personal experience in the subject, f-huh-huh..."

"Fook off, the lot of you," said Rob looking like he was on the verge of a major sulk. He took a lot of stick from the folks at our table, but he always came back for more.

"Anyway, getting back to the subject, I was going to talk to Sef about some sort of unofficial action against the committee thing but getting a word out of him at the moment..." said Colin, listlessly,

"Is like getting a pig out of a supermarket."

Les had arrived.

"Nice one, Les," said Rob. "Actually tha's improving – 'gerrin' a pig out of a supermarket' - If you could drink, you'd be useful."

"How do you know ET was a Yorkshireman?" said Les, apparently trying out another part of the act.

"I don't know, Les, thrill me."

"Because he looked like you."

"Right, you can fuck off an' all, yer four-eyed bastard." Rob looked unpleasantly in my direction but I kept laughing anyway.

"Les, if I may say so," I ventured, "that's quite funny."

"Is it 'eck. Right, if you are really insane enough to go on in that club in Leeds, I'm going to come down there and heckle you 'til you cry."

This was interesting.

"What's this, Les: you actually going to get up and perform?"

"Ah, yes," he replied confidently, sipping his tea. "I think the world is now ready for Les Person, comedy champion in the making."

"I think the world is ready for you to disappear down a fookin' grett big 'ole if you're going to tell rubbish jokes like that, lad."

"Not so much of the lad, young master Rodder."

What did not give me much hope for Les and his ambitions up at the comedy mike was the fact that he was already well over forty. I figured that if he really did have what it took to make people laugh for a living he'd have located it a long time ago. Rob was keen to press home his version of the thesis.

"Les, you couldn't find your arse with either hand if I gave you three days, so I don't know how you think you're actually going to make anyone laugh at you up on a stage."

Rob thought about this for a few seconds, then started laughing, derisively.

"Then again..."

"Alright, Rob, that's enough," said Maurice Butter entering the fray like a boxing referee stopping a one-sided bout.

"You've more chance of findin' Shergar's balls."

"Rob, enough, old son," said Andy.

But Les had more to say.

"If I could make a living telling jokes, I could teach Christopher Reeve how to become an Olympic gymnast."

We all burst out laughing at that, Rob included, while Les just looked straight ahead and grinned at the wall, sheepishly. I had more admiration for the man now, having just seen him take a verbal pasting from a fellow nearly twenty years his junior and still somehow get in the last word. This was partly why I made a point of button-holing him just as we were about to head off to afternoon registration. To be left with the Sef question-mark everyone else carried around in their head wasn't enough for me: I wanted a good answer.

"What do you think about the way Sef is at the moment, Les?" I said, trying to play effective detective.

"There you have me, Tim. He lives miles away from the school, never comes to staff functions and never talks about himself. No one really knows anything about him. Apart from Chris, maybe."

And I'd be better off getting information from a dead KGB operative than from him, Les didn't need to say.

"And you're more likely to get water out of a bath than get information about Sefton from Chris."

"Ah, I don't think that one quite works, Les," I said, trying to be helpful.

"No? Oh, I quite like that one."

Standing outside Susan's office now, I made a quick calculation or two. One, the corridor was empty save for Mary back down the far end, miles away, and two, if I put my ear close enough to the door I could easily overhear the conversation coming to an end and would be a whistling innocent twenty yards away by the time Sef or Susan made an exit. Unless of course they chose to leave via the window, but as we were about twenty feet off the ground this was hardly likely. This teaching game was wearing my head out; I decided there and then on another early night. But I wasn't leaving for home yet; not when I could move soundlessly right up to the door and carefully place my ear against it. It was made of cheap wood, and the varnish had worn away in big patches, including one where I was now gently placing my ear, so I had to be careful - any rubbing movement and I would be in danger of lacerating my lug'ole. I could imagine the subsequent conversation:

"How did you get those cuts, Tim?"

"Oh, listening in to a conversation at my head of faculty's door. Yeah, I've no personal integrity. Don't worry, I'll be alright..."

The gibberish in my head faded and I tuned in to what was being said inside the office.

Susan.

"...well I think it'll do them both a lot of good. They're both doing well and working hard, so..."

"Where is it?"

"London. On a Tuesday. They may go early on the train or they may want to stay overnight."

Who was going to London? Who's been doing well and working hard? If Sef's in there it must be an English department thing. And surely one of 'them' had to be Jez. She was working her butt to oblivion from what I could tell. She rarely sat down with us in the staff room - she was too busy pouring her very soul into the new job, spending lunchtimes marking when she wasn't putting up wall displays or making designer lesson materials. And though she hated to admit it, I knew she worked half the night every night preparing lessons, marking more books, or essays and filling in that blasted planner. You would see it on her desk, the space for each school day overflowing with lesson plans, notes and reminders, while mine looked like a spider with its legs dipped in ink had crawled along each of my spaces for about ten seconds and given up exhausted. Christ, the girl needed a day away from the place alright.

But who was the lucky bastard going with her? Liam. Damn it, yes, it would be him. He worked hard too, or at least liked to make out he did. Shit, *merde, merda* and *scheisse*. And do I trust Liam? A single guy like me? Like I trust estate agents. He'd be grubbing round Jez like an animal, turning on the Irish charm for all he was worth, making that handsome, long, Irish face even handsomer.

Inside the office there was more talking.

"I'm still not sure, though, whether to send Liam or Tim. What do you think?"

Before surprise registered with me that Susan would ask Sef for his sagacious judgement over such matters, it was all I could do not to burst through the door like the police, shouting 'Choose me! Choose Me! Me!' Then I heard the reply.

"Send Tim. He needs it more than Liam."

How would I ever repay him?

"Are you sure?"

"Certain. You think he's doing well? Actually I think he's struggling."

The smiled dropped off my face.

"Liam is very solid now; he's well on his way. Send Tim."

"Okay. Settled. I'll write this down now in my diary before I forget. *Tim and Jez: Green Park Hilton Conference; New Possibilities For New Teachers: An NQT Top-Up Day, Friday November 1ˢᵗ*," she said sounding pleased to be completing yet another administrative task.

And then I started to giggle. Silently. I wasn't going to let myself get caught by Susan and Sef at this late stage. I pulled a foot or two away from the door and punched the air. Twice. And was laughing like a mute jackpot lottery winner, Cup Final goalscorer, man who got to sing with Jeff Buckley. So I was struggling, so what. If it got me a day with Jez, why the fizz should I care? Then I was startled suddenly, and froze. A cough had sounded, just behind me.

"Um, I don't want to bother you, Mr. Weaver, but do you think that listening at keyholes is a very professional thing to be doing?"

It was M.J. Peniston. Of course it was.

15
Drunk with Sage's Eyes
Autumn Term - Week 7 Day 3
Wednesday, October 16th, 2002
Peggy Lane Corridor B /Measby, late Afternoon

When I went back to Susan's office ten minutes later to apologize, the crap was flying. As I approached her door once again, raised voices could be heard doing battle. Up close, a furious tumult of argument was in progress dominated by two men. Initially Susan could be heard trying to calm the situation, but she was too tentative, and quickly withdrew to the position of mere bystander, even though the struggle was taking place right there in her office. This was a two-part disharmony of recrimination and raw hatred. No doubt about it. And I didn't have to press my ear up against the wood to apprehend the fact that it was Sef and Michael slugging it out in there like a couple of super-heavyweights.

I'd actually never in my life heard grown ups behaving in this way. In my family I'd been taught by example to make war against those I disagreed with or wanted to hurt by using the solidly reliable weapons of sullen silence and hostile indifference. I'd been carefully shown from a young age too that blanket refusal to appear at mealtimes was also a useful way to make a point. So the rawness of the fight sent an initial shock wave of nervousness right through me. Then, having been primed to believe that restraint was the first of all virtues, my brain said, 'Jesus, what a disgrace; listen to them, behaving like children.' Even my man Sef had blown his cool completely. Was this a way for two supposedly experienced professionals to behave in front of a young, new teacher? Alright then, behind a door where a young, new teacher was waiting to see one of the occupants?

Then the scraping of a chair cut through the row, as, I assume, someone jumped to their feet. I froze, but then relaxed; this time I had a legitimate reason to be here. If they came out they'd see me but so what? I wasn't moving. I'd come to apologize for listening in at Susan's door and it was my right to stay and wait until I could do just that. In fact, it neutralized my crime somewhat. How was this a way to carry on, the screaming and hysteria making them sound like a bunch of Brooklyn Italians who'd just found out that one of the sons was a homo? The hand hadn't even managed to shut the door properly. A waft of nastiness seeped out through the crack as it slowly but surely fell open wider. I fine-tuned in, and predictably was soon sucked into the battle on the side of The Bald Emperor. He might have been playing catch with land mines, but, Sef being Sef, he just couldn't resist baiting Michael who, by insisting upon pumping up his already overblown dignity, made himself a slow, bloated target.

"...I'll say this again: how dare you turn up for a meeting and sit there reading a magazine. I have never heard of anything so unprofessional in my entire career."

"My dear headmaster, I was merely waiting for something interesting to turn up. An appraisal of the year system might be an appropriate way of passing the time for you and your 'Senior Managerialist Cohort' or whatever you call yourselves, but I'm afraid it isn't for me."

"So why did you go to the meeting?"

"You told me to."

"You volunteered!"

"Come, come, headmaster. Our attendance at one of your Commissariats was a covert command."

"What? What do you mean 'Commissariat'?"

"I hardly think we have time for me to give you a lecture on Russian History now, headmaster."

"Will you please stop calling me 'headmaster'!"

"Why? Have you resigned? If so, then w..."

"Look! We..."

"Could you please *stop* this?" said Susan, having to raise her voice to the level of a shriek to make itself heard.

"No, Susan, we have to do this...Stop being so bloody facetious! I will not be spoken to like this."

"I hardly think that sort of language is becoming of someone in your capacity, Michael."

"You've used far, far worse than that with me and you know you have!"

"That may be so, but as a role model for your staff, do you not think..."

"Alright, that's it, that is *it*! I want to see you in my office first thing tomorrow morning. I shall have the Chair of Governors come in for the meeting too!"

"Are you really trying to scare me with that half-witted janitor of the local Conservative Party?"

Could this get any worse? Could it get any better? I could hardly breathe for my heart pumping blood around my body from the new location of my mouth. I had been scared for my friend initially, Michael having all the power of his magisterial office at his disposal, but I trusted my judgment that Sefton knew what was happening in there and was controlling events with the precision of a Basle watchmaker. By the time the exchanges reached a climax, my ticker had dropped back to its normal place and I was now silently urging Sef to give Michael an absolute pasting.

Then I got a hold of myself. If there was some reason or rhyme in Sef's behaviour, I couldn't see it, unless he wanted the sack, for that was surely where he was heading. No one could talk to the boss like this and survive; it was surely impossible. If he hated a school with Michael in it, why did he not just resign? Why instead go right up to the dragon and tease it, pleading to be professionally incinerated? Why do this if he wanted to stay? Why was he not the least bit afraid of the power Michael could summon against him? There had to be a logic in this I just wasn't capable of seeing.

"Just be there! Half-past-eight!"

"I'm afraid I shan't be there," he said, and unless it was wishful thinking on my part, he was laughing. "I shall be in the staff room, preparing for my first lesson of the day."

"You will be there…and bring your teaching file - I want to see it!"

Seconds later, the door was practically ripped off its hinges as the head, crimson with fury, burst out of Susan's office like the Flying Scotsman at full steam. Ten years older, he was a heart attack waiting to happen. He didn't see me, and blasted down the back stairs that led straight to the admin block.

I'm not sure I still wanted to see Susan; in the circumstances, what I had to say would not now register on any scale of importance for her - but I found myself unable to move. I expected Sef to quickly follow Michael, but a hand slowly pushed the door to and five minutes later there was still no sign of an exit; only the muffled sound of two contrasting voices inside. What they might have to say to each other I couldn't imagine.

After another slow minute had passed, accompanied by the sound of a vacuum cleaner and the echoing scrape of a chair in some distant classroom, I decided to quit and go pick up my things for the trip home. It had been yet another long day and not for the first time that term I had enough material to last me a whole evening of reflective thought. I'd almost reached the bus station about ten minutes later, and had just seen the driver of the 419 climb aboard and start his engine, my mind already revolving like a well-oiled door, when a familiar blue sports car pulled into the curb next to me. I opened the passenger door.

"Get in."

And we sped off into the five o'clock traffic. Gone was the swagger of Sef dancing verbal circles around Michael. He looked about as mad as a castrated bull, so I said nothing through the ten minute ride to Measby. No music this time to ease us on our way.

"Thanks for the…" I started to say as he pulled up outside my door, but Sef had already got out, his side.

"A cup of tea will do," he said.

"Oh," I said. I was honoured, but somewhat thrown. What had I done to deserve an audience? As I was pushing the key into the lock of my front door I was suddenly appalled at the spectacle that would confront him when he entered the less than hallowed portals of casa-Weaver.

"So, *casa*-Weaver..." he said, and his map changed to the shape of a laugh at least, because of the look on my face most probably; how had he stolen the words from my mind?

"I'm disgusted to say I was no different at your age."

There was crap everywhere. Perhaps I exaggerate, but you know how it is when you need to have something perfect and all you can see are imperfections. I suppose it didn't look too bad: just a slew of CDs, newspapers and magazines littering the floor; oh and the chairs and the sofa; and breakfast things not washed or tidied away yet. And that when I looked at the carpet I could suddenly see that it needed a bit of a clean. It wasn't what I had in mind for a first visit from the visiting royal, Sefton Demmler, however, so I cringed with embarrassment for myself. Visiting royalty? Sef? Yes, he was. I wouldn't actually have given a tuppenny crap had the Queen herself knocked at my door and asked to come in for a cuppa and a bit of a sit down. In fact I might not have let her in.

I rushed to the kitchen to put the kettle on, scooping up a pile of stuff as I went, and chucked it toward the paper rack so at least he would have somewhere to sit down, then slopped water all over myself and the kitchen floor just trying to fill the kettle.

"*Eat my fucking bollocks*," I hissed through clenched teeth. I didn't smash any cups, but could easily have done.

Sef was suddenly right by my side. He gripped my right arm and made me look at him. His eyes this time didn't look through me, or into my soul; they simply met mine. For the first time he looked at me kindly.

"Relax. It's only me."

Then he smiled. So I did too, but sheepishly, still.

"Do you mind if I flick through your CD collection? Don't worry," he said, pausing to look over his shoulder at me and again smiling, "I promise I won't say a word."

If Sef really could read my mind, this one would have been easy for him. If I wasn't all that proud of myself and my life, I liked to think my taste in music was safe from too much criticism, despite the only jazz album in my collection being a cheap collection of Louis Armstrong stuff I'd bought one time thinking it might do me some good. I never played it.

"Anyway," he went on, already flicking and leafing, "you've got some stuff here I've either got at home or wouldn't be ashamed of owning myself."

I was stupidly pleased with this as I found a couple of decently clean mugs and got the tea fixings together; tossed a few Jaffa Cakes on a plate to the sound of a CD box opening and the clicks of technological hardware being made ready for use. Then the sound of a Canadian, smoking angel.

'When you're driving into town, with a dark cloud above you....'

"There's hope for you yet: what is a youngster like you doing with Joni Mitchell CDs in his collection?"

I was back in the room, clearing my coffee table.

"It's my aunt; my mother's sister. It was the music I was brought up on - well, some of it."

I lit a tee light under some bergamot. At least this would make the place smell okay, even if it looked like a couple of junkies had blown through. And from there Sef let me tell him a little about my growing up years, and how my aunt Millie Roxiter used to play the acoustic guitar to me, wanting to be another Joni, or Judy Collins, and how she'd try to get me to sing with her, in the long evenings when I'd been off-loaded onto her while my mother was out working somewhere. I was always too shy though and would be more than content just to sit near her listening lapping up the wondrous sound of her voice and guitar. She really could sing. And the chords would float around me like magic before settling on the fixtures and fittings of my mind. Shame for her that by 1982, thirty-ish folk singers were about as fashionable as Formica coffee tables.

I tried to keep my little history brief, desperate not to bore him, and watched his face as I spoke, hoping for approval. I could hear him listening though. Then we got talking about music, where I was much more comfortable. It was bloody typical of the man that he knew more about modern music than I did.

"I can see why you like them," he was saying; we were discussing the rock dead. I was a bit of a Cobain fan. A lot of one, actually.

"But that stuff's not good for a soul like mine."

I think I knew what he meant. "I wouldn't have thought that loud guitar music was your type of thing," I said. The look this comment elicited would have melted a building. It made me realise that I was actually frightened of Sefton Demmler.

"In 1968, when Hendrix was playing the Bag O' Nails and the Marquee, I was 19 years old."

"You saw Hendrix..."

"I didn't say that. One day we might talk about the 60s, but today is not quite the day for it."

Surely you weren't allowed to be this cool in your fifties. It must be in the rulebook somewhere. You were supposed to like musicals; know who Elaine Strich was; or at a push have an Eve Cassidy album alongside your wife's Abba's greatest hits; a Beatles album somewhere for old time's sake. But I should have known better, thinking of Aunt Millie. I hadn't seen her for a long time. I just assumed that somewhere between the age of 30 and 50 everyone from my parents' generation gave up good music like you assume they must have given up fashionable clothes, casual sex and dope. 'I must not be so stupid; I must not be so stupid; I must not be so...'

"Do you play a musical instrument?" I asked, but he ignored the question completely, bar a rueful smile that was actually almost a grimace. Then despite all my better intentions, a thought surfaced: something Rob Rodder said in the staff room one lunchtime.

"Bent as a fookin' spoon, that Sef."

"Straight spoons are very fashionable these days, actually," said Les. "If you go into Leeds and..."

"You know what I bloody mean."

I'd wondered about this from the first training day. The fact that he kept the details of his existence completely hidden made speculation about his sexuality inevitable, I suppose, especially with Rodder around. Homophobia and chisels were his natural bedfellows. However, I hadn't actually asked anyone their opinion on the matter; it seemed disrespectful. I had only asked people like Maurice and Narida questions of a general nature about him. Though Sef had been at Peggy Lane a long time, he was still a man of mysterious identity. No one spoke about him having a wife, nor a partner. No one ever mentioned his having children.

It hadn't stopped me starting to nose around, though. I went to the office after school one day when Sef was away attending a funeral to ask for his phone number. I could then at least start tracking the postal address from the area code. I told one of the secretarials, Pearly Driss that I needed to ring him about an urgent school thing but she just smiled and said,

"Sorry, no can do."

So all I knew was that he lived quite a long way from Peggy Lane. Andy had said something about Burnley, but Narida poo-pooed the idea.

"It'll be some remote village, dear, but you're wasting your time. And you're single, aren't you? Life was made to be simple at your age."

If only.

"You should be out running down a bit of tottie," she said, trying to be helpful but only annoying me.

From Yarrow, a forty-minute drive could put you in four different counties. You could as easily be in the suburbs of Manchester as be buried comfortably in a quaint old farmhouse seven-eighths the way to the Lake District. So a male partner somewhere out there in the north of England? It was only innuendo. Some thought he'd once been married but when you asked experienced Peggy Laners, the conversation seemed to turn into a vague mist and peter out.

This man who loved his secrecy was one the fates had played kind: no one had ever caught him by chance on the streets of London, Paris or Newcastle, walking down the street or coming out of a cinema or a theatre or a restaurant with a lover, male or female. No gay member of staff had ever sighted him in any of the established haunts or was prepared to admit they had. Not that anyone seemed to know who was and wasn't gay in the ranks. In schools, even in 2002, you hid this like you'd hide the fact that you'd lost both your testicles in a wanking accident. The only fact surrounding Sefton Demmler that everyone could agree on, even if they hated him, was that he was the most charismatic teacher that ever stood in front of a class of kids.

"So," I said, "I don't mean to be rude...Sef, you're welcome here any time you like, any time - but, I'm guessing you must have a reason for coming in..."

He looked back benignly and calmly. Very calmly, in fact, for someone who just twenty-five minutes ago had set off the most almighty steaming motherfuck of a fight with his headteacher. In the same situation my nerves would have been lacerated strips of smoking fibre. Just minutes ago he seemed ready to commit an act of bloody road rage. Now he looked as relaxed as a discarded accordion. I don't know how he did it.

"Um, does it have something to do with the row you just had with the head?"

What always got me about Sef was what I saw next: he had this way of composing his face in such a way as to make you think he was about three-hundred years old, whilst trying to read his thoughts was like peering through sea fog for a glimpse of the future. If I'd been twenty years older then maybe I might have been able to discern in those peerless blue eyes some sort of message, but if reading faces were reading newspapers, my level was page 5, *The Daily Screamer*, something about a TV star and a strange relationship with a greasy sausage.

"It has everything to do with the row I just had..."

I took a bolt of energy from that, Sef taking me into his confidence: I could live with the excitement that would bring. I wanted to know everything about the struggle he'd obviously been having with Michael since that first day in his office and to do something to help him win it.

"...and nothing."

"Oh," I said, deflating, "what do you mean?"

"It was time to see you and talk to you anyway."

"Um, what about?"

"About what you want to speak to me about. Let's start with that."

"How do you know what...How did you know I wanted to talk to you?"

"I just know. You want to tell me you're looking for something."

"I'm looking for a lot of things. Well, a few things, you know how it is. Um..." A pair of inquisitive eyebrows.

"You know what you said in the car the first time you brought me home? About Jez? About giving...I mean, me giving her more time. Have you, you know, spoken to her about me?"

"No." He must have seen my disappointment. "But I didn't need to speak to her."

"Then how do you claim to know how she thinks?"

"Tim. Isn't that the reason you've been wanting to sit me down to talk like this?"

"Uggnn!" I croaked in frustration and ran my hands through my hair, feeling I was but a short step away from pulling it out in handfuls. I was leaning forward in my armchair, head pointing at the carpet, feeling like just a silly boy with a lot on his mind.

"How do you know these things about me, about Jez. I'm sorry to sound difficult, but I don't understand what's going on."

"Look. Here's the thing: all you have to do to make things happen is to let go."

"What do you mean? Let go of what?"

"Let go of everything that's holding you down and holding you back."

"Then what?"

"Let yourself fall."

"Can you be less elliptical?"

"No."

"But it can't be as simple as that."

"I didn't say it was simple."

"But fall from where?"

He looked at me without reproach but without approval either. I felt like I was failing an exam.

"Look. I'll say it again, just once: let go; let yourself fall and see what happens. Just see what happens."

I rubbed my head again and closed my eyes and tried to get my hands on what he was saying.

"For someone with a PhD you struggle a lot with ideas."

"You're forgetting: it's only in literature."

"True," he said, his brief smile reminding me of a face I once saw in a painting, and those eyes, looking at me, bluer than the Aegean summer sea.

I was perhaps being a little hard on myself. Or not, as the case may be. It was just that everything that was happening to me now was happening at the wrong time. I'd thought about this meeting for weeks, but now it was here I wasn't ready, I wasn't prepared. Sef's words were slipping away from me, falling down into a dark space from where I'd never be able to fetch them back. I didn't know what to say or how to say it. But I wasn't going to quit.

"You said I was struggling with my teaching...."

"I said that to make sure Susan sent you down to London."

"You see! You've done it again! How did you know I was listening outside the door?"

"I didn't."

"But you must have done! Or you wouldn't have answered me like that: 'I said it to make sure Susan sent you to London.' I wish you wouldn't mess with my head like this...I'm sorry. I'm tired."

"Listen. I honestly didn't know you were outside the door. The point is this: when you just told me you knew I'd told Susan you were struggling with your teaching, you were right: I had said that. How you knew wasn't and isn't important to me."

That took a little thinking about, so the flow of conversation stopped. I got up.

"I'm having another cup of tea: do you want one?"

"No, I haven't finished this one."

"Excuse me while I fetch myself another cup."

I needed to get up and walk around. My adrenalin was pumping. It was tiring talking to Sef but I thought there was a chance that it might be one of the most important conversations of my life. Then the phone went.

"Hello? No, I don't want any thanks." And I slammed it down. Do I want any doors and windows? No I do not want any fucking doors and bastarding windows. I went back to my seat and we carried on.

"So, why is it important that *I* go to London?"

"I don't know whether it will be or whether it won't. I just thought it might help."

"In what way, 'help?'"

"Aw, come on now, don't play the innocent. You're 28; you're not a kid any more."

So I keep trying to tell myself these days.

"Well you've got me beat because I'm thinking, it can't be this simple. It must be more than the fact that I need help in learning how to teach."

I looked from the floor back up to Sef and for a second I think I actually had him worried. His expression looked ever so slightly aspic-like. Caught in a mould. Did he really think I was that stupid? That this wasn't about her?

"Gotcha! Unless...."

"Unless?"

"Okay, I'll come out with it, but this is going to be embarrassing if I'm wrong. You want me to go because I'll be alone with Jez."

The solidity left his face and it again looked almost unbearably human.

"Maybe," he said and tilted his head to the side as if assessing a sculpture or a painting.

"So is it just that you like playing matchmaker? It's not, is it, because Year 8 girls do that not men in their...So it's more than that. What is it?"

"You know the answer."

"But I need it spelling out for me."

I hadn't got to the point of being confident that if I said something to displease the man he wouldn't just up and leave in a second, but it was a risk I had to take. I wasn't feeling like the most intelligent unit in Measby at this point. Sef *tutted*, but didn't storm off.

"That's not how it works, and you should know it. Nothing worth having in life..."

"Comes easy."

"Correct. Nothing."

"So I have to fight for Jez, but I have to work at it a little, is that it?"

"I don't know what 'it' is." He heard me tut in disgust this time, but when I looked up at his face again his eyes were dancing with light.

"But you know Jez would be good for me, don't you?"

"I've no idea. No, really, I don't. She may be, or she may be the last one you need."

"But I want her."

"Okay, so..." He waved his right hand in the air in a rising, fluttering gesture of suggestion.

"Thanks for that," I said.

"Look, you're a good man, you know you are. But..." It was like he was talking about someone else.

"...you've had problems in your life..."

Thanks Sef, for making me want to cry.

"How the hell would you know that?"

"It's written all over you. Don't look like that."

I can if I like.

"Understand this: you simply don't need to be unhappy."

"Everyone's unhappy. Aren't they?"

"And your point is?"

"It's the human condition. To be unhappy. I mean, even you're unhappy, look at the row you've just had."

But Sef was anything but sad looking.

"You think happiness is not possible?"

"I don't know. I really don't and you can't blame me for thinking that. I'm an American Lit. guy for God's sake. But can I ask you one thing: why me? Why are you helping me?"

"Why not you?"

I didn't have an answer to this which wasn't either narcissistic, pathetic or both simultaneously. But I dumped it out there anyway.

"Why me? Why not Liam? Why not Jez?" Did I say that? The notion of Jezebel Treat needing the wisdom of Sef was extremely far-fetched.

"How about your need being strong? How about you're right in front of me?"

"Great. So is this how I appear to everybody? This struggling, weak little kid who needs a life support machine to survive? Lovely. Makes me quite a catch, doesn't it."

I daren't look up at him. I knew this much: self-pity isn't exactly a winning quality to display to the world, but it hadn't stopped me behaving like a child. This was a moment when a cliché really fit: I was hot under the collar, and I could feel a bead of sweat break and roll down towards my left nipple.

"The dark leaves of autumn turn to electric eels in the sand," said Sef.

"What the hell does that mean?"

"Ask Les Person, he talks more sense than a lot of people at Peggy Lane."

Obviously, my time had run out. Then I felt a hand on my shoulder as I stared again at the floor. Sef had got up. I didn't want him to leave.

"Where does a man get a piss round here?"

"Upstairs, first door on your right."

Just Joni and me in the room now for a small while. Thinking about this guy and who in the world he might be.

"You are a holy man on the FM radio...." Not quite, but nearly.

"You are a refugee from a wealthy family..." He might be. It would explain the accent. Or rather, it could easily be me. I could have laughed at the stupid aptness of the timing and the song. At life's collisions and churning of chance. Chance be a fine thing. I went on sipping and thinking. The quiet street outside broken by the roar of another oversized motor vehicle.

"Now then." He was back. "Don't be so down in the mouth. Look, things are going to get better for you, I promise."

"O, you can see the future, can you?" My petulance was so pathetic it was almost funny. But at least it was true: one of the thoughts crossing my mind while he was relieving himself upstairs was that this old bastard actually could.

"No," he said, as he dropped himself down into one of my two leather armchairs once more, "but when you get old, life does have one or two compensations."

"You're not that old." Sef's eyebrows lifted and waggled at that one.

"Look, you don't have to start worrying about me."

"But I could, easily."

"Well don't. Save your energy for the things where you can do most good. And leave some over for yourself."

"Don't worry, I intend to. But, look..." I wanted more.

"What problems have I got that you can see so easily?"

"Apart from the obvious?"

"What's obvious?"

"Tim, come on, now."

"You mean that it's about time I had a truly meaningful relationship with a woman of the opposite sex?"

"If that's what you want..."

It hit me at last that it really was time I shut up. I needed a bigger and bigger shovel, the more I said.

"I know you want me to say more, but I've said enough. You'd say 'there's always more to say,' but now isn't the time. It really isn't. Important as you are, as we all are, more than half the planet is staring down the barrel of the end point of their existence. And there are plenty of people close to home who are struggling, with problems worse than yours."

I'd have to buy him a present for making me feel so ashamed of my petty self-obsessing about, in the end, just a girl.

"Tim. With Jezebel and everything else, your plate is almost over-full already."

His eyes smiled, perhaps at the thought of her, and I could easily have got myself jealous. Sef may have been well the wrong side of the male menopause but he had a great body from what I could see, and I thought, 'how could even someone of 22 not be slain by the sheer force of his presence?'

"She's got a boyfriend as well," I said.

Sef angled his head slightly in mock frustration and looked at me. Fuck it. Maybe he really could see the future. Or Jez had confided in him. That could easily have happened. Only he said he hadn't spoken to her. Would he lie to me?

"Alright, I know. You told me to bide my time. But the way I feel right now, I can't think what I've got that Jez would want."

I knew what was coming: I'd poured out too much self-pity for one day and it really was time he slapped me hard across the chops like Bogey having to calm a doll who suddenly got hysterical on him. I would have deserved it: being down on yourself like this got you absolutely nowhere; it was a feeling or an attitude that belonged only to losers. I know, I know, I should have known better at my age. Also that if Janey could fall for me, so could anyone. She was smart and she was beautiful. But a voice was still apt to caress my ear with all the charm of a talking maggot when I was low, telling me that every time a girl had felt attracted to me, it was a fluke, like an earthquake in Wales, an isolated phenomenon unlikely to repeat itself for a long time. Sef's look killed that devil though. He didn't lecture me. He didn't say anything. He just indulged me with a smile that said, 'stupid boy: one day you'll know to deal with these things.'

Then I had this sense that his magic might already be working. The feeling was beginning to grow inside me for the first time that Jez could be mine. An excitement made its way to the top of my head, like amphetamine. All things are possible in this best of all possible worlds. And the feeling increased and spread as I told myself that with Sef on my side, how could I possibly lose?

Sef wanted some more tea and I glided off my seat like a light cloud drifting across a slow summer afternoon. I put my bi-polar self down to tiredness and the stress of teaching and the tough journey that was just being alive. Perhaps it was God's doing that if you were rich or lived in a comfortable western society, you could be just as unhappy as anyone on the planet - his way of correcting the pitiful imbalance of material luck. Then I knew I was still a child. 'More than half the planet is staring down the barrel of the end point of their existence and you want to talk to me about your tiny, pathetic little problems,' Sef might have said. In the end, he was being far too generous with me. I stopped thinking. I was done, for now. And Sef must have had enough of my whining. But when I glanced down at him as I came back through from the kitchen he was just listening to the music I'd just put on, looking perfectly unperturbed.

"Working night and day, I try to get ahead...."

Slow, wearily sad music for a cool autumn evening coming on, to match a hard, hard day when nothing, it seems, is going right. Sef was leaning back resting his sleek, grey head on my chair-back, and had closed his eyes. I wondered whether he might have nodded off, and felt pleased at the idea that he could be so relaxed in my own humble front room.

"...working night and day don't make no sense."

But as our two mugs chinked in my right hand, the left holding the packet of biscuits, he slowly lowered his head and opened his eyes like a sleepy Buddha.

"I don't know who this is, but I'll have a copy of it if you can get round to it."

"Sef, what was the argument about?"

"That. Nothing. Just Michael playing little boys' games."

"Does this have something to do with the first day when we were all told off for going down the pub?"

Sef was mute, so I had to push this along on my own.

"You gave him a real hard time in there. I couldn't believe it. And I never found out what happened in the office after we left."

At last I'd summoned up the bottle to ask him. Sef looked around my living room; probably noticed the walls, bare apart from a few postcards. I'd meant to get someone to take me out to Saltaire, or get the train, to get some good prints, but the weeks had gone charging by.

"Okay. Michael wants me to leave the school."

"How do you know? Oh, you mean he told you in Susan's office?"

He actually laughed this time.

"No. He's not that stupid. He's just trying to set traps he thinks I won't be able to get out of. Manoeuvre me out the door."

"I still don't understand..."

"Look, it's not really important. It's nothing. He just wants me to run around doing silly little things like filling in a mark book and such like. And when I don't comply....."

"Oh, I see. He can report you to the governors. And if he can keep finding reasons to report you......"

"Precisely, my dear Holmes." We looked at each other and tittered almost guiltily. The blueness of his eyes again made me feel like I was swimming in a warm bath, like I was safe from everything.

"I know you don't look worried about it, but I would if it were me." I could feel myself frowning. "What if Michael wins. You'll lose your job, and I think I know enough about you," I said, stepping out a little bit, "to know it'll kill you to let Michael beat you."

"I'm that arrogant, you mean?"

"I didn't mean that." Did I not?

"But you don't have to worry. He won't beat me." Sef scoffed aloud, the very idea of being manipulated successfully by that man being as silly as Mrs. Manicure dancing around the staff room doing Madonna impressions.

"Tim, you don't have to worry about me at all."

I smiled. He was that convincing and after all, it was what I wanted to believe.

"It's not me you have to use your emotional energy up on. It's Chris. Chris is the one who's in terrible trouble."

16
His Foaming Bejasus
Autumn Term - Week 7 Day 4
Thursday, October 17th, 2002
Peggy Lane Staff room/Yarrow, Bastard Farmer and Street -Afternoon and Evening

Jez came into my classroom at the start of the lunch hour next day. I wouldn't say my heart soared when I saw her, but the first split-second sight of her made every movement in me come to a dead stop except for my eye muscles, which instantaneously stretched, so I must have appeared to her as though someone had suddenly thrust a cucumber into my anus whenever we met.

I still didn't want to betray anything of how I felt to her. I loved to be with her and hated it. I was so sure she could see how she made me feel, it made my skin crawl. I would say stupid, pointless things. Stuff I'd started out having no intention of saying,

"So, Jez, how are you?"

I sounded like a doctor. If I wasn't crazy about her I'd just have said, 'nice jumper' or 'how were your Year 8s?' or 'how many parents have you got coming tonight?' if it was the day of a parents' evening. Every conversation was an ordeal. It was easier when a bunch of us sat together at a staff room table. Then I could just rest back in my chair or the concrete sofa and carefully admire her. She was always talking to somebody, this luscious ball of beautiful, bubbling Lancashire energy, and she would rarely glance at me for no obvious reason, so this was easy. I was a film camera to her movie star. Unless Sef was there of course. Then I would fix my eyes anywhere and everywhere but on her. I would suddenly find Mrs. Manicure's pale pink housecoat interesting, or pick a newspaper up from the table I had no intention of reading. Mostly, however, Sef wasn't to be seen in the staff room, so I could enjoy her. Sounds terrible, written down like that, but that's how it was.

I didn't have a strategy to 'win' her, or anything like that. Hell, no. She had her boyfriend, who - it helped me to think this - obviously was a total jerk - a *'right gonad'* as she put it when she was talking about someone she didn't like or didn't approve of. He couldn't dress, couldn't dance, couldn't sing and had no personality. What else was I to think: ways she would suddenly become free? I know what I said earlier about hope, but I'd snapped out of that. Girls who had a 'boyfriend at home' often married them - and got divorced five or ten years later, but I wasn't going to hang around that long; they weren't even married yet, for arse's sake and this wasn't a Disney movie. And one of the eternal laws of relationships is that the longer they go on, the longer they take to die. The life support machine keeps the body in shallow, superficial motion, though to all intents and purposes the breath has long since left the patient, who is now in reality ready for laying in the ground. It's often a long time before one of the involved can bring themselves to flip the switch.

Where were Jez and Steve on this timeline? I didn't have a clue. Were they somewhere along this line? Did I still have hope? Should I wait? Or get a grip and get out more? I would go round in circles with the same set of questions. Some evenings I would sit at home nursing a sinking feeling deep in the pinkest membrane inside me that I was going to love her until the day I dropped down dead. But when I found myself shocked that she had penetrated my inner workings this deeply, I shook my head and said 'Tim, get a grip: you're a total idiot.'

As the half term progressed, I've got to be frank with you: I didn't make that much of an effort to find out what was happening with her and Steve. There was also a progression in my thinking about my rival: having never met him, I kind of pretended to myself that he didn't actually exist. Excuse me, but it helped get me through my day. All I had on my side was Sef. Though I liked to believe in Demmler, Magic Man of Mystery, I easily fell into dark moods up in Measby in my tiredness, and accepted that obviously no man can see the future or stop it. So the status quo position was Steve 5 Tim 0, and maybe there wasn't much time left on the clock.

And yet Jez, undeniably, was still really nice to me, treating me as some kind of real friend. Every Monday morning before registration she would dump her bag on a staff room chair and ask me how my weekend went and what I'd done with it. This made me clam up more than somewhat, because my weekends were about as interesting as winter in Poland. My lack of activity was embarrassing. To start with I went into Leeds with Liam on Saturdays to do the book and record shops, then we'd sometimes move on to a drink and a movie. But about a month into the term, he asked out Sally Foam from the PE department and that socially, for me, was that.

"Believe me, Tim, the woman's insatiable," he said after their first weekend together. We were strolling the playground on break duty. I was already wincing.

"We stayed in all Saturday. Wet humping. All day. I thought my dick was going to drop off."

"Liam, I..."

"I'm telling you. And it looked disgusting, like a raw piece of dog meat I once saw hanging in a butcher's shop in Vietnam."

I actually stood outside the library entrance with him listening to this. I must have been out of my mind.

"Six o'clock in the evening, it's getting dark and I hadn't put so much as a pair of shreds on all day. I says, 'Sally, come on, let's go out and get something to eat.' But no: she wants me to go at her again from behind. For about the fourth time. Jaysus. It must be all that running and fitness stuff they do all week."

"Probably does something weird to their hormones, Liam," I said.

"Exactly. You'd think...*Hey! Leave him alone!*...you'd think it would make them tired, but it must set off some...some enzyme in the brain or something."

"You'll have to ask Jeff Loin in Biology what he thinks."

"Or it could be Viagra. I wouldn't put it past her."

"But she's only about 26 or something, Liam."

"27. I still wouldn't put it past her."

"She'd have offered you some if she was on it, man."

"I don't need it, boy."

I gave him a look.

"Alright then, sure, I could have used some yesterday."

"Sunday? As well?"

Liam nodded gravely.

"She let me have about four hours sleep...."

"You're joking!"

"Yeah, I am. I slept like the fecking King of China, for about twelve hours. 'Let's go and get some breakfast somewhere,' I said, though it was already fecking lunchtime. 'No chance,' she says, giggling, and turns over, pulls off the duvet, and waggles her arse in the air at me."

"She has got one hell of an ass, though, Liam."

"Watch it. That's my girlfriend you're talking about. *Get off there, Boimer! Today!*"

'For God's sake, Liam,' I thought, but he came around almost immediately.

"Yeah, you're right, she has an' all. You should s-see it in a black thong, Trappy. Jaysus, I'm telling you."

From 'Trappist Tim' I'd gone to 'Trap' and now 'Trappy.' I tried not to picture Liam and Sally. I had to go and teach in ten minutes.

"So...."

"I finally got her out of the house at about seven o'clock and we went down to Headingley. I had fish and chips at Britt's after a starter, and sticky toffee pudd'n and custard to finish."

"Impressive work," I said.

"I was starving again about twenty minutes later."

My brain was beginning to blister with envy.

"Me bollocks have had it. And me nob's redder than a Manchester United shirt."

"Hey, be grateful. It's a hundred-per-cent more than I'm getting."

"Viagra. You're right: I'm going to need some and quickly if I'm going to survive a fortnight with her, Trap. I'm not kidding you. Do you know where I can get some?"

Bloody Liam. Then a thought suddenly occurred to me.

"Have you realized, Liam: you're stammer's gone."

"I know."

We got back to the staff room in time to catch a pause before our next lesson. I needed a good sit down actually. A new arrival interrupted Liam's flow, mercifully.

"Hello, boys. Darlings, have you seen a morning bulletin anywhere?"

"Ah, Narida! Do you know where I can...*aargh, fu-jays!*"

I'd kicked Liam's ankle, making sure to take the bone.

"What on earth's the matter, darling?" said Knickers Narida, looking concerned.

"Ah, cramp, Narida. I'll be fine in a jiffy. *Ah.*" I did not feel sorry for Liam one bit. He ought to have shown more sensitivity to my situation.

Then Jez appeared, her normal bright and breezy self, and threw her purple canvas bag down with a characteristic slump.

"'ello, boys, 'ow was yer weekend?"

Thoughts of black thongs appeared in my head and I had to beat a hasty retreat, much as I wanted to talk to Jez in case it was the last chance I got all day. As I opened the door, Sally Foam rushed past me, a man's caricature fantasy in a short pleated hockey skirt, beaming suddenly as she saw Liam over my shoulder, and looking obscenely, immorally healthy. I wasn't too miffed though. I was happy for Liam that he was getting more action than an African mercenary. You never knew; it could be my turn next.

After a month, he and Sally were still going strong and Liam had become an almost serene presence around the place. But as a result of that, I had no one, really, to hang with at the weekend, but didn't get seriously low about it. I've always liked to go to the movies on my own, so I did, and it didn't make me feel lonely. And then there was the sleep I needed to catch up on. Plus, with all the pure brown shit that had gone down since the start of the term - the Malcolm Incident still preyed on my mind a lot - it wasn't like life was dull. And now the china was really flying: Sef wanted me to help Chris in some way, though he hadn't yet told me what I might do. So, however Life was treating me, it wasn't at fault for delivering me boredom. And I had the prospect of a whole day in London with Jez to look forward to. Which is where we came in, I think.

The door opened. I was sitting at my desk writing up my lessons in my teaching file like a good little boy, and I looked up to see Jezebel. She wore a lilac round-necked wool sweater and a simple pair of black cotton trousers with black, flat, narrow-toed shoes: a little picture. Hair all spiked vertical and dyed dark, fantastic as always. She formed her pretty features into her Jez smile which, I'm not kidding, made me think of things like New York City at Christmas and children laughing wildly on amusement park rides on warm July nights. Then she pulled over a chair and sat down.

"Soah, you. 'Ow ya doin'?"

"Fine. A lot to do though - marking piling up."

"Yeah, me too. Soah, what d'ya think? You and me in Loond'n? Be a bit of foon, woan' it, eh?"

I feigned innocence. "What do you mean?"

"Woss oop with you now, yer dollop? Ya noah whar ah mean."

"No, I don't. What about London?" I put on the most expressive, quizzical mask I could muster.

"You and me; we're goin' on a course to the big citeh; Susan toald me this mornin'. 'as she not toald you, then?"

"Nope."

"A corrse for new teachers. Fust Fridair after 'alf term. She bewked it moonths ago, but she's only just decided 'oo to send from the faculty. Wotja think?"

"Yeah, good," I said, busting a sweat to sound as blasé about the trip as Cleopatra getting her fourth pedicure of the day, and like I had twenty-four other things on my mind right that second, all significantly more important. "I could use the help."

"Noah, I mean, you n' me. On a corrse together down in Loond'n. Wotja think?"

I think, 'what the fuck are you doing flirting with me like this, Jezebel? When you've never moved on to this territory before. I think I like it, but I think I'm shit-scared you're going to end up making a fool out of me. Or I make it out of myself. That's what I think.' I frowned.

"What's the matter?"

"I think I'm going to be sick."

I needed a breathing space to check my situation. What the fucking blazes was she up to? I tramped along to the toilet by the staff room and looked in the mirror. Just what I normally saw. I didn't look pale or anything; it was just me. I stood against the urinal and pissed. Sid Lemon, one of Les and Rob's pals in the DT faculty, came in and stood alongside me.

"Hello there, Tim. How's things, you young fucker?"

"Oh, fine, thanks." We'd had a couple of conversations before. The door opened and Rodder tore in.

"Christ, I need a piss, 'ey oop, Sid."

"Rob, how's your luck, you young arsehole."

"Not bad. Hey, Trap. Jez. She's looking lovely today. Don't you reckon, Sid."

"Aye, she's gorgeous is that one," he said, shaking off the drips.

"She spoken for? Tell you what, Rob, you want to get in there lad, before someone else does. Hell of a pair of knockers."

"Aah," said Rob, the local dialect for 'aye' or 'yes.' Full of local colour were these two. "Like a couple of ripe Mipp and Slinter's mangos."

"What, green are they?"

"I dunno; I'll have to find out."

They both laughed uproariously, as if they'd just written a prize-winning comedy script. I nearly punched the pair of them.

"She's got a long standing boyfriend. They're practically married," I said, and left.

No surprise then that I went back in a bastard of a mood. I launched myself at a defenseless little lad in Year 8 who happened to be in the wrong corridor.

"You! Staff room! Now! Be at the door when I get there in five minutes!"

I kicked my door wide open. I had to get my jacket and my lunch. Not that I felt like eating it. She was still there. A curved lilac back and a gold chain braiding the neck. Reading one of my books. She swung round when she heard the door, wearing an expression of concern.

"You oak-air?"

"Yeah, I'm fine."

"Ah'm a bit worried about yer," she said as I sat down again.

"What? I'm fine."

"You don't lewk it. You lewk tired."

"So do you."

"Thanks!"

"Well, you started it."

"There's noah need ter bite me 'ead off."

I sulked, retreating as usual to the thing that came naturally in the circumstances.

"I thought we were mairts."

"We are." This was in danger of becoming juvenile, though I was comforted to see Jez coming down to a level I was all too easily capable of operating on.

"Well why are yer bein' so coald with me? Yuv 'ardly spoaken to me recentleh."

These are the moments in life when you feel like picking up a large piece of concrete and throwing it through a huge plate glass window in McDonuts or The Burger Centre. Because it feels like fairies doing a tap dance on the nerves of your front teeth. I wanted to scream at the woman,

'WHY ARE YOU TALKING TO ME AS IF YOU'RE MY GIRLFRIEND?'

But of course I couldn't do this. Some guys probably knew how to negotiate their way out of these situations successfully, but the key words or sentences were out of my reach. The first thing that came to mind, 'because I want you so bad it keeps me playing all the maudlin and sentimental music I can lay my hands on,' would have been particularly disastrous, I think. In the movies it's always followed by the girl leaning forward at the guy to give him this tremendous open-mouthed kiss which lasts for about four minutes. The out-music has started by now and the camera pulls away and upwards as if suspended from some silent helicopter. In real life when you say it, the chick leans away from you, looks at her lap, coughs awkwardly and exits, leaving you calling for a large scimitar to plunge into your side. Go out in a blaze of blood and intestines, why not? At least it'll give all those you left behind something to remember you by. And you make the papers and the local TV news, minimum.

"I don't know what to say, Jez. I really don't."

This was potentially bad enough, but I was exhausted by the idea of covering up my feelings completely.

"Well let me ask yer this: are you 'appy about you and me goin' on this trip to Loond'n together, or shall ah pull owt and let your big pal Liam goah instead?"

"I am very happy for you to go on the trip to London."

"Are y' shewer?"

"I promise." And I smiled at her. I couldn't keep up the misery. Much as I would have liked to in a way for strategic reasons - you know the old saying: 'keep 'em mean to keep 'em keen' - but I just couldn't do it. Not to Jez.

"Right; that'll do me."

And with that, she "see yer lairter-ed" and left.

*

"Women, Tim," said Liam later, "working them out: you might as well try doing a Rubik Cube in a blindfold."

A what? I was telling Liam my tale of woe down the Bastard after work before he went off for another bout of prolonged naked mud wrestling with Sally. Or whatever the particular perversion of the moment was.

"But I tell you this, me ol' mucker, for the time being, this one o' mine's very uncomplicated. When she's lying on the bed there, on her stomach reading a magazine, in her PE skirt, all I have to do is slowly push it up towards her waist, inch by inch, slowly…"

"Liam, come on, you know I hate this."

"…and when it gets to the point where I can see she's not wearing an…"

"Alright, Liam! Enough! I can only take so much of this!" I had. Really. Had. *Enough!* of Liam's, sometimes literally, blow by blow account of his PE homework.

"Oh, before I forget. Hetty Kiss came up to me today and said 'had I heard anything about Chris being in trouble?' I said 'no.' Have you heard anything?"

"No," I said, trying not to sound immediately guarded.

"I reckon he's been banging Doris Manicure's head off once a week behind that hatch and he's been found out."

"Liam, you're the only person I've ever met who is capable of the delusional reasoning of someone in the terminal stages of chronic, psychotic alcoholism."

"Thanks, Trappy," he said.

"I know you think you're a sexual conspiracy theorist *par excellence*, but 'par incompetent' would be a better description."

"Oh, very good, you ought to be on Radio 4 with that sort o' stuff. No, Lampeter is a strange one. I wouldn't put it past him. She's not a bad looking woman, Doris."

"You're forgetting, surely, that Mrs. Manicure looks like something Crufts rejected."

"I wouldn't put anything past Lamps the way he sits there in the staff room like a grinning criminal every day…ah, thanks a million," he said as I put another Guinness in front of him.

"You're also forgetting that Mrs. Manicure hit 68 last birthday and looks every day of it."

"Sure but Lamps is a strange one, though."

"You just said that. I think you should go off and write a third series of Father Ted or something." Liam's grand ambition was to write comedy scripts.

"Now, how could I do that with Dermot gone on to the great comedy store in the sky? But I'm telling you, Yankee boy, there may be something in this rumour. There's something about him…"

I went off to pay back some of my beer loan. When I returned, Liam was off again on a familiar theme, unfortunately,

"Timmo, old son, we are going to have to do something about this problem of yours. When was the last time you...?"

"How many times! My love life is my affair, a closed book. So shut up and get me a drink."

"Can't," he said, swallowing the bottom half of his pint like it was a drinking contest, "got to go and meet Sally."

"I hope you're not driving."

"Nah. She's picking me up outside. Then we're going up Moor Lane."

"Moor Lane: what for?"

He took another long draft of his dregs.

"Car sex. It's not what I call a feckin' good idea, but then again, you wouldn't believe what Sally can do with the gear stick..."

And thinking he was quite the most sexually alluring thing this side of the Pennine chain, he flicked his eyebrows up twice towards his curly mop. Then grinned at me in a lunatic kind of sadistic leer.

"I don't think I've ever come face to face with a child molester, Liam, but I know that when I do, he's going to look exactly like you do right now. Don't go and look at yourself in the mirror because you'll find yourself sprinting to Yarrow Police Station to turn yourself in."

"Go home and wank yourself to sleep, why don't ya."

"Don't knock it..."

"'It's sex with someone you love,' God, you're not even original. Woody Allen said that thirty years ago. No wonder you can't get a girlfriend."

"Liam, I have higher things on my mind."

"Thinking of mending the roof tonight are you? Be careful up that ladder."

"Liam, take your oversized, motherfucking ego...hang on. You're not complaining about Sally. And her demands. In fact, you haven't moaned about it for a while....hang on, you haven't..."

"I have." he replied, proudly tapping the buttoned top pocket of his cord jacket. "Loin's dad got them for me, cost price. Works for Counter-Geegy, the Swiss firm. It's like a block o' feckin' marble all night long."

"I don't want to know."

"When it's your turn, just say the word."

"The word is 'bullshit' and if you're still here when I get back from the bog, I'm going to find some and wipe it all over your face."

But he wasn't, and I went for the bus home, at half-past-seven on a Friday night. I was about to cross the road to the petrol station on the Oatley Road to get a paper when I heard a load of shouting and a screech of tyres from under the canopy. A car screamed off down the road in a plume of burning fossil fuel. At the Planet Gas station, a man with sprouting grey hair, was puffing and sweating and gasping out his story to another guy, still clutching a till receipt.

"I was just comin' out the door," he said, still reaching for a good sized breath, "and...and someone drove off in me bloody car. I was only gone for a minute, to pay for me petrol!"

"You want to ring the police."

"They're ringing in there now," he said, pointing back to the shop counter with a thumb. "Bastard!" he cursed. "I only bought that car last week...bastard!"

I dropped the idea of the paper and went on to the bus station. It was some world we were living in. Everyone had their troubles alright. I wondered what kind Chris's were. And what the hell I could do. Sef wouldn't tell me, and I couldn't guess, though I made a mental list of possibilities for a while that Friday night. The look on Sef's face said it was something that no amount of late night music would cure. Or kisses from the one you love. I felt another storm coming on in my head. And you know what usually happens when your thoughts turn to how bad things are...

17
The Chief Inspector
Autumn Term - Week 7 Day 5
Friday, 18th October, 2002
Peggy Lane Staff Room - Lunchtime

...they usually get worse.

The vultures and carrion crows were circling overhead for Chris Lampeter, a week and two days after the 9-2 destruction of Pragmatists School, Oatley. The unfortunately named Rex Lung - oh, yes - he did the damage alright. Andy Crucial is fond of deconstructing major events in the staff room, those that take place both outside the confines of Peggy Lane as well as those within, and of telling us that there is no such thing as a significant occurrence in the world that isn't multi-causal. I'm afraid this is how most History teachers talk these days. He means, when shit happens, it happens for lots of reasons. He was in his element leading the discourse on The Chris Lampeter Affair at a late stage of the lunch hour.

"Er, it's clear to me that what we have 'ere is a classic short-term/long term situation, people."

He actually does refer to groups of staff around staff room tables as 'people,' God love him. 'Hi, people,' he says in the morning, and at break time, and again when he arrives with his Tupperware box of sandwiches bursting with greenery at the start of lunchtime. He does it in free periods too. Only he calls them 'Markin' and Prep' periods' in his glottal Croydon stopping tones.

"Chris has been undone by this feller..." he dictated to us that day, wiping a smear of mayonnaise from his ginger moustache along the way, "...for several reasons. Firstly, short-term, if you will, he's upset because Chris's mob has given his lads a tankin'. Nine goals in the second half and all that. Classic short-term causation."

Also classically, he used the slim finger of the Thudbury's chocolate wafer biscuit he was about to unwrap for characteristic emphasis.

"Blood and sand, it's pissing cold tea out there," said Les, coming among us, having had to cross to the main school from the distant DT block. It was a day of grey October rain and a buffeting wind.

"But underneath that, what do we see? We see a guy who's probably a Tory, outraged by the idea that this teacher is probably having a perverted relationship with his own centre-back, f-huh-huh..."

Andy sniggered, not nastily, or smugly, but because he was pleased that with this image he had conjured a little bathos for our listening pleasure. He continued,

"...and feels that he has a duty, as a clean-livin', law-abidin' Tory citizen, to do right by the young lad, protect him from the clutches of a sexually tortured PE teacher, if you will."

"Even though Chris teaches French," piped Sid Lemon, helpfully, on loan from the DT table three along towards Mrs. Manicure's hatch.

"Which he doesn't know, of course, because he hasn't been at Prags very long. But the interesting thing here, Sid," said Andy, but looking at all of us, "is that underneath all this, Rex rings up Michael Peniston to tell him what's 'appened, because lurkin' in his unconscious mind, as Freud would tell you..."

"Is that Freddie Freud, the Scarborough Dog Strangler?" said Les.

"No, Les, it is not Freddie Freud, the Scarborough Dog Strangler. Nor is it Ethel Freud, the Mablethorpe Saucepan Swallower, f-huh-huh. Sigmund, Les, as you well know."

"And not Mitzi La Freude, the..."

"Shut up, Les!" said four people around the table.

"As I was sayin', in the deep recesses of his unconscious, he's thinkin', 'Cor, slap a delicious, boyish young buttock with a towel! What I'd really like to do is give that gorgeous little hump of soft white flesh a gentle stroke or two, then take it home for a bit of who knows what.' But he's not aware of this, and in his mind's confused state, he thinks what he wants to do is shop our Chris, when really he feels deep-seated guilt and self-loathin' because of 'is latent desires. So basically, what he wants to do is punish himself, not Chris. Therein lays an even greater tragedy, I think we can all agree."

"Thank you Billy Big Brain," said Rob Rodder. "What a load of bollocks."

"No, buttocks, actually, Rob, f-huh-huh," said Andy, taking no offence at this put down, because if he's nothing else, he's a thoroughly nice guy.

"Actually, shouldn't laugh. This is a terrible thing to 'appen to our Chris. Bloody terrible."

There were silent nods and quiet, assenting grunts around the table. If anyone thought that Andy was pushing his luck by trying to make out he was great mates with Chris when he clearly wasn't, they weren't in the mood to pull him up on it.

Michael, the El Supremo of the bottom corridor, was not exactly flavour of the month among the staff at this point anyway. A hopeful and kind expectancy that he'd be able to make a success of his new job had given way to disappointment, suspicion and in one or two cases, deep resentment; and that was only the caretakers. If he'd been a business he'd have ceased trading. The staff room was daily flooded with talk about The Manifesto, as almost everyone was now calling it and almost all of it was negative. While a few thought 'it was about time Pegs caught up with the modern world,' breaks and lunchtimes increasingly consisted of moans and groans, piling on top of each other like plague corpses: the inspections; the committees; the extra work for heads of department writing action plans; the new procedures for staff taking kids out on school trips - the PE, languages and Art staff were in a state of thinly veiled rebellion as a result - and to cap it all, the dreadful angst about Performance Management.

If I failed to impress upon you the full blown horror of Michael's September Spectacular, I apologize. On top of his new surveillance system, he was also itching to implement a new government scheme, 'Performance Management,' another of those phrases which, being a guy with a mere Literature degree, gave me a mixture of the giggles and the creeps. It sounded to me like something from the index of a Sociology text book, or something related to sport in the old East Germany, but I was wrong, naturally. In short, it was a New Labour deal which would jack up our pay a good bit, but only if we could prove we were improving and developing as teachers. It seemed a pretty sensible idea to me but I was in a minority of about one and a half out of ninety on this. Even though the scheme meant more cash, it was going down about as smoothly as a dish of cockroach sorbet. It meant targets being set for everybody – three per year - one of which would be the demand to get a certain number of our kids through the GCSE examinations at a good level. In effect, I suppose, payment by results. And who was to decide what this level should be and working out the kids' potential? Not us. A bunch of supposed egg heads at the Department of Education. If we failed to meet one of the three, we were to get no extra money. And the head in each school would be judge and jury in deciding whether each member of staff made their targets or not. This alone was causing some major freak out stress and outrage across every department bar none. Next summer on results day, we had to get 90% of our Year 11 students with a CAT score of 95 up to or beyond a 'C' grade. Or fail Performance Management.

CAT score? This had nothing to do with identifying those children at Peggy Lane who had a moggy and grading the quality of the food they were putting down on the kitchen floor for Fluffy. A 'CAT' was, and still is, a Cognitive Abilities Test (I looked it up), and all Year 7s took three of them together in their first term of secondary school. The average score across the three was supposed to tell us all how bright the precious one is. A score of a '100' says the kid should end up with about seven good GCSEs and probably do A levels while '110' tells mum and dad that Joe or Mary is smart enough to get to University. '120' means 'prize winner' and a cool scene for all concerned: mum, dad, Grandpa, Grandma, Uncle Tom Cobbly and all will shower the star with gifts, kisses and major pressure, leading to complexes and an incurable eating disorder, etc, etc. A bigger score than that means dad has to go looking for wheelchair marks in the hallway to see if Stephen Hawking's been calling round on the quiet. Conversely, notching a score of '80' means that little Darren will still be needing his mum to tie his shoelaces when he's 20.

Those with a sardonic sense of humour had a clear deck for cheap laughs. We could hardly shut up the mordant Crucial, and when Colin Nostrum, your resident Sociologist, joined the table, people got up and left to find a bit of peace.

"The thing about the 'CAT' score," Andy would say every day for the next week until several of us threatened him with being stripped naked, tied up and delivered to Barbara Lint, the school nurse, for use as a sex toy, "is that it's fundamentally negativist."

"Right," added Colin, "It's a classic example of an élitist structure being put in place to keep the working classes in a state of permanent backward mobility."

"Too true, mon frère," replied Andy Crucial, "it's also New Labour's way of holding down teachers in what is tantamount to a kind of Stalinist straight-jacket."

"You two are so full of shit you could make a better living setting up a sewage farm".

You always had to watch your mouth if Sef was around.

"And thank you, your highness, O Crucial One…"

Andy loathed Sef talking to him like this - his face immediately began to turn the colour of cardboard.

"…for demonstrating what a great historian you are by neglecting to mention the fact that it was the Major government that initiated the CAT test in the nineties. I only thank God I haven't any children in this place for you to adulterate with your two-bob insights and completely inadequate knowledge of your subject."

Colin would have wanted to interject here to inform Sef that it wasn't in Andy's job description to have any more than a working knowledge of recent political history at most, but he wasn't about to destroy his appetite and indeed, the rest of his day by taking on a Demmler who increasingly walked about the place like Hitler just after having had his other nut removed.

Sef was being unnecessarily tough on Andy who was an unfailingly cheerful soul who would always ask you how things were going and actually want to know, and who would give you a lift home even if it was twenty miles out of his way. But Sef was not in a mood to be putting up with anything or anyone who disturbed what peace of mind he could muster in these melancholy autumn times.

Michael made his formal declaration of Chris's enforced absence at an emergency pre-school meeting, the morning of the above discussion. At 8.20.am sharp he marched briskly to the hatch-end of the room, flanked by Elaine and Susan, like a man on a secret mission to save the planet. He surveyed the staff for a couple of seconds, then with handwritten notes held out in front of him, went about his solemn duty as swiftly as a poacher skinning a rabbit.

"Thank you for being so prompt, ladies and gentlemen. I have to inform you that I have this afternoon suspended one of our number, Christopher Lampeter, on full pay, because of an alleged incident that took place off-site on Tuesday, October 8th 2002. In the meantime, a sub-committee of the school governors, led by Chairman Peter Precision, will fully investigate this incident. I have taken this action in full accordance with procedures laid down for all schools by the DfES."

That's the government's Department for Education and Skills for the uninitiated (don't feel bad; I had to ask Narida). So now we knew how deeply Chris was in trouble. O my, o my. My insides locked up for the guy. The room was deathly in its hush. An event like this did not come along every five minutes at Peggy Lane. In fact, no one could remember the last time a member of staff had faced the long arm of the educational law in this way.

Right on cue, rain began to tap at the window panes again, as if deliberately to remind us that it had hardly stopped falling out of the sky for three miserable days now. Elaine Checkman, in the blue suit which always hugged her flesh much too closely, stared vacantly out of the window. Her new managerial colleague, Susan Climer, looked cool, young and sexy by comparison. Trying at least to look suitably and professionally grave, but obviously loving every second of it, the head continued.

"Naturally, such a scenario gives me no pleasure at all."

I'm not sure I could ever put into print Sefton Demmler's later reaction to that comment. The Boss's brisk exit, after taking only a single question from Maggie Tripper, the head of PE, smacked of self-importance, as if Chief Inspector Peniston was sorry but he had an important murder enquiry to dash off to. Susan, who'd tried to hold her face in a rictus of neutrality during the announcement but only succeeded in looking unbearably constipated, and Elaine the dipso, duly padded off in his wake like a couple of PAs, trying desperately as they went to find the correct level of gravitas in their countenance.

'You could hear a parrot eating a Crunchie,' I thought, and realised that after only a few weeks, Les was really starting to get to me.

The room was abnormally quiet thereafter for more than several minutes, until the registration bell pulled us all away. Chris was about as popular as anyone on the staff at Peggy Lane. Daphne Cloth from Textiles looked visibly shaken and Glynis Mapp from the Geography department was almost inconsolable, and actually left the room in tears. Chris's head of department, Pierre Légume, was quickly fuming about the head robbing him, probably permanently, of one of his best teachers. As I made my exit, I looked around for Sef, but he was nowhere to be seen.

18
Luce, Tommy and the Midget
Autumn Term - Weekend After Week 7
Saturday, October 19th, 2002
Measby - Morning

Cllrrrpp! cllrrrpp! cllrrrpp! cllrrrpp! chychtych!
"Hello. Tim Weaver?"
"Alright, fucker? What you doing?"
"Waking up. Ogh! Hold on. How's things?"
"Good. Well, no, not good. I've just come back from the A & E at the hospital."
"Yeah? Working late?"
"Nah. I told you: I finished my stint in A & E two months ago."
"What, then?"
"I broke my nose."
"Ouch."
"You can say that again."
"Ouch."
"Tim,"
"What?"
"Die, would you?"
"Pipe down, Muff. Seconds ago I was still fast asleep. Actually, now I'm awake I can hear you: you sound terrible. How the hell did you do it? Did you get that huge nose of yours trapped in a lift door again?"
"Quit it, you can't do comedy. No, someone broke it for me. Ow! I just hit it with the fucking phone."
"That is one cheap way to get off work for a week. You should have called me down; I would have smashed it so hard you could have had a month off."
"Do you not listen? Look. Someone punched me."
"I'm not surprised it got broken: it's a huge target."
"Fuck yourself off."
"Ah, so I can do comedy."
"Occasionally, look…"
"Neither am I surprised somebody banged you one. Come on then, explain. Minute. I got to get out of bed…go on, I can't wait to hear this."
"Well, I was in my local newsagent, you know, on the corner of Pie Island Road. Mr. Chakwal's. And you know how they have all the front pages of the

papers just inside the door laid out in front of you?"

"No, but go on."

"Well this morning - did you see the papers this morning?"

"Er, no Muff."

"Oh, no, of course. Well, the front pages of *The Stench*, *The Daily Piles* and *The Morning Thrush* all have pictures of Prince Charles on them showing him in town last night with Lally Dibbs at some film premiere. So all I said was 'I hope for her sake he didn't give her one, Mr. Chakwal, she'll catch a disease.'"

"Sounds fair enough. Bit subtle for you, but still..."

"So this bloke, buying a Flake and a *Stench*, turns round and says, 'did I hear you insulting the heir to the throne of this country?'"

"Oh, no, Muff: and you said?"

"And I said, 'no, I'm simply stating facts: but I will insult him for you if you like, mate.'"

"He wasn't a big guy...."

"As if I'd pick on some big cunt - you should know me better - no, he was a little cunt. But I should have noticed his cropped hair though. And thinking back, I should have seen the tattoo."

"The wearing of a tattoo is not normally associated with the reasonable, enlightened man about town, Muff. Did you not know this? What was the tattoo in question, exactly?"

"It just said 'UVF'."

"*Madre mia*, Muff."

"And I should have noticed his Irish accent as well. He sounded like Ian Paisley."

"Oh, shit, Muff, he wasn't..."

"I think he'd just been let out on the prisoner early release scheme or something."

"So that was it, he smacked you one."

"No. Not straight away. So I'd said, 'I will insult you if you like,' and he said, 'Go on then...' And I said, 'okay; if you're a monarchist, I feel sorry for you.' 'Why's that?' he said. 'Because Charlie-Boy's got the looks of a monkey, the brains of a hairy arsehole and the only way he's ever got a woman into bed is either by being the richest man in England or having a four-foot nob extension.'"

"Holy moley, Muff, what is wrong with you?"

"Vodka."

"What?"

"I'd been drinking vodka with Juicy Lucy, Tommy the Hole and The Midget. All night. I was extravagantly Schindler's."

"Oh, man, when will you ever learn? You're 29."

"It wasn't what I said in that initial burst of fabulous wit that was the problem. When I got to the nob-joke he laughed. Well, he sort of looked like he might have been thinking about smiling, if I've got to be exact."

"I don't get it: so..."

"It was when I told him they were a bunch of inbred Germans. 'How dare you call my Queen a German' he shouted, and pulled back an arm that looked like a shoulder of pork and rammed it straight into the middle of my face."

"Hah, hah, hah."

"Well may you express yourself mirthfully. I can only add that it was a bleedin' good job I was elephant's or it would have really hurt. I didn't feel a thing until I came round about two hours ago."

"So how is it now?"

"It feels okay because of the painkillers. I scuzzed some morphine from the drugs cupboard on the way out, so I'm good. My mouth works, anyway. Hang on, me phone's going.....I look a bit of a sight, though. White bandages all over my face."

"Serves you right, imbecile. Thanks for ringing; you've really picked me up. I was having a bit of a black dog on when I turned in last night."

"Was that in a sandwich? Or was it in bed. You want to watch the law don't..."

"Now who's not funny?"

"Okay, so it's the chick then, I assume. What's happening?"

"It isn't really. It's work. A guy at school is going to be disciplined."

"What's 'e done, nicked some paper clips?"

"Made contact with the buttocks of a student."

"With what? Not his James Cobb? You teachers: bunch of homos and layabouts, the lot of you."

"No, Muff, it wasn't like that at all. He's done nothing. It's just that our Head thinks he has."

"What did he touch it with then?"

"A hand. Kind of accidentally."

"Oh, yeah; I do that every day. I suppose you'll be telling me next that your mate was sitting down marking an essay when a kid threw himself arse-first into his lap and he put his hand out to stop him as a natural reaction."

"No, it was larking around in a changing room."

"I know. A bloke who taught at a public school got the push for that the other week. It was in *The Piles*."

"No, Muff, he's innocent."

"It can't just be that that's getting you down. How's your precious girl?"

"Still precious, but I'm wasting my time. She was a little odd with me the other day, but..."

"What do you mean?"

"She bought me a sandwich from town one lunchtime."

"That's it, then. You're in."

"What?"

"When they start doing little things for you, that's the sign that they've got the hots for you."

"You think? What would you know about it?"

"That beautiful girl I trained with in paediatrics, Sophie..."

"Yeah?"

"We'd just finished a shift and she said, 'Raymond...'"

"Raymond!? She called you 'Raymond!?' Hah-hah! And you let her? Hah!"

"Yeah, well, I could hardly expect her to call me Muff, could I?"

"You have with all your other girls! All two of them."

"Yeah, right, nice one. Anyhow, she said, 'Raymond, would you like me to get you some Vaseline?' And naturally..."

"You thought this was some kind of green light."

"Well obviously."

"It's not quite a sandwich."

"Not quite, no, but still, I thought: 'significant.' You know what I mean? And you know what girls are like these days."

"Not everyone is as disgusting as you. Not even young chick doctors out for a good time. So why on earth did she offer to get some Vaseline for you? Did this come at the end of some utterly disgusting conversation full of sexual innuendo? Wait: no, of course not: I remember Sophie, she looked like Uma Therman. So she wouldn't want you doing so much as undoing your top button in the middle of a heat wave."

"Well, I wasn't so sure at the time. You never know your luck."

"Sophie? You'd need more than luck with Sophie. Cranial surgery and a hair transplant for a start. So did you find out why the Vaseline offer?"

"My chapped hands. Said it made her feel like throwing up when she saw anyone with sore hands."

"Good idea for her to become a doctor, then. So why the fuck are you telling me this?"

"I dunno. It must be the vodka. No, it's this: it wasn't the case with Sophie and the Vaseline, but with The Sponge. I knew she fancied me when she kept getting me cups of tea and coffee, and biscuits and brake fluid."

"Brake fluid?"

"For my car. Her Dad was a mechanic."

"But The Sponge was desperate. She was about as attractive as a bucket of blood. Of course she tried to bribe you into bed with coffee and crisps and shit!"

"She never bought me any shit, I'll give her that. Might have been useful if I'd had an allotment, though."

"Or, indeed, if it was a spot of blowington. Go on…"

"Point is, if this Jez is buying you food, that's it: she wants you. She's not ugly is she, this girl?"

"You know she's not."

"So it isn't a case of *nil: desperandum*, then…you're laughing. That's a good sign. And I'm telling you: it's an open goal."

"You're not the first person to have said that. But you know what I'm like. I can't…It doesn't come easy, doing this right. And she's still got this guy in tow. But we're going to London together soon."

"What!?"

"On a course. To London."

"Excellent. So I'll get to meet her."

"Oh, I don't think so, Muff. If she sees you she'll get the wrong impression of me and I'll blow it."

"Hang on. My bacon's burning. I have to go. You won't stop me meeting her - I need to see her to warn her what sort of a mess she's getting herself into."

"Later, Muff. Look, look after yourself. Get some sleep. Go to a doctor again."

"I am a doctor."

"Okay, so, physician, heal thyself."

"That's only the four millionth time you've used that one. And it's a bit hard to re-set your own nose when it's been broken in four places."

"Just take care of yourself. Okay?"

"Yeah, whatever. Look. You too. Take care of yourself, you idiot. And don't be getting down in the mouth about things. About this girl. And if you get really down, give me a call. Okay?"

"Okay. And if you possibly can, get someone to take some photos of you: I want to see your busted face before it heals."

"Go fuck yourself."

"I'll try."

Ccch-cllllykkk!

19

The Plan
Autumn Term - First Half Term Weekend, Day 2
Sunday, October 20th, 2002
Measby – Morning

I was thinking how you see great looking women sometimes, with ugly men. And how this never seemed to happen to me. I might not be fit for a catwalk in Milan, but in my more serene moments I can accept that, like most people, I'm okay: mothers don't hide their children from me when I walk down the street. And I know how to dress myself. I was thinking about this sixth former. A real beauty. Skin like peaches, fantastic smile. And hair. I've got a thing about hair, I think. Good figure. Great figure, actually. Turned my eyes inside out. They wear their own clothes, the sixth formers. So they wear these scooped necks revealing mounds of cleavage, and tops that expose the soft skin on their hips. It's outrageous, but there you go. I tease Muff with that. Can hear him groaning with jealousy at the other end of the line in the distance.

So this pupil, Francesca, I think she's called, goes with this dolt of a lad. Spots, glasses, and I'm sorry, he looks like he couldn't possibly have a personality. Fair play to him though, as Liam would say. But I swear I was miles better looking than this kid even when I was in my sixth form years in the States. I never had a plague of smallpox all over my face. But never could I get a girlfriend who looked like that. Never. Went to sleep gnawing my red, raw heart out night after night after night along with all the rest of the losers.

Then I thought, I shouldn't be thinking like that about sixth form girls. At 28.' Or should I? Where did it say in the staff handbook that it was wrong to imagine myself running naked in the surf with her somewhere on the Cape one hot starfilled night, then pulling her down and Burt Lancastering her with every centimetre I could pull out of the fire. Where, go on, tell me? Nowhere, that's where. It still felt wrong, though.

Could I go out with a girl like that? If she'd done her A levels and left school, of course? 28 and 18 - a ten-year gap. If I was 40 and she was 30 then it would be no problem. Why was it wrong at 18 and 28? You'd be bored. She's ten years younger than you, she'd want to be out dancing her butt off all night long and sucking down Es or some other chemical intoxicant. Which isn't my scene, let me tell you. A suck on a wee slab of hashish from time to time, well yeah, fair enough. But nothing more serious or stupid than that. Man, I must be sliding down. It was illegal as well, now, after that chief inspector guy had it off with a pupil when he was a young teacher. You should see some of these girls in the sixth form, though. You couldn't blame anyone under 30. For looking. And thinking. Or am I unfit to be a teacher? Ah, Chris, if you'd only been caught with a girl not a boy. No. I'm not thinking straight. He'd still get the sack. Was Chris getting the sack? The terminal raspberry? The poor, poor guy. What is he thinking now, I wonder? Nah, don't worry about that, Tim. Chris is a great guy; that much you do know, and as straight as they come, and this charge he's on is going to be laughed out of court, or hearing or whatever it is. Everyone on the staff says so. Les, Rob, Colin, Andy, all the English department. Except for Fiona who never says anything. And Susan we hardly see down the staff room any more.

Half term. Eight weeks done. Eight knackering weeks. I think I've slept most of it when I haven't been at Pegs. It's been...well, terrible, really. No, what am I talking about? It's been okay. I've done okay. It's just the effort it takes to hang it all together: the organizing of lessons; the filling in of files and forms; the marking and the time in the classroom. It leaves you feeling as though a giant pipe is reaching down inside you sucking out the energy from the nucleus of every cell in your body. I keep saying it, but the kids are great, though. They make me laugh. One Year 7 the other day.

"Sir, can you speak American?"

And Joseph, a Year 9.

"Sir, why would anyone be stupid enough to write a poem?"

"Well, Joseph. You should try it. You might find it helps to deal with some of your emotions."

"Sir, I 'aven't got any emotions."

And sometimes I hear myself saying teachery things and want to burst out laughing. I say to myself, 'Weaver is that really you? Listen to yourself: you! A teacher!' And all those faces looking up expectantly after I've said, 'Right, take out your homework diaries.' Waiting to hear what it is I've got to say, waiting for the command. The power you have over them. Not to mention the fact that when you say, 'You! Move to this desk down here! Now!' they do it. Automatically. Apart from the Year 11s. Who at best grunt and mutter as they pick up their books cursing you under their breath. Sef still watches over me. He'll invent a reason to come in and see how things are going, as he did the other day; and I saw Sandy Smart, who sits in the front row, looking up at him as he strode comfortably over to my desk, and smiling with this look of warm and total adoration. She's great looking too, is Sandy. Looks really fine, even in a blazer and stupid blue tie and I'm forced to admit to myself that I'm jealous. Sef smiled back all pleased with himself but trying not to show it. I'd give a lot to get that sort of reaction from kids. Will that ever be me?

In short, no. That I doubt. How many of these people are there in the world? Sefton Demmlers do not come around every day of the year. 'Mould,' 'Threw,' 'Away,' 'The' and 'They' are words that spring to mind. God, I hate that. It's not funny. So why do it, Tim?

I am going crackers. Two days into the holiday, Sunday morning, ten-past-eleven and I officially start to lose it. Or am I just exhausted? Put on a CD. Find something soothing. What do I need at this point of the morning? Not The Stones, shit, no; too loud. Certainly not Nick bloody Drake. Don't want to end up throwing myself off the Measby church tower and ruining everyone's day of rest. Ah, this'll do. The Gunks: *Pitiful Inside*. Just brilliant from start to finish. Not too doleful, but not happy either. Don't want music to cheer me up, want music to wallow in. This'll be fine. And find a book to read. Or shall I just lie here. And let the morning drift by. Maybe cook some dinner later, and phone Liam, and Muff. And maybe my Mother. She expects it and she'll only make my life hell if I don't. But for now, just lie here and let my mind empty itself. Harmlessly float away down a river, along with the voice of Andy Pea., not Andy C, f-huh-huh, and the peace I still have left inside my mind. Floating with guitar strings, lazy, listless and slow as The Gunks play a ballad for a change. For once not give a bloody damn. If I fall asleep, who cares? On a long, slow Sunday morning. Whooze…gonna…kna…?

There was a knock at the door. I must have drifted back to sleep. When a sharp rap brought me back. Out of that warm fuzz. I pulled myself to my feet. Not a Jehovah's Witness, please. I always feel like I've caused a malnourished African child to die every time I send them packing. Simply asking to save my soul. It'll be someone collecting for something. Or a neighbour? But I hardly know anyone. Could be Barney. Better not ignore it. Else he'll be getting his stepladders out to see if I'm hiding upstairs. On a cold doorstep, it's Sef. Clear from the moment I see his face, the downside of his ocean personality. Grim is his expression. And Jezebel. Blimey. There's a surprise. Eyes flick from one staring to one smiling, neat little hands playing with a pair of sweet purple gloves with no fingertips. Smoke-like breath on the autumnal morning. Eyes of Jez wide with the zap of the air temperature on her face. What the hell are they doing here? Together. My guts did a roll. Sef's blue car on the road there.

"Come in. Come in."

"Soah this is where yer live." Jez looks up, down and around, stuffing gloves into pockets, and crinkles her mouth sideways, as if to say, 'typical.' At least I know it doesn't smell, what with my oil burners doing their stuff most evenings of the week.

"You bin tekin' droogs in 'ere, or what?"

I couldn't tell if she was kidding me or not.

"Do you guys want some coffee?"

"Yeah, great," said Jez while Sef just nodded. He was weighed down, I could tell that. Wearing a green Israeli bomber jacket. He does it again. Black denim. Clean shaven, but tired as hell around the eyes. Dark circles there even I could see as I tried to come round. They were standing well apart. Either they're carefully acting their separateness or I'm as paranoid as I think I might be. The fear stopped.

"So, what's all this about then. Is it social?" I said as I moved around pulling milk and coffee canister from the fridge. Jez followed me into my kitchen.

"Smells nice in 'ere, atsh'lleh. Wor is it, *au de dope*?" said Jez.

"Not social. No," said Sef.

"It's abowt Chris." Jez leading. "It's abowt what we're going to do."

"What do you mean?" I said, lighting the gas under my silvery pot.

"We're not going to leave Chris, um, to rot." Sef. "Michael is going to take him to the proverbial cleaners."

"Sack him, you mean?"

"'Take him down', they say sometimes in your country of origin, do they not?"

"Yeah, they do. They do."

"Well then. I think that describes it with perfect accuracy."

Made me think of that phrase, 'Chris has left the building...'

"Unless we can do something drastic..." Sef paused, and stared at my blank wall, lost to pure, dark thought, "he's going to be a goner."

Sef made it sound like we were already carrying his coffin on our shoulders towards a cold January graveside. This was a new Sefton to me: self-doubtful - the God-figure showing his mere mortality. The Emperor with odd socks on. Then I had a thought about Chris.

"But, this is one offence. This isn't so serious that he can get the bullet. For this one thing? That can't be right." I could feel the anger rising in me.

"There's something you should know. About Chris. He has two written warnings on his record."

Sef paused. He didn't find it comfortable to tell me this stuff. As if it was spilling his own guts. Bringing back bad memories. So Jez took over the reins.

"Sef'uz toald me, so I'll tell yer. Last football season he poonched a parent at one of 'is Year 10's matches."

"What?"

Jez was nodding at my incredulity. "Yeah, flattened a big mouth who was shoutin' abuse at the ref an' 'is players."

"Sorry. Whose players?"

"Chris's players. He's had them since they were eleven. He's very protective."

"Jeee-zus. Laid him out?"

"Broken jaw."

Sef still looked grim. Then walked back into my kitchen. Soon heard cupboards and cups.

"You're kidding?" I said to Jez pointlessly, knowing full well she wasn't.

"Did he get taken to court?"

"Noah. Funny thing was, it was a copper 'ee 'it, apparentleh. But for soom reason he didn't want t' press charges."

"It could have been worse, then."

"It's bad enough, dear boy," said Sef coming back with a fist full of mugs. "If it hadn't been for the head of that time being one of Chris's biggest fans, he'd have lost his job. The Chair of Governors, Precision, wanted him out. 'Not in keeping with the traditions of the school -'" he spread the mugs around - "as if we were Eton."

"Thanks, gorrany sugar?"

"Yeah," and I went to fetch my darling some muscovado.

"Brown sugar? Whar 'er you then, American posh?"

"It's muscovado: a lot better for you than white muck."

"You're supposed to 'ave prawns wi' that, aren't yer, as a starter?" she said stirring, with a glint in her eye. Her tone was all wrong. This obviously shouldn't have been the time for humour.

"If you two have quite finished...but we were able to buy him off with a majority vote of the governors in favour of a let-off if Christopher went on an anger management course. But that, unfortunately, was not his first offence."

"Okay, so what..."

"Was the first?"

Sefton went inward again and trod quietly in his black desert boots on my bare polished boards to the window. Gazed out at what was left of the quiet village Sunday morning. Steam coming off the top of his coffee. Jez looked across at me and silently shook her head, serious now. The facial expression was crystal. He didn't want to talk about it.

"He woant talk abowt it," she said, seeing Sef turning back to the room, "the silly oald git. Do yer good to gerrit off yer chest, lad."

Sef let slip the faint edge of a smile. It was one of those situations where the Mafia boss indulges the one who dares to cheek Il Capo, because they have the cajones where everyone else grovels or keeps a safe distance. But he still wasn't telling.

"The point of the matter, is that Chris's career is over if we can't come up with something to save him."

I was wondering how soon I should butt in to say 'what on earth makes you think I can do anything worthwhile to save him?' but I didn't want to insult Sef. If he was here and was asking me to participate in some kind of crisis pow-pow thinking I had something to offer, then I had to accept that he had to know what he was doing. So I did and we all sat down. Miraculously I'd cleaned up last evening so Jez didn't have to work a space in piles of papers and magazines with her shoe to have somewhere to plant her feet. All the soft surfaces for seating and lazing were free of debris too.

"Ooh, nice roog. Did you gerrit from IKEA? Can I put it over meself, I'm cauld."

"No. I got it in a mall in Rhode Island. I'll switch the heating on."

"Thanks."

"So," I said, sitting back down in my one armchair, "what....?"

"We need a plan. I thought, with your background, you must have read hundreds of books. Somewhere in one of them is the answer."

"Dr. Tim. Yer kept that one quiet, di'n't yer," said Jez with some look in her eye I couldn't quite place. Some sort of sub-textual shit going on I wasn't quite awake enough to appreciate. I wasn't pleased that Sef had told Jez about my PhD, but I'd have to forgive him. This would have to do with Chris and the reason we were all together now. I wasn't proud of my alleged expertise in deconstructing symbolism, metaphor and allegory in American *noir* literature from the 1920s and 30s, but good God: surely it wasn't actually going to ride to the rescue here, was it? That would be something.

"So, I'm not saying we have to come up with a solution right now. But we do have to inside a week. Chris has his hearing with the sub-committee on the Friday after half term."

"They're not in such a hurry to stick the knife in, then?" I said.

"I think they would be," said Sef, "but the mighty Precision is out of the country 'til next weekend. Why they're waiting until the following Friday, I can't say. I don't care: it's to our advantage to have the extra time."

But if we could come up with something now or at least start the thinking process, so much the better. I had a question, an obvious one:

"Before we go any further, how can the head make this stick when the kid didn't complain and the parents didn't complain? Aren't they supporting Chris? Hasn't Peniston talked to them?"

"Of course they support him, of course they do. But Michael can override them."

"But why is he so desperate to get rid of Chris, what threat or...oh, I get it. He gets rid of Chris to hurt you. And – if Chris goes, you're going to leave too, right?"

O, my aching heart.

"We'll see about that, but yes, you've got it. I seem to be weighing heavily on Michael's mind at the moment. If he can hurt me, he will."

"Ah can't work out worrit is you've done to upset 'im. There's soomthin' yewer not tellin'."

I looked at Jez.

"It's something to do with that one-to-one he had when we left his office on that first day. He won't tell me either." That end being now tied up, I went on.

"So let me get this straight: a headteacher, of a school...is actually being...this petty."

"Wakeh, wakeh, Tim. Where 'ave you been all y' life?"

"To use a loathsome expression, Jez, 'in fairness,' Michael is not quite guilty of mere pettiness. Much of this is because he thinks I can bring his whole project down."

"The modernisation thing. But you can't do that."

"No. Of course I can't." I willed Sef to look regretful about that, but failed.

He remained at my front window without a change of expression: worried, thoughtful, but with a hint, a shadow, of something else that he had to deal with that had nothing remotely to do with Peggy Lane. How different he was now to the Sef who'd sat just over there with his eyes closed listening to my music the last time he was present in this room. Would I see that again? Like a favourite film, I wanted him to last indefinitely. Be there for me when I needed him, on one of my shelves.

"Soah, Tim. Get yewer 'ead round all that American stoof you spent all that time on in Loond'n."

And all the time I wasted on it before I got there.

"What about you, you're probably smarter than me."

"Booger off: 19th century English is my thing. If Jane Austen was sat 'ere now, she'd be no bloody use. Nor Billeh Wordsworth."

"Mmm, I don't know..." said Sef in reply to that, before his voice trailed away across fields of deep thought once more, between short sips of liquid. So I sat there and sipped my own cup, and mulled the thing over. Obviously, what we needed was something to attack Michael with.

"'ow about threatenin' 'im wi' violence?"

Sef's look was withering.

"Ah'm oanleh brainstormin'. It's what we've been taught to do wi't kids all the time."

Sef sighed, but turned away from the window to us.

"Okay, let's play games, then. No good: he'll bring the police in."

"Would he, though? If we threatened him, how would he prove it unless he had his office bugged?"

"There's a further problem: I haven't personally got any connections to Yorkshire gangland. Have either of you two?"

"Ah noah a bouncer in Rochdale."

"Would he be prepared to come over with a couple of friends and threaten Michael with a baseball bat or two?"

"For a price, probableh."

"Which of us has a spare few hundred quid, then," said Sef, amazing me that he seemed to be on the verge of seriously considering threatening the Head with GBH or worse. But even if it was no more than an exercise in the use of heavy irony, at least it got the juice in the thought processes moving. In response to his question, I could perhaps have straightened out this wrinkle. But no way was I going to get involved in any violence. I didn't want to end up in fucking jail. So I shook my head.

"Don't lewk at me. Ah've got student loans to pay back. Wor about you, Sef, you must be loadid."

Sefton produced a laugh that was dryer than a vista of Moroccan sand dunes.

"Don't we need to investigate his past, see if we can find a skeleton or two?" I said.

"Take too long." Sef. "We've only got six days."

"Tim," - Sef again - "in a detective novel, how would someone like Michael be brought down."

I thought about it. If not violence...

"Easy, if not violence, blackmail."

"But we 'aven't got time to goah into 'is past and find an affur, or..."

"I don't believe he's gay," said Sef.

"Then why doant we gerrim involved with a woman now?"

"In the next week?" I said. "Come on..."

There was silence for at least a minute while we chewed and chewed.

"Well, in the literature it's always a *femme fatale* who's the bait," I said again.

"And a set of compromising photographs," said Sefton softly, a hand working and worrying his chin.

"Soah, if we can gerra woman, and a photographer, an' a camera with a zoom, we joost need to pur 'em in a plairce where we can photograph 'em at it. Soah, a car?"

"Then we'll have to follow them. That'll be hard, if not impossible. And face it; we aren't going to get this guy in the next week and a half, screwing some chick in a car. Or kissing her. It's insane. He's married for Chrissake. Has he got kids?"

"No. He hasn't."

"Is 'e 'appily married?"

None of us knew.

"But it's too far fetched," I said.

"Unless he's having an affair already," said Sef.

Now that was an interesting thing to ponder for a minute. I switched the CD off; it was getting in the way. Jez pulled the rug around her again and made a thoughtful face.

"If 'ee is, then 'oo?" said Sef. I'm kidding, Jez. The more we got into this, the more her use of correct English disappeared over the hills towards home.

"I don't want to be too controversial, but it would not give me a heart attack to learn that Michael and Susan are somewhat closer than is professionally desirable."

This was a thought that hadn't occurred to me before.

"Susan: she's not the type, is she?"

"Everyone is the type," said Sef authoritatively, "given the right or wrong circumstances."

"But let's assume they're not involved. We're back to square one. Because we can hardly go to Susan and say, 'Susan, throw yourself at the head in his office and we'll be outside taking a picture – don't forget to keep your hand firmly on his groin.'"

"No, because, as I seem to keep having to remind you, Timothy, Susan is Michael's blue-eyed little darling at the moment."

"Soah, she's off t' list, then."

"Yes, but try this." I was beginning to warm up now. "If Michael isn't happily married and if he is up and ready for some action, if we can get a woman into his office to come on to him, and we get one photograph of them getting too close, or him kissing her, then we at least will have some shit to throw at him. Am I right?"

Sef and Jezebel didn't reply. They thought it over for what seemed like a long spell. I couldn't sit or stand still – I paced the floor next to my stereo, nerves spun tight with tension.

"Your supposition may well be correct about the state of his marriage. Or not. If you're right, and actually, even if you're not, then the right woman may well be able to extract what we need from the dear man, for - and I may have arrived here before you or I may not - Michael's office has a large picture window which happens to be on the ground floor of the building. And twenty-five yards or so from that window is the craft block. If we can get hold of a good enough camera and photographer, we may get what we might call, 'a result.'"

Sef almost savoured the last word, starting it with a precisely enunciated drum roll of 'r's.

"Soah, one kiss, one photoah, we send it to 'is wife, or threaten to, unless 'ee finds a way of callin' off the meetin'. Can he call off the meetin', Sef?"

"Oh, yes. If Precision wonders what's going on, Michael needs only to say he's bottling out of the hearing because of Mr. Doosen's support for Chris. I know Precision. He'll only go forward with this if he knows he's taking his headteacher with him. And if we have Michael on a string anyway...no, that won't be a problem."

"But come on," I said, dousing down the excited flame of hope that I could feel rising in me, "this isn't real. One: we get a woman into the Head's office and get him in a clinch? It's alright in American fiction, but this is reality we're talking about, the here and now. What woman is going to be insane enough to do it? Someone on the staff? You're crazy. We find an actress? Also crazy - where are we going to get an actress from? Second: if it backfires, we are all up the stovepipe."

"I will take the rap for you."

"Christ, Sef. Don't tell me: you've had your career, ours are just beginning. Sounds like The Waltons. In Chandler or McBain, we'd all three of us go down the crapper. Which is much more like real life."

Sef was now in a thoroughly calm state of mind. He spoke quietly, looking at both of us in turn with deadly seriousness.

"It's only logical. If you two aren't seen taking the photograph, no one will know you're involved. And tell me: what is the point in all of us losing our jobs when it need only be one?"

"Are you going to do it all then? Take the picture? Organise the woman?"

"I won't be taking the photograph. I know someone who'll do that. And I won't be asking you to kiss the head, Timothy. So relax."

It was time to stand up and be counted.

"I won't let you go to the wall for me."

"Grow up."

It looks worse on the page than it was at the time. Sef narrowed his gaze at me and raised an eyebrow, but in such a way as to let me know that I hadn't lost his beneficence.

"Now who sounds like something from pulp fiction? Sorry. But you're not thinking straight."

"Tim, 'ee's right. There's noah need for us all t' be 'eadin' for t' Job Centre if it all goahs wrong. Unless you want me ter snog Michael's 'ed off, Sef..."

I may have blushed at this, and my stomach did indeed turn to water at the thought.

"Sweetly put, Jezebel. And thank you for the kind offer: I'm sure he would find you impossible to resist, but I already have the person for that."

"WHO!?" we both practically screamed.

"Mrs. Twyford-Sounding."

There was a silence in the room while Jez and I drank this in. Then it suddenly looked possible; God, yes, Fiona: a master stroke. She was hotter 'n Alabama in July. Pretty great looks and a sensational profile, to put it mildly. Her whole aura was one of sex, danger and money. Danger for Michael anyway, if he was weak enough to take the bait. That was the question, it seemed to me.

"*Yes!*" I practically shouted as I put my cup down on the crowded mantelpiece. Smacked my right fist into my palm.

"O yes, she fits the bill alright. This is it!"

"Calm down, calm down," said Jez. "An' anywair, are yew shewer she's attractive enoof?"

Sefton and I immediately exchanged glances, like two experienced operatives exchanging a microfilm in a Berlin back street in 1963. His eyebrow twitched just a faint amount, but it was enough. Even if his marriage was made in heaven and stronger than the atom, if that woman could make the right moves he would be extremely hard put not to blow his stack right there and then, never mind return one little kiss. So we at least had a chance. Not a good chance, perhaps, but a chance nonetheless.

"You shewer she'll do this, Sefton Demmler?"

"Fiona and I go back a long way, and her – um - account with me, if I might put it that way, is in deficit in terms of favours. And she is, Jezebel, I can assure you, for many men, an exceptionally attractive woman."

And she wasn't married. She was divorced. Michael was not unattractive either, so we didn't have the problem of her having to kiss a stinking monkey. Only a modicum of good acting was required on her part.

"And don't worry about Fiona's ability as a practitioner in the stage arts. I once saw her in an adaptation of *Madame Bovary*: at the interval half the men in the audience rushed for the toilets and their cars to relieve their, um, emotion. She was - I have to admit - absolutely stunning."

Jez was not looking all that pleased to hear this, a little womanly jealousy going on, perhaps. I didn't blame her. To me, it was music, like an undiscovered album by Nirvana.

"What about the photographer?" I said.

"Come on; you know who runs the photography club in school, do you not?"

"Les? Do you think he's up to it?"

"Have you...? No, you won't have seen his work. Surprising as it may seem, he has a very good eye. Goes tramping about the cities of the north at weekends finding all sorts of interesting stuff to shoot. Most importantly, he's got a zoom lens that'll give you a close up of a man picking his nose in Leeds with Les standing on a tall building in Leipzig."

"When, then?" said Jez. "Have we got t' time to ger' everythin' readeh?"

"I've got all week to persuade Fiona, and I think getting her agreement should not, in the end, present too much of a problem. Then we need to get her inside Michael's office on Monday, if we can. That's easy enough. Les develops the film on Monday night. Tuesday morning I can pay Michael a visit. This gives him three days to think the matter over and make a single persuasive phone call to Precision."

"Job done, cum back Christopher, all is forgiven."

"That'll be one round to us, anyway," I said, feeling as though we'd already pulled off something miraculous, just to have come up with this scheme.

"'ave we won one, yet?"

"O yes, my sweet little Jezebella," said Sef, suddenly looking for the first time that he thought we might be in business. "We have one in the bag, at the very least."

"Doant tell meh: you and 'im in 'is office that first Moonday of term. An' yewer still not tellin', are yer?"

Sef tapped the end of his nose with a very precise forefinger and I believe, looked very pleased with what we'd knocked together in only ten minutes or so.

There was still one thing though:

"S..." I hesitated; I still felt like it was virtually sacrilegious to use his first name.

"Sef, you do know how immoral this is, don't you?"

"An' 'ow oon-professional."

"You're both forgetting something."

"What?"

"The bastard deserves it."

20
The Way Up
Autumn Term - Half Term Week, Day 1
Monday, October 21st, 2002
Peggy Lane Headteacher's Office - Morning

Michael Peniston and Susan Climer sat five feet away from each other in opposing armchairs at the far end of the headmasterial office on a grey Monday half term morning. It was the sort of day when you wake up, look out the window, think 'soon it'll be winter' and resentfully realise you have to plod on regardless. However, for our Michael, there are no seasons in his reality, because he wakes up every day with the type of euphoria that can only be experienced by those who love their job.

Do not be fooled by the positioning of the chairs. Since the start of their professional relationship back in September, Michael and Susan have worked together with increasing closeness. Despite, to use a typical Colin Nostrum phrase, the 'cleavage in their mindsets,' they quickly found that they could work easily and efficiently as a partnership, gathering thoughts, collecting ideas and producing policy documents. The September Manifesto, or 'September Strategies' as Colin was trying to re-name them, with zero success thus far, was the outstanding example of this, though the work they'd already done on a school action plan which Michael wanted published in time for Christmas ran it close.

Something else was also increasing: the Peggy Lane supremo's tendency to rock back and forth on his sleek black chair of a morning, in the quiet before his staff arrived for their working day, wondering why it was that he and Susan got on so well. To begin with, they both liked the ideas which passed for modern in their particular corner of the working world. That was one reason. Delving only slightly more deeply in this ascending young headteacher's mind, though he was still master where Susan was pupil, they could both speak educational jargonese. As befitted the relationship, Susan tended to be tentative and faltering on occasion, but she was learning fast. Michael, of course, was native, and savoured every phrase. He radiated pleasure when he spoke education.

"Come and see this normative distribution curve for the GCSE Maths results, 2002 cohort," he'd said to her quite early in the term one late afternoon. On a piece of light yellow paper laid out landscape-wise were the vertical and horizontal axes of a traditional graph, with a line sweeping across the page, first up from the bottom left-hand corner to the top-centre, then curving round like a northerly by-pass, before re-descending to leave the paper edge about halfway to the bottom. The page was also covered by a disease of crosses, each one a sixteen year old pupil with a GCSE Maths grade. Most of these Peggy Lane crosses were below the line, where in a good school the majority would have been above the line having a party.

"It's scandalous," said Michael, knowing that even if Susan failed to spot the trend immediately, she'd be up to speed in about three seconds. She was a smart cookie and he liked that a lot.

"One thing we have to do one night next week, if you have the time after school, is identify the departments where measurable outcomes aren't good enough and from there, demand an emergency interim action strategy from each head of faculty. What do you think?"

It sounded a sensible, if a little obvious thing to do.

"Fine," she said.

"Great," said Michael, trying to look serious and professional, which was silly, because at school he never looked anything else. Four or five other ideas bobbed around her brain too, not involving short-term scenarios of the interim action plan variety, but she thought it not appropriate to raise them. Perhaps when she got to know Michael better, she would. Run them up his flagpole and see if they fluttered in the new Peggy Lane wind of change, so to speak.

They were both capable, actually, of sitting down after dinner in their respective homes - both made of fine old Yorkshire sandstone - with documents that described and explained all kinds of educational developments and initiatives - from both government and free-standing agencies - and eating them up with a spoon as if they were dessert. If a leaflet entitled: *'To the Classroom and Beyond: School Inclusiveness in a Modern Setting, a four strand day-course. Chief input: Frank Strides (choices of venue: London, Manchester or Leeds)'* plopped into their pigeonholes for attention, they could quickly assess the level of advantage likely to accrue from their attendance. And without precisely knowing why, where even a year ago Susan would have looked at such a thing and immediately scanned the room for the bin, now she paused and wondered if actually it might not help her to, well, develop her career. Now, when examining the aforementioned course, if at the end of the plan for the day, Part Five was described as *'Wash Up: a chance for teachers to raise points extruded from the day,'* not the slightest objection did she take to it. If the term 'plenary,' which been used both to the comfort and discomfort of teachers up, down and across the length and breadth of the country for the past twenty years, was now in the process of been eliminated to make way for a new twist of linguistic modernism, why should it trouble her? Where, at the end of the day, was the harm?

But what of the Nostrum Cleavage, I hear you ask? Here is part of it in a nutshell: from a Penistonian viewpoint, if the movers and shakers of the educational firmament wanted to insert the new usage, 'Wash Up' to describe what used to be termed merely "anyone got any questions?" at the end of a course, consigning 'plenary' to the dustbin marked 'Dead Jargon,' then the point was that they had to be right. Logically, one day, Michael might be in a position himself to brush 'Wash Up' aside if he so desired, planting the term 'Spliff Up' or 'Day-End Evaluation Epiphanous Moment-Possibility' in its place. And if ever that time arrived, using such power to initiate would be essential. Otherwise, how would the education system develop and progress?

As far as Susan is concerned, the exposition of her feelings about this subject two paragraphs up the page is incomplete. True, she had felt revulsion for the continuing despoilation of the beautiful English Language by evil linguacrats for some time now, but she had - and it mystified her - come to a point in her life where she not only didn't mind such wilful destruction of the semantic landscape, but felt it thrilling, naughty even. It gave her the same feeling she'd had when she choked on her first cigarette in Deardsley Park at thirteen years of age, the same evening Nicky Spunk had tried so hard to get two gritty, fat digits into her knickers. It was such a long time since she'd done anything rebellious she'd forgotten what sticking two-fingers up to authority felt like. She decided it felt so good she would keep doing it. She saw the irony in this and nearly laughed at herself. There was another reason too: she wasn't stupid. There was money, kudos and even further elevation for her in this change of heart, and who, let's face it, isn't attracted to at least two of the three?

The move for Susan from English classroom to Management Suite had not been without difficulty. She, as much as anyone with an English degree, loved books. She adored poetry and used to write it: deeply personal stuff, bleak slabs of what she hoped was somewhat Plath-esque verse, much of it really quite moving. Here, take a glimpse.

You are like the paper which spews from a photocopier
Thin.
Like a blade of grass in my raw, rude red hand, green with my envy
A Post Office, teeming with the people, eager to push letters into slots.
Like the chip shop where I watch warm vinegar run through my fingers and down my scrawny arm and onto your
saveloy.
I bite it, and heavenly meat, spills from my mouth like
A beast drooling on dead liver.
The flesh was like a birdsong, like a heartbeat, like a head being crushed by

A crude, laughing bulldozer.

Not bad, I'm sure you'll agree, but not that great either. So she gave it up at the age of 26 because she found she was so content with her life, her heart seemed to be empty of existential misery; there was no longer any darkness in her soul to dump onto the page. She also gave up because she thought she was rubbish at it. Which is always the way for those who are brought up on the best and must measure themselves against it. If she couldn't be as good as Sylvia or Emily Dickinson then what was the point? She considered the idea of following in the footsteps of Wendy Cope but two seconds later she said out loud, "face it, Susan, you haven't got a sense of humour." When it came down to it, she wasn't even capable of being good enough to give what's her name, the Somerset one who she'd seen as a child winning Opportunity Knocks every week, a run for her money. So that was most definitely that, as far as the life of poetic muse was concerned.

Happily, she actually liked being in the classroom with young people. This was easy for her because the kids at Peggy Lane, as everyone said who came in from other schools, were well-behaved and friendly. They weren't arrogant or spoiled; they were down to earth and grounded, most of them, having come from good, no nonsense, Yorkshire stock. Safely married, she was happy to have come here as head of English after a long spell at a school in Worksop where she'd shown an outstanding ability for organization and discipline. With the help of an outstanding female mentor who had shown her how to talk to children, how to raise her voice at children and how to teach children, she flowered to become a top-notch classroom practitioner technically, one whom even the great Sefton Demmler respected. Thus, even though not exactly overflowing with charisma, she soon established herself at Pegs as a very accomplished professional who got on easily with everyone she came into contact with. She may not have been the first one you thought of inviting to your party, or of putting onto a list of the first twenty even, you'd put an invitation in her pigeon hole because she was so damned hard to dislike. And she was now as much a part of the Peggy Lane wallpaper as…well, Pegs didn't have any wallpaper, it was a school of painted plaster and breeze block, but you get the picture.

However, to her surprise, she soon became fed up with this. Sliding past 35 and having tucked away six years service at Pegs, she came to the conclusion that it wasn't going to be enough for her just to wile away the rest of her working life doing this. Sadly, she couldn't have children, and no amount of modern fertility treatment was going to re-make her fallopian tubes. This she had come to accept without rancour or bitterness. She would have liked to have hated Mankind or God, or both, and to have railed dramatically at the stars, but she just wasn't made that way. Her husband was adamant that they wouldn't adopt and she wasn't prepared to take on the long term task of overturning his mind on this one. So. She could now see the future: a long, straight empty highway stretching to the distant horizon. It no longer offered anything remotely unexpected and unexplored. Instead, it crowded her head with fat bored clouds of everyday dreariness. It's blindingly bloody obvious, she often thought, pottering around the back garden trying to fake an interest in the natural world of green and coloured wonder that Tuesday night Dutch yoga wasn't going to fill the void. Neither were monthly quiz nights with Mark down at the Labour Club in Oatley.

She would have to do something or commit quiet suicide, she thought watching a re-run of Morse Code late one Monday night. 'Don't be silly, Susan,' she said to herself immediately, 'you're not the suicide type.' Which of course she wasn't. She toyed for a time with the idea of going into politics. She could get herself elected up here as a Labour councillor fairly easily, and her appetite for hard work and the bureaucratic process would tie on the wings she'd need to fly to higher achievement in a grubby but earnest and committed environment. Trouble was, though she cared about people, she doubted that she cared about them enough. Then again, the thought of getting away from the flat predictability of the working week aroused her temporarily. She was a Virgo, and true to those who made their entrance onto the planet at that period of the astrological cycle, she hated routine. Pegs was easy, teaching was easy, but once she'd got a handle on its new stretches and strains, so was the head of faculty job. The thunder of the need for change rumbled in her head.

The life she imagined as a Westminster woman, if she could get that far, was different enough, but in the end she decided she didn't really care enough about cockroaches crawling across babies in cots in desperate housing estates, so she dumped the whole notion one night in the middle of practicing the Leiden Theory of Detachment at Bidworth Village Hall one evening. She decided to focus on winning the quiz with Mark once a month instead. He was wanted to break the Labour Club Quiz Night record for most consecutive wins in a calendar year.

The thunder in her head rumbled and brooded like a distantly terrifying threat while she waited for something to turn up.

Or someone.

Michael's arrival had given Susan - not Sue, because she's never liked Sue: it makes her sound like a hairdresser - the opportunity for change alright. She was surprised to have been singled out with lightning rapidity for promotion and though it had been obvious to some of the smarter observers of life at Peggy

Lane, her further elevation on account of Malcolm's accident surprised her again. She was flattered, obviously. She thought about this suddenly emerging career path to higher management opening out in front of her like something pre-ordained during the capital of Bolivia question one evening, and said, 'why not?' instead of 'La Paz.' Mark would know that one anyway. Now that her career game was to be played on a completely different pitch, she simply, and blandly, struggled to find a good enough reason not to make whatever accommodations were necessary. What surprised her about her new situation was the ease with which she was making the transition. Apart from one ghastly faculty meeting it had been an absolute doddle. Dealing with the new language was just a minor issue really, and so far no task had been put in front of her that she hadn't dealt with smartly and quickly.

In fact, without her even being aware of it, Susan Climer was developing the attitudes of mind that could easily make her a superstar like Michael. She had the aptitudes. She sucked up discussion documents, pamphlets and action plans like an industrial Hoover while Michael, ever the mathematician, wondered how she did it so easily. The answer was trivial to Susan: it was because she could read like lightning. She'd been the fastest in her class at primary school and was discarding five books a week by the time she was 9. She didn't let up as she got older. The expansion of fiction writing, self-help writing, travel writing, sports writing and writing writing in the 1990s had been a Godsend. She still read everything she could get her hands on - anything that fitted her Susanesque spec. that is. History interested her, so did biography and, it goes without saying, poetry and modern fiction. The house seemed to consist of books and little else. They were like triffids, like giant hogweed, threatening to suffocate occupants and visitors alike. Mark's mother couldn't stand to visit, said it made the house smell. Fine, thought Susan: she hated the interfering cow anyway.

Mark was an architect, and he'd planned the extension with great effort, ensuring that Susan's obsession with the printed word was indulged. Nooks and crannies of various and interesting sizes and shapes were lovingly created, just for the display and storage of her books.

It was in bed two nights after Malcolm's accident, while Mark toiled away manfully trying to conclude a connubial encounter by giving his wife a big orgasm, his finger twiddling with her clitoris as if tuning-in a faulty short wave radio, that she decided to really embrace Michael and what he stood for. While Mark, evidently having difficulty in bringing the project to fruition, worked a change of strategy by slithering southwards, Susan decided conclusively that as the boss had turned Malcolm's accident into such a big door for her, she might as well stroll through it. Elaine, the other deputy, was a hopeless piss artiste who couldn't do her job anymore. By rights, either of Pegs' two senior teachers, Trevor Money or Molly Factor, should have been pushed upwards into Malkie's slot, but before he vacated his high place for Michael, Andrew Covely had marked a few cards for Mr. P., apprising him of a couple of relevant scenarios. Firstly, Trevor wanted to spend more time on his own novelty thong-making business (a margarita pizza-flavoured number made out of stretched and dried mozzarella was really taking off - Asda were even considering taking it in all their stores nationwide). And secondly, Molly wasn't capable of getting arrested in her position as assistant to the pastoral deputy and staff development officer so couldn't possibly be promoted further. The bright spot here was that as she increasingly toiled moistly with stress-induced depression and chronic asthma, early retirement was an increasing inevitability. It was this tin lid on the negative historico-futurish situation that caused Michael to decide that he had to act quickly to move the Peggy Lane agenda onto rigorously bureaucratic terrain. 'Kill or cure,' he thought. By nature he was impatient anyway: 'so what the heck, go for it,' he thought. 'Promote Susan and if it's unpopular with some, too bad. This is what you wanted to become a headmaster for. In the end, it's your school.' He remembered Sef's words that first day, and dismissed them with an audible *hurrumph*. "What the Billy Blazes does he know," he said out loud that night as he undressed.

By the time Mark's tongue resembled a shredded length of bath towel, Susan had decided to go with whatever Michael wanted. The 'why not?' was becoming a 'definitely.' She'd been given this new Reporting, Recording and Assessment post, which offered the chance to bring in all sorts of changes and 'new strategies for school improvement,' to quote a current buzz phrase, and Malcolm's fall had opened up other new areas. If anything else was in the offing - and you never knew, with Molly's health and Elaine's drinking quite what was around the next corner - she was up for it. Decision made, she quickly faked as large a climax as she could, and packed Mark off to sleep. So, when Michael asked her to come into the plot to undo Sef, she thought, 'oh, to hell with it, yes.' She'd come this far, she'd crossed Stamford Bridge, so there was no going back. The danger it promised made her heart pound uncomfortably, but it also made her more awake, more alive. She liked Sef, but any squeamishness she might have felt about the moral consequences of such action she put aside easily, knowing that if her betrayal caused him to lose his job, he was too brilliant not to survive, or indeed, prosper somewhere else, perhaps somewhere outside the teaching profession. She was coming to realise perhaps more clearly than dear old Sefton could, that the profession was moving further and further away from the teacher he was and had always been. There was no way it could reach back and pull him in.

She'd often thought he was wasted in teaching anyway. Surely he could produce some great fiction if he could be bothered. She'd never really understood why he hadn't. How could he be satisfied merely with teaching children? 'I'll be doing him a favour,' she thought, as she mopped herself up in the bathroom. She felt no guilt at the thought of bringing him down as she went to sleep that night.

Well then: here they were, in Michael's office. Half term Monday and starting to rain. A couple of weeks ago, he'd said casually to Susan, 'hey, by the way, if you're not too busy at half term, perhaps you could come in and we could get some of this new assessment stuff finalised and start to think about some curriculum ideas for next year.' And Susan has said, 'yeah, sure, sounds like a good idea.'

They'd immediately begun to motor through a robust agenda, which included a decision on whether to bring in a GCSE Leisure and Tourism course, something Simon Cupboard the head of Geography was keen to get going, and how to implement the new target-setting scheme for Years 10 and 11 after Christmas. But though it was signalled for discussion at the end of the meeting - for Michael liked to work an agenda for every meeting without exception - after 'Item 5: Development of Blended Learning at Key Stage 3,' they could hold out no longer. They began to talk about the hot topic of the moment at the school: the fate of Chris Lampeter.

"A lot of staff are very upset about what's happened to Chris, you know," said an initially hesitant and slightly bored Susan.

"Mmm. I'm aware of that. But you agreed, Susan: that if we want to get rid of Sef, it's too good an opportunity to miss. And you know what's going on in the States: three strikes and you're out. He's had his chance, Susan. He's been asking for it."

'I feel sorry for him,' she wanted to say but kept it down. 'He's a good man, you know,' she wanted to add, but she kept that down too. She stared at Michael. Even in half term he wore a blue pin striped office shirt with white collar and cuffs and a pair of blue denim jeans. She didn't like his trainers: too lumpy and young, and too white. But she looked at him and wondered.

"What do you think the governors will do?"

"Oh, they'll fire him. What he did to that kid was practically a sexual assault. I've had a talk with Peter Precision. He doesn't like Chris. Never has. 'Loose cannon,' he says. 'And a fool to keep making mistakes.'"

"I know, but it's the first time he's done something like this and Lip's fa…"

"He's irrelevant, Susan," said Michael. She was taken aback by how determined he was to be ruthless. And a little attracted to the sexiness of power. Or aroused by the eroticism of the newness of her relationship with it.

"He'll be gone come next Friday."

"Aren't you being a bit hard?" she said.

It really was all new to her, this power politics. Dealing with people as if they were pawns to manoeuvre and manipulate on a chess board. It was like shunting crushed cars onto the hard shoulder after bad dual carriageway collision. It disgusted her, yet sucked at her insides at one and the same time.

"I'm afraid you have to be hard sometimes to get on. If you want to make it to the top, these are the things...the things you have to do," said Michael.

She reflected on this. 'No, you bloody don't,' she thought. Not all heads coped with challenge by trying to stab it in the throat the first chance they got.

"Have you always wanted to be a Head?" she asked.

"What do you mean, 'always?'"

"Since you started, I mean."

"No. I don't think anyone's like that. It just sort of happened. I worked at a school down in Sussex, my second job, and I got to know the Head very well. After a couple of years, he took me aside and said, 'you know, you should think about being a headteacher: it'd be the right sort of scenario for you. You have the talent.' So...and then the idea grew from there really."

He fiddled with his pen on the blotter and drew a house. A neat one, with a lot of windows.

"And now you're there, how does it feel?"

"Good. Great, actually. Most of the time."

"What do you like about it most?" said Susan, genuinely curious about this stupid but marginally handsome guy, an ex-Maths teacher, but one with something her internal womanly mechanism was unconsciously picking up on, now that he'd edged a fraction past the *verboten* line into her personal space.

"Being here with you. Actually."

"Oh, I see: I'm one of your 'Smart Targets,' am I?" 'God, what am I saying? That was pure education-speak. Damn,' thought Susan.

"Well, let's see. You're not simple. Or perhaps you are. I don't know."

Michael, it must be recorded for posterity ('Must it, Tim? Are you sure this isn't a reflection of your own conflicted unconscious?' I can hear Andy Crucial warning me, as he smears away some granary bread crumbs from his wiry lip brush), felt a surge in the trouser region. He could have bottled it at this point, but he thought of who he was now, his new position in the scheme of things in this place. This checked him though. "Headteacher makes absurd sexual advance at colleague." It could get him the sack. Only no one else was around on a grey, quiet Monday morning of half term. No one to disturb or observe them at all. And Susan didn't seem to mind in the slightest him edging his chair so close to hers, their knees were almost touching. It was enough to draw him forward to the finish line.

"Um...you would appear to be measurable," he went on, his heart pumping hard, seeing clearly an opportunity for an exceptional learning outcome. He felt himself blush.

"Am I attainable, do you think?" said Susan, quickly homing in like a heat-seeking missile on Michael's overplaying of the bishop. She thought she might as well go through with this. The rain was beginning to depress her.

He laughed, a little embarrassed, and looked sideways out of the window. But he couldn't because he'd already closed the curtains earlier, when the sunshine had been dazzling. No one could possibly see in.

"I'm beginning to think you might be a realistic, um, proposition."

She had a good mind to blow him out of the water right there and then for that. She thought about it for about a second that seemed to last an afternoon, as the troublesome implications of all this passed across her mind. 'No one can hear me say this,' she thought, feeling a nice clean hit from climbing up into this position of power over the man in power.

"How time-specific do you want to be on this?" she said, feeling herself cringe from anus to gizzard, but leaning towards him slowly at one and the same time.

"I..um..." he was lost for words. After all, this was his first time.

'You're really not very worldly, or clever at all, are you Michael,' she thought, as a wind picked up outside the window. 'But you're almost a catch, being a headmaster with your big car and your seventy grand a year. Plus, here you are urging my career forward with machine-like authority. And it doesn't have to last for ever.'

'Bugger it,' she thought, and opened her slim but not unattractive mouth ready to kiss him.

21
The Brakes Complaining
Autumn Term - Half Term Week, Day 3
Wednesday, October 23rd, 2002
Measby/Leeds - Late afternoon/night time

I am Tim and I am sad.

I walk through the streets of Yarrow in the cold October rain and the flowerbeds are full of the poor green remains of dead flowers that now look like weeds. The wet stuff falls out of the sky like people emptying buckets in your face. I think I might be going bald and two of my back teeth hurt. I can't chew on them any more and I'm too scared to go to the dentist. And Chris is headed for the wrecker's yard.

What's more, there's this: Jez rings me on the Wednesday afternoon of this same half term and after making me pick over the plans we made with Sef for about ten minutes - and I'm quite enjoying myself, just to hear her voice and know that for a while, even though it's only for a while, she is spending her time on me - she says,

"Guess what…"

And I think of the possibilities these two words throw up: 'I just bought a new car,' maybe. Or 'guess what, I've got a big boil growing on my fat arse. Just what I need.' She hasn't got an oversized behind, she's got a lovely behind, but she'd say it was fat. Even, 'guess what, I'm really looking forward to our trip to London. Just thought I'd tell you that I wasn't joking there in your classroom.' It might be Jez being unkind or shallow, teasing me because she knows how I feel about her, but, y' know, after much deep reflection, I decided I could live with it. But no. She says this:

"Guess what?"

And I'm daft enough to have let my good mood get the better of me, and reply, "you've got a huge boil on your arse," really going to town on the English version of the word, which I don't normally use. And I hear her laugh at that down the other end, a small laugh, so rich and fetching it's all I can do to stop myself dropping the phone and running the four miles barefoot to her house in Yarrow, right there and then, to pick her up gently in my arms and swear my undying love to her. But of course I don't, even though I really, really feel like doing just that, and instead hear her say to me,

"Steve and me are gerrin' married."

I did drop the phone. In despair. But I picked it up double quick to cover my tracks. Why do we bother? For good reason, I guess.

"Shit, sorry, Jez, I dropped the phone. Right. Where were we? Yes. What? You're getting married. Great!"

A pile of twenty CDs neatly stacked on the floor went flying across the room having just made contact with the toe-end of my right foot.

"What was tha'?"

"What?"

"That noise. Is there soomewon there with yer?"

"Eh? Oh, that was a pile of CDs falling over; they just toppled on to the floor. I knocked them. I was just sorting them out."

I looked down at my light blue sock. Don't laugh. I like light blue. And saw a small spot of blood expanding slowly in the big toe region. Fuck, it hurt, too. Look, Jez, I bleed for you. Actual blood.

"And no, there's no one."

"Look, if you've gorra girl in over there, you can tell me, yer noah."

I didn't know how to play this. I didn't know what she was trying to say, if indeed she was trying to say anything.

"I know, Jez. No. I'm definitely on my own."

"At least ah think we're gerrin' married."

What?

"Oh?"

"Steve's asked me ter marry 'im."

"Oh, well...that's nice. That's, um, cool."

"Well 'e 'asn't exactly asked me."

"..."

"He says he wants to. What d' yer think?"

What do I think? What a fucking silly thing to say. A stupid thing. What do I think? I think I want to shoot him through the head with a high-powered air rifle. From a distance of about five feet. Thus giving him no second chances. And get clean away with it. Then there'll be some sort of hope that you might one day marry me. How much to let go? How much to hold on to? I have no idea. I suddenly think of the poster outside the King's Hall in Yarrow advertising a concert by the Dribble Valley Hand Bell Choir, and I don't know why.

"Jez. Please tell me. Why on earth are you going on like this?"

"Oh, alright, be like tha'. Ah thought you might be interested, that's all."

I give up. I had never come across a woman who complicated things so much.

"What makes you think I might be interested in whether you marry Steve?"

It's funny how when you're not consciously trying, you can produce a quite intelligent response while living on your wits in the middle of a conversation where you feel like your whole life's on fire. This might at least reveal whether Jez really has realised the effect she has on me.

"Oah, I...I joost....well..." There was a deep sigh of frustration, I think, from the other end at this point.

"I....oh, I doan't noah, Tim. I just thought you might."

Which gets me precisely nowhere.

"Do you mean, 'Do I think you should marry Steve?'"

I think Jez had suddenly realised what a bone-headed question this was, assuming I was going to take her situation seriously. Seriously, I think she was screwing me around, out of boredom, or pure mischief, just as she was in the classroom about London. And I was beginning to think for the first time that Jezebel Treat might be just a selfish, manipulative bitch. The phone was all but dead at the other end. Then this small voice.

"I think ah'd better goah. I'll see yer."

I was broken and speechless with everything: frustration; pain; the senselessness of two grown ups with a couple of degrees between them being completely unable to communicate, even in their own language. It was as if we'd been forced by some higher authority to converse in French, when neither of us had taken it in school. I tried to leave a long gap, but not long enough so she wouldn't be able to say she hung up.

"Yeah. Later, Jez."

Thunk!

I pulled on a jacket and ran out the door. Crossed the road and waited for the bus into town. It came in ten minutes. By which time I'd had to go back for my wallet. I got off at the bus station and walked up the hill towards the school and found The Yarrow Car Hire Centre. Within a quarter of an hour a bored middle aged fat guy had put me in a white Mégane and I drove off towards Leeds. It was the first time I'd driven since I rammed my own car into the central reservation of the M25 just south of Guildford the previous winter. A new gold Fiat Baggio my darling mother bought me. I'd had it five weeks. Top of the range: lovely Pickard CD/cassette with four-speed change potential, Muttler Bucket Grope Screws on the rear suspension and aluminium Toiler Bum Valves on the carb. Plus, extra-zizz airbags to top off the deal. Real nice. But I thought I was going to die when after swivelling the rear end like a championship ice skater I careered headlong towards the barrier thinking; 'this is it! I'm gone.' I swear to God, I really did think that.

"Oh, no, it's designed to bend inwards on impact, sir," said PC Delves, as I sat in his passenger seat in a total daze merely minutes later. 'Thanks, man,' I thought, but it didn't change the fact that minutes before I was on course to find out lickety-spitly whether God made me or not. Now, none the wiser, I am Tim, I am angry and I am back in a car.

I changed down into second as I approached a roundabout near Oatley. Then stopped dead and stalled it trying to pull away.

"Fuck!" I screamed at the windscreen. Not used to the clutch yet. Five o'clock was coming on but for once it was a fine late afternoon, golden everywhere with all the leaves now turned colours and starting to fall.

"The *fuck* I care!" I said out loud again. A slow procession of cars all the way down through the outer city suburbs. If I wanted to get shot of this anger by driving like an eighteen year old out on the Friday night pull, I'm going in the wrong direction. But I can't be bothered to turn around and head back toward open country. So I crawl past places, neither village nor town towards the city. There are fields, then shops, and houses lining the road, big detached ones. Then a proper settlement, apparently with no name. A smart and warm looking coffee place has a woman sipping contentedly from a big white cup in the window.

"You look happy enough, you fucking *cow!*" I shout. "What about me? What about *me!*" Now I pass a cemetery and government buildings. Soon I'm past the ring road and university halls of residence, the sort of place where once I strutted my young stuff so indifferently. In another city of course.

Leaves and leaves and leaves. Fallen on parked car windscreens. Beautiful russet browns and luscious, rich reds seemingly everywhere each time I look to the side of the road. Students begin to appear and an old man carrying his bag of shopping, walking through a path of grey paving stones either side of the light brown mulch. Hate this time of year. Shortening days until winter. Makes you glum, like the retreating summer took all the fun with it and disappeared for good, especially when things just aren't going so well. When there's too much time and not enough to do with it. Not that that should bother me now I've made the big step into the white collar world. But look where it's fucking getting me. Still crawling along, reach Headingley. Shop lights now bright and strong in the creeping dusk. Sky a darkening but brilliant light blue, backlit by a silver sun. Incredible sight, but wasted on me. I tramped streets like these last year in Nottingham and was as miserable as sin. Had nobody. And autumn was like a sad cello playing a lonely concerto. Only the stress of a teaching practice got me through by occupying and annexing every thought in my head. I am not impressed at all by any of this. And hardly know where I'm going. Stomach empty, but I feel nauseous. I recognize the streets and shops from coming up here one weekend to see a friend called Stan. We went in that pub. The car behind hoots me on.

"Fuck *off!*" I scream at it, not that it can hear. And not that it matters. Buses in front. Picking up students at bus stops. This way to the university and the city. Up past the park over on the right with its rows of dark trees. Away over yonder out my left window, row upon row of terrace rooftops from lost industrial times. Crest the hill past cheap curry places and dark little desolate shops. Or is it my mood? The thought of people scrabbling to make ends meet selling worthless crap to the poor always depressed the hell out of me.

The university is now all on my right, the white stone engineering building. After another third of a mile on a whim I turn left, suddenly, and park. A horn screams at me. "Go fuck yourself in the ass," I scream back. Not exactly the stiletto-like wit of the PhD man, but it's all I have at this moment. Not a great place to leave the car either, but I must be confusing myself with someone who actually gives a fuck. Walk to the main road and cross. Look up at a tall white tower and vast steps in front of me. University main building. I follow walkers through an archway to the left where I know the Students' Union building will give me a welcome. My head stares down at the flagstones when I'm not checking my way. In disgust. At what? At everything. At Jez playing games with me. Then, I think...Oh, here we are. No one checks me on the door, it's too early. I know the way to the bar. I walk through but it's ten-to-six and not open.

Then I think, 'what if it all fell into place with this woman? If it was like it was when I first met Janey? Would it change the way I feel? Would it really?' I sit down and jam my hands down into my jacket pockets. Fuck, I nearly ripped one. Anger still feeling like it's going to bust out of my jaw bones. And feel a kind of grinding in my chest. A grinding in my chest? What am I talking about - a grunching in my stomach is what it is.

One or two guys pass through to another part of the complex. I hear a pinball machine in the distance and a call for someone on a loudspeaker. Funny how I think that having been a university student in another part of the country gives me the right to sit here. Where it isn't my party. But students are the same everywhere. They look the same in every place. Same clothes, same haircuts, same expressions. I love them. I'm 28 but I swear to God I feel just like them. I still feel I belong in places like this.

Good. The bar shutter clatters up to begin the night. About bloody time. I walk over. A guy about my age with small, oblong, trendy glasses doesn't smile - just looks at me like his are the same problems as mine.

"Pint of Black Dung."

I fiddle for my money and he's not getting 'please' from me if he's not going to say 'hi,' like a bartender would in the USA. 'Hi, g'd-evening and what kin I git ya?' All friendly. And isn't it always hard not to say 'I'll have a beer and a shot?' White strip of a tab placed discreetly on the bar when your drinks arrive.

A pint glass is not far short of dumped in front of me on a beer towel that's seen a lot of ale.

"This one's for Chris," I say out loud and take a whopping slug from the glass. The bar guy looks at me like I am totally off my head. It's lovely beer. Big waft of sweet flavour, but with that alcohol hit that you need. Especially at times like this. I walk to a table and sit on my own, placing my thin glass carefully on top of a beer mat. 'Beefwell's Old Squirt' it says on it. I always carry a paperback with me wherever I go. So I reach for my inside pocket and sure enough, there's my battered copy of *It Might Be a Brick* by Sally Knowles. So I sit there, drinking and trying to read.

But it's hopeless. I sup and stare at the people drifting in for an early drink. Some boisterous lads at one point, full of the joys of young life, pints and shorts ahead, some spliff in their pockets and maybe a jump on some young chick's bones later on. A girl comes in with a striped tea cosy hat over her head, nine inches of hair hanging down below like streaming tales of rat. She looks sad and alone and I start to worry about her and fret. Then her boyfriend comes in and her face breaks into a beautiful smile, and when she takes the hat off he kisses her and whispers something and she laughs, her mouth still touching the side of his. And I notice her hair isn't in fact greasy at all. It's fine and he strokes one side of it with the outside of two knuckles with great tenderness, then speaks again, and again she laughs, full of student love.

I drain my Dung and leave.

It's dark now and growing cold. Frost tonight, probably. The sky is empty but for two stars spread distantly across the sky like a sulking married couple. I retrace my steps to the arch, but instead of crossing the road, turn to the right and walk down the hill, past a church with a spire as black as soot from two hundred and thirty years of smoke and grime and find the pub Stan - or Hippie, as we all called him at King's - took me to one Saturday night. The Frinton. It was worn and old-looking from the outside and at first sight looked absolutely spent on the in. Those three-legged tables had been there for donkey's years and it was lit like a catacomb. But as I remembered it there was a snug, comfy room off to the right-hand side and a kickin' juke box. It hadn't changed since Stan the Hippie had me in here celebrating an election. The same dark wood climbed up to a high ceiling, veined yellow with a decade of accumulated fag smoke. The barman was cheerful and much older than me; in his forties I would have said, but with two silver earrings in each ear and a shiny head. He had a tattooed neck as well, a spider's web, and I thought, 'what the hell, I might get one of those myself one of these days, make myself more interesting.'

Another row of beer pumps beckoned me.

"Pint of Smoky Box, please, and a shot of Bowmore please." The row of malts behind the bar at the bottom of a broad mirror, like a huge silver window, looked promising, so I dug in for one. Have to have a Smoky Box, not least as it's got a huge reputation.

"No problem, surrr," he said in a broad Scots accent, and went about his business, seemingly pleased with his existence, anyway. How did you do it? How was he able to pull off this marvellous feat? Was he shafting a girl of 20? A crude thought, but I imagined at 40, it must take a lot to put a smile on your face. He must have been aware, surely, that he was way past his best; that he was possibly even going to die soon? He was a handsome, tough-looking guy, though, muscles like knots of solid oak, pushing the sleeves of a black t-shirt out of shape. Maybe he was in love, maybe he was gay; what the big shit did I know? Lucky bastard, anyway, if he can look this cheerful in October.

I pulled out my Sally Knowles again and re-started chapter four, but I couldn't concentrate. And I loved reading on my own in bars and cafés. I hit my pint hard again, and walked across to the bar to ask the man for some water for my Islay malt. I'd forgotten it.

"Heeere y'ahrrr," the guy said in his kindly way. Nice people, the Scots. Back in my chair, I thought, 'Okay - time to put things to rights; time to try to sort out my thinking here and now about Jez.' If I could get that right, maybe the rest of my problems would fall away into the bottom of the universe and stay there forever. The hard thing was knowing what you wanted. Jezebel, I wanted. To lie on her lap somewhere and have her stroke my face, tell me everything would be alright. Love. Has to be the answer. Must be the answer. Doesn't it say so in all the songs? Love is the only cure, Love is the only answer, Hate is the root of cancer, all you need is Love. Putting aside the fact that love is also the drug, if I could get Jez to love me, then its heat and brightness would burn the melancholy out of my soul like a veruka. Shit, this is not the poetic imagery we want on a night like this, Tim. What if all the songs are baloney, what if there was nothing mystical about Lennon; what if he wasn't touched by genius, by an infinite power? What if the only love that is real is platonic love, holy love, the love for one's fellow human being? What if romantic love, sexual love is doomed always to fail? What then?

"Another Smoky Box please," I said, back at the bar.

I took my pint back to my corner table. Another delicious drink. Customers are trickling in now, and the voices at the bar no longer carry a slight echo from the high ceiling and hard, solid floor. The chill has gone from the place too, even when the door opens to let in another drinker, and I begin to feel a nice cosy warmth beginning to grow. A layer of comfort against the nasty fear I can still feel right here in my shining plexus. And this anger at Jezebel that won't quite go away. But as I wipe some creamy white froth from the head of my pint from my top lip on the back of my hand, I don't feel quite so mad with her. Things could be worse,

Tim; she could easily have exhibited absolutely no interest in you whatsoever. She could easily have rung me, or not rung me, just told me matter-of-factly at school, 'Tim, guess what, I'm getting spliced. Yeah, it's love alright. The real thing. You? Don't be silly.' Or worse, I could have heard it second-hand.

I replay the phone call again in my head for the three-hundredth time. Every nuance of every word of each sentence, spring cleaned and dusted, swabbed for the last trace of meaning. Do words have DNA? Can you buy a bottle of sub-text unraveller? Pour some in this wonderful pint and know instantly exactly, precisely, how she feels about me. What she wants from me. Or buy some truth potion and force her to drink deeply. More difficult, that. Have to get her to Measby first. How am I going to pull that stunt off?

Tell Steve you're coming to see me tonight so we can smash his life into pieces. Must get another pint of this great beverage and tell you what, another short. Might make this a McFrechtish this time. Take my jacket off to make it clear to anyone who wants to nick my place that I'm staying. So watch out.

Takes longer to get served but my empty chair and beer mat is safe. Still no Sally Knowles read. It's not really any good anyway. Stupid story of a bishop who gives up the cloth to go looking for himself up the Amazon river. I could have told him he was right there underneath his habit the whole time. Or whatever it is these guys wear. Only made it to page 25. Should ask people in the bar if they want to take it off my hands for nothing. Should stand on the table, really. Announce the fact that I'm selling. And announce the fact that I'm in love with a woman called Jezebel Treat. No longer just a girl. I'm sure all these people will be pleased to know how great it is, in this modern age of sex and cynicism that love still exists in the hearts of young people. That we don't all want to fuck off to clubs and shovel drugs down all night and writhe like demented robots in the eighth circle of hell, to that...that industrial, inhuman noise that passes for dance music these days.

I nearly fall over on my way to the jukebox but manage to hold on to my grip on the planet's skin by reaching out my left arm for support on this girl. Unfortunately I have to grab hold of her substantial right boob to pull off the balancing act. She seems to understand the unavoidable pitfall of gravity inherent in the situation, but the bloke she's with gives me a filthy stare.

"Very sorry," I say, and try to make a friendly face.

The girl smiles and I know I haven't offended her, whatever I've done to her boyfriend. Alright, then. What do we have, here: Springsteen? No, not in the mood for The Boss. REM? No fuckn' way, man. Stones. Ah. Here we are. *Bitch.* That'll do. That'll rock this joint. Oh, I can be so funny when I want to be. What have we got here...three for a quid. So what else. Beatles. Nah. Not tonight. All sorts of modern shit too, but yeah! A Motown section here: so *Tracks of My Tears* will do the job and what else? *Signed Sealed Delivered, I'm Yours*, baby. Fantastic choice. And won't everyone in here love me. Punch the buttons. What do I need here: D4. *Plack.* Hold on...*Plack.* J9. Where the fuck is that J? There. *Plack.* 9. Oh, 'sorry, mate. Sorry.' Bumped into someone carrying a tray of drinks there. No harm done though. *Plack.* N5. Come here you little bastard. This is for Jez. *Plack* and *plack!* There. Great choices, Weaver.

Get another malt while I'm waiting for them to come around. What a great, great pub, this is. Fine - no: tremendous beer and nice friendly people. Students mostly. My people. Noble in the art of the taking of the degree. Educated people. The best kind. Which is why I am in the honourable art of teaching.

"Mind where you're goin', mate!"

"Oh, sorry, sorry."

Oh, it'd be nice to be back at a place like this. Reading and writing the days away. The peace and tranquility of philosophical contemplation. Dreamy winter afternoons of the diligent scratching of the pen and careful perusal and selection of the quotation. To illustrate my sagaciousness.

'Have you read Weaver's treatise on Bryson?'

'No, not yet; I'm still putting the finishing touches on my life of Michael Parkinson - fourth and last volume.'

'Oh, you must. Weaver's textual analysis has no equal. And his prose? Wondrous. Flows like a velvet cascade. We await the first novel with breath absolutely plastered with bate.'

I amuse myself so much that I burst out laughing in front of all these lovely people. And take another mouthful of beer. Christ, that mouthful of.... *Ccoerrqchoufffff!!*

"You alright, mate?"

"Yeh, I'm *Ccccccoourrrechhch!!! Ccccoourrrechhch!!! Fine!*"

Just like in Yarrow, the bloke sitting behind me leans over and bangs my back for me. A drop of beer went down the wrong hole and landed penis-upwards in Africa, ha-ha-ha-ha!

"Thanks. Yeah. Cool. Thanks, man."

I fight it, but rapidly have to accept the fact that the room is going round and if I shut my eyes I feel as though there's a giant chandelier up there in the middle of the ceiling and I'm being swung around on it, hanging on for dear life. But I tell myself I'm fine. I can hear music. Blaring horns of The Rolling Stones and it sounds absolutely great. I have to get up though to go for a piss. So I do.

"This is my song! I put this on," I say to a mixed group of Maths students or something, a real square bunch, anyway. "Isn't it great?" I continue, beaming, to the next knot of drinkers, three girls standing by the wall. One of them smiles at me and another smiles at the third. Part of my brain says, 'Tim, they can see you're totally shit-faced and they probably think you're a fucking idiot and feel sorry for you.' But the rest of the grey matter reads this as 'Timbo? Go for it, lad, these chicks think you're great fun.'

I manage not to pee down the front of my trousers, something I've done a few times down the years when ee-aawed to the gills, and feel as though I have every right to be pleased with myself. I have to splash water on my face and down the back of my neck though, to make myself feel more awake.

That's better.

I stride out of the toilet feeling fantastic. I beam a massive smile at the three girls.

"Hi, girls. Isn't this a fabulous song?"

"And *lerrrve, it's a bitch*," I sing in my best Jagger. "My aunt yoosh do a great Mick Jargger. You shuh meet her shumetime. Pirry Dockshrer"

They smile back at me and two of them are laughing. See Tim? They think you're great! So I am great and I feel great.

"Isn't this the best song?" I shout to all of them.

"Yeah!" grins one of the girls, looking not at me, but at her friend. I swerve back to my seat, which waits for me safe and sound. Still plenty of Smoky Box in my glass. I drain most of what's left of that, my throat feeling better, and wag my head to the music. Tap my foot too, as it fades.

Now Smokey Robinson and the Miracles. I don't know if you know this song. It's famous. It's considered to be one of the great singles of the Sixties, possibly ever. It's sweet, it's soulful, it's well-written and beautifully, perfectly arranged. Loved for that inimitable Motown sound and the smooth, classy singing of a decent melody. A story of lost love. The next thing I know, I'm feeling a little sleepy, so I bury my head on my forearm, head almost on the table. Still listening to the music. Then I feel myself shaking. And tears streaming out of my eyes as if I'd spent a whole day peeling onions. I don't feel okay any more. I need water. Must have water on my face and in my mouth. I get up quickly, much too quickly, feel my foot catch something on the way out from under my chair and in a gruesome splinter of a single second realize that my control of destiny has flown as suddenly as the hard floor comes up to meet me and speaks into my ear as I crash. Sounds like, 'O that this too, too solid floor would melt into a nice soft bed.' But the last thing I remember thinking though, is

'Malcolm.'

22

A Friend of Spirit
Autumn Term - Half Term Week, Day 4
Thursday, 24th October, 2002
Leeds - Early Hours of Morning

Everything is a blur at best after that. I remember people around me. I remember the cool concrete feeling wonderful against my skin. But I remember the word, 'hospital' making me not so happy with my change of situation. This said 'all is not right with your world, feller.' Then I collided with half a sentence that had 'blood' near the front of it. And felt so tired. I recall that too. Not so much exhausted as obliterated. As if all my energy had gathered itself together in one ball somewhere inside me and decided to take its leave. I thought I could see it, dust-coloured, waving me goodbye. 'Thanks for everything,' it said, 'but we've all had more of you than we can stand. No hard feelings.' I wanted to stay there forever, with all my bones melted into the floor. Then my brain began talking to me again.

"You remember the word 'hospital,' I sent you earlier?"
'Uh-huh.'
"Here it is again, only this time you're in one," it said.
'Let me sleep,' I replied, 'I'm hurt and I'm drunk.'
"Only after you've let these good people mop your blood and sew up your head, you moron, you bum. You're damn lucky they let brain-dead assholes sleep off drink in their cubicles on nights like this."

So they did – fix up my head. I know that because someone told me afterwards. At the time, though I have it on excellent authority that I was technically conscious, the record of the next hour in my memory is like a single blank piece of paper fluttering in the breeze. I tried blocking the whole experience from lodging in my mind with everything I had. Then the work on my wound finally stopped and they let me shut my eyes and shut down.

When I came round a second time, I saw a bright glare from a harsh light and white tiles. Boxes on a shelf. A thin white glove poking from the side of one. And a familiar, if still peculiar smell.

One side of my face was holding on to plastic. When I moved my head, it peeled slowly off a green, warm surface like my cheek was the sticky side of Sellotape. That made my head hurt, so I stuck it carefully back in place. I think I groaned. A short electronic surge of everyday worry poured into my head. Car? Keys? Money? Are they still in my pocket? I could feel panic spreading suddenly from my stomach up towards my chest. What if I've lost them? How will I drive it back to Yarrow? How injured am I? I was at sea on a raft and I wanted some dry land under me. To hell with Jez and all of that. For the time being she was a luxury I could no longer afford. I was on my own here, and I was scared. I thought of Mommy and Daddy; they used to be here to sort little Timmy out and make everything alright. Not any more.

I defied gravity with my head again. Either it didn't hurt so much or I was just more determined second time around. I tried to sit up, but couldn't manage it. But realized in the process that my bed was a trolley. The light was way too bright. There was a curtain in front of me, which didn't cover a gap on either side. A nurse passed by behind; I saw a flash of mid-blue. Once. Twice. A swish of uniform. Then as my senses began to boot up and move through a bunch of whirring clicks, I could hear a man's voice above me, muffled, its sound arriving stage-left, from a cubicle next door. It was coming back to me: my grand arrival in this here A & E. With my own Doctor Green, a nurse and my own personal drama. And still here now: an inert form occupying a small space in the quiet business of the night shift.

Which made me think: what time was it? I pulled my arm around slowly and looked down at my wrist. There was nothing there but a white band of skin.

"It's ten-to-twelve," said a voice. I tried to twist my neck half-behind me to see who it was, but it made me feel sick so I had to stop, then lie down again. Did I say that out loud? They were getting up anyway and coming over to me. The sound of someone leaving a chair. It wasn't a nurse. She wasn't wearing a uniform. She had on a grey duffel coat and she kept her hands in her pockets. Everyone was doing it these days.

"Hi."

I was flat on my back so I couldn't see her properly. But she was sort of leaning over so I could at least get the general idea. She smiled. It was the girl with the boob. I wanted to ask her how it was, whether I'd damaged it, but thought better of it. I looked at her and tried to connect things up. But there was only a misfire of threads. One of them sent out a signal which made the words, 'oh, no' form in the middle of my head.

"Do you remember what happened?" she said.

"I fell over." Logically, I must have. Even I knew that.

"…and smashed your head. You've got six stitches…"

She paused, as if I probably wasn't capable of taking this in.

"…concussion, but no fracture. You've had tests…and you've been x-rayed."

I wanted to say, 'that's not all I've been,' but it took too much effort to shift the message from my brain to my mouth. She was Asian. Indian-Asian. Or

Pakistani. Not far-eastern is what I meant. I hadn't noticed that in the pub, but then I don't think I'd noticed much after about half-past-seven.

"When?"

"Oh, hours ago. It was only about eight when you were brought in. I think..."

"What?"

"I've only been here a couple of hours."

I looked out from my thick head at her again, dazed and confused. Her face passed through different phases, one of them something of an encouraging smile. She had nice white teeth.

"I'm Safeena." Eyes uncertain now. I tried to smile back but I'm not sure I managed to pull it off.

"I know what you must be thinking..."

I was thinking through the demented light that my fucking face hurt as well as my head.

"...but you don't need to...to try to...you just need to get home and sleep it off. Not that I'm a doctor."

'No, I'm a doctor,' I thought. I pressed gingerly at what now felt like a monster package of sticky tape and wadding at the front-right of my head. I don't know how I could have missed it until then. Safeena brought her hand up to it too, but pulled it back, as if she might hurt me. She looked at the white mass and winced.

"Nasty," she said. "You were unlucky; The Frinton's got a hard floor."

I tried reaching into my memory for the events which now seemed to belong to a different age.

"It was a nice pub."

"I've never seen you there before."

"You, um, a regular, then?" I was beginning to find that my mouth was regaining its form, which was something, but it came with a side order of jaw pain.

"Mmm, two years, on and off...Tim."

"How..?" I started to say but pain started to emerge in a red throb from the general direction of the wound and it stopped me dead.

"A nurse must have gone through your wallet or something to find out who you were. When I got here, she said, 'are you a friend of Mr. Weaver?'"

If my mouth wasn't actually open, in my head it was, as some of the smashed threads were starting magically to grow and re-connect again.

"I asked her your first name."

My God, who was this angel? No, she wasn't beautiful, like Hollywood make-believe come real, but her smile was like someone sent down from heaven. 'When have you ever needed someone to come to your aid more in your whole life?' my brain said to an aching self.

A nurse came in. Young. Bloody fresh looking for midnight.

"Hello, Mr. Weaver. How are we doing, then? Do you want to try sitting up?"

She had that patronising voice, like I was 5, or 95 but I tried not to take offence.

"Steady now. You've got a slight concussion. Let me prop you up."

Slight? Then what did you have to do to get the full certificate: put your head in a cement mixer? She did something behind me with her foot and her hands, flipping and turning. My top half came up suddenly, and I felt like I was going to throw. It passed.

"Okay?" she said, smiling, obscenely cheerful for someone working at that time of night. "Now, can you swallow these?"

"What are they?" I managed to say.

"Pain killers."

"Oh." Hard little blocks of white from her hand. Then water from a cup in the other.

"Good, 'boy,'" she nearly added. "The doctor's coming in a minute to see if you can go home."

I didn't know what to say. Jez appeared in my mind suddenly and the reason for me being here. I fought back that dreadful, dreadful urge to cry. Found the silent words to fend it off. You got to be a man in here; and you're simply too old. You mustn't and you can't. I stared as hard as I could at the name, 'Nurse J. Bradley,' on the blue plastic tag on the nurse's uniform. 'Leeds R.G.I.' it said, above her name.

"Could you check my keys? I mean, my jacket."

"Car keys?" she said, and looked at Safeena with some complicity. "Don't worry. We've got those. And your wallet and your phone. I'll bring them in and see if the doctor's ready to see you." Then she left - a spruce bundle of smooth blonde efficiency.

I turned to - who was it - Safeena? Puzzlement sat there in my mind, left-centre, but coming up from the back all the time was the return of comfortless memory.

"I...I'm sorry you…"

But why did I have to apologize to this girl especially? She didn't have to be here. Thought processes were starting to crank successfully: she must have seen the worst of everything I did. And wasn't repulsed and revolted. I reached further down and found the pictures from last evening appearing. This girl was crazy. Whatever she thought about the way I behaved and the fuss I must have caused, I was filling up with hot, sticky humiliation.

'Whatever you've got, you deserved,' I said to myself. The girl, Safeena, laughed a rueful one, and shook her head a fraction at her own confusion.

"I know: you want to know why I'm here..."

Well you can tell me if you want.

"It's just...you needed someone. You were on your own."

She was a little embarrassed, so I helped her a little; I should have been the only embarrassed one in the room.

"Thanks for what you've done." What else could I say? "You can go, though. I can ring someone to come and get me if I can't drive."

I tried to think quickly: did I have some numbers with me? Actually, no. Bugger. Okay then. Scraps of paper in my wallet? No. Perhaps I could remember Liam's, then. Er, no. A lot of thanks I'd get ringing him at this time of night anyway. Sef? Nobody knows his number. Jez? I couldn't ring her even if I thought she'd come. Can't I stay here? Thoughts of bed shortages told me that my thought processes were now pretty much all switched on, red lights glowing in the dark. All systems soon to reach normal status once more. Good. Then I might be able to find a way out of this mess, despite the shame I was covered with here.

"Can you? But look, it's okay. I'll stay for now. You still need someone." She smiled a little. And now through the last veils of mist I could see her eyes, dark brown, giving off a warm, inviting light. Her hair wasn't long; it rested snugly against the hood of her coat in loose curls, centre-parted in front. Yes. I suppose my first reaction was right: angel is what she was. The first ministering angel to have appeared un-asked for in my life.

I didn't have the energy to be more of a detective. It was easier to lie back and listen to my head throb like an engine and be grateful that I wasn't facing this on my own. This Weaver-shaped mess on a new scale. But it was still weird to think, 'I hope she stays. Whoever she is.'

We only had to inhabit another pool of silence for a minute. Nurse Bradley returned and did a test on my feet, which were bare, pushing them hard "to see if you've got any weakness."

I wanted to ask her for a big notebook and a couple of hours: I could have made her a belting list. But according to this professional, I didn't have one. Then a doctor came, a knackered-looking guy a bit older than me with hair like wire, a thick green shirt and a wild tie, loose at the neck. I was wondering about the lack of a white coat when he started to examine me. He looked deep into my eyes with a thin torch for what seemed like a long time.

"Okay," he reported, tucking his torch into a shirt pocket. "Good. Your tests came back: blood; urine – both fine. You have a way of getting home?"

"Yes. I think so. Yes." I didn't look at Safeena. If she had nothing figured out, I reckoned I could drive at a push. If I really had to. But as things stood, I couldn't even put my socks back on; J. Bradley had to do it for me. 'We all know you're pathetic,' said the voice in my aching, swollen head, 'but we're still not going to let you cry.'

"Let's get you on your feet, then." J. Bradley helped me with some precision to carefully put my legs down on the floor and I was walked up and down the narrow cubicle.

"How does that feel?"

"Okay..." I said, feeling just about able to keep my head from crashing sideways into the wall. It felt that heavy.

"I'm okay."

"Right; we'll let you get dressed then."

So there I was, looking at the rest of my own clothes on a chair next to a plastic tray with my keys and wallet in, thinking about getting back in the game. I pulled on my things, with assistance. It was slow going, and I felt sick again trying to get my legs into my trousers, but like the first time it passed. I left the cubicle and the girl in the duffle coat was waiting for me outside, the hands buried, the eyes watching me. As if we actually knew each other. This was what going on? But I hadn't any better idea of what to do than to go with the flow. The situation would right itself one way or another. That was all that mattered. I thought, 'if only life were always this simple. If only it was a plain matter of making it from point A to point B.'

"I'm going to hold on to you, okay? Just in case."

I nodded as she carefully threaded her left arm through my right to keep me steady. I could feel the pressure from her and manly thing though it wasn't, I liked it, never mind whether I actually needed it or not.

"So," I said to Safeena, as we walked, I assumed somewhere out of the hospital, somewhere in Leeds, "have you...I mean..."

"Have I a plan?"

"Yes."

"Not really. Well sort of. But I haven't got a car, if that's what you're wondering. Where's yours?"

"Um, where are we?"

We were moving steadily down one of those long corridors every hospital I've ever been in seems to have by the mile. Like long worms. Worms? What am I thinking. Intestines, then. Tubes?

"The Infirmary."

"Where's the pub?"

"You want another drink?" She stopped and looked at me as if I was a complete loon, and I would have been.

"No. That's the last thing - I mean the pub from earlier."

"Just a few minutes walk up the road. Where did you park?"

"Erm, let me think." I paused to consult my memory again; there it was, just back from last night's first beer.

"Just across the road from the pub. If it's still there. It didn't look like a nice neighbourhood."

"It isn't." But she kind of half-laughed, which kept me from worrying.

"Look, you shouldn't drive, you're still concussed. You heard what they said."

"How am I supposed to get home at this time of night?"

"To Nottingham? I don't know."

"Nottingham?"

"There's an envelope in your wallet with a Nottingham address. Sorry; standard procedure, apparently."

"I used to live there."

"Oh, I thought it was a bit strange. You're a long way from home if you're from Nottingham. So where do you live?"

"Yarrow."

"That's...that's past Oatley, isn't it? I haven't been out that way."

"Oh, sorry, I haven't even asked you. What do you do?"

"Philosophy."

"Student?"

"Final year."

"Where do you live?"

"About half a mile away, if that; beside the park. Hyde Park."

"I'll drive you."

"No. You can't drive. You're not safe."

"What else am I supposed to do? Find a hotel?"

"Is there anyone you want to come out to get you? I can phone them for you."

I could still have used my phone. I wasn't an invalid.

"No."

"Oh. Well, I could help you find a hotel. But you can stay at my place."

I tried really, really, hard to see through a new kind of fog, but we were still walking and I still had to save some thinking just to do that. We reached the main entrance and stopped and faced each other. She took her arm away and put it back in her pocket. She looked uncertain, like she was working something out in her head. I really hadn't a clue about her motives and frankly, I didn't care what they were. Standing made that awful tiredness kick back in. Fuck, I was so finished, it wasn't true. I just wanted to sleep. That was the best part of what I knew.

"Let's get a taxi," she said and I didn't argue. She sounded organized and that was what I needed.

"Montague Mount, please," she said to the guy as we got in. He was Asian, like Safeena. They exchanged words in a language I didn't understand - a few practical sentences by the sound of it. We up-geared along a road deserted of people past another tall white building towards a main drag.

"We're going past the pub in a minute. Did you park down a side street?"

"Yeah." We drew past the pub, now shut up and dark. It looked impossible that I could have been in there only a few hours before. A strange drinker in a strange town. What on earth was I doing, going in there? None of this felt real. I knew where the car was. If the car was still there and hadn't been nicked I'd be able to see it, even in the dark. I'd been cheeky, sticking it right next to the main road, past the yellow line. Dangerously parked really; some idiot could easily already have clipped it turning the corner. I craned my neck forward from the left side of the cab, looking.

"It's there," I said, too tired to point. You couldn't miss it, almost sticking out into the main road, white and on its own.

"You can get it in the morning."

"If it's still there."

"It'll be there," she said, and patted my hand. I looked at her, or tried to, but she was looking straight ahead. I sat back and tried to relax, which was easy. When we stopped, I was already asleep.

"Come on," I heard her say from miles away. "We're here."

Then Safeena was talking in another language again and paying the driver. Up steps from the pavement we went, to a door. Safeena opened it with a key and then there were stairs, just past a row of bicycles. Did she live in a fucking bike shop? I may already have fallen asleep again at that point, I don't know. The stairs. I made them with Safeena holding my right arm as I gripped a stair rail, and with gentle pressure placed upon my back. Taking me to a place where the light couldn't find me. I collapsed onto something soft. Ah, bed. A lamp went 'click' but it didn't matter, for I was only seconds from finding my own darkness again - at the end of a day now done, the hard day's night well and truly over, ended by an unknown girl and a strange bed.

23
Only Particles of Change
Autumn Term - Half Term Week, Day 4
Thursday, 24th October, 2002
Hyde Park, Leeds - Morning

When I wake the next morning, it's already late. My eyes have finally opened. Thick mental blankets trapping consciousness being pulled away. Revealing awareness of sunshine through the window I was turned towards coming out of sleep, giving light to a still unfamiliar room. Night wrappers stripped from my hearing. The ticking of a clock finds me, a circular timepiece in vivid yellow by the bed. I make my ears work harder, to listen beyond the quiet door. A single chirp from a bird outside the window interrupts. Says, 'Oy! don't ignore me like everyone else in this neighbourhood!' I look and see backs of terraced houses. Then I listen to this place again. Stillness. Peace. Noiseless but for the intermittent clicks and cracks of a house breathing. A house of students all gone for lectures and tutorials. And the lovely hush of the library. I think again about time. Two yellow hands point in opposite directions and show me a quarter-past-eleven.

I can see from down here that it's a woman's room. Or a girl's, if a university student is not a woman. It smells much too nice to belong to a man. A perfume of something heated in an oil burner, a home-from-home smell. Coming from where? There. Three of them, ceramic, in different colours, on a shelf facing me. Photographs and trinkets, knick-knacks. Elephants. I sit up and look around me. The ceiling is high, as if trying to keep itself as far away as possible from an old, scruffy carpet. I know this place from years of my own gone by. All the same, these student houses. Old, raggy-edged and everything I know. I don't feel so bad.

The big purple duvet I'd just crawled from under was warm and comfortable. Sleeping the sleep of the dead in there almost, I was. Near the window there's a chair with clothes: tops, trousers and a cardigan. Coats and bags hang from the back of the door. And a scarf. Walls, a deep pink, are strangely comforting.

I sit on the edge of the bed still, and touch the pad on my head. It's still there, holding back a pain throbbing with some malevolent illness underneath. Have to find some tablets. I try standing up and I feel okay - well enough to get going. I walk to the shelf above a dresser and see a picture of three girls laughing on a hillside. Another frame has two girls with their arms around each other, posing for the camera, smiling widely in happy times. In a blue wooden frame, one of the girls from the last picture has an arm around what must be her mother in a close up heads shot. Both of them look like Safeena. It's Safeena's room. I feel a pressure drop in my guts. And I well up. A film of moisture in both eyes which I fight back. What a girl. What would I have done last night without her? 'Tell me that, clever dick.' I have no answer. I don't know what we all deserve in this world, but I can't think what points I've earned with the Almighty in recent times to deserve her. Her milk of human kindness. The cynic in me gets off the bed, comes over to where I stand and says,

'She's lonely. She's a loser. She just needed some grinning idiot to take care of last night and along came Dimbo-Timbo to provide a free service.'

'It won't wash,' I tell him. 'She wasn't alone - that I do remember. She was with a guy in the pub.'

'*Tschah!*' my cynic replies, struggling now.

'I may be dim but I'm not stupid. She's way too nice to be a loser. And look at the photographs. Go back to fucking sleep.' He falls away behind me and I move on.

I'm still in my clothes from last night but I'm not really bothered. 'Not a bother on me,' as Liam might say. Except there's blood on my shirt. I had black jeans on last night, so if the red stuff dropped on them, I can't see it. I scan the room for my jacket. I don't remember taking it off, but I must have. It's there hanging up on the door. I missed it just now. I go over, feel inside for keys, wallet and phone. They're there, untouched.

Outside to look for a bathroom. I find it next door and a mirror. Splash myself with water and soap. Wipe a towel across my face and look at myself. I've got to say, I look either ghostly or ghastly. I make myself laugh at the mirror but see this strained and desperate face peering back at me. Apart from the huge bandage, I have a lump over my right eye that seems to be more closely-resembling my borrowed duvet by the second. Got to lift off this bandage. I do, with great care. Great move. My head is shaved in a four-inch single track road from my brow towards my crown up the right-hand side. A dark-red line carves through it, accompanied by tiny cakes of dried blood to keep the stitches company. I look like the monster's brother. All I need is a bolt in my neck. A hat to cover the whole lot up with would be good. Or a cardboard box. As would a mouthful paracetamol tablets. I open the cabinet and pull out a blue and white packet. Hand full of water, then suck it down with two white bullets.

So what next? Go find some coffee. Just as I do every morning of my life. Wonder where Safeena is. Have at least to say 'thanks' for everything. Just then a door downstairs shuts with a 'bang.' One member of the household is home anyway. I'm thinking, 'should I go downstairs and introduce myself?' But I look such a sight. And I've left traces of blood on the towel. A fine kind of guest. I go back to the bedroom to think this thing through. Whoever it is will probably make a drink and go upstairs to their room. Or downstairs if there's a bedroom down there. Out of my way. For me to sneak into the kitchen and make myself some java, which I'll drink rapidly and slip away. Better still, just slide right out the door. Really don't want anyone to see me like this. Not even Safeena, who must have seen me last night looking like my head had fallen into industrial machinery, looking fit only to be pronounced a totally sad idiot. I can get coffee up the road where that wealthy lady sipped so carefully to herself on my way to the university yesterday eve. If my car's still in place, that is. But for now, wait in Safeena's room. 'Saf's room?' 'Saffy?' No. Only 'Safeena' sounds right.

'Tick, tock,' goes the clock. Locate her bookshelves to find something to read while I wait. A lot of philosophy stuff. Names I recognize, like Plato. Plays by Sophocles. And later guys: Kant; Déscartes and Sartre. Some novels. Slippery Jones is there. I like him. And what do you know, Sally Knowles: *Salty Tears Fall*. Hope it's better than the disaster I'm reading. But pick up another. *Leaving This Town* by Slicky Warp, a little known American crime guy. I've read three of his and written about his best book, *Gutbucket Strength*. Safeena, you dark horse. I open the page hopefully, but I still can't concentrate. I stare at the walls and the window for two minutes, maybe three, but boredom falls on me all too easily. There's no choice. Time to be the best Tim I can be. Have to muster some sociablility here in case I need it. Make the supreme effort. I walk over to the door.

Gingerly, I grab my jacket and creep out on to a huge empty landing. Was tiny to me last night, groaning for the velvet padding of unconsciousness. Now find the top of the stairs and descend. There's the sound of a cupboard opening and closing, and the movement of feet. One pair, I think. A rising *whup!* as a fridge opens, sounding to my left as I make the bottom of the stairs. The front door is about four metres away down the passage to the right. Look both ways like I'm crossing a road. And creep like a criminal. If I'm discovered, one of Safeena's flatmates is going to scream the place down and accuse me of all sorts. If this was the States I'd be in danger of being shot. Slip the safety catch, squeeze the trigger and ask questions later. But this is not America, it's the UK. So get on with it. Check my pocket for keys and wallet. All is sound. I'll be creeping off, then.

"Where do you think you're going?"

Turning, I see Safeena in the passage by the kitchen door, arms folded.

"Don't be such an idiot: come and have a drink." I hear her accent for the first time. Southern. London.

I expect to feel annoyed to be thwarted, but feel something changing somewhere inside me to see her. Changing the way I'm seeing this person. It's maybe in the way she looks at me.

"Sorry," I say, like a small boy.

"You should be," and she turns and goes into the kitchen. I follow, into an unusually big room with a high ceiling again and the usual appliances, but this one has a big round table in the space between the door and the sink by the window.

She doesn't wear great clothes or anything; just blue jeans and a navy cotton sweater with a round neck. But a silver pendant hangs down and looks smart and expensive. She reaches up to a high shelf to get a canister. Her top rides up and I can't help noticing a wee roll of fat round her middle that she probably doesn't want. I feel awkward, guilty even, to look her over, but I do anyway. She turns and looks at me and her eyes make their hit. New daubs of liquid chocolate in front of me. Dark with flecks of daylight. Or something. And I think, is it a physiological thing or is it the personality that comes out of a face? The soul? If this was someone on the make, would I have looked at her and see what I have just seen?

"Cup of coffee?" she says.

"Sure. Thanks. Be great." I suddenly want to stick around. For a little while anyway. The usual mutual questioning develops, after she gives me a glass of water and a couple of tablets which I quickly deal with. Four might be too many but I'm hurting like shit. So I tell her where I'm from.

"How about you? Where you from?"

"Hertford."

'Where's that?' I think to myself.

"Don't you know it? It's north of London, less than an hour on the train."

"And originally?"

"Hertford," she says, and looks at me hard, but decides to drop it after a couple of seconds. "But my mum and dad were both from India."

"Whereabouts?"

"Nowhere you'd have heard of, I don't think. Uttar Pradesh. In the north."

"Cool." Tim for God's sake. You hardly look like James Dean with wild lawnmower tracks carved across your head.

"Whereabouts?"

"A city called Lucknow. Have you heard of it?"

"No." I smiled at her to offer embarrassment for my ignorance.

She smiled back but narrowed the eyes a little to check me over. I wanted to ask her right there. 'What are you checking for: racism?' Or does she know, instantly, what a white guy thinks of her colour? I can't ask her. But I will, I start to decide, if she gives me the chance.

She made the coffee, instant, but Splendid Cotton Calypso isn't that bad if there's enough of it in the cup and the milk isn't that skimmed stuff that doesn't taste of anything. She put a pot of sugar down on the big table where I sat and I made sure I took plenty. I sipped. It wasn't bad, actually. I suddenly realised I was starving. I stopped a second and thought about it: I hadn't eaten for the best part of a day. And now a thought inserting itself at the front of my mind: 'hey! you don't feel so bad.'

I smiled again as she sat down. I might well have been overdoing it. Whitey apologizing for the Empire. Geeze, what a prat. You weren't there and it wasn't your fault. And this is hardly your country. I felt I was still riding on the borrowed goodwill of my bang last evening. So already it was starting to go ugly and stupid as I watched Safeena take one sugar. In which case, as I probably won't see this person again, I might as well plant my tanks on her lawn.

"So. Safeena. Um. If you don't mind me asking; erm…um…why did you come to the hospital?"

She stirred her cup and looked down into it for a minute.

"Why? I felt sorry for you." She was looking back up at me.

"Oh. Thanks. That makes me feel good."

She leaned over and inspected my wound with her fingers.

"It's not too bad, actually. You're going to need a good hairdresser, though."

Then she probed my eyebrow with a touch I could hardly feel.

"Ouch. It's come up a fair bit in the night."

"Thanks for the bed…" Shit, I've got to do this. To hell with it.

"…and for coming to the Infirmary. It doesn't matter why you were there. Just that you were there." My turn to look into my coffee and stir it some more.

"I hope you had somewhere to sleep."

"Don't worry, I was fine. I had two empty bedrooms to choose from."

"So why were you at the hospital?" I wasn't going to let go of this. When it comes to the opposite sex to mine, I'm no genius, God knows, but you don't, I presume, walk through the outskirts of one of the most dangerous cities in England at night just because you feel sorry for somebody.

She didn't say anything. She just looked around her, at the ordinary kitchen, then at me, and made a face. I had to feed this thing again.

"It was the middle of the night. There were a million reasons not to be there."

"I was just around the corner, actually, at a friend's, just chillin'. So you see? I wasn't putting myself out all that much."

I think even my Year 10s would have spotted the fact that she was trying to convince herself as much as me.

"You were such an idiot in the pub. You were in such a state."

"What? No. I just fell over."

"No, no," she said laughing. I liked that she seemed to be enjoying this. "Come off it, you had your head on the table. You were crying your eyes out!"

No. I wasn't. She must have been lying.

"Hey. No! No way!" I couldn't have been. "I am the last man to sit in a pub and cry."

But shit, then again, she was there in the place with me and I...was sort of absent.

"I wasn't, was I?"

"Oh, you were." Still she was chuckling away at my expense, but that light in her eyes hit me like music. The more I looked at her, the more I fell in to them. Her sitting there, hair tied back today in a crinkly pony tail. Her ears perfectly proportioned, neat little things, with silver drop earrings hanging down. I kept looking. And thinking: 'was that eye-light Jimmy Page's shimmering guitar on *The Song Remains the Same*? Or Tord Strang's soaring, ethereal warbling on *Inevitable Probe*?' I think this is where I usually go wrong in these situations. Start thinking about music, get distracted and lose the moment.

"What are you looking at?"

"Nothing," I said, giving out one of those nervous laughs to try to keep it light.

I was looking at her nose. It wasn't exactly snub; in fact it was slightly big, but I didn't care: as if it mattered. And then I thought about Jez, the woman I thought I loved. If my mind made any sense of the thought, it just put a wall in front of me, a big, blank wall. Way barred, no information. If there's a pen for me to write something on it, it was up to me to go find it.

"The whole place was looking at you last night."

"*No*, don't say that!" Fucking hell.

"Dancing at the jukebox, dancing all the way to the toilet and back. To the Rolling Stones, I think it was."

"No, *no*," I said, dipping my head over my coffee. The heat of the steam was making my cut sting. 'But I don't dance,' I thought, 'I never do. I'm the last one on the dance floor.' Mind you, I never get drunk. It's one of my things. A little stoned or a lot stoned once in a while, like I told you, but not smashed out of my face on alcohol, for God's sake. I hung my head, and tried to cover my shame with laughter. But the way Safeena was looking at me, I'd only amused her.

"I'm going into a state of permanent abstinence from this moment, swear to

God." I wasn't joking, either.

"Knocking people over, I don't know," she went on, shaking her head. "I had to work really hard to stop the bloke I was with punching you..."

'Christ, was it the inadvertent boob grab?' I wanted to say.

"...my friend Simon. You spilled your pint all over his new coat."

"You did? I did it for him, though, in the end," I said, meaning to sound rueful.

"And you nearly sent me flying - nearly injured me, actually."

I think I might have blushed, because when I looked at Safeena's face, it was turning colour too.

"And then minutes later you were slumped over, crying like a baby."

Maybe this was the time to think about leaving. But who exactly was this guy Simon?

"Then to cap it all, you got up, got your foot caught in the strap of this girl's bag on the next table and crashed into the floor, in a way I would have said was impossible, but you did it. I saw the whole thing."

"Tell me about it."

She looked straight into my eyes again, looking for something.

"No, I mean really, tell me about it!"

"People were rushing around you, genuinely worried about you. And there was blood everywhere. The crack of your head hitting the tiles almost drowned the jukebox."

"Was it you who called the ambulance?"

"No. The barman was on to that in a flash. I was just in the crowd. I picked your book up. It's over there."

I followed her eyes to my Sally Knowles, adorned with its own unique spats of blood down the page ends.

"So the ambulance came; did anyone go with me?"

"Yeah, the barman, Frank."

"The one with the tattoo?"

"You owe him."

"You're not wrong there," I said "I'll have to go see him."

"You should. He came back after about an hour. I was still in the Frinton with Simon; Jolene and Leah were there too by then. He told us all how you were. You were still unconscious, but not permanently damaged, they didn't think. They put the stitches in while you'd gone bye-byes."

"But you came later. Why?"

"I told you. I felt sorry for you."

If these encounters aren't international chess matches, I haven't a clue what

I'm talking about. So there we were, sitting pretty close together, sun just about still rising and throwing warm, bright light into the room. I looked at her hard. I may have said this before: that I may resemble a greenhorn in love sometimes, but I'm learning as I go. I checked back in the memory bank again. 'So last night, you were laying there in the Infirmary, and when you woke up a strange woman was there and took you home.' Right then.

I made sure my cup of coffee was steady on the table, looked at her again to measure up the position: situation critical, possibly terminal. Safeena, I thought: see this look in my eyes? If you don't like it, get up from the table now and change the subject before I humiliate myself - again - and embarrass you; before I do something which is going to change everything. 'Don't be melodramatic, Tim. You've only just met her.' Fuck off; it's not easy; you don't know how many crime novels I've read in my time. I've even got a piece of paper telling the world I'm supposed to be an expert. If you'd read some yourself, you'd know how hard it is to translate love scenes from the page to real life. The days of grabbing a woman by the frock and kissing her hard when she least expects it are over. 'Don't you believe it,' said my alter ego.

Safeena didn't move. She looked at me square into both eyes and held her gaze. So. *Madre mia*, here we go. Kiss her, Tim.

I edged towards her lovely brown face and she didn't scream. She held a perfectly still gaze on me, as if losing it would kill the both of us. She lifted her right arm towards the back of my head. I saw it, noticed it didn't contain a blunt object and relaxed. I braced myself, body holding its breath in case she didn't know how to kiss, but a split second later, as her hand caressed my hair, my mouth made contact with lips that turned into soft, melting little pillows of flesh and I was back in dreamland and a long, long way from Canada, baby, a long way from snow chains.

Relief, excitement and strangeness. Where has she come from, this woman? On the one hand, what am I doing here? On the other, my heart is thumping like a man on a door being chased by a wild animal. And my mind is in orbit somewhere near the Andromeda Spiral. The acceptance and approval of the first kiss is an unbeatable thing. The second was even longer and almost presented me with more physical damage.

"You look terrible," she said and smiled, a drugged look on her face. And I could feel myself beginning to sweat, which was not promising.

I didn't know what to say.

"I don't know what to say." Suddenly complications were falling into my mind like blocks of rubble tossed in the air by an earthquake.

"You don't have to say anything you don't want to."

"There speaks the philosophy student."

"No. There speaks Safeena."

"I don't know anything about you."

"Don't you?"

She was a smart one right enough. Probably smarter than me. With Jez I didn't foresee that being a problem. 'With Jez.' Man, why did I have to start thinking about Jezebel?

"Have you got anyone?" I asked.

"A boyfriend? No."

"What about Simon?"

"He's gay."

"And he beats people up?"

"Only when they make him angry. And he's got the fact that he's a screaming queen to live down remember."

"Oh," I nodded, and tried to look grave.

"So no, no one. You?"

I think she knew the answer. I hesitated, hating to admit to her a weakness, a failure. And to myself.

"No. N-Not really."

"But you like someone? Love someone?"

Oh, my. This wasn't fair. How could she be so direct. Would even Jez have been this close to the punch?

"You really know what questions to ask, don't you."

I looked at her face, watching for how much I could disappoint her. I really didn't know anything about her. What if she was one of these chronically possessive types? What if I decided I wanted her out of my life and she stalked me? Well you don't know, do you? There are some mighty strange people out there. She says she has nobody, and she's not so nice looking she's going to have men following her up the street like crazed dogs.

"Who is she?" she asked, drawing away a little. I picked up my mug of coffee, stalling. What could I say? I decided to do the outrageous thing: be honest.

"There's a girl I work with. I really like her. But she's getting married."

"Doesn't mean you have to stop feeling what you feel for her."

"True. Where did you get be so smart for twenty years of age?"

"21, and thanks for treating me like an idiot."

"Sorry. Okay, true. But, for what it's worth, I haven't got anyone, to all intents and purposes. No one from my past, anyway." Lurking there like a bad smell. I sort of grinned but she didn't laugh because there I went again, making the inappropriate gesture because my face heard words that only existed in my head. But she still sat there close to me. I wanted to stroke her arm but thought, 'no Tim, bad move.'

"What about you though?"

She thought and shook her head.

"Clear decks, right now and behind me. Do you think I'm desperate?"

"No. You don't need to be. I think you're lovely." It felt good to let it out for once. I usually held it all back; held it all in. But she got up now, annoyed. What did I do wrong? She went over to the sink and rinsed her mug.

"You don't have to say that to me, you know."

I got up and went over to her.

"Look. I don't go around the place kissing people all the time. I don't go to clubs trying to pick up chicks."

"Chicks?" she said, startled.

"Sorry, but where I've just come from that's the word a lot of men use. I use it in the post-modern sense. Naturally."

"Oh, naturally. *Naturellement.*"

"And if anyone's desperate around here, it's me."

Her face opened right up in horror, eyes wide, and mouth drooping open like a rubbish chute.

"Shit! No! I didn't mean that!"

"Don't swear."

"Why?" I said.

"Because you don't need to."

Oh, wow, a girl I like who objects to profane language. This was a new one.

"I didn't mean it like that. Honestly."

She still wasn't impressed.

"What I mean is, if there's anyone round here who has to be the one to feel sorry for, it's me. You said so yourself."

"I was joking!" she said, animated enough to swipe a hand at an adjacent tea towel, pick it up and throw it at me. "You obviously do think I'm stupid."

I went to her to hold her. She let me. I held her real close and her me. Weeks and weeks of thinking about Jezebel, then all of a sudden there's this person right here in front of me. This Safeena. Coming out of the sky like a Stuka. No, Tim. Like a painting by Rembrandt. 'But paintings by Rembrandt don't fall out of the sky you stupid twat.' What was I doing, thinking about the Second World War in the first place? I could hardly suppress a giggle.

"What the hell are you laughing at?"

She pulled right away from me and folded her arms, really cross. Leaned on the wall and stared out the window. Then she realised that the sun was shining right in on her and she had to look back towards me, shielding her eyes. I exploded with laughter. What a mistake. But no, I was wrong as usual. She laughed too, and came towards me.

"You...you..."

"No swearing, now," I said.

Now where was I? Sometimes you just have to let go. We came together again, smiling hopefully at each other, and I moved in as close as I possibly could, to feel the simple warmth of her. The newness of this was fantastic, even if it was all just a complete aberration. It hadn't been quite like this for, wow, a long time. My past romantic record I shroud in mystery for good reason. 'Never advertise your weaknesses and failures' is a motto worth keeping in your wallet. This was the best I'd ever felt in the close company of a woman, even though Jez was there in the background, a ghost in the machine. I pushed a strand or two of hair away from Safeena's face, like I'd seen a hundred times in the movies. Held her face gently and looked at her. Too close to see her expression almost. She made that narrow-eyed face at me again, the one she made in the hospital. It made me laugh again.

"What?"

"I told you. I like your face."

And I kissed her the best I knew how.

"Do you know what you've got?"

"No."

"Neither do I. But you've got something."

"That's a relief."

We seemed to be doing a lot of laughing that morning and for the moment, we were happy. Happier 'n hell. At least, I was.

24

His October Symphony
Autumn Term - Half Term Week Day 4
Thursday, 24th October, 2002
Hyde Park, Leeds & University - Mid-Morning

Of course, a couple of great kisses in the kitchen didn't solve all that much, wet and comforting though they were. We did a lot of talking before I left. If you wanted a bedroom scene, I'm sorry to disappoint you, but it didn't happen.

"Sorry, I don't go to bed with monsters before midnight," she said. I tried briefly to persuade her to make an exception for me, but she was having none of it. In truth, I didn't even do that. She made it clear that it wasn't going to happen and that was that. So all we really did was talk, and me, I was trying not to make too much sense of this. I just wanted to stave off Jez somehow, so I could keep this floating in a bubble feeling of unreality.

"So what do I call you: 'Saf'? What do your friends call you?"

"'Saf' or 'Saffie'; 'Big Tits' when I'm being especially annoying; your eyebrows can come down now. And before you say anything, 'tits' isn't swearing."

"Oh. Right. 'Saffie' makes you sound like a stuck up bitch, and 'Saf' makes you sound like a nickname for rice. I think I'll stick to 'Safeena' if that's alright with you."

"Aha. Watch yourself."

"What?"

"You've practically committed yourself to seeing me again."

"Of course I'm going to see you again. If you let me."

"What about this...Jezebel of yours?" she said, trying to hold a face that was everyday-normal, and missing by a mile.

"Look. We've only just met..."

"You and me, or you and her?"

"Both."

"...and you don't know how you feel about her."

"Well, maybe 'yes' and then again, 'no,' I don't know. Can you cope with that?"

"No. But I'll have to, won't I?"

"You'll just have to be philosophical about it, won't you."

"Ow. Ouch, that hurt."

"Be serious, then."

"Okay. Sorry. Well, I don't...this is just so unexpected. I didn't drive into

Leeds with the intention of finding myself a woman."

"Yeah - what *were* you doing just hiring a car like that?"

"Didn't I tell you? I just wanted to look around; I hadn't seen the city yet."

"In the dark?"

"It's got pretty strong headlights, the Mégane." She might have wondered what she was taking on. I was wondering what she might be taking on. "And the sunset over the university was spectacular."

"I bet. Look, going back to um, Jez: you haven't...er...by any chance...?"

"No. Nowhere near."

"Have you kissed her?"

"No!"

"Oh." She was busting herself not to show she was pleased. If it had been me, I'd still have been fretting like someone unable to eat their last meal on Death Row. I was jealous of her almost for being able to take this. I'd have kicked me out and been watching daytime television whilst contemplating a totally Weaver-less future if I'd been her.

"And you: there's really no one?" I could not believe my luck. It was like leaning right over a mountain top and not falling. Normally girls I went out with did so out of boredom or for a break from the real thing. I was like a branch of Filmbusters: you didn't buy Tim, you rented him.

"The only problem I can see for you is the fact that if you ever decide you want to meet my family, you'll have a job getting within a mile of the place."

"Because?" But I could see this one coming.

"Because you're white."

I frowned. This was way beyond my experience.

"My Dad says I have to marry a Muslim."

"And are you going to?"

"Not if I don't want to. But he doesn't know that yet."

"Have you been out with white guys before?"

"Of course - we're practically the only Asians in Hertford."

"I think I'd like to meet your family."

"We're getting ahead of ourselves here, aren't we? This time yesterday you didn't even know me. And there's this little thing between us."

"Thanks."

"Don't be so crude. *Sir!*" she giggled and put the kettle on for some more coffee. "I've never been out with a teacher before."

'Me neither,' I thought, pulling at my chin.

"And I've never been out with someone whose accent is vowels in one continent, consonants in another. You're not putting this accent on are you?"

"Yeah, I put it on so chicks really dig me. Especially young students who don't know the first thing about the big wide world."

By the time I'd steeled myself for another cup of Calypso, my shin was aching from two whacks from the Zamani trainer. Stopped me thinking about my headache for a while anyway.

"I have to go in a minute. So what next?" she said, trying to make my hair move across to cover my race track. This time I ran my index finger along the skin above her left wrist, through hair I kind of liked, to the pushed-up sleeve of her sweater. She looked down at my finger sliding gently up and down.

"It's horrible, isn't it."

"What is?"

"All the hair on my arm."

"No, it isn't," I said, and pulled her arm to my mouth and kissed it, turning a very fetching down-curled bottom lip first into an unconvinced smile, then a real one after I looked at her hard to tell her 'hey! I'm serious.' I felt the pleasure of it right deep inside me. And damn. Felt a hole where I thought Jezebel was one day going to be. Perhaps the best thing would be to get two conkers, hole and thread 'em; paint a 'J' on one, and an 'S' on the other, get Liam round, and the conker which survives the contest is the one I'll go out with. No? Well, it was more appealing than tossing a coin. Then I thought of Sefton, my Master of the Universe. I thought he'd lined me up with Jez because he could see the future. His master plan seemed at the moment to be disintegrating like an old map.

"A lot of Asian girls get rid of the hair on their arms."

"Oh, really?"

"And white girls too."

"Oh, yeah? That's very interesting."

"That's it. I'm dumping you already. If you're going to patronise me."

"No, look, seriously, it is." I kissed her arm again.

"Alright, lay off. Be serious for a minute."

"You mean you're not dumping me?"

"Not yet. Listen, what next?"

"What next? Well, I get the car. Then, I drive it back to Yarrow before they charge me an extra day. Then I'm going back to my house in Measby. You can come with me, if you like."

"You know what I mean."

I didn't feel like being serious about anything. The next place I was going to after this was confusion and if I could only put that off for half an hour it would be another good thing to come out of my ridiculous foray into Leeds. But that's one of the shit things about life. You never can. Wherever you are, whatever you do or gets done to you, you have to keep rolling. The wheel won't stop turning just for you.

"I know what you mean. Okay. Well: we take it a stage at a time, don't we?"

"I suppose." A frown.

"I'm sorry. Look, you can go off me, you know. Tomorrow you might regret this completely."

"Yeah, I might. But I don't think I will."

"Well, that's all I can think of for the moment. You don't drive, I don't drive, but the bus runs past your door, practically, to Yarrow all day long, doesn't it? I've seen it at the bus station enough times. The Leeds bus."

She nodded and I could see her looking into the future and thinking.

"Don't worry. It'll be okay."

"I'm thinking about what I'm going to have for dinner tonight, actually. It's my turn to cook."

"You rotten cow!" I said and grabbed her under the ribs, digging my finger ends in. She leapt up, screaming, almost tipping the chair on to the floor, but I caught it.

"Thanks," she said, "it's about time you did something for me."

So I grabbed her again, and again she screamed and jerked until I stopped and kissed her again. Found her neck and kissed that too.

Well what do you expect? You should try tickling your partner now and again. You never know what it might lead to. Eventually, that morning, it led to Safeena looking at me very seriously again.

"Time to go," she said. "Oh! Take this." She took a striped woolly hat from her coat pocket and pulled it very carefully over the top of my head and down until it touched my brow.

"There. That's better," she said, and stepped back to judge the view.

"I bet I look a sight in this," I said, looking around for a mirror.

"No, you look quite cute, actually. And don't pout. You look like a girl."

"That's a lifetime's ambition achieved, then. Thank you."

"You'd make a nice girl."

I could only smile ironically. I'd worry about that later. In a month or something. Because I was on a roll. We walked to the university, hand in hand, which, I have to tell you, blew my fuckin' mind. Me in my silly hat and I didn't care. Through Hyde Park we went, like something from a film, kicking fallen leaves out of the way. A man in a donkey jacket a hundred yards ahead was sweeping them into a black plastic bag. His cart was beside him. I thought, 'I wouldn't change places with you for the musical talent of all the people I like put together.' Realised what a stupid, illogical thing to say to myself that was and laughed out loud. It must have been National Laughter Day or something.

"What?" she said.

"Nothing," I said.

We walked on. Twenty-eight years and five months I've been on the earth and all of them without this girl. Now I feel like I've been knocked on my ass sideways. But at the same time like I'm up to my knees in cold water. Feel as if I'm always going to know her. But then I think of Jez again without meaning to and my mind melts uncontrollably, like ice cream in August. Shake my head as if there's a fly in my ear, to shake off Jez. I can do it. Students in ones and twos walking along the paths to the first lectures and tutorials of the afternoon. An air of lovely learning about the place; an October symphony of study and contemplation, peace before the raging sea of future times. Days that could still be full of possibility. Reminded me of my past and tugged at my insides as if someone was cutting my intestines with a chef's knife. Dead pangs of sadness because teaching just isn't the same. My car, like some kind of miracle of the urban age, was safe and solid, tyres fully-pumped and in place. Then I crossed the road again with Safeena and walked her to her lecture block, a tower of grey, haggard concrete in the middle of the huge Leeds University campus. Hugged her at a big red door as people carried bags and folders in plastic wallets, taking not the slightest notice of us. Kissed her and said,

"I'll call you."

"You will, won't you...?"

"Of course I will. Call first if you want. Don't wait for me," I said.

"We'll see about that," she said. She rubbed my hat quickly with her long brown finger ends, careful to miss the wound, and went inside.

So I turned and felt the sun in the sky and wanted to dive right into the deep pool of shining water, then come up again to show the world I was reborn.

25
Over The Hillside
Autumn Term - Half Term Week Day 4
Thursday, October 24th, 2002
Hills above Aysgarth, North Yorkshire - Morning

On any normal half term Thursday, Chris Lampeter would probably be out walking on some Yorkshire hill. Judie, his wife, would be at work, so he'd take his two children to his mother's in Oatley, still quite early in the morning and drive up north, perhaps to Kettlewell, or east across the Great North Road above Richmond to the valley of the sweeping river Swale. He'd park his car in a quiet pub car park where he knew it would be safe all day long, then take a small rucksack from the boot, pull on his favourite walking boots and be off.

On a sunny autumn day like today, he would stride unhurriedly up and up, until he reached a commanding view, then pause. He'd pull down his yellow rucksack and take out a flask of tea and a slice of home-made cake. Most people in these situations would gaze across at the miles of emerald green fields, studded with autumn golden trees and farms, at distant rolling hills and moorland on the horizon, notice how utterly other-worldly and stunning it all was and take stock. Flick one side of your mop of brown hair out the way for the hundredth time that morning if you were Chris Lampeter. He didn't like caps or hats, didn't Chris.

Even if you weren't one who liked to indulge in fancies of what you might accomplish one day in the future, or in dwelling wistfully on the past with regret or nostalgia, you couldn't help reflect, looking at this sacred wonder, on the way things were with your life: how the kids were doing in school; whether they were happy; how your life partner was doing; how she felt about the state of things and what you might do to make them better. Once in that frame of mind it was almost impossible not to think about how far you'd come in the world. And what you still might have left to do. Chris did not belong to that group of 'most people,' but today was different.

He wasn't normally a deep thinker because he was not one of life's intellectuals. He knew that and it didn't bother him. He had no intention of writing a biography of Jean Paul Sartre or reading Racine in the original French.

But then if you weren't one of life's talkers it was hard to avoid thinking, a lot of the time. There wasn't anything else to do if you weren't one to lose yourself in books or television. He was happy to lose himself in the garden, mind, tending plants, flowers and vegetables, or in the shed where he liked to make things out of wood. Nothing fancy: doorstops; name and number displays for the outside of houses; bookshelves. Best of all, he would forget himself there almost completely and be quite content to, feeling as though he was dissolving as he fed total concentration into the task that lay right there in his large hands.

He did not go out walking because he got miserable or depressed. Far from it. He liked his life: his woman; his kids; his job; going to France a couple of times a year, where they ate better food and drank better and cheaper wine than they did at home. He liked being alive did Christopher David Lampeter.

His life really would have been simple, an unexpected family tragedy excepted, of course, but for one thing. The complicating factor was something weird in him, like a virus - that manufactured something popularly known as 'anger,' of the type that needed 'managing.' Almost every other day the infection would make a door open to a dark place inside him whence came a hot, burning oil of nasty, bitter feelings. He could be reading an article where the selfishness of factional leaders in the Congo was causing a civil war to rage, resulting in half a million harmless, innocent people starving to death. The inevitable photographs of pathetic infants lying on the parched earth waiting for the end, when they should have been laughing in a hot African sun that could turn primary colours into a riot of joy, would make him feel so riled that he would find that he'd torn the offending material into litter before he'd realised that he'd moved his hands. If there was someone in the room he might only throw the bloody thing at the wall, but that was worse because the result was hot, bright, scarlet anger turning to orange sweating embarrassment. If Sam or Becky were watching the TV he might hold himself in, in which case he would grind his teeth together, or shake his head ten times over, or both at the same time. And he'd have to go out to the shed to calm down. It would happen away from the house too. A man in the street carelessly throwing an empty fag packet on to the ground would set him off. A bloke throwing stuff out of a car window absolutely infuriated him because he could do nothing to put it right. It wasn't worth chasing him in the car, though he'd done that once or twice. But if you dropped a chocolate wrapper in the street, you might find Chris rapidly overtaking you from behind, grabbing your right hand and slapping the offending item back into it.

"I believe this is yours," he would say, and with six feet and three inches at his disposal, and the bulk of a solidly constructed centre-forward, you didn't argue. His stare would make you want to say 'sorry' very quickly and promise you'd never do it again.

He had no idea why he got so angry - though he suspected a psychologist would no doubt find something - but it came swelling up from an inner darkness with the unfailing regularity of television and nothing could stop it. In the workplace, the problem was in danger of having the potential to destroy the things he loved. This he could understand, at least. The job, as everyone knew now, was one of the most stressful you could do. But thankfully, the pressures on a teacher to refrain from taking his problems out on the kids were so extreme these days, he was never tempted to let his anger misdirect itself. 'It's not kids that get to me anyway, it's adults,' he once said to Sefton Demmler: 'Kids, they're young, they've got an excuse, what do they know? But grown ups: they've no excuse.'

Two things left him exasperated. First was the fact that the rest of the time he was a gentle and quiet man; a large but tranquil presence wherever he sat, wherever he stood. Those who'd seen Chris explode, and they were few and far between, were shocked to witness such a change in a man they thought they knew well and whose behaviour they believed to be flat and predictable.

The second maddened but also encouraged him, as he nodded and said "mornin'" to a bloke in his late-fifties out walking his yappy little dog across the hillside just above Broker, was the fact that he was finally getting the problem under control. He could feel himself getting older now, and changing. So when the rage appeared, most often when he heard a moronic parent at one of his team's matches throwing puerile abuse at a referee - which often was Chris himself - about an offside or a tackle one of his lads had put in, though it still made him want to walk over to the offender and grab him by the throat, he didn't. He wanted to, badly, but nowadays the pestilential miasma would burst out of the black hole only to be choked off and contained by a new strength of mind. Instead of feeling the liquid rage racing through his body faster than miles an hour to form a cloud of rage in his head, he could change his focus to a point in the sky, or an object in a room, concentrate on it for just five seconds, and using a mantra he'd learned on the anger management course in Sheffield, he could trap the liquid somewhere below his throat and disperse it.

Those whom he trusted told him that the second disciplinary hearing had given him no choice but to turn things around, but it hadn't been so easy to feel that he was beating this thing. Determination hadn't been enough. Neither had simply thinking about everything he had to lose: his job; his wife; his children and his team. He'd known for a long time that he needed help from outside, from people who were trained in understanding what the virus was and how to deal with it. But going to them, finding them wasn't a simple matter of coming to his senses and dialing a couple of phone numbers. Only his second and near fatal collision with authority had given him, not so much the strength, but the lack of an alternative to going through with facing the embarrassment of confronting his demons publicly.

But the rewards that accrued to him from this were so satisfying. Each match these days would bring the same parents as last time, doing exactly the same thing as last time, the same thoughtless mouthing off at whoever it was thwarting their feeble ambitions for their child.

"Crap decision, ref; that was never a foul!"

"Get 'im in the book ref; disgusting tackle that were!"

But though the virus would unfailingly release the same black emotions once again, he would fight it and win. And as the weeks passed into months, he would win the battle more easily than the time before. The urge to strike was not as strong now as the power of his mind to achieve self-control; to use the techniques he'd learned that enabled him to stay his powerful arms and hands. 'Perhaps the worst is over,' he'd thought, 'now I've turned 40.'

Then, not long after this massive turning of the tide had come, the ludicrous event in the Pragmatists's changing room arrived to mock it completely. When he was summoned to Michael's office to hear that someone had made a complaint, he wanted to find them, pour petrol over them and light it. Then when it dawned on him that the biggest problem here was Michael, he wanted to pick up a chair and hurl it through his large office window. Followed by Michael himself. But he hadn't. He had gazed way down deep inside himself again and proved that he had rounded that bend in the road. Though he could see the end of his teaching career waving and beckoning him a few dozen metres further on, he knew it would benefit no one to let his top blow. So he did all that was left to him: await the verdict of the governors of Peggy Lane school and in the meantime start thinking about another career.

He realised he was sweating a little after an hour's walking. *Phew!* October could be quite warm these days. He stopped to rest for a minute. It was beautiful up here – it really was. This simple thought was such an obvious one, but it was one that refused to wear out. He wasn't ready yet for a drink, so he walked on and upwards towards a blue sky buddied up with fat, short harmless clouds of white. It wasn't going to rain today, though.

Then despite all his best efforts, the shitty, pitiful irony of his situation, the nonsensical stupidity of it, smashed into his face again on the hillside there. And it dawned on him why he'd been so keen to come out onto the hills this particular morning; why he'd wanted to get out of bed hours before the massed ranks of still exhausted teachers had begun to stir, this Thursday of half term, and walk out into this huge wide-open space, into all this solitude.

His eyes became unfocussed and his tear ducts opened as he walked, and for the first time in his forty-two years he was happy to let huge, fat tears drop out of his eye sockets onto the stony, muddy path beneath him. He walked off the track for a few paces down the hill and squatted down on his haunches as if winded. He wiped his face with the back of his hand; then using his hearing to ensure there was no one around, he got to his feet and looked across the valley. He saw mile after mile of still velvety green hillside, spreading to a broad horizon, blessed with autumn-coloured trees, a violently rushing river in the valley bottom and a flock of sheep standing stock-still in its field. He looked and noticed their complete indifference to his plight and felt everything inside him fall apart. He slumped down to the floor, not bothering if his arse got wet, and sat there, not caring now whether anyone saw, hair flopping down untended, and he would stay there, waiting as long as it took for every last tear to empty out of his soul onto the tough Yorkshire grass.

26
Madre Mia
Autumn Term - Half Term Week, Day 5
Friday, October 25th, 2002
Measby - Afternoon

As my first half term week off was drawing to a close, life was a riot of action and recovery. At least I thought it was until I realised that the action was all in my head. Like my recovery. It still hurt like hell along the line of the cut and I hadn't been outside without pulling on my new woolly hat. I didn't give a raining piss what I looked like. Actually, I'd only been out to get some food and milk from the local shop.

"You've had a nasty bang, haven't you?" said the guy who ran the village shop, Mr. Khan, politely. Nice guy; a sort of small and ordinary feller somewhere in his fifties, unless he'd led a hard life. My eyebrow was still bulging like I don't know what and was turning from a deep muscular blue to a dark livid purple. Then as I was walking in my front door clutching a pint of full cream m. and a couple of king-sized Blart bars, Barney Plough was just leaving his.

"Bloody 'ell. Has one of yower kids given you a bit o' revenge for all the 'omework you've been givin' out?" he said, grimacing as if he was reaching to scratch a deep itch in an awkward place, which was the closest I'd yet come to seeing him smile.

"Thanks, Barney. I'm just going in now to add you to my will. I'll see to it you get all my compost."

He looked warily at me as if I'd just threatened to fart in front of his mother as he inserted a key into his van door. I thought the comment would have flown over his head like a 747, but there we are, what did I know about these people?

If injuries come in threes, that should be it, I thought: Malcolm; me and Muff. I was stretching the superstition a bit, what with Mr. Went's accident being two months ago nearly, but what are straws for if not for clutching at when it suits us. I hadn't forgotten that Day One disaster. I was going to pay him a visit to apologize and see how he was, but the word came through at school that he still didn't really want to see anyone, which was fair enough, I suppose. He wasn't talking very well yet apparently, and was still only able to suck soup through a straw or accept his wife feeding him porage like he was 90. Poor sod. But now that I felt fate had got even with me, Malcolm was a weight slowly sliding off my mind.

Life was not so much happening to me now as flowing towards me like lava. The rest of Thursday, after I got back from Safeena's, the home front was quiet, so I just tried to rest and let the fantastic shock of the escapade in Leeds hit and pass through me. I felt like a soaked sponge: I couldn't take any more of anything. So I got home and crept onto the sofa like an exhausted soldier and stayed there all evening. I only gathered up sufficient strength to crawl up the stairs to fetch a pillow and duvet, then came back down and crashed into a kind of dark temporary eternity. Stayed there all night long. Somewhere beyond the wads of surgical cotton covering my mind I heard cars passing down the high street like they were miles away across distant hills for about a minute, then zonko.

Friday began with a gradually arriving then exploding sound of a telephone clanging like a fire bell. After that it went off so often I nearly ripped the cord out of the wall. This may have been the action I was telling you about. The key call happened to be from Jez, who'd gone to Bury and her parents' for the best part of the week, but had left her number for Sef and he'd rung her with a report on the progress of The Plan.

"'ello? Tim? 'Ow are yer, petal?"

"Hi! Fine," I said, physically awful but psychologically on the up, despite having sat there all morning with my head being pulled in two directions like a doll being fought over by a pair of Scorpio twins. "I'm great, how're things with you?"

"Me moom's gone off with the milkman, but apart from that, ah'm ecstatic."

"Ha-ha-ha, Jez." Good one, ever the comedian, our Jezebel.

"Noah, really. Shiyazz. Mind you, yer should see 'im: rilleh fit lad is Nairthan. But, well, me broother's goin' owt of 'is 'ead and threatnin' to batter the crap 'owt of 'im."

After five or six days at home, her Bury accent was off the scale.

"Hold on. You're serious, aren't you - and your milkman's really called Nathan? Mine's called Alf and he's about 80."

"Well owers is Nairthan, ees' 25 an' 'ee's abowt to start a career as a model."

As if things weren't crazy enough. The image I had of Jez's mother was someone of about 50, wearing curlers in the morning and smoking 60-a-day. Bingo and Karaoke in the evenings.

"Isn't she cradle-snatching, your mum? How old is she?"

"Forteh; vereh good lewkin' and twice as sexeh as me."

This under normal circumstances was something worth stopping and thinking about, and called for a calculator, but normal times had gone out the window like cassette players. Or something.

"What's happening with The Plan. Have you heard anything?"

"That's why ah'm ringin' - apart from findin' owt 'ow yew are - Sef rang."

"He rang you?" I was jealous. Why hadn't he rung me?

"Great. What's happening, then?" I was anxious now.

"Well, first: Fiona – it's in the bag."

Unbelievable. Unreal.

"I don't believe this, Jez. What we're saying is: she is going to try to get the headmaster of Peggy Lane…"

"Ah-noah, ah-noah, but is it excitin' or what?"

"Y'know, the thing is, I cannot believe that someone who I reckon right now is in Venice sipping Black Cows is actually going to go through with this."

Jez said nothing, obviously thinking about what I'd just said.

"D'yer not troost Sef, d'yer not?"

"I suppose so. I mean…yeah. If that's what he's told you."

"D'ya not think shiz gorgeous, tho'?"

I had to think. Had I any reason to lie? I couldn't see one.

"Yes, Jez, I admit it, she's hot. If you're over 35."

"Cum on; yer tellin' me you wouldn't take her oop the lane if y'ad aff a chance?"

"Up the lane?"

"It's a lawcal expression. Yer noah wharra mean."

"Not at my tender age, Jezebel, dear. And I have my standards. Older women. So tacky for a guy with a bit of class."

"Ah'd ah thort you'd be desperate to 'ave a goah oop the lane wi' Dolly Dancer, never mind Fi-Fi Lamore. And she's got the class, not yew, boy."

Dolly was the head cleaner, a fearsome woman - reigning all-Yorkshire arm wrestling champion, apparently.

"Thanks for the vote of supreme confidence, darling."

"Flamin' 'eck; what 'ave yew bin oop to this 'arf term? I do detect a certain soomthin' in yer voice."

She was right. Normally during an exchange like this I'm way behind the baseline struggling to know what to say and how to say it in case I give my little two shilling heart away.

"Let's say I've fallen on to some good times, Jezebel. Now come on, The Plan; let's get back to it. Fiona."

"'ang on…"

I could hear her brain ticking over all the way down the other end. I wasn't in the mood to be trifled with though.

"Get on with it, Jez, I haven't got all day. I've other things to do."

"Oo-oooh..," she said, her voice rising and falling, saying 'alright then, cocky bastard.'

"...alright then, fair enoof. 'ere wi goah. Fiona. In plairce. Les. In plairce. The time: Moondair brek. Ten-past-eleven. That's Plan Ayer. Plan Bee: Moondair lunch, start of, five-t'won. Fiona, smooch, smooch, smooch. Les. Snap, snap, snap. Result, won-nil, full time."

"I'll have to come and watch you teach Shakespeare with this sixth form class of yours. It must be something to see."

I didn't have a sixth form class, a fact that made me very jealous of Jez indeed.

"Wotja mean?" She knew what I meant.

"With your accent, I think Postman Pat's the only thing you're fit for teaching children about. Maybe Noddy."

"Wor-azz gor inter you, Timoteh."

"Nothing, why?"

"Noah. Cum on: tell meh: 'oo is sheh, I want t'noah."

"You're way off, Jez. But I'll tell you the truth."

"Gowon then."

"Ma Weaver's won the state lottery: two million dollars. She's giving me half. That's why I'm so up."

"*Boll-lerks.*"

"What?"

"Bollocks yew've won the stet lottereh. Cum on, what's 'er nairm? I want ter noah - ah insist!"

"I'll see you, Jez," I said, and put the receiver back in place. I screamed the fucking place down with delight.

"The worm is turning, *baby!*" I shouted to no one save my own ego. My head hurt again, but it was well worth it. "I've got her! She's on the run! I've got her!"

It was true. I'd heard it. That thing in her voice. Jealousy. Never had I experienced such an open and shut case. It's what they say, isn't it: if you want to get a woman's interest who quite likes you but isn't sure, get another woman.

About an hour later the phone went buzz-buzz again and it was my mother. My engines shut down.

"Hi Mother."

"Timothy - now how are you?" You'd probably call her 'posh' in the UK or well-spoken, depending on your rung on the ladder. Either way when she asked you a question it came out as an outright accusation. In America she was just plain 'English,' our cousins across the water not being able to or not being bothered about the niceities and nuances of the class system the Brits still jump to.

She'd fit in with the Betty's crowd if she ever came to Yarrow. The classy tea room I was telling you about way earlier. All fancy cakes and overpriced bread and exiles from the south-east, la-di-dah-dahing their way through a mid-morning *café* or afternoon pot of tea.

"I'm just fine. How are you?"

"Lovely, dear, just lovely. Hank from across the road has just finished putting in my storm windows, so I'm at peace with my environment. For the time being, at least."

The weather can get somewhat wild in Boston in the winter, when some nasty cold air blows down from Canada.

"That's good. So. What are you up to?"

"I was going to ask you the same question."

Were you. About time. She hadn't called me since the second week of term. And only then it was a lightning call to confirm that a bloke called Milton wrote *Paradise Lost*. She'd suddenly discovered the existence of the crossword, for some reason. One of her fads, like singing in the local church choir and learning the violin. She's 53 so I wasn't saving up for a Stadavari for her just yet.

"Oh, you know, this and that. The teaching's going really well, you'll be pleased to know."

"Oh, is it, dear? That's lovely. I hear that English schools have gone to pieces in the last few years. No shootings, I hope, at your school. What is it? *Pretty Something Girls?*"

"*Pragmat Harbiss Grammar*, mother. I told you last time."

It wouldn't make any difference. Next time she'd be calling it 'Stabat Mater Sisters of Mercy.' Or 'The Praline Centre For Distraught Juveniles.'

"Oh. I see. Sounds like a nice school, dear."

"Well it is."

"Is there any chance that you'll be home for Thanksgiving? Don't you have half term still, over there?"

She'd lived in England for twelve of the last twenty years but she'd go on like she'd been exiled permanently like PG Wodehouse, or something.

"Yes, mother, but the two holidays don't coincide."

"Oh." Silence. She was easily distracted on the telephone, especially if there was a magazine open on her lap. Or one of the televisions pouring grey sludge into the room. Anything to distract her from taking a genuine interest in her youngest son.

"Frederick and I are going down to Florida this year for Christmas."

"Oh. Well, I was going to fly over to see you in Boston for a week." I wasn't sure why, exactly, seeing as it made me utterly miserable, but you know how it is. You do these things for parents. And I had only one left.

"I could come down to Florida, I suppose."

"Well, you could..."

"But?"

"Frederick wants to invite his children and his two sisters. So there won't be much room at the apartment. You could stay at a motel, though, dear. There are some lovely ones now in Key West. Some right down on the water."

"Key West!" That was a long way south. "I thought you didn't like the heat."

"I don't, but Freddie has a friend with a place down there. The fishing is, what did he say? 'Spectacular.' So I'm going along with it, for this year anyway."

You always do. She doesn't work, what with her second husband being a semi-retired orthodontist who only needs to work five months of the year to sit on his fat ass all day drinking Gin Slings with his bridge pals or shooting the shit on the golf course about the vast wads of cash they're all sucking out of people's wallets.

"I'm sorry, Mother, it's a long way to come just to stay in a motel."

"Oh, Timothy, I do so want you to make the effort. You know how it upsets me that you're over there in England. Why don't you come and teach over here, darling, with your Masters you could walk into a good college."

I couldn't and it's a PhD. And anyway...

"Let's not go over that again..."

"Dr. Weaver. Sounds so lovely. If you only put more effort into your life you could still make a success of it just like Nicky. And he'd be so proud of you."

Nick - my older brother who practices gynaecology in Denver - would just be jealous of the competition for mother-love. He'd have hated me getting some attention for a change. Even though it would only last five fucking minutes before she was attending to his every need.

"Do you think, Mom, that we could just once have a conversation without you throwing him in my face?" He had a massive house, paid for, from what I could tell, for doing the best cosmetic penis work in the city.

"It really doesn't help the two of us to get along if you go mentioning him every fu... every time we speak on the telephone."

Silence. Then a sniffle. Here we go. Every time... "It's not my fault that I'm proud of him. Remember, your father and I..."

"Had nothing when you got married, yes, I know, mother."

"And I just want you to make some money for yourself and settle down..."

"With a nice girl..." Look at the luck I got here: stuck in the plot of an American TV show from the 1950s. And now she's crying. Or more likely, pretending to.

"Mum, I didn't mean it. I'm sorry; I know, it wasn't easy for you…"

"It's too late. You've done it now. You've upset your mother. You just don't care about me any more, I can see that…"

Sniffle.

"…all the years I spent worrying myself thin, practically into the grave, caring for you when you were ill."

Oh, God, let's not go there. Pause while she reaches for the tissues. I'm going to puke any second.

"…the easy life you've had that Nicky didn't have while he worked so hard to qualify."

Another dramatic pause so I have room to feel guilty enough to surrender. I'm not going to let her win this round anyway.

"I can't do this, mother, I'm sorry."

"It wouldn't have done you any harm to have got yourself a real profession. But anything to make me miserable, I know that."

"Okay. Look, I'm hanging up now, Mother. Bye."

Sniffle.

"Mum? I have to go. I'm sorry."

I hung up. Two in a row. This time I lifted the set above my head and threw it into the wall three feet in front of me. It made a ding and a dent in the plaster. I stood there feeling like I was going to spontaneously combust. Then I picked up the phone. Listened to the tone. It was still there. So I put it back down on the floor where I kept it. You feel so stupid. But I was glad I didn't have to go out and buy a new fucking telephone. What do you do when you're in a stew? I'm not rushing off in a blind fury to rent a car this time. I paced up and down my front room trying not to ludicrously collide with the furniture. I do so need dignity in my fury. Put on another CD. Decided it didn't fit my mood, so changed it. Then changed it again two minutes later, then switched the whole thing off altogether about three minutes after that. It was like trying to eat at Gordon Ramsey's after someone's just stubbed a cigarette out on your face. So that was my afternoon ruined.

So. So. So. Fuck. Fuck. Fuck. My. Fucking. Brother. Fuck his eyes. The insufferable smug bastard. With probably the biggest prick in the state of Colorado. And my equally impossible selfish bitch of a mother. Despite what I tell people to make myself sound more interesting, about as authentically American as the tripe on Bury market. And all that 'Timothy darling' crap when she was brought up in a back-to-back slum in Huddersfield in the late days of rationing. Used the movies to develop delusions of grandeur. Going along three times a week to the Doxy on Mill Street and coming home copying the voices echoing massively from loudspeakers in the cavernous picture house. The scrupulously polished accent of Dorothy Tutin and the wholesomely sexual apple tones of Hayley Mills. Produced a strange mixture. Stuffed her father's socks down her dress to imagine she was Priscilla Gush, lappy-breasted Brighton blonde bombshell from the late-50s. Met my father, Colin, on a train from Leeds to London. A kindly engineer from Hull with a face like Montgomery Cliff. Older than my mother. Born in 1942 as bombs began to die away, a father on the railway and a mother who scrubbed the step and bore six children. Mother, then called Deirdre, was running away at sixteen the day she accidentally spilt tea on my Dad in a dusty carriage. Changed her name to Constance. Dad going south to find work. 1965. The lure of a capital just beginning to swing. Goodbye to all that grim north, with its cheap suits, bad teeth and backstreet abortions. Pathetic plastic toy Christmases. Grime and poverty even George Best and The Beatles couldn't wipe out. My antecedents. Struggling in the south until a stranger met in a Shepherd's Bush pub one rainy night gets my father a job in the labs at the Hoover Factory. Works his way up and ten years later finds a small kind of fame, inventing the Slip-Joint Dust Bag. Wealth to raise mother's sights even further. She meets a glorified American dentist at a small-but-special dinner at the Savoy in honour of my dad and runs off to Massachusetts with this mouth-hacker who has an inexhaustible supply of confidence and a pocket full of flavoured condoms.

 The slug trail down the past sounds ugly and feels worse. When my dad has a full breakdown and is hospitalized in deepest Surrey. One year after Deirdre took flight for America. Where Nick and I now follow, forlorn little boys, to make our own sense of the future. To somehow escape the clutches of her bullshit schemes. Sometimes I wish Nick had died just so I can believe some force somewhere has seen fit to punish her. Hate myself for such an unworthy snot-stained thought. But is anyone guilty in the end? Aren't we all merely victims of time and chance? Loose and afraid in the universe, atoms untended and unwanted, we are. Arrive in places un-chosen to grown ups unlooked for, as useless and as blameless as all the dead generations bred in squalor and misery. Surviving somehow on bread, beer, potatoes and dull dreams.

 A life without dreams is a life of living bad breath.

 Who said that? Sophocles? Paul of Tarsus? No. Les Person, sipping a desultory cup of coffee in the staff room after one of his jokes had fallen flat yet again.

 "That's my life all over," he said. I felt like giving him a ring. And terrified, I am, because I have had this recurring dream for years that the phone is going to ring with Connie on the other end telling me that in actual fact, Colin wasn't my real dad; that it's really Vic Bladderwick, the famous one-eyed Yorkshire boxer who was put away in 1975 for multiple child molestation a year after, in a moment of more extreme psychosis, he fucked Deirdre - back home to visit the family holding her fingers over her nose - in the back of an old Cortina, thus procreating poor little me. Wakes me up in the first light of any old dawn you care to mention, stopping me from going back to sleep, while the cold fact hits that I'll never be able to see my Dad for to get me some DNA and a test of complete finality. For the simple reason that the fool went and threw himself from a high church tower in 1979. The day Margaret Thatcher won the election. Is it any wonder that I keep my intense interest in politics to myself? And that I lie about my father to people, wishing him more than the world to be still alive and here with me? While instead Deirdre continues to live the life of Riley thanks in part to the royalties from his wondrous invention.

27
Tonto
Autumn Term - Half Term Week, Weekend 2
Saturday, October 26th, 2002
Measby - Evening

Brrrppp! brrrppp!; Brrrppp! brrrppp!,
"Hey. Muff."
"Timbolina. How's things?"
"How are you? Shit, it's been ages."
"So what you been up to? Don't tell me: nothing but being a dreary fucking English teacher, while I've been here in the beating heart of the country saving lives."
"Yeah, you're right as usual. You got me beat, man."
"Hah. Well, it's about time you admitted it. This is the show, right here: fantastic new leukaemia treatments and prosthetic arms being made like you wouldn't believe and get this: next month the Henry VIII is going to be the first hospital in the world to do a dick transplant. What do you think about that?"
"Congratulations on being brave enough to come forward for the operation. It must have taken a lot of spunk."
"Hold it. I'm ringing Eddie Izzard right now to pass that one on…"
"What's this about, though? I take it you're smashed out of your face or hooked up to some amphetamine drip you've robbed from the hospital."
"Wrong. If I seem even more ebullient than usual, I can only put it down to love."
"Muff, have you been hanging around the Psych ward again? You really must stop bolstering your ego by bedding poor young girls with chronic personality disorders. I've told you this before, but you never seem to listen."
"Nothing you can say can ruffle my sweet feathers, ladyboy. Love has given me so much power I could listen to your cheap jibes all day without it raising my heart rate one beat."
"Okay, so don't tell me, she's 51."
"No."
"60, then."
"25."
"Blind."
"Doesn't wear glasses."
"Stupid."

"Degree in Civil Engineering."

"A lesbian."

"What?"

"Testing what she thinks is her true sexuality by trying to fuck you without throwing up afterwards."

"Tim."

"How did you meet her? Did she come in for a haemorrhoid operation?"

"Tim."

"Did you look at her anus and think, 'now this is a woman I could do business with?'"

"Tim, what's the matter?"

"I...I...I don't know."

"Take it easy, feller. Take a time out. Breathe, feller, breathe; slowly now. Do want me to call back later?"

"No! Stay there!"

"It's okay, Tim. I'm not going anywhere. Just keep breathing calmly for a bit; then when you're ready, just tell me what this is all about, slowly."

"Sorry, Muff..."

"There's nothing to be sorry about; it's okay, it's okay. Take your time."

"Okay. Stay there, okay?"

"I'm here."

"Thanks, man. Thank you."

28
Stuck Inside of Yorkshire with the Measby Blues Again
Autumn Term - Half Term Weekend 2
Sunday, October 27th, 2002
Measby-Yarrow-Measby Morning & Lunchtime

I woke with Sunday blues and my head still hurt like shit. The words 'vinegar in custard' were on my mind, going round and round. 'Vinegar in custard,' I kept thinking, 'vinegar in custard.' Slept so badly I sat on the edge of the bed after I woke and felt like I was going to throw. Knowing how the day usually develops when it starts like that, I should have quickly applied to have the whole thing cancelled. Vinegar in custard. Vinegar on custard?

My joy at a victory over Jez was short-lived. There was something fundamentally wrong about the way I'd reacted to the phone call. If I really felt something deep for this woman that was no way to treat her. I moved that idea around my mind a while, only for it to meet up with another uncomfortable thought a minute or so later. Or was it a second? I wasn't sure. If I felt about Jez the way I had the previous Friday afternoon, where did that leave my so-called feelings for Safeena? Stinking in the crapper, that's where. I was in no mood for prissy Jane Austen imagery this windy morning. All of a sudden it felt like all my defeats were coming back to haunt me. On a day where I should have been thinking a lot more about Chris and his wife, who really did have problems.

Each age to his own though. I couldn't suddenly become 40, fretting about where my old age pension was going to come from two decades down the line, or whether to take out a bigger mortgage or not. I was Tim and I could buy my house outright. So? It's not my fault my father lards my bank account from the grave. You get the problems you're dealt and by those shall ye live. If Chris were me, would he not be eating existential dust? 'Of course,' I said to my kitchen. 'Mais bien sur.'

The morning was already falling into midday when I found myself drinking even more coffee and trying to face up to the main business of the day: I was meeting Safeena off the bus in an hour. Should I call and put her off? If there are three things I love, none of them is oiling out of previously made commitments at the last minute. I loathe letting people down and making excuses. So, like it or not, Safeena's going to see me in a tsunami state and that's that. It could be for the best. She cops a load of Tim in meltdown and thinks it's the last thing she needs in her life. And runs screaming for the nearest taxi she can find back to Hyde Park. At least it would un-complicate the situation. Vinegar in *the* custard would make more sense. But I didn't want the word in the sentence. Had I dreamed this? Vinegar? In custard? Sort of summed up the way I felt though. Vinegar in custard. Not a taste you want in your mouth. I do remember I dreamed last night of a spider, its body just out of sight on a block of weathered wood. Just its legs, bent and creepy, were all I could see. And cobwebbing. I hate spiders, so that was no surprise. But did I dream a dish of delicious home made vanilla custard ruined by drops of sourness? Tim, you'd better get a hold of yourself before your wheels go rolling off into the roadside like tumbleweed in Nevada.

Eventually I pulled on a coat and got the one bus of the hour into town. Chilly this morning with the wind trying to bite, but clear. A blue sky but weak looking light, like someone forgot to turn up the switch. So I got to the bus station with just ten minutes to go before her bus got in, but the clock said ten-to-eleven. Had to be wrong. When I asked a hapless Sunday bus stop woman what time it was, she said, "It's just comin' oop to ten-to-eleven." She must have seen my vacant expression and said,

"The clocks went back last night. Dint yer noah?"

"Oh, no, I forgot," I said, feeling like the town idiot.

'Tssuh,' I went. Typical. Fucking useless Sunday. I was grinding my teeth, and my jaw ached as I walked to find somewhere open for coffee. Stop grinding, Tim. You got enough problems without losing the enamel off your teeth.

'Take a walk in a winter town,' came the line from the song in my head. 'Feel your life's all upside down.' Melancholy music filling up my mind. Not what I would have prescribed for myself at this time. 'Fuck you,' I said to the song. 'And you've no one around,' it continued. 'Not the problem,' I replied. Too many around, and one of them I'm an hour early for meeting, thank you very much. A huge cup of chocolate and a read of the Sunday paper in *Avanti!* took the edge off the seasonal gloom and my other ailments, but I was still in no shape for this as I walked back out to the bus station. Especially as I started wondering where that big glowing feeling I had for Safeena on Thursday went. Was it the idea of romance that made me fall for her? When we kiss someone for the first time when we're not drunk or stoned, do we play make-believe because that's the way we're made? Are we genetically programmed to feel attraction so we replicate the species to stop it dying out? Or is my mind just screwed at the moment? Did I dream the way I felt about Safeena on Thursday? Did I imagine being with her made me feel happy? I plodded towards the bus station again, thinking about how much I hated Sunday streets, always looking empty and forlorn to me. Not much open on this day of the week in Yarrow, even in this age of the perpetual corporate retail jamboree.

I saw the red Leeds Metropolitan Rider turn into the square and come wheezing up the street from the roundabout to the pull-in near where I was standing. Fourth off the bus was Safeena in her grey duffle coat again, but sweet blue braids in her hair and I didn't know whether to cry or throw a large brick through a shop window thus buying myself another problem so I didn't have to deal with this one. So what are you, Safeena, the vinegar or the custard?

She came off the bus smiling sheepishly at me, but hopefully. She couldn't keep that unmistakable look of 'girlfriend' from her cute little face. I say 'little': it wasn't at all. It was nicely shaped and strong, but dominated by those eyes, all deep tones of smiling brown. You're as lovely as I thought you were on Thursday.

"Hi."
"Hi, how are you."
"Okay."
"You?"
"I'm okay."
"Where's your woolly hat?"
"Oh, I forgot to put it on." I had. "I've been wearing it, though."

We embraced, but didn't kiss. Her eyes and a slight movement of the head told me this was not what she was expecting and I hated myself. But I took her hand and we walked to where the Holmes Farne bus was already waiting to go out. Conversation was stilted. The sky had clouded over and big drops of rain began to fall on the window and drip slowly down. I suddenly remembered I liked watching them as a kid, waiting to see how long they could hold out after their initial fat plop, before sliding in a trickle down the pane. I always felt safe on buses. When it was wet outside it was always warm and steamy inside, and folk were always so pleased to be out of the rain, red cheeked and smiling, and not too shy to tell the driver,

"Oh! That's better!"
"What's up?" she said. So I told her what I was thinking about.
"When I got on the school bus I used to cower in the smallest corner I could find hoping no one would notice me."
"Why?" I said. I found it hard to imagine a shy little Safeena.
"So no one would call me 'Paki'."
"Did you get a lot of that?"
"Yeah, some. Not at primary school. But when I went to big school - we used to call it 'big school' when we were in primary, did you?" she said, smiling.
"No. Don't think so." I couldn't really remember.
"At High Tuffs I used to get huge Year 11s picking on me."

"Bullying you? Physically?"
"Yeah, a little."
"Wow, how did you cope?"
"Snitched on them," she said, enjoying the telling. No scars present as far as I could see.
"Did you?" I said eyes wide.
"Yeah; and all my friends in my form came with me."

I sighed in relief. The thought of Safeenas all over the country being treated like this, all friendless and catastrophically miserable as a result didn't bear contemplating, especially in this Sunday mood. If she hadn't been so matter of fact about it, and if there hadn't been a happy ending in the story, her little Year 7 halfling mates there to support her, I think...I don't know what I think I'd have felt. I just didn't need to dwell in someone else's pain this morning - afternoon, now, actually.

We pulled up in Measby at the stop right by my house and I thought about Safeena being the first girl I'd brought here. I thought, 'Tim, you could be thinking lascivious thoughts right now, and probably should.' But the thing was a non-starter, I could tell. Not that Safeena said anything. Perhaps it was because it was the obvious thing to do, two young people being alone in a house together. It was what practically every other young couple in the world would have done. Not us.

We went inside and talked about - well, everyday kind of stuff. I made some coffee and we sat on the sofa and gassed about work, universities, families, the people we knew – friends and such. It suited me. And what was going on in Safeena's mind I didn't know, but this territory seemed to be fine with her too. She held my attention without the remotest difficulty. How can I say this without it sounding patronising? She was an interesting girl - woman - and she could talk for England, I'm sure, if she were ever given the opportunity. No, that's not fair. She just seemed to find talking - fluently and intelligently - a more natural thing than anyone I'd ever met, I think. She seemed a very open person too. I got the feeling she hated secrets. And lies. I only wish I could tell you what she talked about in detail, because the whole time we were there, I wasn't really listening properly to a word she said. I think she has three sisters. And likes Monet and that singer called Dildo. But aside from that, my mind is a blank page. I should have done a lot better. Don't think I didn't feel bad, because I did - bad, confused and unable to get myself together.

"So, do you want to go to the pub, get some lunch?" I said after about an hour, feeling on the whole that this was going to be another complete disaster of my own making. I didn't feel like eating, it was just that the only other option was moving on to the territory of what the hell we were doing here with each other at this point in our two existences.

*

The bus pulled into the station and Tim was standing there, hands in pockets. Just like me. I do that. He had a black coat on. Like a donkey jacket, but more expensive. Much more. I looked for his head to see how that cut was. It was really incredibly bad the other night. He'd combed his fair hair over it to try to cover up the stitches and actually, he'd done a good job. For a man. I tried to improve it with my fingers, stroking the strands of hair into position as gently as I could. I thought he might be wearing the hat I gave him but he wasn't. Not that I minded, because he looked a bit of a prat in it really. I think I got carried away with things the other day – no - the morning after we first met.

My heart was beating so hard in my chest all the way down on the bus I thought I was going to be sick. Then I felt my inside leap when I saw him. You know that feeling: like there's a lift inside you suddenly jerking up. I hadn't been able to stop thinking about him since Thursday morning. Life is funny, isn't it? People say, 'Safeena, oh, she's outgoing and confident,' which I am. But I still don't know what possessed me to go to the Infirmary to see how he was. It was like I just had to go. Something in my head, almost separate from me, said, 'Saf, just get up and go to see him.' Something down deep in there said, 'don't stop to think about it: just go. He needs you.' Yes - thinking about it here and now it was almost like a voice was really talking to me, saying, 'he needs *you*, Safeena. Not somebody else. You. You've got to go, don't argue.' So I went.

I'd seen him in the Frinton behaving so pec...pe-cu-liarly - sorry, I can't get my mouth in gear this morning - and it wasn't as if he was amazingly good looking or anything, though he wasn't bad either. But what do they say about women? Some of us anyway. They respond to the vulnerability of men sometimes. And although he was being loud and smiling and talking to people he obviously didn't know, you couldn't not notice he was lonely and in a right state. Maybe it was that which lodged inside me straight away. I say that, but when he fell and got taken off to the Infirmary I had no intention of doing anything. If I'm honest, it was at Mairie's that the voice in my head went, 'Go, Safeena, this is it.' And the weird thing is that it's against everything I've been taught. Most psychologists don't believe there's such a thing as intuition.

I thought things were going incredibly well after he stayed the night - not with me, he slept in Antonia's bedroom - but then when I got to Yarrow the next Sunday he was awkward with me straight away and I thought, 'Oh, no, this is all wrong.' But you can't just turn round and go back when you've just arrived. And you think, well, maybe this will pass, but it didn't. He didn't even try to kiss me when we met. He held my hand but he was so half-hearted about it he may as well have not bothered. And I thought, 'here we go again, here's another of your disasters, Safeena.'

On the bus to the village where he lived I really did want to go back to Hyde Park. Even writing essays was more fun than this. He was so uncomfortable with me but I couldn't ask him why. I knew it was the other girl though. It was obvious. And the bus isn't the place for a heart-to-heart and a break-up before we've even started. God knows what we talked about - yes, I do remember: we were talking about when we were at school. Anyway, it made me think back to the feeling I'd had sitting drinking coffee at Mairie's and I thought 'how could you be so utterly idiotic.' So I had to just stay and hope that it would stop. That one of us would say something to break the awful spell. If it's meant to be, it's meant to be - and if it's not, it's not. So tough it out, Safeena. We'd only just met so I hadn't much to lose. But actually, that didn't work.

By the time we got to Measby I thought about going home again and suddenly I wanted to cry - I could feel my lip start to tremble. I don't know why I was doing that because it would just have been total embarrassment if I'd quit and left. And I'm not the type who goes blubbing at the first sign of something going wrong. I'm usually the last actually; I've got a reputation for being a bit hard. So I forced myself to think about something else and luckily it stopped. I tried to console myself that if it disintegrated from here, then with Tim being white, it would have probably been some hassle anyway. A few fundamentalist guys gave me a hard time around the campus last time I was with a white guy. It's the last thing you need, really, in your final year.

So anyway, his house was pretty cool and it wouldn't have come cheap. I was half-expecting mice, but it was clean and tidy. Amazing for a bloke. It smelt nice too. Incense and oil. Reminded me of home. He had a patch of art postcards on his wall. A lot of them were really eye-catching. Mostly modern stuff but really beautiful. Art isn't really something I know a lot about, but, you know, 'I know what I like'.

God, I was nervous. If we couldn't make some sort of connection again, every minute was going to be completely dreadful, and after an hour or something I would have left, and obviously Tim would have been relieved. Why can't we as people talk about what's real except when there's a crisis or something? I mean. We...I should have said to him straight away, 'what's going on?' when I knew he was feeling uncomfortable. But no - we started talking about stupid stuff. Well, mostly I started talking about stuff: my course, my friends, the weather. We even got onto politics, for God's sake, when it was obvious in two seconds that a) he isn't interested in the subject and b) he doesn't know the first thing about it. And I talked about my family, of course. And as all of my friends will tell you, I don't mind talking about myself, not in the least. I told him more about where my family came from in India, and about my background. But the more I went on, the more I began to feel sick inside. What was the point in telling this guy my personal stuff when it looked as though it was all going to be a complete waste of time? It was like throwing away perfectly good food.

Mind you, I couldn't help feeling relieved that he was interested in my background. Very interested and not at all put off. That kept me going - for a bit anyway. That somehow, if we could get out of this mess, he might be someone I could, well, you know…how shall I put it? Let's just say I felt drawn to him from the start, without really knowing at all why. It was a bit weird, really. But he's an odd one. He's got a doctorate but I had to practically drag it out of him. And he would tell me nothing about his family. The only thing he talked about with any enthusiasm was his job and all the people he worked with. Except Jez - he didn't mention her, which was daft because once he got on to the subject of his school, she was like this huge presence there in the room anyway. Of course it would have been so much better to have used that to get the whole thing out into the open, but I just…just could not find a way to make myself brave enough to do it.

He got annoyed when I laughed at one point and called him 'Doctor Tim.' I nearly asked him to examine me but the atmosphere wasn't right for that sort of thing. Would I like to have slept with him? I know it seems like everyone is screwing the whole time nowadays, but not me. Perhaps that's my conditioning coming out. And fear of my father. I shouldn't laugh. No, well, yes, at some stage then, I wanted to sleep with him. To be close to him. As well as for the, um, excitement.

Do I think he wanted to sleep with me? Isn't that what all blokes want? I started to think at one point, because he was being so cold, 'is there something wrong with me? Doesn't he think I'm attractive?' But I knew that that was the least of the problem. Because on the Thursday, Tim was, well, passionate, considering. So there was definitely something there for him. Otherwise he wouldn't have rung me on the Friday asking me to come over to Yarrow. Measby, sorry. To be honest I didn't expect him to. I thought there was some sort of chance I'd never see him again. With another woman hanging around it wouldn't have been surprising, would it? I mean, on paper, or if I was sane, I wouldn't have let what happened in the kitchen at no. 23 happen. In theory it was completely wrong. But it was all strange territory for me – this all having started with the voice saying, 'Go, Safeena.' I suppose I just thought I had to keep going with the flow of things, to let go of all my doubts. Because aren't there always reasons why we shouldn't commit ourselves these days? There always seem to be with me.

Anyway, we went to the pub for lunch. It was a relief to get out of the house - you know, change of scenery, some people around, giving us something different to talk about - but there was still this space between us, and a tension, and we weren't going to solve the problem right there and then. We walked up to the other end of the village by the church and we stopped in a little craft shop that was open. Stuff was too expensive for me. Then we got to the Rusty Bucket or whatever it was called, and had a drink and some nice food. But with more small talk. Actually it was pathetic, in something like the true sense of the word. There we were, two grown people - I know I'm only 21 but I'm supposed to be an adult - trying so hard to be nice to each other, but completely unable to communicate. It's enough to make you weep. Of course, when we got back, it was obviously time for me to go: I'd been there long enough for us both to feel that it hadn't been a complete embarrassment - you know how the English are with their manners - and that would have been right: 'embarrassment' would not have been the appropriate word for the thing. If what happened hadn't happened, I'd have always looked back at that day and described it as completely, bloody, wretchedly, awful.

But of course, I didn't go home.

29

Go On As Three
Autumn Term - 2nd Sunday of Half Term
Sunday, October 27th, 2002
Measby - Afternoon

We got to the house again and I was taut like an athlete's hamstring in the face of this stalemate. We could only go on for so long talking about whether Britain was a more racist society than the USA. It began to look as though the only sensible thing I could do in the circumstances was to check the bus times at the stop on the way to the front door, go down town on the next one with her, wave her off back to Leeds, then throw myself in the Whardle.

There weren't so much lines as whole staves on my forehead by the time we got back through the front door again. I looked at Safeena to see if she was keeping her coat on - thankfully she took it off; though I can see her so clearly now, hesitating fractionally before she placed it on the chair, as if she was thinking, 'really, I need to get out of here.' It still makes me wince to think about it. Yup, I can see her clearly in my mind's eye, in her ribbed smoke-blue sweater, rolled at the neck, her head looking at the floor as she pulled the hem down over the top of her trousers. Uncertain. Doubtful. Her hair, parted carefully today, but falling onto a troubled face, as if she wanted to hide.

Or maybe she probably wanted to scream in frustration as I did, but it just doesn't do when you're English. Even part-English. We both had the disease.

I went over to my stereo system and put on a CD Sef had lent me. Actually, given me. 'It's rather a cliché,' he said, 'but you might like it.' I knew what he was saying. 'This will be good for your musical education, dear boy.' I didn't mind that, it being the province of knowledge to speak and the privilege of wisdom to listen. It had this very cool cover: a black guy playing a trumpet, in a great suit and elegantly immaculate tie - bright little diamonds in yellow and crimson on a navy background, throwing a beautiful shadow onto his white shirt. If the music was as good as the photograph it might be something. I opened the case and slipped it in the player. I don't know why I chose it except that it was right there staring at me. Perhaps it was a subconscious thing, blue being how I felt under a layer of pure, concentrated exasperation.

This piano sound came out of the speakers, and a bass - an acoustic one - the tall upright one that looks as though it needs a man with fingers like sticks of rubber celery to play it. Suddenly they do this thing together, a short middle-eastern sounding wavy line of notes. Then the bass starts playing this melody and the drummer comes in tip-tapping on a cymbal, then the trumpet and a sax enter together. And the sound of it came out into the room and it was instantly hypnotic. The music charged the air with some kind of mystical electricity. Like suddenly it was a different time and a different place. We were suddenly alone on a new stage.

We were still standing up. And I found I was looking at Safeena straight in the eye, and she at me, and for once her look straight back into mine was something I could read like a kid's book. My instincts took over. I went up to her and slowly opened my arms and she came inside them. Then we started moving to the music - with the music - just slowly, shifting our weight in rhythm, side to side, round and around, gently - smoothly, easily. She rested her head on my shoulder, and it seemed to fit there so perfectly. I felt my life suspended in the face of the moment; felt my everyday self closed down and my stomach gripped with a new tension. Then I felt her body right up against me, warm and soft, even through her clothes. I was careful where I put my hands, but I lifted up her sweater at the back and found her skin, and began stroking it softly, as softly as I could. She kissed my neck and we kept moving to the beat. The music was just out of this world - coming out of some other place entirely. The drummer was still clicking away on the cymbals and the saxophone player was soloing, fast, but in control. An intense piano was still talking away out of one speaker, while I tried to hold Safeena even closer and her me.

Three times, four times she kissed my neck - five times, in steady succession, and no sign of letting up. I let my index finger stray lower, pushing the material at the top of her trousers up, then away to see if gave me the freedom to work a little lower. Then I found the top of her knicker-line and gently stroked the soft flesh underneath. And still she was kissing my neck, now moving down to my throat. This was a situation you could no longer hold on to. It was slipping fast from both of us. She had relaxed her whole body, or it had relaxed for her, and I could feel she'd surrendered, all of her, right there in my arms. She began to pluck at my shirt, at the back of me, loosening it from my trousers.

Then the door went. Tap, tap, tap.

We had to stop. There was no argument, and no choice. Something about the knock was too urgent. We pulled ourselves apart. I was not enthralled. The Plan. Something could be wrong with The Plan. It might be Sef. Or it might...

Be fucking Jez. Couldn't be, surely.

I went straight over to the door and opened it. And there she was, wearing a coy smile and a navy blue hoodie. She looked at me hopefully and questioningly as people do in these situations. The music was still playing behind me, and the thought flashed past my mind that I wanted Safeena to have the presence of mind to go and turn it down, or better still, off.

"'ello. Oh." She must have read my face, just as I was studying hers, like a difficult menu.

"'ave ah called at a bad time?"

"Er, well."

Jez's face had already dropped like a man going over Niagara Falls in a bucket. Then I said something I immediately regretted. But how could I send her away? How could I be so impolite? You can't defeat your upbringing, when all is said and done. Did I feel sorry for her? I didn't think so, not when I'd spent the last two months mooning over her like a goon, but why else would I say this?

"Do you want to come in?"

I hoped she'd say 'no'. Or did I? Down there in the netherworld at the back of the brain, who the Bob Monkhouse knew what muck and chaos was churning around. Not me, man, not me. I only read books for a living and a life, and none of them were about psychology.

"Oh, noah, I doant think soah if you've got someone there."

I didn't say I had someone there.

The way the door of my house is positioned, Jez should have been able to see almost all of the room, though I was blocking as much of the doorway as I could. There was just one chair out of sight where Safeena might now be sitting if she'd wanted to make herself scarce. Unless she'd leaped into the kitchen or up the stairs as I opened the door. Or was cowering behind it.

Ah, what the hell.

"Come in, come in," I said, and moved out of the way so she had a path into the room.

"Are yer shewer? 'kay, then."

And in she came, something like a woman who'd come to collect money but didn't expect to get any. I shut the door and turned around expecting to see Jez and Safeena looking at each other, like two cats, but there was only Jez, standing awkwardly in the space between pieces of furniture.

"Would you like a drink? Cup of tea? Coffee?" I knew she drank only tea, but I wasn't drinking straight. I mean, thinking straight.

"What thee y'ell 'appened to yewer 'ead?" she said, coming over and reaching up on tiptoe to almost be touching my stitches. I instinctively and unthinkingly bent down to help her. I might have been lowering it in supplication. Barely five-foot was Jez 'in me stockin' feet' as I'd once heard her tell someone in the staff room. Her hand flicked my hair.

"Wow, that is soom cut. 'ow the flippin' 'eck did yer do that?"

"I fell. In a pub."

"Pissed again, were yer?"

"Drunk? Yes, I'm afraid I was. Drinking with some friends. Stan and his mates - y'know, my mate in Leeds."

"Noah, I doant know your mairt in Leeds. Anywair. When did'ja do it?"

"Thursday. Friday? Thursday…Thursday."

"Yew doant seem to noah what day it is, lad."

"I didn't hardly know what day it was afterwards, let me tell you."

"Did you goah t' 'ospital? Moost a' done wi' that..."

"Yeah, Stan was very good. Stayed with me until they took me, um, up to the ward."

"Stayed in overnight, did yer?"

"Yeh-yeh. One night. Then I spent a day at Stan's house. Came home yesterday."

I don't, as a rule, make a very good liar, and I wasn't about to rush out to the bookies and put money on me having made a good start here.

And where was Safeena?

"I'll go and make the tea."

I scurried off to the kitchen too fast. I might as well have had a big sign around my neck, saying "DISAPPEAR NOW, JEZ; YOU'RE NOT WELCOME." She could tell I was nervous. Where was Safeena? She wasn't in the kitchen. Then she must have flown upstairs. Corpus Christi, she must have moved like a greased streak of lightning to get to the top before I opened the door. Then it occurred to me she could have left via the back door. I found myself staring at it now. Don't tell me you've left, Safeena. Then I thought about her coat. Was it still on the chair – where Jez couldn't miss it? Holy heaven – I was fried.

I put the kettle on, fetched the teapot from the cupboard and got some milk from the fridge in about ten seconds, to get myself back out there to Jez quickly. I was in a panic when I had no need, really. Well, not until I went through the door and saw Safeena treading carefully down the stairs. I closed my eyes for a second as momentary panic gripped my gut, thought 'this is it' and got ready to deal with the shit-field as best I could.

"Okay. Right. Jez? This is Safeena. Safeena? This is Jez. She works at Pegs."

She knew straight away who Jez was. Oh, my heaven, this was it. Suddenly the thought occurred that Safeena might be thinking I knew Jez was coming round. Like I'd set this up. I would have to have been about as sane as Hannibal Lechter to be carrying on with that kind of caper, but you could never predict the level of a person's thought, especially if they watched a lot of soap opera where, I believe, things like this happen oh, all the time. Because her face was like a bag of explosives. Jezebel's was more quizzical. Confused. Like she had no idea I had any

Asian friends hanging around. Or whatever they might have been doing with me at my house.

"'ello."

"Hi."

It couldn't have been a frostier exchange if they'd met in the Arctic Circle to discuss patterns of seal migration. Lord, what was I thinking? Nothing much and a hundred things at the same time. If only real life could be like the movies - because hey, I could deal with this by running out the door and carrying on up the road, leaving them to it. But instead I watched Jezebel and Safeena eyeing each other carefully, examining each other for flaws, permanent damage and weapons, by the look of it. Then I suddenly had an epiphany: what a pleasant and highly unusual change to have two women apparently competing for my attention. I wished immediately that I had a video camera to hand, both for posterity and to show Muff and all my friends, none of whom would have believed me if I'd tried to tell them how I spent my Sunday afternoons.

"Do you want some tea, Safeena?" I said, deciding to try pretending that nothing remotely untoward or interesting was happening here, to see if that worked.

"Er, yeah. Thanks, Tim."

I winced at the intimacy that stuck like Araldite to my name, wondering whether Safeena was laying claim to me, whilst I slid away to the kitchen, as Jez said,

"Soah, 'ow long 'ave you known our Tim?"

"I'm a friend of Tim's cousin. Alan. He's at Leeds."

"Oh."

"We were both going to come today but he's not so ill - so well!"

"Soah you decided to coom on yewer own."

I was back with a tray of mugs and the sugar bowl, trying to remember if I still knew how to whistle. I hoped that wasn't a nervous squeak I just heard in Saf's voice in response to Jez playing police inspectors. That I'd just imagined it through this haze of terror.

"Yeah, that's right."

This I heard over my shoulder as I returned kitchen-ward. Good move, Saf. At least this way Jez might buy into the notion that she'd come out here because she wanted older man Tim to screw her brains out. And that I was merely being the well-brought up adult, simply being hospitable. And if she detected a little *frisson* in the air, it was just me demonstrating how all single men operate biologically. That given enough time between bouts of copulation, I would eventually screw Mrs. Manicure up against her tea trolley.

"So, you work with Tim?"

"Yeah, and what do you do?"
"Leeds University. I'm there stu..."
"What do you...sorry...studeh?"
"Philosophy."
"Oh, interestin'."

Only Jez wasn't really interested. At least, not in the conventional sense. Her face was a composition of dark and manic activity; a cross between something out of that flaming Brontë novel and *Return of the Living Dead*. It was all I could do not to drop the tray.

"Cuz ya can try bein' philosophical about this: I'm norra fan of bein' lied to so fookin' blatantleh - right to me face."

"Jez..."

"Don't fookin' 'Jez' me. I don't care who you 'ang about with, Tim. But don't try to cover it up in such a...a fooking..." she was falling and I couldn't catch her – I so wanted to make this easy for her. But I saw her spit shooting across the room like venom.

"...pathetic fashion." It was odd to hear Jez sounding her 't's to speak such good English. 'Good English;' I should know better: conventional English. The thoughts flash across the brain like horizontal lightning. For the first time I wondered whether the broad Bury accent was just a put on for everyone. A mask. Then I was thinking 'thank God she can speak the language properly.' I dreaded to think what kind of complaints she'd be getting after the sixth form parents evening if she gave them the Jez I heard almost all the time. Then I was riding the wave of the event. Only it was the one that had me as the man going over the falls in a bucket. Safeena was gaping into Jez's face and didn't know what to say.

And then Jez started to cry. Words ran out like the water supply on a day when they're digging up the road. Not a good simile. Words ran out of road, and water dropped out of her face and her mouth was open like a tunnel. I thought - actually I don't know what I thought - but I was still holding tea mugs in my hand and must have been gaping myself at the poor girl like a dumb ass. Safeena was still gaping too about five feet away. If she'd gone over to Jez and hugged her I wouldn't have been in the least bit surprised. I then watched as Jez dropped on to the sofa in front of us and hung her head.

Then Safeena was right there with her too.

"Whatever's the matter?" she said, as if this couldn't just be about me.

"Everything." It took us about a minute - a long time if you sit there and count to sixty – to get Jez to start choking her story out, through sobs and tears and a running nose. A face broken into pieces like a Picasso in deepest cubes. Safeena produced a tissue from somewhere but a huge Sunday tablecloth wouldn't have been enough to wipe her sorrow dry. Then Saf did have her arm around her and Jez leaned into her and I thought, 'typical: bloody Women's Mafia.' Sworn enemies they were two minutes ago.

So I got to play tea boy for a bit and Jez drank some in the time-honoured English way. We all did. Before we found out what all this was about for Jez. I would have been kidding myself if I said I didn't think that some of her tears were for me. I liked the idea of that, of course I did. What bloke in the world, person even, doesn't revel in the thought of being fought over by two women? Or men? You know what I mean. Unworthy - but I didn't care then and I'm not so sure I do now. It was a whole lot more than that though: parents desperate for her to marry the childhood sweetheart; a father who'd always dominated her - wanted her to do this subject and take that job; go to university near home; dealing with his problems and pain by inflicting it on someone else; supposed to be his pride and joy, his only daughter, but that wasn't the way with Dad, apparently, Jez receiving only the endless torment of paternal cruelty instead. Then there was the disconsolate Steve who last night was on the receiving end of the verbal Dear John routine after five years. Jez saying 'thanks for everything and I never really loved you anyway so I don't want your ring or your life anymore.' Thoughts of 'goodbye cruel world' for Steve, but he'd get over it. The disappointment of Steve's parents who think the world of Jezebel Treat, along with lots of other local friends and extended family members, but who never cared so much for her that they were prepared to put Jez's father in his place. Just when I thought she was about to turn into an enemy, into a bitch, or a witch, she turns into - well, just someone else trying to make it through. It's not a very profound thought, but that's just the way it is, isn't it: we all just trying to do this seventy-year fandango the neatest and sweetest way we can, trying not to fall over. Perhaps pick up some applause on the way. If there's a trophy or a prize in there, well, we'll take that too. Maybe enjoy the pure pleasure of a neat turn or a bit of a strut when we can get our confidence up.

Right there and then, in the two hours it took to get the whole story out of Jezebel, I felt like a winner, like a star with the rose between my teeth, in my black hat and gaucho pants, because this poor girl's life was in the shithouse and mine, for a change, suddenly wasn't. Several times in the midst of all this, Safeena looked across at me, smiled and said, in the language of her body, that when we'd seen Jez off into the afternoon, she was going to take me upstairs and make a man of me. To which I thought, 'If that's what you want of me, go girl. Go get it. I ain't going to stop you.' And hoped that she got the message: that for me and Jez it was over, although in truth, as you know as well, if not better than me, it had never really started

30
I Didn't Come to Crawl
Autumn Term - Week 8 Day 1 (new half term begins)
Monday, October 28th, 2002
Peggy Lane Staff room, headteacher's office & DT block - Morning Break

Monday break time arrived on a fresh and already well-advanced day, the clocks indeed having gone back, stealing a whole hour of precious daylight from our afternoons. As if they weren't hard and tiring enough already. A week off made the return a bitter one as the September Manifesto bit. Minutes of the Pastoral Care Committee's opening meeting were already pasted on the wall, recording the fact that 'The role of the form tutor in the 21st century educational arena' had been the main agenda item and that six points had been made and logged. More committees were soon to meet for the first time, staggered across the next few weeks. Mark book inspections were about to pass through the staff like dysentery, while the head and his chief lieutenants began a vast round of lesson inspections that would slow many a recovery from the onslaught. At our staff room table a bunch of unhappy gatekeepers of knowledge were working on the new school motto in response to Michael's briefing notice that we should all bend our thoughts in its direction for a spell. '*Pulando in Dumtandis Noblatum,*' we could all agree, was miles past its sell by date:

Nobly We Bestride the Day

'Reflect on a new motto' Michael had said, so this we were now doing.

"I've got an idea," said DT's young glamour boy, Rob Rodder, heartthrob especially of his form, 10BX, "he can stick his school motto up his slimy arse."

"Such a way with words," said Maurice Butter. "You should have been an English teacher."

"Ah'm not a poof," said Rob of the sleek, high cheekbones. You wondered sometimes whether he came out with these comments from feeling genuinely affronted by such humorous rejoinders - or whether he was once sexually abused with a copy of the complete works of Shakespeare. The two PE teachers in our midst at this time were in the vanguard of the hunt for the new mantra.

"How about 'We Crush the Opposition,'" said rugby specialist Andy Chap.

"Or what about, 'We Take No Prisoners,'" said Bobby Coulson, his partner-in-chief.

"*Per favore*: boys, isn't it time you learned to read? Your thinking is stupefyingly lamentable. That means 'shit-awful,' barely worthy of a couple of five year olds." Sef had deigned to join us. He was unusually chipper. I hadn't seen him like this for weeks. He continued.

"How about 'Resistance is Useless.'"

This was met with one chuckle and four long faces around the table, while Messrs Chap and Coulson naturally enough determined to concede Sef nothing, looking like they were planning murder. I'd have felt the same and I don't know how Sef got away with it.

"But is it, Sefton?" said Maurice Butter. "If you're talking about it from a staff point of view? Are we all just going to fall under the crushing yoke of the new managerialism and become slaves?"

"That I wouldn't know, my dear Maurice, but I suspect all will be steadily revealed as time inexorably unravels."

Back to our stirring debate. Rodder was still trying to impress us all with the serious weight of his wit.

"What about summat to do wi' all these exams the kids 'ave to take these days: 'We stuff 'em full of knowledge.'"

"Hmm, now that has a supreme elegance Fred Astaire himself would have envied, Rodder."

"Fred 'oo?" said Rodder.

"But if I'm honest with you, a transcription of a cat's fart would make a better motto."

Rob, always the last to know when he was way out of his depth, grunted moodily.

"Cheer oop," said Jez, "you'll grow a breyn won daih." This was a brave response from her considering she looked as though she'd woken up to find her pet rabbit hanging by chicken wire from the bathroom ceiling.

"How about 'We shake 'em and bake 'em'?" said I. I rather liked that one. I looked at Jez but she was staring out the window into some impenetrable middle distance.

"'ey oop, Quasimodo's woken up. We don't want none of your bloody Yankee rubbish 'ere, lad," said Rob.

"So nice to have a professional Yorkshireman at the table. So enlightening. Any racist jokes you'd like to perform for us, while you're here?"

"Easy now, girls," said Knickers Narida Harrington, arriving with her cup of Mrs. M.'s instant.

"Sefton, go easy on the youngsters, dear. We don't want them so upset they can't teach."

"I'd loike 'Failure is Not an Option.'" This was Liam piping up.

"Or more like 'Success is Not an Option,' the way things are going round here," said Hetty Kiss, sweeping in and sitting down with us.

"Bloody Numeracy Committee I've got to chair tonight."

"Numeracy, Hetty?" said Maurice, incredulous. "But you're the head of fucking Drama!"

"Michael says you don't need to know anything about the subject under discussion to chair the meeting well. It's all about management skills, apparently."

"Fook a kebab," said Rodder, eyes swivelling like an anti-aircraft gun around to his left. He was hung up on the door.

"Bejasus."

"O my Aunt Maisie's hairy fanny!"

"Maurice!" said Hetty looking at the last ejaculator in surprise, but like everyone else he was gaping at the form that had just crossed the threshold.

Fiona had just entered looking like Everyman's idea of the perfect way to die. She had on a perfect black, sleeveless wool dress that clung to her desperately, like a motherless child. If she had a bra on, it really wasn't doing a good enough job. Now, I'm not a one for high heels, but I think among the men I was in the minority judging by the way Liam spilled half his coffee into his trousers and Rodder unintentionally let forth a meaningful groan that was way too loud in this setting. Fiona's legs were indeed a thing of high art in that get up. As she walked down the length of the room towards Ma Manicure and her hatch her hips swayed like a rope bridge in a gentle breeze, rendering every male thence engaged in conversation a useless article. Facially, she'd gone for an understated approach, with a minimal amount of slap, except that her lips had a maroon-coloured layering which made her mouth look like a…well, let's put it like this:

"There is no way a woman looking like that should be allowed to walk around freely in society," said Maurice who had been so uninterested in sexual topics up to this point in the term I would have laid 5 to 1 he'd been professionally neutered by a skilful vet. He ventured further.

"If every workplace had a woman looking like that, the economy would collapse within a month."

And she was nearer 40 than 30 too, which shook me up a bit. Jez was looking eagerly at her too, but in a crushed kind of way.

"Try not to come all at once, boys," said Narida.

I even saw Sef wearing an exceptionally enigmatic expression. I wondered whether this was something beyond his sitting there knowing full well that he was the one responsible for encouraging the futile illusions of the Peggy Lane manhood.

"*Thong!*" went Rodder in the sound of a bell, and it was understood instantly around the table that he had disgraced the whole male gender by being so cheap and transparent, though really we were all guilty and knew it. Coulson shook Jez's water bottle in Rodder's direction, spraying him with Buxford Mill Best Sparkling.

"Hey!" he shouted, springing out of his seat, "ah've got to teach in a minute!"

"I don't think you're fit for anything apart from a long, slow wank," said Coulson.

"Could you be a little more graphic?" said Susan, who was passing, unexpectedly. She hadn't really been seen in the staff room at break time for weeks. I looked up. The staff room clock said, 'five-past-eleven' - fifteen minutes before the end of break. Time for me to leave.

"What the feck is she doing coming into school dressed like that?" said O'Neil-Neil as I got out of my seat. His mouth still drooped open like a busted door.

"What indeed," said Sef, barely able to keep a smirk off his majestically lined face.

*

Fiona Twyford-Sounding walked through the staff room and out to the work room where she picked up her bag and checked her looks in a hand mirror. She went back through to the main staff room and out the door whence she'd made her unintentionally spectacular entry only ninety seconds earlier. By the time forty-three more had elapsed she was standing right outside the Peggy Lane headmaster's door ready to knock. She lifted her right arm to a small patch of wood just under Michael's nameplate, a pair of delicately inlaid silver bracelets sliding back down her forearm to the elbow as she did so. As she hesitated, the door opened at a leisurely speed from the inside. She instinctively dropped her arm. Her stomach fluttered.

"Oh, hello, Fiona." said Jesse Frump, the school secretary.

"Michael's free, if you want him," she said, all greying hair swept up in a tight bun.

"Oh. Thanks."

Jesse smiled through a pursed mouth and left the door a few inches ajar for her. Fiona slipped inside, a long, lingering look from Jesse following her in.

"Hi, come in, Fiona," said Michael, managing to look busy whilst standing still in front of his number one filing cabinet, holding an official-looking white document.

"What can I do for you?"

*

At eight minutes-past-eleven I entered the DT. block through the double doors and turned left into a classroom. Les came walking towards me from the back office holding the most enormous camera I had ever seen. If that was a telephoto lens it was so big that never mind Leipzig, he could point the thing at America and get a good close up of George Bush scratching his arse in the White House.

"Crikey, Les, Michael will see that thing if he so much as glances out of the window. It's a howitzer!"

"What? The 400mm Caforth Super Lensical? They don't make these any more, sonny Jim."

"They don't make the Ford Anglia any more either," I said.

"More's the pity. Don't worry. She won't let me down. I've been using her for twenty-five years since my father fell down a mine shaft and the definition is incredible. And the touch you get on the trigger. It's like handling my own..."

"Les! It's Michael! He's near the window."

Les had already scuttled into action, bending low at the waist and lurking his way to the window. He got there and slowly raised himself until the top five inches of his head loomed dangerously above the parapet.

"Excuse me, sir."

Holy spanners. A kid, a little Year 7 by the looks of her, was at the door and about to come far enough into the room to see past a lathe and find Les looking like a stalker or worse at the window. If I was quick though I could hold her at the threshold where she wouldn't be able to see one of the teachers apparently losing his mind, the room starting narrowly before opening out into a rectangle like an igloo constructed by a conceptual artist. I had to be as bright and breezy as I could. I knew what to do, having seen Sef in action for weeks now with little ones like this little lady intruder.

"Now then, my *petite* halfling, what can I do for you?"

"It's Fiona, sir."

"What!" I almost screamed at her.

"Fiona Bright, that's my name."

"Oh, right. Fiona. Yes, fine, right: what is it you want, then?" I was practically dribbling whilst trying to usher her back into the passageway without touching her. I didn't want a lawsuit on my hands to cap everything.

"I was looking for Mr. Person. I've got my DT homework."

"Oh, is that it?" She was holding a see-through plastic folder, a Polly Pocket, with some pieces of white A4 paper inside and I was holding out my hand. "I can take it for you."

"He said to give it to him myself. It's my project. I've done a lot of work on it in half term."

"Fiona, I promise you. He won't mind. I'm about to see him myself. I'll take it."

"Okay then." And she offered it to me.

"Thanks then, Fiona. Bye."

"Have you hurt your head?" she said.

"Yes, now you better get going; the bell for next lesson will be going any minute and you don't want to be late."

"It looks painful," she said.

"Look, I'll hurt your fucking head in a minute if you don't piss off out of the way," I didn't say, but may have done if she'd pushed me any further. Not that she'd have deserved it though, the little sweetie.

"No, it doesn't, I'm fine. It just looks bad. Thanks for being concerned. Look Fiona, I have to shut this door now, excuse me, won't you?"

"Okay, 'bye," she said, and I shut the door on her and turned back to our very own David Bailey crouched at the window, huge weapon at the ready in his right hand.

*

"Hi. Michael. I've come to see you about the trip to Stratford I want to organize for my sixth form group."

"Oh," said Michael, "Have you? Sounds good. But under the new system you'll have to put your request in writing. Make a copy for me and one for the Chair of Governors. And there are some risk-assessment booklets you'll have to fill in. If you see Jesse, she'll..."

"Oh, is that a photo of your wife?"

She moved smartly, but not too swiftly towards Michael's desk, still in place in its snug position in front of the big office window, as if the most important thing on her mind at that moment was to admire an image of a Grace Peniston superbly captured in the middle of being attacked by a hair-do from the mid-1980s.

"I didn't know you were married, Michael," she said, her voice ascending to the end of the sentence with a teasing tone, now at the desk fingering the frame. She actually was interested in the photo, not just because she'd built this into The Plan, but she really would have liked Michael to explain to her why anybody would choose a style of clothing in, by the look of it, 1999, that made them look like a rejected backing singer from a Spandau Ballet audition.

"Twelve years," he said, reaching a hand out to reclaim the frame. He'd arrived at the window. Fiona gazed into Michael's eyes waiting for a return examination and guessed hard where his hand was about to be to ensure that it made accidental contact with hers.

"Oh, sorry," said Michael and realised that this woman was standing much too close and looking at him as if he were Mr. Darcy in the wet clothes get-up.

"It's okay," said Fiona softly, now holding him with a gaze dripping with lust. She had to squeeze her left eye three-quarters closed from the sunlight that suddenly, but only momentarily, streamed onto her face as she pressed her lips onto his left earlobe before going on to exhale just a touch higher with ravishing slowness.

Peggy Lane's headteacher was unable to move. Fiona thought she heard him swallow very, very hard. Michael tried to say, 'I don't think you should be doing this Mrs. Twyford-Sounding' but all that came out was a mid-to-high pitched squeak, as if he were a mouse that just had its knackers trodden on. 'You're mine,' thought Fiona, now wondering and hoping in equal measure that Les had already got half a dozen snaps of the scene by now. Her prey was so static she had time to glance down at her wristwatch. '11.17-and-a-bit,' it whispered up at her, 'time to finish the job, Fi,' it said, before returning to silence.

And this she did. She shifted him sideways and pressed herself up against him and, tongue first, wiped her mouth slowly across his. He did not demur. Neither did he kiss her back.

'Damn,' she thought, and in the next instant slid her right hand where she thought his penis ought to be. 'Contact,' she said to herself as her open hand closed around a chunk of solid, tubular flesh.

'Rigid just about sums you up,' she thought.

Still the bell didn't go, but Fiona didn't think she should push her luck any further. She let go her hand and four seconds later she was out in the corridor, breathing heavily.

"Everything alright, Fiona?" said Susan Climer, about to do the same as she had three minutes and seven seconds ago, only without knocking.

"Yes. I'm just having a tiny flush, that's all," said Fiona, trying to keep things perfectly smooth. "Time catches up with all us, Susan," she added, finishing the exchange with a forced, truncated laugh, before pushing off down the corridor at a lick. When Susan went in, she found Michael Peniston in a state of confusion in his beautiful Richano reclining chair.

*

The sweat was pouring off me. My watch said fourteen minutes-past-eleven and there was no sign of Fiona in Michael's office. There was only the man himself to the left of the window - we could just about make out his ass, that's all - standing by a cabinet reading a piece of paper. Then Jesse Frump came into view.

"Come on Jesse, get out of the fucking way," I said, on the verge of panic. "And where in the eighth circle of bastard is Fiona?"

"If you can keep your head when everyone else is throwing daisies in the park…" said Les, passing each word out into the air at two miles an hour, staring across at the head's window unblinking, face perfectly immobile until he pushed his glasses frame up above the bridge of his nose with a wrinkle.

"There she is," he said quietly.

"Get ready!"

"I am ready," he said, "Do…not…worry."

Then in a sudden flurry of activity Les stood half-upright, stepping back from the window as he did so and swung Big Bertha, with its two-foot lens, up to his eye. The next instant, the whole contraption went off in a series of rapid *clicks! schrapps!* and *whhrrsss!* that sounded like a flock of swans taking off for Africa in my right ear. I lost count of them. Then as quickly as Les's blur of commotion had begun, it stopped.

"Michael has just burned his budgie," he said quietly but emphatically, dropping below the head's sightline and placing Bertha carefully on the floor by his side. By which I think he meant he'd just captured a portrait of Michael that once seen, he would never forget.

"Right, let's get out of the way," he said, and before I realised what we were doing we began to crawl on our hands and knees to Les's back office, my magnificent *compadre* struggling to keep his pride and joy above the hard floor.

"If someone comes in now and sees this," I said to Les,

"I shall walk out of this school and keep going 'til I hit the airport."

I came here to teach, after all.

31
Tighter Than China
Autumn Term - Week 8 Day 1
Monday, October 28th, 2002
The Moor above Yarrow - Lunchtime

How I got my mind back on to teaching that day I don't know - you'll have to tell me. I don't remember a thing about it. Was I doing Macbeth with my Year 10s? Come to think of it, it may have been Thomas the Tank Engine. The other criminally tough thing was keeping what we'd just done to myself. There were only six of us in the loop: the five players above mentioned and Chris, who sat at home through all of this gnawing at hope. He had a way to go yet but we'd torn the ass out of the sucker, no doubt about that. Whichever way you sliced it, Michael was fucked, butt to the sky, and we'd won. Sure, blackmail was against the law but Sef had convinced me utterly that there was more chance of the moon falling to earth and crushing us all than there was of Michael going to the law. I could see the logic in that too. If he was as ambitious as Sef said he was, then we were as safe as cheese. I looked at the moon that night and it was locked up there as tight as China. It was a thing of peaceful beauty - almost full and shining out of the sky like a gigantic reading light.

We'd agreed to get out of the school at lunchtime to take a look at the situation as it stood, very briefly up on the moor. We staggered our exit at five minute intervals, though quite why, I don't know. The victim either knew what had really just happened to him or he didn't. If Michael knew, he'd have been on to us by now and would have called Les out of his lesson for starters, and no doubt Sefton Demmler. I couldn't see him sitting on the information that one of his staff was taking paparazzi-style close up shots of him exchanging mouthwash with a hot English teacher in his office in school time. I think I knew enough about him to know he'd have frothed at the mouth like a cappuccino machine and gone steaming out of his office for instant revenge. So I figured I'd know we were in the clear if Les showed up straight after the bell.

As soon as I could dismiss my class, I headed for the car park, trying to control my body movements: I felt like I'd been connected to a badly wired toaster: my backbone felt like rubber and my head like it was in space. In the rush of adrenalin my girl problems seemed like they were happening to someone else and suddenly trivial.

Les was already in his car - an old red Volvo estate - waiting for me and we set off, negotiating our way carefully out of the school as gangs of kids headed down town for lunch. They weren't watching us as we slowly tooled down Moor Lane. Out of a bunch of tall-looking uniforms I saw my old pal Adam Taylor with his mates, laughing and throwing berries at a parked car. Within three minutes we were on the top of the moor pulling over into a lay-by custom-made for cars and campers to ogle at the view. We couldn't see a thing. The fog of November always hit Yarrow early in the year and though it was clear in town we were in the clouds up here.

We were the first out of school so we had a little waiting to do before the unmistakable sight of Sef's light blue sports greeted us, droning quietly up the hill to the pull-in looking like something from the age of Harold Wilson. When he turned in, we got out. It was cold up there. With Sef were both Fiona and Jez, who was doubled up in the back with hardly room to breathe. After looking around us in case police cars and vans were roaring up the hill to call us to account, we all came together in a mood of laughter and celebration. Jez punched the air with both fists and said,

"Yess!" as she walked towards Les and me. Les was grinning at Sef, who walked across to him nodding his head almost imperceptibly, but he was doing it repeatedly, as if to say 'great job, feller.' He didn't say anything at all though - not at first. His face was like reading difficult poetry. He looked exultant, but also as if he were about to break.

"Yew flippin' stah!" Jez said to Les, and went up and hugged him.

As soon as we'd formed ourselves into a ring he began to talk us through the coup: how he'd struggled to hold it together for nearly fifteen minutes at break time hiding in the back room, praying that no one would come looking for him.

"We should have locked the door, really, and given Tim a knock code," he said fretting.

"Don't worry, don't worry," said Sef, "it's done, it's done. You got it, didn't you…"

"Oh, yes, I've got it. It was like eating fudge, but I managed it."

I wasn't sure whether he was trying to be lucid and failing or trying to crack a funny. I was grinning anyway. That Les.

"Where's the camera?" said Fiona, face like stone as usual, cuddling herself because of the cold. She'd changed out of the dress. She was all in black: thick sweater that looked like designer cashmere; trousers that also must have set her back about a hundred quid and smooth suede on her feet.

"In the back of my car."

"You'd better move it, hadn't you?"

"Don't worry, I'll finish the film at home and process it tonight. I'm not going to let it out of my sight."

I began to see Les in a new light. It was hard to imagine him being this serious and this organized but he had a look in his eyes like steel. And according to Sef he was one hell of a photographer. I thought about what I was doing here. What did I owe Chris Lampeter? Nothing. I suppose I'd just followed Sef blindly, though I thought I knew Chris was a good guy the first time I saw him in the pub on my first day. I still knew I was mad to be doing this, putting my career in jeopardy before it had begun. I looked around at these people: one bald, ageing man who could still turn out to be a false prophet; a geek in thick glasses; a glamour puss who was wasting herself in the classroom and a young English teacher who had no more of an idea how to run her life than I did. It dawned on me that I didn't really know any of them. A chill went through me.

"Come on, Sef, take me back, I'm cold," said Fiona. And she was due to get into her car and make herself scarce for a few days with a mystery illness, a move distinctly lacking in professionalism, but a tactical necessity in Sef's view and hers.

"So is it you, Sef, who's going to take the evidence to Michael?" I wanted to check that the next stage of the operation was unchanged.

"Are you going to take a witness?" Les wanted to know.

"I'm not sure yet. Maybe. Just give me a package of prints in the morning. I'll go and see him at some stage tomorrow."

"You can have them tonight, if you like. I'll be finished by, ooh, ten o'clock, roughly."

"No, it's okay. Take them across to your room first thing; I'll come over and get them as soon as I get in."

Sef was never in school early.

"Fiona," said Les, shyly or sheepishly, possibly both, "can I say this? I don't know how you did it, but you were absolutely fantastic. Chris is going to owe you for the rest of his life."

I was moved. So was Jez. Her eyes began to glisten in the mist unless I was mistakenly sentimental. It was the tender way Les said it. Fiona looked at the speaker and the studious composure of her face suddenly cracked wide open into a glorious smile. It was gone in a flash, though, put back in its box until the next rare occasion it demanded some air, but in that tiny, yet huge moment, it was abundantly clear to me that here was another soul full of pain. Sef doubtless knew its cause; and it probably connected up with her motivation for becoming involved in The Plan in some way or other. The thought calmed my fear - that in the end I had to trust these people and was right to. And if the whole thing fell to pieces, what the hell: there were other jobs out there and other places to go. When it all shook out – however the pieces fell back to earth - we'd all find a way of earning a living one way or another.

So we got in our cars to go back to what we were paid to do for the time being at least, feeling that with just a smidge of luck, and Sefton Demmler in control of the final scene, the last act of this crazy melodrama would soon be played out on the Peggy Lane stage and we could all take a deep breath and move on.

32

Job Done
Autumn Term - Week 8 Day 2
Tuesday, October 29th, 2002
Peggy Lane DT Block Rm 1 - Morning

The photographs were perfect. Les had more than proved his worth. Four of the ten colour stills framed Michael Peniston and his lover beautifully, excitingly, their mouths embracing in a moist-looking kiss. Undeniable. Indelible. In stills one and two, Michael's face expressed neither surprise nor discomfiture. By the sixth it was clear he'd been given something to think about and by the tenth he looked like he was ready to get stuck in, though he never quite did. The highest paid defence lawyer in the land would have been unable to pluck his wriggling client from the hook, though, unless they could prove that he and Fiona had been rehearsing for the Yarrow Players' autumn reading of *Sex in the Headmaster's Study* by Rory Lewd. And then explain why break time on a full working day was an appropriate time to iron out that wrinkle in the third act.

"There's something about the way he's tilting his head," said Les Person as he and Sefton Demmler carefully handled the evidence in the former's back cupboard.

"He wants it...here," he said, handing full possession of the bomb over to his colleague. He was neglecting his drink. Steam spiralled temptingly into the dusty atmosphere from a squat turquoise mug of hot tea, as he drew it to his mouth for a first sip.

Les fair enjoyed his morning cuppa - two sugars, dash of full cream milk - getting him started, helping him to prepare mentally and physically for the day ahead. Same time each morning, about half-past-eight, regular as. Les could hardly tear his eyes away from his recent artistic endeavour as he went "*slurp*" and sucked in the first draw to the back of his throat.

'Lovely,' said his bright beady eyes.

In terms of photography this Tuesday morning, "hmm," was all Sefton wanted to say at first, but after another half-minute's careful perusal, he added,

"Lesley, Lesley, Lesley, you have nailed the parrot to the perch."

"To nail the parrot to the perch, you first have to place the nun on the emperor's shoulders."

"I couldn't agree more, my friend. There's no catching the wasp until you've spun the teacup on the edge of the mud flap."

"Absolutely right."

Still they stared and studied.

"You have to admire Fiona..." said Les.

"She looks there like five feet six inches of pure walking, talking rear-entry..."

"A nicely measured sentence, Timothy."

"Oh, sorry." I felt my face go *zap* with a sudden blush. It felt like I was betraying her.

"No, you're right," said Sef. "I doubt that Michael will ever recover. However, that is not our concern. At least, it isn't mine."

"When are you going to present him with these?"

"I was going to do it sometime today..."

"Have you worked out exactly what you're going to say?"

"I think so, but unfortunately we have to wait. I've just been in the office. He's out all day assisting a course for prospective heads."

"God help us all," said Les.

"He may call back at about four, but he may not."

"That's us on tenterhooks all day. Is he in tomorrow?"

"Yes, in all day."

"Does that give us enough time before the hearing, do you think?" said me.

"Oh yes. I would hazard a guess that even if we failed to bring these marvellous images to his attention until half an hour before Friday's meeting, we would still save our man. Precision wants him out but we know what kind of fucker we're dealing with here, do we not."

"When the lemon hits the tugboat..."

"...he'll automatically support an idea or policy of the head of Peggy Lane, whether it's Michael Peniston or a plastic blow-up simulacrum of Kylie What's-Her-Face replete with velvet vagina."

"But he won't be able to," said Les. I was getting lost.

"You mean...but..."

"Timothy-*rrb*," said Les, taking another mouthful of tea. "The Chair of Governors normally does what the Head tells him to, give or take. But he's going to want to sweep this whole thing under the sugar bowl when he sees these."

"If I have the measure of the man, he will no more want a public scandal than he would want a caravan holiday in Skegness," said Sef looking at me somewhat like one of his pupils. I did still feel dumb sometimes.

"So when he learns that we're prepared to send them to *The Yorkshire Excreter*, *The Turd* and Michael's wife..." I got it.

"Here, take them, Sef," said Les as if he was handling chemical weapons.

"Okay."

"And take this."

"You don't want to keep it?" Les passed a small black canister containing the negatives to an open hand.

"I have enough trouble keeping all my stuff in order as it is. Matty's putting pressure on me to have a complete clear out of the office. Tonight might be the night when he goes berserk throwing things away. No, you have it. It'll be safe enough won't it?"

"Oh, I think so. Okay, then…Have you made copies?"

"Give me a chance, your honour. I didn't finish these until nearly half-past-one this morning."

"Lesley…" There was a doubt in Sef's tone of voice I hadn't heard before. We needed copies. "Listen: you keep the photographs. And the negatives. Make another set of copies tonight, if you will, and keep them safe. Bring the negs and one set of prints in again tomorrow morning."

"Sure?"

"I don't think we want to risk leaving these lying around today for someone to walk off with. I would much rather we do exactly again tomorrow morning what we'd planned for this morning. Then I'll go straight into Michael. If my form doesn't get registered it won't be the end of the world."

"If you're form don't get registered it'll be the end of Michael's."

Sefton raised his right eyebrow toward the ceiling and trained the eye underneath on his friend. The ascending curl of his mouth at each end revealed his approval of the remark.

Les slid the photographs back inside the envelope with great care, and popped the small, neatly formed canister in there with them.

"I'm going to keep them in the car. I don't like the thought of having them anywhere in school."

"Whatever you think. Lesley," said Sef, placing a right hand on Les Person's shoulder.

"You are an oyster among pearls."

Lesley smiled. And you could see how much he loved Sef. How could anyone not? The answer was, for me, you couldn't. Unless you were one of life's natural born tossers. Les P., package in hand, left his back cupboard where he kept a desk and a filing cabinet, then walked down through the classroom and out of the building to the tiny adjacent car park. He clicked open the boot of his Volvo Estate and placed the buff envelope on the right-front part of the boot carpet. Then he shut it carefully again with a satisfying *thunk!*, locked all five doors, and went off to fetch his register from the Year 8 office. He whistled a tune based on a confused double remembrance from his record collection that should have sounded like a cross between *Go West* by the Pet Shop Boys and *Under My Wheels* by Alice Cooper. However, it came out sounding remarkably like the twelfth minute of Ginger Baker's drum solo, *Toad* (studio version).

"Morning, sir," said Trammel Tater from Les's Year 11 GCSE group, meeting Les Person at the near end of corridor A.

"The lark is on the wing, Trammel, and the Spurs are in mid-table once again."

"I support Leeds, sir."

"That's entirely your fault," said Les.

33

Losers
Autumn Term - Week 8 Day 3
Wednesday, October 30th, 2002
Peggy Lane Staff Room and Room 2 Corridor B - Morning

On Wednesday morning the Peggy Lane staff waited with tired resignation for Michael's briefing while it poured in buckets outside. Charles Dejong, that spruce and ever-inspired Maths teacher, saw fit to allow himself a cavernous yawn, while Boris Fairbanks, second in the Drama department, had bags under his eyes the size of tobacco pouches, suggesting that preparations for the Christmas production of *Some Like It Like This* weren't going to par. Others stared ahead at rain splashing down windows, or at notice-covered walls, contemplating the day ahead or considering their lives. Many sat with stiff, tired faces or collapsed troubled ones.

"It's that time of year," said Maurice as we got ready to receive. But that was only part of the deal. A few dozen of us inhabited pools of school anxiety, but a smaller group of piteous wretches carried a heavy load brought in from home. There were unhappy marriages, a pending separation and two impending parental deaths. Nathan Byas (History) was chronically upset by Leeds' home form. Eight were desperate for love, or at the very least, sex, and two had just registered with internet dating services in a sterling effort to get it on the quick side. Jamie Nice (Music) was agonizing over an audition for Singing Idol and three were hitting the anti-depressants hard because of surplus flab.

A terrible state of affairs all this, I hope you'll agree. And that was just the men, ha-ha. But we're not stopping there. Mura Fleece-Ravings (Art) scratched nervously at her hand bringing blood to the surface because her oldest daughter had a Chinese boyfriend. Jane Fairey (RE) had an as yet unexplored breast lump, while a colleague (Glynis Mapp – Geography) who'd just rushed off to the office to take a phone call suffered from the constant terror of one day getting one. A middle-aged PE teacher (desperate to remain anon.) had serious erection problems and wondered whether Pelé had the answer. Another three just had erection problems. As for the numbers of both sexes who had a dubious relationship with the bottle, well, we'd be better off not going there.

Every teacher at Peggy Lane had worries, coming in a myriad of shapes, sizes and textures, but in the every day world of the classroom teacher, you just didn't see them. Eight weeks into the school year, I had only had conversations with about fifteen per cent of my colleagues and none of them groused about their problems apart from tiredness, but we all moaned about that.

I loved sitting at our table. I looked at the here-assembled. Rob Rodder, whose only problem seemed to be the recurring one of deciding each night out which eager young bitch to brush off and which one to take home, produced a likely winner of the *Pegs Outstanding Yawn of the Day* award. Maurice Butter immediately followed suit, threatened by the loss of oxygen. Knickers Narida dropped an unsheathed marker pen on her skirt.

"*Fuck!*" she said, emphatically, "I just washed it."

Alex Carfman, not normally one of us, looked up momentarily from his paper then went back to an article about Prince Chuck complaining about the declining quality of writing paper in Britain. Then the staff room door was pushed open at speed and through it bounded a fit young Labrador with eyes like comedy and a fresh pink tongue lolling out of his mouth ready to lick you like an ice cream. In reality it was our headteacher, Michael Peniston. Joyful he was, this October morning.

"Morning everyone!" he said, face now beaming like a pair of Muttler Top Group Radium Headlamps, his skin glowing as if he'd just come from a four-hundred dollar massage. His audience, almost to a chalk-face operator, felt like groaning back at him. Those carrying clogged up, nose-red colds just about did.

"Here are the Wednesday notices. Notice One. I'm proud to announce that Jessica Planet has just been selected for the England Under-15 swimming team and goes to Prague next week for her first international competition."

He paused for his staff to register their pleasure and pride at this wonderful accolade for The Peregrine Lane Grammar School. Three did so vocally. "Well done!" said Molly Factor, yelping with suppressed lust. At the thought of Michael, it should be stressed, not Jessica.

"Wonderful to see her life moving forward like that...and would Jessica's teachers please organize some work for her to do on the trip. You should pass it to her form tutor, who I think is...thank you, Dainty....Dainty McFormage. Notice Two. The New Vision Committee meets tonight in C4 at 3.40.pm, tea and biscuits provided as per usual. The Motto Sub-Committee..."

I was bedding right in at the school now quite nicely. I knew this not just because of the comfort I found in sitting with my new friends in the staff room, but how sick I was of picking up on Molly's thinly disguised 'fuck me, Michael' interventions in all these tedious meetings. And she was about as attractive as a rusty calculator.

"..Notice Seven. I ought just to warn you that if I'm not in school tomorrow it's because I'll be at Leeds Infirmary after a heart attack."

He left a stage pause so we could all enjoy the joke. Molly and a couple of others cooed and giggled, but the rest remained totally out of sync with the level of comic energy being put out from the podium.

"This afternoon I shall be taking the Y10 soccer team for their National Trophy Third Round match with Darkside High School..."

"Soccer?" said Rob at the level of a murmur but not disguising his disgust. "It's not fookin' soccer, it's *football*."

Michael's linguistic quirk was also noticed by Colin Nostrum, another Elland Road season ticket holder, who briefly considered its sociological implications before becoming lost in a reverie of analysis as he reminded himself of the cardinal factors in the development of league football in the industrial northwest and midlands in the late 19th century.

"...because their normal teacher, Bob Coulson, is still off with shingles..."

"What a fookin' Nigel," said Rob, again low in decibels, who didn't like Bobby the C.. "I bet he's in town doin' 'is Christmas shoppin'."

"...And as I haven't refereed a game for a number of years, I'm a little worried, ha-ha."

"Nice work if you can get it," said Rob, who had more on his mind than a featherweight intellect this day. Probably worrying about the world's supply of condoms running out. Next to me, someone was in a state of poisonously intense amusement at Michael's gratuitous self-confidence.

"There speaks one who's never refereed a game of football," whispered Mr. Nostrum carefully.

"...that is if it stops raining. Perhaps that'll save me. Finally, Ofsted: I'm expecting the inspection date to arrive on my desk any day now..."

I'd looked for Sef, Jez and Les as soon as I came into the staff room, but none of them were there then. Jez came in halfway through Notice Six and was immediately engaged in trying to attract Susan's attention up the front next to Michael with a mimed apology. I thought for a long minute that Sef was absent too, but he was here – I just couldn't see him until Notice Ten because Nostrum's huge head blocked what normally would have been a clear view a couple of tables away. Les definitely wasn't there. When I did finally clap eyes on Sef, I could see straight away that something wasn't right; his eyes, though still blue, were far away and glazed, like fine Wedgwood. Jez wasn't listening to Michael either, as he completed his formal announcement of the meetings, directives and urgings he thought needed our attention that day. When she'd finished gazing out of the window towards the Conference Hotel across the road and finally reacted to me making faces at her like Lee Evans, she just looked at me and shook her head.

"Okay, that's it: good teaching, everyone!"

Michael had recently got into the habit of ending briefings with his little message of hope for us, as if he'd just discovered the first series of *Hill Street Blues*.

"Thunderbirds are Go," said Rob.

"Let's do it, Comrades, f-huh-huh," said Andy Crucial, punching the air.

I stood and let those around me troop off to registration, and looked down at Sef whose eyes simply stared out at a fixed point somewhere in the future.

A hand on my arm. Jez.

"Coom outside and I'll brek it to yer."

She should have been striding purposefully off to her squad of halflings, while I was about to speed my way to the Year 9 office to ask Alana whether any staff absences needed plugging. But I followed Jez to a kink in the corridor by the library, a gulf of horror opening at speed in the depths behind my diaphragm.

"It's all gone wrong."

"What!" She was wrong; the plan was foolproof.

"Les 'ad his car stolen last night."

"Not..."

She nodded gravely. "The envelope was in the boot."

"But the negatives must be..."

"They were in t'envelope."

"You have to be kidding," I said without the least hope. "The stupid, stupid man. Why didn't he take them out of..."

"No, no, noah, you've gorrit wrong: Les didn't even make it 'ome. He left work at about half-four and stopped to get petrol..."

"Where?"

"That one on the A65 in town. Filled 'is tank, went to pay for 'is petrol, then when he came owt, a couple a blokes had fiddled with the wires, started oop 'is car and driven off. He forgot to lock it."

"So much for the eyes of steel." My voice trailed away to nothing before I finished the sentence.

"What?"

"Doesn't matter...why didn't you ring me last night to tell me?" I wasn't really annoyed at the idea of being excluded; it was just something to say to try to mask the God-awfulness.

"I didn't know until fifteen minutes ago meself. Sef didn't know until Les rang 'im at seven. He 'asn't bin ter sleep; 'ee's bin waitin' for the cops to ring and tell 'im they've found the car. But they 'aven't."

"Shitting, bloody bollocks."

"*Shush!*" hissed Jez at me. Staff and students flowed past towards registration in ever thicker numbers.

"Ah noah. Lewk: got to goah. Oh! Forgot. We're meetin' at your place at loonchtime. Be in the car park as soon as you can. Sef's car."

She rushed off to 7VD, who'd fallen in love with their Miss Treat in the first week of term and fretted when she was seconds late for the register. I now had to try to get through the morning somehow. I started with my nice Year 10s and decided to set them an essay on *Macbeth*. We'd been working on the role of Lady Macbeth in the first part of the play last lesson, so I set them a piece of writing on her character, posting the title up on the whiteboard with a black marker in my scrawny writing.

"Sir, you never told us we were going to do this last lesson." This was Rich Baffle, whining again.

"What's your problem, Rich?" I said, wearily.

"I hate writing essays."

"Don't worry, Rich, you'll do a great job, I'm sure."

"I doubt it."

I half dead-eyed him to let him know I thought he might be trying to cheek me, so he'd better be careful.

"Did you understand what we were doing last time about Mrs. Cawdor, Richard?"

"It's Rich, sir. I y'ate 'Richard.'"

"Sorry. Rich?"

"Yes sir, a raight nasty piece of work; 'the nipple and boney gums' and all that stuff."

"'*boneless gums...and dash'd the brains out, had I so sworn as you have done to this.*' You've got it, good. Okay, then. You'll be fine. Find page 32, everyone: act one, scene two is her first scene, remember. And don't forget: plenty of quotations from the text, now."

They were wonderful. They were all dutifully writing the title down in their exercise books without a peep apart from those who'd already done it and were leafing through their paperback copy of the play to find the relevant Lady Macbeth bits.

But I'd have been better off not setting up a cop out lesson, because for the next twenty-five minutes I sat at my desk trying to do a little marking while I was thinking, and ended up doing nothing but worrying myself sick. What were we going to do now if that car didn't come back? Guiltily, I thought far more about Sef than I did about Chris. The thought of life without him was unbearable, especially as I'd only just found him. Somehow it didn't seem possible that if Chris got the sack, he'd hang around at Peggy Lane. He'd be gone. I knew that.

He came in through my door at the halfway point in the lesson. I always sparked up like an engine plug when he visited me and I did now. I believed in his miracles, I guess. Sobrione Balkan looked up from her page,

"Hello, Mr. Demmler."

"Hello, Sobrione. How are the adjectives?"

"Sparkling, sir," she replied. An in-joke, I observed, envious as usual for this sort of intimacy with my own students.

"Good," said Sef, managing a weak, January afternoon smile, though it was still just October, and morning.

"Outside," said Sef, to me, and we went out to the corridor. I closed the door behind me, quietly.

"Les has just been in to tell me that they haven't found the car. You know what I'm talking about?"

I nodded.

"Have you got a plan?" I said.

"No. Not yet. But there's still time. The hearing's not until Friday night."

"But…"

"But this: if I have those photographs in my hand just five minutes - two minutes before the meeting and Michael right in front of me, it changes everything."

"But what if we can't get them? What if they don't find the car?"

"There's nothing we can do but wait."

"But…"

"Before I forget: we're meeting at your house after school. If that's alright…"

"Okay, no problem." I flapped through the pages of morning memory for information on the state of the place but still managed to feel honoured at the same time.

"Back car park, twenty-to-four."

Lesson two I had my Year 8 class. Similes.

A year and a half-term down the line and they're halflings no longer, really. Some are shooting up like sunflowers, while on one or two others, spots are already sprouting on faces like an outbreak of tropical disease. They're a bit more boisterous in the line outside, and noisier coming in. I still hadn't tamed this lot yet.

"Okay. Who can remember what a simile is from last year?"

A hand in the air.

"Yes, Dominic."

"It's when something's similar to something."

"Not bad, Dominic, not bad. Can you give me an example?"

"Erm, when an apple is like a washing machine."
"Nope, you haven't quite got it."
Another hand.
"Naomi?"
"A simile is when you compare two things to make your point. Like 'as nasty as a nasty person.'"
Most of the class laughed, but nicely.
"That's not a good example," she battled, "erm, erm, 'as nasty as a witch.' Or something like that."
"Good, Naomi, you've got it." I scrawled her example up on the board quickly. "Another example would be, 'as nasty as an English teacher.'"
Half a dozen of them laughed at this, feeble though it was. I tried again.
"Or, 'as nasty as a headmaster,'" which wasn't much better, but it seemed to strike a chord.
"He's a prat," said George Portion, setting off a lot of giggling from the back.
"Hey! Easy, George, we can't have that."
"He is though, sir. He told me I ought to lose weight, sir."
I looked at George. He was indeed as fat as an overstuffed cushion, only it wasn't so much his fault as his mother's; she'd already been in to see me about her little Georgie-Porgie for giving him too much homework. 'As overweight as a groaning galleon, bursting with bullion.' Pity I couldn't slam that lot up on the board.
"Well, George…"
"Fat bastard."
"Who was that?" I barked, well- annoyed.
Silence, then answers.
"It was Stockport, sir."
"No, it was Jiffy, sir" and I then had to spend the next thirty-five seconds shutting the back corner boys up. There was nothing they loved more than winding each other up. Eventually there was order again, with Stockport seeing me at break.
"Sir…" said Thomas Prime.
"Thomas?"
"You know the headmaster?"
"Yes…"
"Does 'is wife work at the school, sir?"
"No," I said, "why do you say that?"
"I saw him 'olding 'ands with a teacher in his office, sir."
I looked at Thomas inquisitively, leaving him in no doubt that I wanted an

answer.

"Our tennis ball went over the roof and landed in his bushes. Bibble went to get it and saw him through the window, sir."

I wasn't sure I should be letting this go on, but it was far too interesting to shush up. I just made a stern face as if I thought it was probably lies.

"Holding hands with Miss Cleaner, sir."

"There isn't a Miss Cleaner, Thomas."

"Miss Climer."

I looked over at the speaker. Francesca. Immaculate, middle class and sweet. Certainly no liar.

"Francesca?"

"He means Mrs. Climer, sir. I was there when James Bibble was telling everyone. 'The English teacher in the suit,' he said. Isn't that..?"

"Okay, that's enough. Let's get back to similes."

As fanciful as a trip to Jupiter. As far-fetched as a Hollywood script. A lie as big as George Portion's appetite for junk food. The lesson passed. Break arrived and then I was free, period three. I sat in the marking room and tried to get some work done but it was impossible to concentrate. I went for a walk. Along B corridor a halfling was walking towards me. Several sniffles and a pair of red-rimmed eyes told me he'd been crying.

"What's the matter, little one?" I said.

"It's me bag, sir. I've lost it. Me mum's gonna kill me."

"Hang on. Where did you have it last?"

"In the PE block. I've just been down there but I can't get in."

"No, it'll be locked. Go at the start of lunchtime; it'll be open then."

"Can't, sir"

"Why not?"

"I'm going to the dentists, sir. I'm going now - I won't be back in school until tomorrow."

"What make was the bag?"

"Lingo, sir."

"Ooh, nice. What colour was it?"

"Black, sir." That was a big help. The kids' sports bags all seemed to be black these days. "But it has a Leeds United badge on it, sir, and my name on a white sticker."

"What's your name?"

"Saviour, sir, James Saviour."

"Okay, James. Look, try not to worry about it too much. It'll turn up, they always do."

"Do they, sir?" he said, trustful little eyes looking up at me as if I was a cross between Florence Nightingale and his favourite TV presenter.

"'Course they do. You go off to the dentist. Is your mum coming for you?"

"Grandad, sir."

"Okay, then. Tell you what. I'll have a look for you later on. A good look. And if I find it I'll pass it on to your form tutor. Who is it?"

"Miss Wellbrowser, sir."

"Okay. Right. Off you go."

I didn't have anything particular to do, so I strolled over to the PE block via the corridors, as it was still coming down like a scene from Blade Runner outside, and tried to find Tom Reaks, the caretaker, or his assistant Alf. Their office was just to the side of the changing rooms, but no one answered when I knocked, though the inside light was on. Maybe I'd go back later for poor little James. From there I went to the library where *The Morning Marauder*, my favourite newspaper, was delivered every day. They also had *Rock And Roll Mouthwash*, the legendary music magazine which covered the 60s and 70s.

So I buried myself away quietly for forty-five minutes, with the humming breath of a nearby computer and the narcoleptic drone of nearby Alex Carfman in the semi-partitioned library classroom for company. At lunchtime, we were in the staff room as usual. I wanted to tell Andy, Colin and Liam, though not Rob, badly, about the crisis, because they may have been able to offer us an idea or two. It felt now as though between us we just didn't have enough know-how or enough strength to beat this thing. I'd racked my brains but I could think of nothing, short of gaining time by burning down the school or shooting Peter Precision in the back of the leg on his way to the meeting with an air rifle. Trouble was, I was back at our original meeting: I didn't want to go to prison and I didn't have an air rifle anyway.

Then Sef poked his head round the door and beckoned me with an eyebrow. Les was out there in the corridor too with a face like an ashtray. I didn't bother asking them whether they were supposed to be in a classroom. If they'd gone AWOL for a few minutes, the world wouldn't stop. We walked out the front door into the rain, then round to the back of the main building to Sef's car. I crammed myself into the back.

"They found the car."

"Great!"

"In Darlington. Joy riders." But there was no joy, not even relief, in their voices.

"They dumped it outside a factory and set fire to it."

"But the boot?" I said.

"Burnt to buggery. Nothing left."

"The photos..." I said.

"They're gone," said Les, sounding plain beat.

"That's it, then."

"There's still time to think of something," said Sef.

I didn't need to say, 'so you haven't thought of anything?' If they had, they'd be telling me.

I'd seen the actor Michael Caine on television once being asked about his philosophy of life. 'When anything bad happens to me,' he said, 'I always try to take something good out of it. And there's always something you can learn from even the bad things, whatever it is that's happened to you.' I thought about that now and for me it was obvious. There was nothing to learn from this at all. Apart from the plain bleeding obvious: that horrible, wet, brown stuff happens to all of us. And in the end, all you could do was take it and hope it didn't kill you.

34

A Marriage Of Convenience
Autumn Term - Week 8 Day 3
Wednesday, October 30th, 2002
Peggy Lane Playing Fields - Afternoon

By three o'clock the rain had almost stopped. Michael had been worried that he'd have to call the game off but was assured by Andy Chap in the dinner hall that the Peggy Lane pitches drained "like spaghetti, boss;" so with the drizzle easing off through the early afternoon, he'd worked through some admin for the DfES knowing that his day was fairly certain to end in sports gear and a healthy run around Football Pitch 1.

He was looking forward to refereeing this game and then again he wasn't. He was a pretty good footballer was Michael: in his young days he'd played for the school team and loved it. 'A skilful centre-back who isn't afraid to tackle,' ran the line in the school magazine when he was 14. Trouble was, as he moved inexorably through his teens he was slow to put on height so he was more regularly bested by tall, bustling young strikers who knew how to throw their bony weight about. He lost his place in Townery Hill's team in the fifth form but wasn't too disappointed. He still had his interest in model aeroplanes and cycling, and he was now able to throw himself even more energetically into his studies to ensure that he would make a success of himself there. At 17, his major ambitions had nothing to do with sport. But he'd played again at University - just second team stuff - and he'd always intended to play for a club when he started work, but what with one thing and another, he'd never got round to it.

Neither had he ever been a school team manager during his teaching career. During the days of his first professional flowering, the schools he worked in only wanted PE specialists to take teams, then later, when the opportunity was there, he had already taken to concentrating so hard upon shinning his way up the greasy pole there didn't seem to be time for this sort of extra-curricular activity. Junior Maths Club? Yes; Saturday mornings running around blowing a whistle and getting rained on? No. But with Bobby Coulson's unfortunate shingles coming on top of his own ejection of Lampeter from the role of coach to the school's football pride and joy, the Under-15s, here he was, Mr. Johnny on the Spot. Messrs Chap and Tracker were taking rugby teams over to a school in Keighley that afternoon, and the remaining candidate for the task, Mick Trance, was away on a head of department training course in Manchester, so Michael was actually doing the department something of a favour. In such a crucial game, Andy Chap did not want the refereeing of such a game to be handed over to Darkside's notorious Robin Tracker. Though always terribly pressed, Michael was actually too happy to oblige his lower-lying colleagues. If there was one thing he couldn't resist it was the opportunity to prove himself as a manager. We're not just talking about the noble game here - any form of management. He was Chairman of the Wine Society in his village and treasurer of the Carnival Committee, or was, until he resigned last summer soon after achieving his elevation to his first headship. If asked to take up a post of responsibility, any post, he normally found it impossible to refuse. After all, if he didn't accept the challenge, who would the relevant organization find that even came close to having the ability and experience Michael Peniston could bring to the situation? So naturally, when Andy Chap came to see him on the first morning of the half term to myther him about having no one to take the under-15s that week, Michael had offered before Andy knew he'd finished moaning.

Things were going so well for the Peggy Lane headteacher at this point in time thanks to his talent, acumen and dedication, he felt he could afford a little school-based recreation. So, at 2.50.pm on the nose he strode down to the PE staff changing room with an even stronger tang of anticipation in his mouth than usual for his main afternoon task. There was only one thing niggling him as he gathered the red and gold shirts around him for his team talk outside the changing room ten minutes later; one teensy little thing...

"Have you ever refereed before, sir?"

Nicky Crimms, who wasn't averse to winding up a teacher or two himself, drew his breath in sharply when he heard Blue Mole's question. This wasn't Mrs. Kiss or Ms. Mapp here, or even Mr. Tick, the Maths buffoon who everyone tore to pieces as regularly as Yarrow market day. This was The Head. Michael, immaculate in expensive leisure clothing: navy Dragonage drill top; Run Hills track pants and a pair of Dragonage Interceptor Specials on his feet, stared extremely hard at his inquisitor.

"And your name is?"

"Blue Mole."

"Sir."

"Blue Mole, sir. Sir."

Michael stared at Blue even harder as he bounced the white leather ball he'd been flipping over and over in his hands on the concrete floor under the changing block canopy where he and the team stood sheltering from the rain while they still could. The Darkside boys had already trotted across to the pitch forty green metres away where white nets and corner flags billowed tantalisingly in the breeze.

"Don't do that, sir, you'll damage the leather, sir," said Tyke Triff.

Before he could react again, Michael said,

"Oh, sorry," remembering that indeed, you didn't use a leather football on a hard floor for this very reason. He flicked off a look of disapproval at Blue Mole anyway to assert some authority then got down to the business he wanted to conduct: Item 24 in his Tuesday night list of jobs for the next day: Team Talk.

"Alright then. This game..." He bounced the ball on the floor again forgetting himself then clutched the ball to his chest as if it were a threatened baby, to show the boys that he wouldn't do it again.

"You know your positions, yes?"

No response.

"Yes?" said the Head, more loudly, pushing his head forward from the neck at the team like a bossy chicken. There were a few quiet 'yeahs,' a couple of grunts and a nod from Scotty Mint as he fiddled with his shorts.

"Okay. Team talk - usual formation: what do you play?"

"4-4-2," replied skipper Crimms immediately, arms tightly folded with resentment.

"Okay, we'll see how that goes."

Skipper Nick looked at a couple of team mates with an expression that said, 'You'll see how it goes? We always play 4-4-2 and we always win. What a prat.' Nicky began to worry. What if the Head started tinkering? He looked at Jamie Spooner, the team's ace goalscorer, for a reaction to compare against his own, but he was busy admiring his boots and checking them for flecks of dirt. Whatever the conditions, and they would probably be filthy today what with all the rain, he insisted on leaving the dressing room with perfect boots. It irritated Nicky, but he had to admit, Jamie was a fantastic finisher.

"Now I want you to give it your best. I know you're used to winning but never underestimate your opponent. No complacency." He stopped at this point to look at his charges - he wasn't quite sure they all knew the meaning of this word. He was none the wiser when he'd finished his brief facial expression-survey either. It irked him also that they didn't seem to be paying him the sort of attention he was used to receiving from the pupils and staff at Peggy Lane. The irk quickly sped to outright annoyance. If they're being sullen with him because they'd lost their precious coach then he'd have to prove who was boss - prove too that now Lampeter was gone they'd have to learn to play without him. He continued, making sure he was firm; that there was pure steel in his voice.

"Tackle hard, be first to the ball. Okay? Keep it tight at the back. Mark tightly at corners."

'Huh,' thought Lip Doosen, 'if he'd bothered to come and see one of our games he'd know that we hardly ever concede a corner, never mind let a team score from one.'

"Now in these conditions, the ball's going to stick. So get it forward quickly; no fancy stuff."

You could have collected the silence and put it in a box. Mr. Lampeter had always, *always*, even when they were tiny boys in oversized school kit that made them all look as though they were shrinking, trained them to be a passing side. The team may not have been overstuffed with kids from the top English and Maths sets but to a spotty pubescent they knew it was their ability to find each other with the ball on the floor that made them a great team 'at this level,' as top TV pundit Gary Cripes might have said. So when they heard Michael's instructions, they stared into their boots or looked over at the pitch with a mixture of disgust and longing and waited for his blether to stop.

'Miserable lot for such a successful team,' Michael thought.

"And when you get a chance to shoot," he now pronounced firmly, "shoot! And whatever the scenario, even if we go a goal down, keep going! Above all, keep playing to the end!"

With this emphatic finish, he felt sure he'd made a good start with the lads. 'A good team talk,' he thought to himself. 'Professional. Sensible. Intelligent.' It suddenly occurred to him that he may have found another excellently useful acronym: 'PSI. Yes, I could use that; it's so smooth and neat.'

'What a pile of shite,' thought Scotty Mint. And if the lads had been able to converse by thought transference, Scuffer Mole would have replied, 'I can go one better than that, Scotty: what a load a' bollocks. And speakin' o' bollocks, one o' yours is stickin' out of your shorts.'

"Right, let's go," said the stand-in gaffer, and they all trotted off to the pitch to have a five-minute warm up before kick off.

The Red and Gold Under-15s had won all their matches since the season began in the first week of September. Thus their record so far was: Played 8; Won 8; Drawn 0; Lost 0; Goals for: 49, Goals against 1. Two of the wins had come in the national knockout trophy. The first two rounds were regional, so they'd played Richmond Grammar, thraping them 10-0, then Nonna's Park, Sheffield, who they dispatched 6-1 despite having four players missing. This match had not pleased Skipper Nick, however. It was their first game without Mr. Lampeter, and the lads hadn't played with their customary style and exuberance. The whole game things didn't feel right and the score flattered them. On top of that they conceded their first goal of the season, Crimms stupidly handling from a cross that constituted Nonna's only serious attack of the match.

It was a useful thing that they didn't know much about these next cup opponents as the information might have sown one or two seeds of doubt among the ranks. These Darkside lads were no mugs. Shropshire champions last season, they too were unbeaten this 2002-3 season. The tell-tale signs of their prowess were there if you knew how to look. There was something in the absolutely pristine condition of their kit that would have scared any team but Peggy Lane. The sparkling white Promo! socks were enough on their own to intimidate the usual rag-bag collection of whey-faced Year 10 skinny arses they normally came into contact with. In the language of sports apparel this articulated the fact that here was a team that took itself very, very seriously indeed. Above they wore navy shirts and navy shorts and knew that in these unusual and distinctive colours they looked as sharp as...well, no one in the team would have come up with anything better than 'as a very sharp knife,' so we'll use our authorial power to suggest the image that they looked as sharp as a squad of Mods on their way to a rumble with a bunch of Rockers in Brighton circa 1965. The way they stroked the ball about in the warm up was worth a goal start too: the passing was smooth and accurate even as the players laughed and joked with each other. They were apt to show off their tricks too, midfielder Bim Dancer, for example, loving the feel of the ball balanced perfectly on the nape of his neck. He would hold the position long enough for half the other team to notice and have most of the stuffing knocked out of them before the skippers had even tossed up. Then he'd let it trickle down his back and arse before executing a back-heeler that sent the ball arcing magically back the way he was facing to the feet of a colleague twenty metres away, making the opposing defenders want to walk off and get changed.

Meanwhile, manager Tracker was a tall, slim, no-nonsense PE teacher with a nasty streak that made him hated but also feared; he was a legend in his own mirror, and was becoming one further abroad as he neared thirty and made his way forward in the world of education. The only boys who liked him were his football team. He cosseted them, nursed them and praised them; bought them fish and chips after away matches. And the more they played under him, the more they became like him: mean, bordering on the nasty and as competitive as a bunch of wired Italians.

The first Michael knew of this was when he blew up for a foul in the second minute by a Darkside midfielder with cropped hair on Blue Scuff. "God!" said the cocksure little so-and-so loudly in dissent, making sure he faced away from the ref, thus reducing the chances of a booking to a minimum. Michael was going to take the lad aside for a word but he was ten yards away and counting by the time he was ready to open his mouth. 'Next time,' he thought.

Five minutes in, things were going well for the virgin referee. One offside and one other foul was all he'd had to deal with apart from throw-ins, and he was already getting used to giving the running commentary he remembered one of his old masters always giving during his own school days.

"Pegs throw!" he now barked, pointing an erect arm in the direction of the throwing team's opponents' goal, or simply "goal kick!" when the ball ran out behind the byline. 'This is going okay,' he told himself, as pleased as the kid who lost a quid but found a fiver; 'this is easy.' By the time of the third goal kick about ten minutes in, he'd begun to point extravagantly at the six yard line, holding a knees-bent pose for a full second before running backwards towards the centre-circle. He'd seen the Premiership refs do it on TV. Then Peggy Lane won a corner and he pointed to the flag with the same flourish. He liked himself doing that. "Corner ball!" he shouted for emphasis and sheer pleasure.

"Who the bloody 'ell is that new ref," said Mr. Doosen as he arrived, late, because of the early kick off. "What *does* he think he looks like, pointing like a bloody traffic copper."

"That's 'eadmaster," replied Joe Gofrey, father of Paulo, the Pegs goalkeeper. "Ah know: I'm not sure he knows't rules, either. Look."

Bim Dancer was about seven yards away from the ball at the kick, not the required ten. Michael hadn't noticed. He had an excuse. He'd seen *Match Of The Week* enough times on the television to know that referees had to watch the penalty box carefully because of all the pushing, shoving and shirt-pulling that habitually took place, and he was looking for it now like a true professional.

"Oy, ref! Ten yards!" shouted Miff Mole, father of Blue (and Scuffer).

Michael looked over to the touchline at once. He was immediately annoyed at being shouted at. He felt a shiver of discomfort run down his back. Who was this parent? Didn't he know this was the headteacher he was dealing with? He ran over to the source of the comment, becoming aware as he did so, very disapprovingly, that this was a Pegs parent doing the rabble rousing.

"Do you mind not shouting like that? We must have good behaviour on the sideline."

"Do you not know the rules, man?"

Michael could scarcely speak. He was livid.

"Of course!"

"Well the player should be ten yards away at a corner; he's virtually breathing on our Blue!"

"Our blue what?"

Miff *tutted* in disgust and gave Michael the dead eye.

Michael felt as though he needed a full meeting of the Senior Management Team to give him an inkling of what this parent was going on about. Why was he talking about 'our blue' when Peggy Lane played in red and yellow?

"Just let me do my job," he told the testy parent.

"Well bloody do it properly, then," said the squat and chunky Monsieur Mole, but after Michael had begun to sprint back into position. Livid, he blew his whistle for the kick to be taken. *Peep!*

The struck ball arced through the air with beautiful curvature to the back post where six yards out, Nicky Crimms, making a tremendous late run from the penalty spot, busted a header up into the near corner of the net.

"One-nil Pegs!" shouted Le Mole, pleased as anything. His grin was broad but he wasn't ready to exult. He was too used to seeing the team go one-up in games; it was normal, it was routine. But it wasn't good enough for Reg Ramm, who'd come all the way over from the county of the Shrop with a half-dozen other parents to see the big game, the last before Christmas now the clocks had gone back. For Reg and some of the Darkside parents had seen something Michael had missed: as the ball swerved in from the corner flag their goalkeeper had been impeded by the early jump of Stuart Pitchfork.

"Foul!" they screamed. Not once, but over and over. And as Michael ran back to the centre, they shouted some choice comments at the man in the packet-fresh green Dragonage top.

"The goalie was impeded! Are you blind?"

"You're useless, ref!"

"And you look a right ponce in that shirt!"

Michael didn't hear the last comment but he'd already run over to talk to Robin Tracker.

"I'm sorry, but you need to keep your parents under control. I'm not having this."

"But it was a foul. Didn't you see it?"

Michael held his cold, narrow gaze, but his mind was ticking over in a state of mild shock.

"It's your linesman in this half. Look, he's not flagging."

'Damn,' thought Robin. And of course, his opposite number was right. Lonely Deems, father of Rudi, was pacing back towards the halfway line. He hadn't seen it, the blind twat. He should never have asked him to run the line. Defeated, he looked at Michael one more time, and skulked back to his established position beside his subs and the parents.

Inside, Michael was a cauldron of churning emotion. He thought this would be a cinch, this refereeing lark. He was The Head, after all! He would bestride the pitch like the towering giant he so obviously was. Only it wasn't turning out like that. It was like suddenly being cast on a rocking and rolling boat when you've only ever known dry land. He began to tighten up with stress. He detected a trace of fear in his guts. And he found himself wondering now if he could really do this.

He *peeped!* the whistle again to restart play but the confidence had gone out of him. As the game developed once again, he made more mistakes. He blew for fouls that weren't fouls; failed to react to trips and elbow shoves he saw but couldn't get his mind in gear to whistle at. They were so fast, these boys, he could hardly keep up. His chest was heaving at each stoppage so that after 20 minutes he longed for the oasis of half-time. But he was only halfway there. And he wasn't noticing the flow of the game well enough. He would have to give another team talk at half-time but at this rate he wouldn't have a clue what to say. He didn't know who was on top and who in the Red and Gold was playing well - who not.

'I'll just have to start going to the gym,' he said to himself, wondering with displeasure which fraction of his nightly paperwork he would have to forego to accommodate the new demand on his out of school hours.

On the touchline both sets of parents, naturally, thought Michael the worst referee they'd ever seen. True as it probably was, they said this about most referees, most games. Darkside thought he was hysterically biased, while Peggy Lane thought he was a hopeless nit, totally out of his depth. The team were one-up still, but the locals were worried that for no apparent reason he might suddenly award Darkside a penalty, or miss a blatant hand ball when Pegs were on the attack. The only saving grace for Michael was the fact that at the half-hour mark there was nearly a fight on the sideline. However, a true free for all was narrowly averted.

"Bloody dirty lot, you," Mr. Mole had shouted after an elbow banged into Tyke Triff's ribs without Michael noticing. "Deliberate, were that. Disgraceful."

"You shut your mouth," came the plucky reply from Jack Strap, father of Lanky, the Darkside centre-back. "Or I'll come and shut it for you."

Then it affected the play. The lads on both sides heard the fathers squabbling like rats over the last corpse, and started throwing themselves into tackles, pulling shirts and pushing each other off the ball. There were so many infringements Michael didn't know which ones to punish and when. In short, the game had gone way beyond his grasp, and as the afternoon grew slightly darker, he was hanging onto his whistle for grim death, willing his stopwatch to reach forty minutes up.

At thirty-eight-and-a-bit, Darkside equalised. Their captain, Mark Pin, his team playing with the breeze, swung his right foot through a rare loose ball in midfield without intending to shoot but succeeded in accidentally launching a scudding missile at the Pegs goal. Paulo Gofrey dived spectacularly, pushing the ball as it began to come in to land brilliantly onto the underside of the bar.

"Great save!" shouted his dad, as the ball bounced down and hit the line, bounced up again four feet, dropped again with inevitable gravity and landed on a boot-made divot on the goal line. But from here it bounced up weakly, dropped to earth one last time, fatally, and trickled towards the back of the net as twenty-three spectators nearly expired with the breath they were holding in. 1-1 and everybody breathed out.

There was hysteria among the Darkside parents.

"Told you they were rubbish," screamed one.

"We've got these bastards, now," shouted another.

Mole senior was ready for fisticuffs but Cliff Triff literally pulled him back by the coat.

"No, Miff lad. Let them. You'll end up with a fine or worse if you set about 'em."

"I didn't know folk from Shropshire could be so wild," said a shocked Joe Gofrey.

"It's all the sheep shaggin' they do over there – sends 'em crackers. Anyway, calm down," continued Cliff, "we're going to win. You watch."

At the last kick of the half, a lunging tackle whacked the ball out of play 10, 20, 30 metres towards a copse of trees in the direction of the moor. As it sped towards him, a man in a dark donkey jacket, hands moodily entrenched in its side pockets, swiftly withdrew himself into the shadows.

35

Winners
Autumn Term - Week 8 Day 3
Wednesday, October 30th, 2002
Peggy Lane Playing Fields - Afternoon

    The Red and Gold trooped over to the sideline and fell upon a tray of oranges that Mr. Gofrey kindly provided for every game. Then Mr. Mole came along with his crate full of Boosterade bottles. Michael hadn't thought about this and was grateful. Looking over at the opposition, he noticed them all swigging contentedly from blue plastic bottles of Morning Power. Next time he'd be better prepared. He blew hard, still trying to recover his wind and his composure.

    The boys turned inwards to form their customary loose cluster ready for the team talk. Nobody wanted to speak. In truth, they were confused by what had happened so far. The sense of rhythm they always played with as a matter of custom or instinct was completely absent. There were two obvious problems which stuck out like jagged metal into the team's collective psyche: one, the pitch was sticky, turning into puddles over in the far corner where the grass fell away at the start of a long slope down the valley towards the town. This was hindering their passing game. Two, the opposition, it had to be admitted were handy. That much was now obvious. The boys looked at one another and the uncertain faces they saw were living proof that the Peggy Lane invincibles had been knocked out of stride. They began to verbal this out amongst themselves as if they were going to do their own team talk. The head was busy sucking on a troubled orange segment and didn't look like coming up for air quite yet. On the second of the major points they were agreed: Darks were niggly, dirty even, and sledged like a bunch of Australians going down to a rare test defeat. Michael was brought into the discussion almost immediately, but for practical reasons.

    "There's a lot of talking going on, sir," said Captain Crimms, "it's putting us off. You've got to do something about it."

    "Yeah," said Will Gaffy, "disgoosting things, they're sayin': callin' my mum a whore."

    "Right," said Blue Mole, wanting to add his tuppence halfpenny. "That short little twat, the six, keeps saying to me, 'your mum's shaggin' the milkman, the coalman and the whole of the Yarrow fire brigade.'"

    "Alright, that's enough of that!" said Michael, outraged that one of the boys would use this sort of language in front of him quite so openly, even if it was reported speech.

"If he says it to me once more, I'm going to belt 'im."

"And get sent off: brilliant!" said Nicky looking at the ref.

"You should pass him on to me," said Stuart Pitchfork, "I 'aven't got a mum."

"I didn't know we 'ad a fire brigade," said Joe Gofrey quietly, still sulking about the goal he'd conceded. Blue Mole wouldn't have minded laughing at this point, but knowing Nicky might belt him one later if they lost, went back to sucking his bottle instead.

"Look," said Michael, trying to take control. "I told you before the start: you're trying to pass the ball too much - it's too muddy."

He suddenly remembered his striker in the gold boots and how quick he was off the mark. "Get it forward to...to..." he was pointing at Jamie Spooner.

"Jamie, sir."

"Yes, Jamie. Hit it long and let him chase after it. And..." he pointed again.

"That's Stuart," said Nicky.

"Right; Stuart. You're quick too, Stuart. So play the long ball. You might as well. They're breaking up the game with their fouls and not letting you play," said Michael, suddenly seeing the light. He'd actually perceived more patterns of play than he'd thought.

"It would 'elp if you blew your whistle a bit more often," said Mr. Mole, who'd strolled over to listen.

For once, Michael not only realised he was in the wrong, but felt he could be honest.

"Okay, you're right, I should be doing better; I'm struggling to keep up. But I promise you, I'm doing my level best. That's all I can do."

Shocked by his frankness, both players and parents relaxed and let go of their intense annoyance at the very presence of this posing interloper. The bottom line was simple. They wanted to beat this bunch of fit, strong, competitive, cheating scum. These were the approximate thoughts of skipper Nick and he was not alone.

"Come on, we can beat these," said Blue Mole.

He clenched his fist and bent his gaze at as many of his team mates as he could without moving his head from side to side. His mate Boyce Allinson had put him in a headlock in History earlier and it still hurt if he jerked it.

"Come on, let's fookin' do these cheating cunts."

"You didn't hear that, headmaster," said his father.

"I did, but for this one time only, I'm going to pretend I didn't."

They broke for the second half in much better spirits.

For good reason or bad, Pegs tried the new tactic. As often as was feasible, goalkeeper, defenders and midfielders when they were deep, lumped the ball up the park for Stuart and Jamie to chase. And though it hadn't yet paid off as the clock ticked right up to the half-hour mark, it often looked as if was going to at any point. Stuart and Jamie were as quick as shit off a pair of shovels, and though the navy Darks had a back four which in the summer could have doubled as a highly successful 4 x 100 North-East Shropshire District Sprint Relay Team, they'd struggled to catch the attackers all afternoon and had been forced to resort to a lot of skulduggery to contain them. However, the passing - if thirty and forty yard whacks up the pitch can be so called - had yet to achieve the required accuracy, so for now they were able to hold on.

For Michael, the first thirty second half minutes passed much more peacefully. It had started to rain; not heavily - it drizzled, but it was incessant. In contrast, the wind had dropped so it wasn't that hugely annoying rain that slapped your face and put you in a bad temper, but that steady wetness that almost loped down on you, slowly drowning any good mood you might have started the match with. For Michael it was truly a God-send. Parents wrapped up, found hats and umbrellas and shut up. They had too much liquid to cope with, and couldn't find the adrenalin to produce the anger and outrage of the first period. There were grumbles and groans for sure, as every tackle, throw-in and free kick decision was contested, but that was all; as if they'd all turned from spirited middle-aged, blood-is-thicker-than-water potential hooligans into bumbling, grouchy young geriatrics.

Michael was soaked now, big waps of rain dripping down his hair onto his forehead and thence into his eyes, but he didn't mind now that he had the game under closer control. The rain had slowed it down so he wasn't running about like a badly-made mechanical toy. The long ball stuff helped too, there now being fewer close tackles, barges and pulls. His linesmen were doing a sterling job with the offside flags. They were no doubt as biased as each other, so cancelled each other out. That was fine as far as he was concerned. He wasn't going to be doing this every week, he'd decided that. As for the Darkside's sledging, he'd caught a navy shirt 'effing and blinding as he chased a ball alongside Stuart Pitchfork right at the start of the half.

"Your mother fooks animals...." he'd heard the lad say before they both left him trailing, hurtling off like a couple of eager young hounds in the direction of a thump towards the Darks' penalty area. He caught up with the offender at the goal kick and yellow-carded him.

"Any more of that and you're off. And that goes for the lot of you," he said with raised voice, swivelling the studs on his Interceptors neatly through 360 degrees.

As he looked at his stopwatch, thirty-two minutes of the half gone, only one thing was wrong: Darkside had just scored.

Pegs had been unlucky. Though they'd not looked their normal superior selves, they'd scrapped and fought as well as any team could have, and hadn't given the Darks a sniff of goal, until a fatal slip on the wet surface by Will Gaffy let that Bim Dancer in on Paulo Gofrey. Bim's shot was low and hard and skidded into the net impressively, again off the woodwork - the post this time.

"Bollocks," said the young Gaffy.

"Fook!" said Paulo, throwing the ball out of his net disgustedly as if it had just thrown a brick at his dog. At the side, the crowd of eight Darkside parents cheered wetly but loudly.

"We've got 'em now!" shouted Reg Ramm.

"Yiss!" said Lonely Deems, "we're going through! We're going through!"

"Come on, lads," said Michael surreptitiously as his charges slumped back to their starting positions.

"Nine minutes left plus stoppage time. You can do it."

'Maybe we can,' they thought, and got stuck in again.

There was more scrapping and fighting - in the footballing sense - in all areas of the pitch now; twenty outfield players going at it for all they were worth. 'If only everyone in Britain was like this,' considered a proud Michael Peniston, 'this country would be a so much better place to live in.' Then Nicky Crimms put in one hard tackle too many. He mistimed a lunge at the ball down his left flank and took the legs of the winger. 'Ohgh!' he grunted, the wind taken out of him as his ribs hit the wet grass. Michael yellow-carded him.

"Dirty bastard," said Sally Marshland, mother of Rhodri, the Darks' fearless midfielder.

"Hey, watch your bloody language," said Miff Mole, petulantly.

"Bloody watch yours," said Alice Kabb, mother of Darkside goalie Keith.

Six minutes left.

The free kick came in high and hard but Paulo was off his line in a flash and jumped up and caught it, no problem. He looked up, saw Jamie beginning to turn, ready to run, somewhere in the direction of the halfway line, and wellied it as hard as he could, both feet leaving planet earth momentarily as he did so. Seventeen players turned tiredly and watched the flying ball descend and hit the ground with a splash well inside the Darkside half. The water held it up; otherwise it would have been in the arms of Keith Kabb before the weary muddied mob had dragged themselves out of the Peggy Lane penalty area one more time. Instead, the ball bounced almost vertically, making it hard for defender Abdul Malik to judge its flight. Stuart Pitchfork was right behind him as the centre-back raced as fast as he still could back towards his own goal to deal with the incipient danger. Fatally, he paused, while Stuart got both feet off the ground in the rain and nodded the ball forward. Unlike Abdul, he hadn't stopped, so in one second his forward momentum took him five yards clear in pursuit of his own header.

Keith Kabb arrived on the scene hoping to catch the ball in his box before Stuart could make up the required ground but its second bounce again took pace off the ball, leaving Keith a fraction from stranded. Twenty yards out, the ball reached the top of its new arc a foot above Stuart's five foot seven frame. Goalie Keith was closing in on the ball, but he'd have to head it clear if he made it on time.

"I can't look," said his mum on the touchline.

"Go on, lad," said Michael under his breath, urging Stuart on.

"Go on, my son," said the man in the donkey jacket coming forward out of the trees.

Stuart rose that foot off the ground and nodded the ball beyond Keith Kabb and was past him in a flash to finish the job, the Darkside fans' hopes sinking as he went. The third bounce was followed by Pitch' chesting the ball forward perfectly, so as it fell to earth again in front of him he easily poked it in from the six-yard line. A huge cheer rose behind him. Some boys, a few girls and one or two teachers had joined the Peggy parents to make it so. 2-2.

Three minutes left plus stoppages.

There wasn't time for much thinking. *Peeep!* They kicked off again, Darks now trying valiantly to attack. However, Lip Doosen was now an increasingly dominant force at the back. He stopped Bim Dancer with a tremendous tackle, just as his would-be nemesis was throwing his last everything into an attempt to score from a half-chance near the penalty spot. Having snuffed out the attack he now tried the heroic: a slide rule pass of thirty yards along the floor which would give Stuart another clear run on goal.

"Shit!" he said loudly, as the midfield mud slowed its path. Michael waited for the ball to go out for a throw-in and produced yet another yellow card. Fair's fair. There was little dissent from the touchline; the tension seemed to be choking off the spectators' words, as if the vocal cords were saying to the brain,

"Oy, give it a rest, there's a great game going on here!"

Stoppage time.

Gaffy smashed the ball forward for the last time before extra time. It landed in a dangerous area behind the Darks back four, but full back Dobbin dumped it out for a throw. This was met with a roar from the home fans that surprised everyone. 'Do we have a long throw expert?' the newly arrived fans thought.

'No,' Miff Mole would have said had he heard one articulate the thought. Scuffer Mole, again sent on as substitute thanks to Doosen Senior, who'd reminded Michael that his team had some ten minutes earlier, had a go. It didn't make much distance into the Darkside box and a defender hooked it away. It bounced and hit Tyke Triff just below the chest. The tired, aching football dropped to the floor two feet away from TT's body, then rose about eighteen inches, and he thought, all in less than a second, 'Ooh, good height for a volley; I'll hit this; I've bugger all to lose.' He swung his right boot at what he thought was the dead centre of the ball.

"Shit," he said not very loudly in view of the recent Crimms yellow card, but still proving that when it came to profane language, the team was limited. He'd struck his shot hard alright, but was comprehensively wrong about the required direction: it was missing the far post by at least six feet. Then he saw his shot hit the refereeing headmaster on the knee, and begin travelling in a left-right diagonal across his sight line towards the goal. His mouth opened as he followed its path. Goalie Kabb had already moved to his right in case he had to make an important last-minute save, but with the deflection he was now frantically trying to shift his weight in the opposite direction to head off the pill, now travelling at speed dangerously towards his left-hand post. However, he only found himself trying to pedal a non-existent bicycle at the speed of a Keystone Kop and slithered to the ground with a *thlush!*, at which point the Mitre Supreme, with a *reeeyeeesshh-hh!* hit the back of the net a foot and a half off the ground with a finality that was truly shocking to all who saw and heard it. 3-2 to Peggy Lane.

"No goal, no goal!" shouted the mums who didn't know the rules.

"No goal! No goal!" screamed Reg Ramm, who, like all men who watched football, thought he knew them, but was prepared to admit he was wrong if the ref would only disallow the goal.

"Goal! Goal!" roared everyone from Pegs, some of whom actually knew the rules.

"The silly useless bastard'll disallow it," said Miff Mole to his friend Rip Doosen.

"Goal!" shouted Michael, trying to disguise the triumph in his voice as he pointed to the centre spot. The Darkside players protested, but not with much ardour. They were knackered, too gone even to take much notice of Tyke Triff being buried by a mound of delirious Peggy Lane team mates.

Michael picked the ball up from whence a disconsolate Darkside player had left it, and got the match kicked off again. Just two Darkside passes from the centre-spot later, Michael looked at his stopwatch. It hit 00.00 and *ppffwwh-heeeeeeeeeeeppppp!* sang his Acme Thunderer. The game was over.

The man near the trees smiled broadly, gave the air a small punch and took off through the trees for home.

36

Saviours
Autumn Term - Week 8 Day 3
Wednesday, October 30th, 2002
The Peregrine Lane Grammar School, Yarrow - Late Afternoon

I was just inside the staff room door at the end of the day on my way to get my coat when Les caught me. He still looked pitiful.

"Change of plan. Sef says can we meet later at the Cleft, instead of your house. About seven; is that alright?"

"Yeah. Why?"

"Sef's had to go somewhere. I think it's to see Chris to break the news."

"No new plan then," I said, lacking hope.

Les shook his head and looked at the floor as if it might split open, enabling our solution to emerge in the form of a magical missive from beyond. He looked so defeated I felt like spilling tears. He shook his head minutely and I thought he might be the one to crack into liquid misery. I didn't want to see that happen.

"Come on, Les. Let's go and see what's left of the match."

"No. I'm not going to watch that man cover himself in glory."

"Don't worry, he can't take any credit: they always win, don't they?"

"Just about. The power of the stocking over the rudimentary awakening."

"The cultured left foot over the unpardonable dining table?"

"Dans le nutshell," said Les, looking up at me suddenly.

"Me neither," I said.

Liam came in. He'd been off sick the first two days of the half-term, so I hadn't seen him since before the holiday. I was pleased to see his ass, looking quite the academic today in new black spectacles and leaner than ever in the body. I thought he might help me forget this headache I'd had all afternoon.

"Liam. How's it hanging?"

"Hanging off, actually. We should never have taken the first Viagra tablet."

"We...?"

"I'll see you, Tim. Liam." Les turned from us. I was about to say 'see you later,' but remembered in time that Liam was still outside the loop. This was unfortunate as I liked him more and more; but according to Sef, his mouth was as loose as a dockside trollop's morals. We sat down and slung our legs across chairs and tables now the place was nearly empty. Only the dribs and the drabs came in at this stage of the day for bags and books from the work room on their way home. Hetty Kiss and Livvy Lovejohn, the queens of the Peggy Lane drama department were earnestly discussing the Christmas production, every word of which we heard as their voices threw echoes off the walls in the near empty room. Mercifully for everyone there were no meetings tonight, something I pointed out to Liam as I tried to rest my weary self.

"Good feckin' job too. You know they've got me on this New Vision Working Group; Jasus..."

"I know."

"...and I need it like a catheter up me langer...You smile, but it's no joke when you're having to listen to someone going on about the need for setting up 'structures of inspiration' and shite like that."

"How were your classes today?"

"Okay, but the rain always gets them playing up a bit, and two of me Year 8s came in covered in mud. 'Did you miss the Ark?' I said. 'What sir?' they went."

Liam was mimicking them, making a face so gormless I didn't recognize him any more. On this form I could have sat here for the rest of the afternoon. What was left of it. The light was already beginning to fade, what with dark, threatening clouds still sweeping across the sky like an illness.

"Hadn't a clue what I was talking about. That's the thing about this country: no one has a clue about religion."

"Just as well, probably. You going out to watch the football?"

"Nah. You?"

"No. Can't be bothered."

"Isn't it typical, Liam:" I said, apropos of nothing much, "we dream all our lives from the age of about sixteen for an insatiable woman to come along, someone who'll do it day and night..."

"Up every orifice."

"Speak for yourself...mind, you're a catholic, aren't you?"

"No, I'm Ian Paisley's rent boy. 'Course oi'm a cat'lic," he said, slipping right back into the vernacular. "You're spot on. It's the guilt they put into you from the age of four. The only way I can cope with it is to bang as many women as I can up every hole I can find."

"No wonder you look like a worker on the bridge over the River Kwai half the time. I suppose you're making up for lost time now you've found the woman of your wet dreams."

"Do I look that bad? It's the lack of sleep. I'd sell me grandmother's knickers for ten hours kip."

"Tell me: is there any danger of an emotion or two coming into this relationship of yours?"

"Oh, Christ, yeah. It's a hell of a relief when she falls asleep."

"Lookout, here's the girl herself. Hi Sally."

"Tim, hi. Hello, you," she said to Liam, slapping him on the thigh.

"Ow! Bloody women PE teachers; you've better biceps than a lumberjack, you know that? Tim was just telling me, you get testicular cancer from too much sex. Did you know that? Ow! Don't!" Sally had some of Liam's sideburn hair in a nasty looking snag and had locked her jaw in concentration so as to inflict something near maximum pain. I almost envied Liam, erotically constructed in the extreme as she was and friendly personality that she had.

"That's for blabbing about our love-life, idiot."

"I've told him nothing, honest!"

I made as innocent a face as I knew how, though I doubt it was enough.

"Come on Irish boy, I'm taking you home. See you, Tim."

I found a weak smile for both of them and said 'g'night' and they left still picking at each other in that way that only people in love do.

So, I sat in the chair there on my own, my thoughts coming and going. 'I'm not very good at showing affection for girlfriends in public…I'm going to let down Barney Plough's fucking tyres one night, he's really getting on my nerves…I'd managed to kiss Safeena outside the university library now, hadn't I, but it had been a stretch…Maybe I was getting better or maybe I was still under the influence of a wallop on the head…I need something for my dinner. What have I got in the fridge?' I took my battered-looking mobile out of my jacket and rang her, just to hear her voice, but she was switched off.

No one was coming into the staff room now, and the Drama Queens had gone off to their purpose-built theatre to look at some props. There was just me. Ten-past-four. I folded my arms and rested my eyes for a little while under bright buzzing strip lights, trying anyway to induce a feeling of much-needed well-being by thinking about my girl. I saw her smiling face in front of me, surrounded by jagged grey shading, as if in one of those old photographs from the start of the last century, and began to relax. Such a friendly face: so wide and warm; so trusting; so full of young life. 28 plays 21…am I too old for her? 28-21…21: is she too young for me? I felt my consciousness dissolving in a pleasantly suffocating sort of way, my head easing of pain slightly. The face was laughing now, as I slipped under. 'Tim,' she was saying, smiling like mad all the way, 'Sef was right all along: but it's me, Tim, me! Not Jez, it's me!'

When I woke up half the staff room lights had been switched off and it was pitch black outside. My neck ached as I pulled myself up straight. I forced my eyes to reach down to my watch. Ten-past-five. There was goo leaking out of the right side of my mouth as usual, but not so much I couldn't wipe it off with the back of my hand. This was no good; I had to get myself awake and moving. I was cold, so I found my black coat and put it on. What time was I meeting them in the pub? I still had plenty of time. I yawned and felt essentially like shit, with the memories returning of a bad day that started in a mess and proved incapable of improving. Still, it had been an exciting thing to be involved in so early in my time at Peggy Lane. Intrigue almost rising to criminality. Ridiculous. To think that we'd almost pulled off that stunt. I checked I had my phone and patted my inside pocket for the safety of my wallet. I wouldn't mark anything tonight. Not with another crisis session pending later on. So there was nothing else to take home but myself. I stood up and went to the door. It was open and I heard the sound of the electric cleaner in a distant corridor as I left. I yawned again and looked forward to a big cup of java when I got home and some hot food. I had to start cooking properly. My headache was coming on again. I tried to turn right to the front door but I was waylaid.

"Oh, sorry; I nearly bumped into you!"

"Oh!" echoed my new friend. "Sorry, my fault," said a friendly-looking woman in smart work clothes: a two-piece navy suit with a 'National Rich Bank' identity badge on the lapel. She was swinging a party of keys around her forefinger that had a black leather Monstar car fob.

"No, it was mine; I was miles away." 'Jackie Saviour,' the badge said.

"I wonder, can you help me? I've come to look for a bag. My son lost it earlier today at school. I'm sorry it's late; I meant to get here earlier but I couldn't get away from work…"

I ransacked my head quickly for recognition, because the word 'Saviour' sounded familiar, and found it.

"Yes, I know about this. His name is…"

"James."

"James! That's right. So he hasn't found it yet…"

"No."

"Obviously. Sorry, I fell asleep; I'm not quite with it."

She laughed one of those silly laughs people make out of a polite nervousness.

"So, where does he think he left it? Oh!" I said, coming round a bit more; "the PE block, wasn't it?"

"Yes. He tried to get in to have a look at 3:30 but 'the changing rooms were locked,' he said."

"And there were no caretakers around…"

"He's a bit shy, actually. I don't think he tried very hard to find them to be honest."

"Sure. Right, well, I'll take you along there and we'll see if we can't get in and find the thing. This way…"

I started up B corridor heading for the outside door at the far end with Mrs. Saviour alongside me. As we went she took a paper tissue out of a black shoulder bag and blew her snout politely.

She saw me looking.

"Sorry. Cold."

"It's that time of year, isn't it," I said. 'Stone me,' I thought, with dread; 'it'll soon be Christmas. And I'm learning to make pleasantly meaningless conversation with people. Look at me.'

"It's always that time of year with me," she said, and laughed again in a silly way that was already getting annoying.

"You're cheerful, considering James might have lost his bag; it was a Lingo, too, wasn't it?"

"Yes, it was …You haven't got kids yourself then, I take it," she said, still smiling. They must have some money, the Saviours, to take the loss of an expensive bag like that this lightly.

"No, that pleasure as yet awaits me." Again she giggled. 'It doesn't take much to make you laugh,' I thought.

"You'll have to get used to this when your time comes, especially if you have boys. Always leaving things behind and losing them," she said. We reached the outside door and moved into the gathered darkness. I expected it to be cold, but the air was mild and heavy with moisture, though it wasn't raining. There were outside lights to help us on our way.

"It's through here." We passed the science block on our right then made a left turn towards the sports field and changing rooms.

"Leeds United fan, isn't he?" I said, fighting hard to stave off an impolite yawn, as the back of the changing block came into view. The left-hand windows, below a flat roof, were in darkness, and so were those on the right, but there was plainly a yellow glow from a window in between.

"Ah, there's a light on. I wonder if there's a cleaner in there mopping up or something. There's been a match." I was thinking aloud, really. "So if the doors are open, we're in business."

"Good," said Mrs. Saviour simply and stoically. "Mind, knowing our James, he probably left it somewhere else."

Fifteen metres or so from the building I could hear running water, which in the space of seconds became the hiss of a shower. The window with the light on was split into horizontal panels, like strata, and they were slightly ajar in a pleasingly neat line. It occurred to me that the match might only have just finished, but the thought was rejected in a second because I could see it had been dark for a while. Then some silly idiot must have left the shower on by mistake. Or did the cleaners wash the mud away after a school game?

"Good news. If the showers are on, the door's open," I said, cheerfully. I must have stunned myself with my own genius use of logic. "And if the door's open, someone's there with some keys that'll open the changing rooms."

"Yes," piped Mrs. S., following my inanities expertly.

"Bear with me, this is the first time I've been round here: I'm still new."

"Oh..."

The doors were round the other side of the building. I thought, anyway.

"...Do you like the school?"

Now that was a question. If you've got a couple of hours I'll answer that one for you.

"Yes, very much."

The sound of the shower was loud now as we swung left at the window slats on our way round to the other side. Luscious looking steam was strippling out and making its way up into the early autumn evening. 'I could do with one of those myself,' I thought. When we got round to the other side there was a weak, pasty light in the under-canopy roof illuminating a door in the middle of the frontage. The shower was in here; we couldn't be wrong because above the door was another row of frosted glass slats allowing the same sickly light to escape that we'd just seen around the other side.

"You'd better wait here," I said.

I still thought it might be a changing room but as I entered I thought 'probably not.' I was still waking up. My thoughts were still tired and stumbling. The bloke cleaning himself will have some keys to the changing rooms, anyway. Then I'm out of here. But I'm going to have to suffer the embarrassment of a naked male body probably, to get them. Drat. Why did I have to get involved?

Opening the door I remained half-expectant that space would fall away from the door showing me peg racks and low wooden seating, dust and pieces of half-remembered lost property on the floor. But no. I was straight into a large PE staff office, well-lit as it turned out, with three untidy teachers' desks to the left and right, a pile of muddy kit in one corner and the smell of mud and stale sweat unmistakable in the warm, wet air. Straight ahead of me, well in front of the back wall only a short underarm throw away was an inner wall of white tiles. Halfway across it was a doorway about a metre or so wide. The shower entrance. A metre further back, another neatly-tiled wall rose most of the way to the ceiling to protect the modesty of those losing the grime of their sporting exertions behind. To be safe from spying eyes.

But not protecting sounds from keen ears.

I was rooted to the spot. Above the sound of the hissing hot water, it was evident that someone was dying in terrible pain back there. But it couldn't be that. Not when there were two voices in pain, one in a lowish register and one rather higher. Time seemed to be rushing by in a supernatural whirl, but each second was enough for the world in which I swam to splinter apart into a million fragments and come back together again. I thought at first of Liam and Sally, but unless Sally's pet name for Liam O'Neil-Neil was 'Michael' it couldn't be them. The male voice had loudened to a regular stricken groan. However, judging by the rhythmic squeak of pleasure from the female participant in this extra-curricular activity, the dying was only an outmoded euphemism; they were fucking like desperadoes in there.

Then the sudden excitement of fireworks hit me as I realised what I had to do. First, I turned around to lock the door – which would have been a mistake had I been able to do it. When I put my hand to the bolt it was already across but there was nothing to hold it in place - it was broken. I looked down to see a thick bunch of keys in a mortice lock. Someone had been careless. Very careless. They hadn't turned the bunch over to protect themselves from the cast-iron finality of an outside world they assumed they were holding at bay. Quickly, I opened the door, grabbed Jackie Saviour by the wrist and yanked her inside. I turned towards the shower again and examined the expanse of white tiles. Nothing. I rotated my eyes left, then right, down, then up, and there I found what I needed. High up near the dusty ceiling was a small red wheel that played a vital part of a pipe system. The shower on-off switch. I walked to it in a trance and on tip-toes, turned it, which way? *Clockwise*, as fast as I could.

Whether the hissing stopped before the ardent gasps of fully-committed physical effort I couldn't say, but within three or four seconds of meeting firm resistance at the end of my wheel-turning, all noise in the room ceased save the buzz of the strip light and the 'drip...drip...drip...' of cheap education plumbing. I looked at Jackie still holding her hand and tugged gently at her to follow me. She gave in to my silent request with perfect submissiveness. I led her to the shower entrance and we were there in three steps.

We stopped.

'Drip...drip...drip.'

The bogus loneliness of this sound exploded with potential in the hideous tension as we tip-toed towards the inner shower. If my heart were held in my body by elastic, the bonds were at the snapping point, but I pressed on as if moved by hypnosis. At the entrance we made one step forward, two to the left, one to the right, then made a 180-degree rightward swivel to bring us to a full view of the performers.

Caught, they were, like rabbits in our 4x4 headlights. Trapped like wild animals in cruel iron.

He wasn't quite tall and he wasn't quite slim, and his light hair didn't need finger combing at that precise moment in time. It was impressively thick, I could vouch for that directly now. The poor sod held a pair of balls and a red, mangled-looking schlong in two crossed-over hands. I looked at the horrified face, frantically appealing to me for pity.

"Mrs. Saviour…" I said, in the best teacher-voice I could muster, "…have you met our new headmaster, Michael Peniston? And by the way, you don't, by any chance, happen to have a camera on you, do you?"

Michael turned away from us and clasped his lover, protecting her from view, but still showing us a bare bottom. She'd been behind her man trying vainly to grasp anonymity in these moments of terrible discovery, but I could see her hair tumbling down and even wet I knew it was that of my boss, Susan.

Many thoughts zizzed in my head: from 'what on earth was going on? This was supposed to be a fucking school!' which it literally was by all accounts, to 'Susan, please stay behind Michael, I'm too embarrassed to look at you' and several others in between. I wanted to say, 'Michael, you stupid, stupid man,' but I wasn't brave like the characters who said such things in my favourite books. Jackie Saviour wasn't saying anything either.

I tore my eyes away from the nude scene laid out in front of me to check that she was still there and she was, a fraction behind me, doing a good impersonation of a concrete sculpture. Then I watched as she unfroze and pushed me aside; pulled her shoulder bag around to the front of her and unzipped it. After a brief scrabble around she produced a mobile phone, pointed it at this pair of Bambis and pressed…waited for some seconds to pass, then pressed again.

"I won it in a raffle at work," she said, apparently as stupefied as I was. And if I hadn't thought she might, in the circumstances, take it as some sort of opening gambit, I would have given her a very big kiss indeed.

37

Make Your Mother Sigh
Autumn Term - Week 8 Day 3
Wednesday October 30th 2002
Peggy Lane – Very late afternoon

We left the PE office, carelessly crashing through puddles, and went back into the main school building. Jackie Saviour followed me when I ducked into the first classroom inside the door, breathing heavily.

"Look," I said, "if you like you can leave the reporting of this to me. I don't want to put you to any more trouble."

She was white with shock. She may have had a better grasp of what we'd just seen than me.

"Okay," she said, coming out of a trance, brain switching back on after a temporary breakdown.

"But you will report it. We can't..."

"Don't worry, Mrs. Saviour," I said, "I'm going to make sure that the chair of governors knows about it as soon as I possibly can. Tonight, if possible."

"Here: you'll need this phone then, won't you? Or shall I..."

"No. Yes. I'll take it. How about I ring you tomorrow and we'll find a way of getting it back to you."

"Okay. That'll be fine."

So I said 'goodnight' to Mrs. S. at the school main door promising to ring her as soon as I knew anything concrete and raced down to the admin area to find an empty office with a phone. My bowels were heavy with the thought of Michael chasing me down corridors to stop me. The door of the Head of Upper School, Chris Barton-Jones, was slightly ajar, and I slipped inside. I didn't switch on the light: there was enough illumination from the corridor for me to see the phone on the desk and use it. I dialled '9' for an outside line and got the buzz. I wanted to get to Sef but I still didn't have his number. I mistyped Jez's number twice and looked down at my hands to see them shaking. I stopped, to get a hold of myself, troubled by a racing mind that said 'O God, O God, O God' to me over and over, then tried to hit the Jez buttons properly this time.

Bbbrrr! Bbbrrr! Four times. Come *on!*

"'elloah?"

"Jez, it's me."

"'el..."

"Listen. You'll...I...It's..."

"Whatever's the matter? Slow down, slow down. Tek a deep breth..."

I was trying, but both my lungs were trying to climb out of my mouth to take a holiday.

"Okay...I'll try....Okay..." I had to shut my eyes to do this. I visualized in my mind what I saw. It wasn't difficult.

"It's okay. We've got Michael."

"What do you mean? You've not bloody kidnapped him 'ave yer?"

"No..." I still struggled. I wanted so much to laugh. "You'd better sit down. You won't believe this."

"Spit it out, man, spit it out..."

"Are you sitting down?"

"Noah, just get on with it!"

"I'm at school. And I've just caught Michael......"

I couldn't say it.

"Caught Michael what? What?"

I couldn't.

"WHAT! FOR FOOK'S SEK, WHAT?"

"Just come to my house now. Now!"

"I y'ate you, d'y'noah that, Weaver?"

Clrrk.

I replaced the receiver in its cradle and sat down in the swivel chair at the desk. A photograph Chris Barton-Jones had put up on the wall was caught in a wide beam of light from outside. Two children in Peggy Lane sports kit were holding up a trophy, looking almost unbearably happy in all their flowering of youth, rosy-cheeked and beautiful. They dissolved out of focus as two big gloopy tears swelled across my misty eyeballs. I thought about slumping down on the old scratched wooden desk and really letting it out and for a number of seconds it felt like a fantastic idea. But instead, I pulled a tissue from the box on Chris's desk, wiped it across my upper face and left. No one saw me leave the school except for cleaner Mary, who stared at me as I rushed past, heading for the front school door. Thirty minutes later, I stepped off the bus in Measby and could already hear my phone, ringing and ringing and ringing.

38

10 Things to Do in Yarrow When You're Dead
Autumn Term - Week 8 Day 3
Wednesday, October 30th, 2002
Measby - 7.46.pm

"Is that Tim?"
"Yes, it is."
"Hello...um, it's Michael."
"..."
"Michael Peniston."
"Hello."
"...It's about earlier."
"Oh, yes?"
"Yes, I...Can we talk about it?"
"Sure."
"I mean, can I come up and see you?"
"Sure. Do you know where I live?"
"Measby, isn't it? High Street. 21?"
"Yes, that's it."
"Can I come now, are you busy?"
"No. Come up anytime you like."
"Okay. I'll be there in twenty minutes."

He was there in less than fifteen. His knock was as I expected: hard, urgent, impatient. Three short raps. I may have imagined desperation, but I doubt it.

"Come in," said Tim who stood with his arms resolutely folded in the middle of his living room. He held the pose of a Roman centurion: proud and determined. I doubted, however, that this would be easy for him; he was still a young man, and of the many truths surrounding Michael Peniston, one was that a decade and a half in teaching had given him a certain amount of street wisdom. The outcome of this meeting was by no means certain to be a positive one for us.

At the start of the knock I retreated rapidly to the kitchen, but made sure the door was open so I could track the conversation precisely. Then the rattle of a latch and the squeak of huge hinges on an old wooden door announced the arrival of our esteemed guest.

"Hello," said a tentative voice. I couldn't see him, but I imagined a figure in a wet coat, looking strained, battered but far from without hope.

"Hi," I heard Tim reply, casually. "Come on in. Can I get you a drink?"
"No. No, I'm alright."
"Sure?"
"Yes. I want to get straight to the point, if I may."
"Okay."
We'd had only one hour to rehearse this - less - but Tim, though he thinks he's not that strong, has something very solid at the core of him.
"I suppose you weren't expecting me to call you."
"No. I was."
Well done, Tim, remembering not to say 'we.' Our friend Les Person had rung me shortly before six to break some startling news and we immediately speculated upon the possibility of Michael wanting to set up a visit such as this. We'd undertaken a certain amount of preparation, but we could not, however, predict how Michael might tackle what for him was, whatever his level of expectation, a situation of acute difficulty.
"Oh."
It was apparent that Michael hadn't the remotest idea of what Tim and Jezebel euphemistically called 'The Plan.' This did not surprise me. You may know how ambitious men are: their minds work in narrow funnels, missing the wide open expanse of the larger picture. To be in tune with his appreciation of the broader context, consider the mental sharpness of a pair of nineteen year old clubbers staggering onto a British city street at three a.m.. Michael was only this much aware of what he had done.
"Are you alone?" said Michael.
We decided, of course, that Tim ought not to be alone; not because I thought His Headness might pull a gun or a blade, but for the most obvious of reasons.
"Yes."
"Have you spoken to anyone? Apart from Mrs...Mrs...?"
"Saviour, no. Not yet. I plan to, of course."
"Oh," said Michael. He was trying to remain calm, but an audible ejaculation of relief revealed his feelings. Then he made his pitch.
"Before you do, let me ask you something."
"Sure. Fire away."
"How would you like an immediate promotion? After Christmas, I mean."
"But I'm still in my first year of teaching; in my first term? It's not possible."
"Oh, it is. I'm the headteacher. I'm looking to give opportunities to young teachers anyway. I've already consulted the Chair of Governors. It's all going to happen, whether it's...it'll happen anyway."

He was lying. He wouldn't have spoken to Precision about the event.

"Like what? What promotion?"

"How about ICT co-ordinator for the English Faculty?"

"I don't know much about computers, I'm sorry."

"It doesn't matter. We can train you."

"Well..."

"How about I make you assistant to Elaine as chair of the New Vision committee? I can give you an allowance for that. Or how about co-ordinating a new initiative for gifted and talented students? That's about to happen. With your PhD, you'd be perfectly placed for a scenario like that."

His voice was running away like an overloaded lorry down a one-in-six. And getting higher. I could hear his breathing becoming heavier also. Tim was out-performing himself. His face, which I could see in profile, was a convincing wall of blank indifference that was clearly having the desired effect. Michael now found himself in a position of enormous difficulty. Events were unfolding more favourably than we had planned. He'd begun the game with a very limited hand and had played a Queen of trumps. But he had nothing to back it up with unless he was some kind of Lancy Howard.

"I'm not sure," said Tim, slowly, as if he was considering the offer with meticulous seriousness.

"But Mr. Peniston..."

"Michael."

"Michael. Why are you making me this offer? You honestly think I'm not going to tell anyone about what I saw?"

"Come on, now; any promotion you want; name it."

"Have you been in touch with Mrs. Saviour?"

Here Michael stumbled, his mouth full of doubt and a grossly swollen tongue, judging by the noises he was making.

"Nnn...yy...ww...I.I.I...wwee....gnn...I haven't yet. Why do you want to know?"

He wasn't the quickest car round the circuit, our Michael, but perhaps I was underestimating the pressure he was under.

"I want to know whether you've tried to buy her off. Is it money? Something from the school accounts you can make disappear with a little sleight of hand?"

"You really think I would try to bribe the stupid woman?"

"Sure, why not? I would if I were in your shoes."

"Would you?"

"Of course!"

"I haven't spoken to her; I rang her; she wasn't in."

"So you have tried to bribe her."
"No, to sympathize with my situation; to ask for her forgiveness."
"I think you'd better leave."
This was taking too long.
"What do you mean?"
"You tried to bribe her."
"I...I haven't."
"Okay, thanks for coming; it's time for you to go."
"Alright, alright, yes, I rang her to offer her something."
"Thank you. Now. Let's think of what else you might do for me."
"Okay..."
"How about something for Sefton Demmler?"
I could have garrotted him. He was trying to be clever. To put on a show for me, probably. I just wanted him to concentrate precisely on the job in hand. Then a pause.
"I have a lot of respect for Sefton. He's a fine, fine man. A great teacher."
The sound of a man groveling, and lying, is always excruciating.
"How about giving Sefton a promotion?"
"I...erm...such as what?"
"Deputy Head."
"I'm sorry, that's ridiculous..."
I nearly knocked a kitchen chair over. He was betraying his inexperience now, overplaying his hand dangerously and stupidly. If he didn't calm down, he would ruin everything.
"...how about head of Faculty? Would he take it?"
"What about Susan?" said Tim, his tone of voice pressing Michael now much too hard.
"What about Susan?"
"You mean she won't be staying?"
"She'll have to go if I stay."
"Really? Is that fair?"
"Tim, this is the real world. I can't afford to keep her. She'd have too much power over me. I can buy her with a fantastic reference: she could be a deputy head in a year with her brains and talent."
"Have you offered her money?"
Better, Timothy, better.
"No."
"Tell me the truth."
"No."

"Okay, that's it. I want you to leave. Now."

"Alright, alright. A couple of thousand pounds. But she wouldn't take it. I was being very stupid at the time. I…"

He was stuck.

"Okay, I believe you. But where will the money come from?"

"I have money."

"School money?"

"Of course not."

"But you could get some."

"What are you asking?"

"Twenty thousand pounds. For you to keep your job. And keep you out of the newspapers. I don't care how you get it."

"You obviously know nothing of school finance. Um..."

His breathing was becoming more and more laboured.

"Alright. Five."

A third pause. A long pause.

"Okay. I can get that."

"Alright. I've heard enough," said Tim.

This was our moment.

"Sefton!" he shouted.

I looked around at the table behind me where Jackie Saviour sat, looking as though she had been hit by an amnesia bomb, but I was sure even so that she had heard and understood every word. She came up to Peggy Lane from work just to look for her son's lost bag, but walked into this. She did not look well, but she was Nicole Kidman alongside Michael, who fell to his knees as we walked through into the drama. His hair was plastered to his head like a piece of wet cloth and his pale beige Princedom raincoat had dark stains on the shoulders and chest. He looked in need of a saviour himself.

"Hello, Michael," I said. "How the devil are you?"

"You!" he moaned, exhausted. "You......I should have known."

I smiled, which caused him to bow his head at the carpet. The gift had not been given to me to feel sorry for him. Instead, I watched Timothy go over to his mantelpiece. Behind a number of trinkets: an oil burner; a clock; two small, brightly coloured earthenware vases and a collection of three tiny elephants, he kept a framed photograph of himself with a girl. From behind this he retrieved a Richness Sonic 300.

"Rather decent tape recorder, Tim, is it not?"

"It has nothing less than the Hausfink Weltmike 2000 as standard, Sefton. A snip at $399.99."

"Michael," I said, "you deserve to be hosed down with horse shit. You're finished. Now get into your car and fuck off home. Apologies, Mrs. Saviour."

"It's quite okay, Mr. Demmler. 'A fucking prick' I'd have called him; but 'horse shit' will do fine."

We watched him as he grovelled to his feet, turned with the speed of an ancient tortoise and slowly made it to the door. He opened it, walked out into the rain and didn't bother to close it. I wouldn't have either. As his car moved away, the three of us looked at each other and simultaneously shook our heads, as if worked by a puppet master from above. Jezebel then came down the stairs to join us and only when we'd taken in her smile, wider than the Humber estuary, did we allow ourselves the pleasure of a group embrace, many smiles and a certain amount of laughter.

39

The Fairest of All Yarrow
Autumn Term - Week 8 Day 4
Thursday, October 31st, 2002
Peggy Lane Staff Room – Morning; afternoon ride to Measby

The first the staff knew of the Peggy Lane earthquake was next day, Thursday, as events began moving with the speed of a military coup. There was an emergency briefing of the staff first thing presided over by the school's *Eminence Trés Annoyant*, Peter Precision, and in person himself, Derek Clemenceau, the West Yorkshire Director of Education. I have to admit I felt something of a dude sitting there with all the usual faces, knowing every detail related to the startling facts that had caused this occasion to come about. I should have been sitting there moodily strumming a blues guitar in a pair of Keith Richard shades. Precision, in his pompous 'I Am the Voice of Yarrow' solicitor's drone, opened the ceremony saying,

"It is my sad duty to inform you that as of this morning, Michael Peniston is no longer the headteacher of this school."

The air reverberated with charged particles of shock. At this point you could have run up and down the staff room stark bollock naked shaking a dead monkey and no one would have paid you the slightest bit of attention. My colleagues listened in various gradations of disbelief. Over the course of the term Michael had been accepted as the new Head of State, King of the Peggy Lane lands, destined to rule 'til we were all dead, but he was suddenly gone, decapitated, toppled.

Precision, with a face like a miserable frog, looked up from his carefully prepared script, a document Clemenceau had probably pulled out of the drawer in his Leeds office for him, and observed our reaction briefly over half-moon spectacles. Experienced observers noticed the absence of his usual smugness.

"Michael has been found to have been in breach of the rules binding the conduct of any professional teacher, and this being so, he last night decided to offer the school governors his resignation, which we have accepted."

On the rapt faces around me it wasn't hard to discern many instant revelations of pleasure at Michael's demise, but I could easily have been feeding my own bias into the mix. I looked for Sef's monstrous delight but he was a photogenic study of the Sphinx, arms folded as usual, eyes studying his kneecaps. People looked at each other in silence. But as soon as the tall, dark-suited Clemenceau had tried to persuade us of the essentiality of our not talking to the press, and had asked us not to speculate on what Michael might have done, thus bringing civic proceedings to a close, the noise level rose to an immediate crescendo. The infamous 9GR would have been hard pushed to match it doing Drama on a Friday afternoon with Livvy Lovejohn. Top of the agenda was the rush to guess what foul misdeeds Michael had begotten. It was broken up much too soon by the bell for registration that called us once again like drones in the hive, but at break everyone was going at it hammer and tongs, so to speak.

"There's been a secret revolt by all the heads of faculty and heads of year to County, that's what it'll be," said Liam, who was practically prepared to lay down his life in defence of the plausibility of a backstairs rebellion.

"I'm telling you," he said, desperate to convince himself, if not us.

"I think they buckled under the heat Greenbattle put on them on account of all the trees that have had to be cut down since September, f-huh-huh," said Andy.

"You're quiet, you two," said Maurice, looking at Les Person and me, "sitting there on the sofa there, a pair of inscrutable Chinese. You know something, don't you."

"Oh, they're merely listening contentedly to the warp and weft of this delightful lunchtime symposium on Michael's premature exit. Do let them be, Maurice."

Sef had surprisingly joined us with his occasional cup of Mrs. Manicure's Grestcafé Continental and in fact was sitting back in leisurely fashion, fine dome shining, his own home-brought blue china cup resting on his knee like an afternoon cat.

"He was poking Susan in the shower after the match. That's all it was."

Sef's blue eyes momentarily flared up like an angry wave at Les, who sat there wearing his normal weasel-like deadpan mask. Sef had made it clear to The Plan Crew that we were to play completely dumb on the whole firework display. For Fiona's sake especially. But the response around the table was a roar of genuine laughter to which I thought it wise to contribute. No one ever did take Les seriously.

It wasn't long before some were trying to re-write their own history.

"I 'ated the bastard," said Rob at lunch time when the shocking news had sunk in somewhat.

"That didn't stop you trying to force your tongue down the back of his Dharmani trousers half the time," said economist Trevor Money, a rare visitor to this part of the kingdom.

"You what?"

"I've seen you at least twice this term sucking up to him: 'I'd like to take some students to Russia, headmaster, I think it'll be an excellent scenario for their ongoing development, headmaster.'"

Rob said nothing, but looked as though he wanted to eat Trevor's liver with a ladle full of fava beans and a good Chianti.

"Easy now, Trev. Just because you thought Michael was a bit of a sex God, doosn't mean you 'ave to take it out on poor Rob."

Jez's intervention produced more mirth round the table and the locked antler moment blew over, though Trevor was less than impressed with being put down by a youngster in public. He quickly took off with a folded copy of the pink *Finance Digester* under his arm.

"And I hope that's not Alex's *Morning Torygraph* you've got there, brother, f-huh-huh," called Andy, after him.

"He won't be back in a hurry," said Colin.

"Capitalist swine, eh, Colin? F-huh-huh," said Andy.

"He's right about you though, Rodder, don't deny it," said Maurice.

"I was only lookin' after meeself; nowt wrong wi' that," replied Rob. "And don't think I'm runnin' away – I'm goin' to the bog."

"Don't forget to leave some hairspray for me, brother, f-huh-huh," said Andy.

Jezebel was getting back to her old self. She looked my way and gave me the first proper smile I'd had in ages, eyes glittering again a little, cheeks pushing back the air pink with perky health. We didn't know how long it would be before the real reason for Michael's going became public knowledge, but it would leak out somehow. The only question was whether it would take hours, days or weeks. We wouldn't need to give evidence at any future hearing; that much we did know. Sef did the negotiating with Precision, who was desperate to keep the lid on the whole writhing mess, and thought he could, as if we'd phoned him the previous evening to report the scandal of Peggy Lane's headmaster failing to keep the school lawn in trim. He would have had a better chance of persuading Sef to dress up as a pizza and stand in the middle of Yarrow giving out promotional leaflets for a new takeaway. Murder, as someone once wrote, will have out. Especially these days, what with most people having no more scruples about betraying confidences than civil servants eager for another newspaper cheque.

'Impossible,' he'd told Precision on the phone. The C. of G. wanted to battle it out. 'He goes, it's as simple as that. Unless you want me to phone *The Daily Turd* and regale them with the whole story....No, I didn't think you would....Fine, okay then.'

Precision immediately contacted Clemenceau who within an hour had phoned Sef to have one final word before bowing to the inevitable. The only concession he got from us was our allowing Michael to resign before he could get the sack. But some of my happiness was tempered because of Susan: she would be going too. You could say what you like about her apparent lack of basic brain power, getting caught like that, but I would have still defended her as a good person. But why she'd hooked up with Michael defeated me.

"If you want to water your horses at McDoodles, you have to eat the ketchup," said Les sagely, and the others nodded.

"You ought to go on the stage, Les," I said.

"Funny you should say that," said Les, who smiled to himself happily. It was a day for stupid grinning.

"I'd like to fill that twat Precision's arse with gelignite and light it with a Molotov cocktail," said Liam, as if trying to plunge us all into a dark, gloomy place.

"Our esteemed Chair of Governors, Mr. O'Neil-Neil? Why so?" said Sef.

"He doesn't like the Irish."

"How d'yer noah?" said Jez, stifling a giggle.

"His sort never do," said Liam, before speculation began about who might step up into the vacuum left

"...by it transpiring - that means 'turning out,' Rob - that Michael's old chap was bigger than his brain," as Maurice expressed it.

The most satisfactory thing about the aftermath was the arrival of Chris in the staff room that lunchtime. During the same above-mentioned phone call, Sef effortlessly released Chris from bondage by telling Precision that if he wasn't, and quickly, he would be straight onto the news desk of every tabloid in the country. With the ball having landed at his feet six yards out and with the net gaping, Sef did not mess about. Or to move metaphors, he rammed the needle straight in the vein. There was no decision for the C. of G. to make: *The Turd* and *The Morning Shite* would have had an all-night party with the story if they got hold of it, and might yet. It didn't help Precision that Michael had from the first been very much his appointment.

Chris Lampeter slipped quietly through the door five minutes before afternoon registration and was practically mobbed before he could come over to us to sit down. He looked pale and had lost weight, but his smile did a good job of pushing aside the strain; eventually it would be wiped completely from his face.

"Christopher," said Andy, attempting to speak for most of the staff, if not all, "welcome back, mon frère. Let me say that only once did Colin say you were an arse bandit who deserved everything he got, f-huh-huh."

"Thank you, Andrew. Colin, thanks: I knew I could rely on you to let me down completely."

"You know me, Chris, always the supporter of the status quo."

"Crap band, Status Quo," said Rob.

"Detention for that joke, Rob, f-huh-huh." Andy Crucial's smile was a picture of profound glee, I noticed. Then it hit me. It was only the few of us who had been in on The Plan who had the doldrums upon them. I looked around the table, then the whole staff room, and all I saw were happy smiling faces. Hetty Kiss and Misty Wellbrowser were both cackling like witches who'd just downed a magnum of Champagne each. And the bods on the Science table: Loin; Barton-Jones; Waft; Bunsen et al, were making such a commotion at one point that Alun Christian-Grieves, the head of RE, had to tell them in no uncertain terms to pipe down, at which point they did, until his mouth busted into a loud laugh to show them it was just a wind up. The staff room was normally a more cheerful place at this time on a Friday, with the weekend about to be born, but it was never like this.

"How did you hear you were coming back?" said Liam.

"You mean, 'how did I get my job back,' Liam, don't you?"

"Er, yeah, I do actually. How did you g-get your job back?"

"Simple. I got a phone call from the Chair of Governors this morning to tell me that County were dropping the charges."

"Do you k-know why?" said Liam, whose nervous energy seemed to have got the better of him again. Chris looked down at the mug of coffee Mrs. M. had lovingly filled for him and thought about the question.

"I think it was that Mr. Doosen finally got it through to Precision that what I'd, um, done wasn't a problem to him; that he was happy for his son to be in my care. I'll have to find out whether he had to go to County Hall and beg on my behalf. Yes, I'll have to find that out."

There was an ecclesiastical quietness now as we regarded a Chris who seemed just a couple of thoughts away from breaking down.

"So there's no story of heroics and derring-do, then," said Andy.

"Not that I know of," said Chris.

"Coom on, lads, this is Peggy Lane: nothing like that happens round 'ere," said Rob.

"Too true, comrade, too true. Apart from Chris's team coming from behind to win in the last minute last night. Apparently they're gutted about Michael leaving, f-huh, huh."

We all smiled. "The way he was going he'd have ended up this season's top scorer."

"Your team weren't the only one who came from behind last night," said

Rob, triumphantly.

"Robin, that type of unreconstructed Tarbuckian rejoinder is simply not welcome in this staff room. Kindly reform yourself or go drink your coffee in the Sixth Form Common Room," said Sef, passing by.

"Is your name 'Robin'?" said an inquisitive Chris. "Fuck me, I never knew that."

And we all laughed, with Chris forgetting himself and suddenly spilling over with words, while Rob scowled like an England cricketer making yet another duck.

So Chris Lampeter was back, and all was restored at Peggy Lane.

40
Ferry Cross the Whardle
Autumn Term – Week 8, Day 4
Thursday, October 31st, 2002
Car to Measby – afternoon

Well, no, it wasn't. I was not alone in hoping it might be, so I could actually start to enjoy my teaching at the school, without all the horrors of The System watching over you like it was Russia in 1957. But we were 'dreaming' according to one expert I trusted. Sef drove me home that afternoon. I don't know about him, but I was hollowed out with exhaustion as much as I felt serene and exultant. And still there were questions, questions, questions.

"What'll Susan do now, do you think?"

"I shouldn't worry about her," said Sef turning the wheel effortlessly as we turned onto the road out of town and not swearing at the traffic for a change.

"When Susan went into teaching, there were other roads not taken."

Sef glanced at me slyly to see if I'd taken in the reference to the Robert Frost poem. I knew it.

"Two roads diverged in a yellow wood, and sorry I could not travel both..."

Sef nodded, looking not pleased, just straight through the windscreen, a little preoccupied again, maybe. But then at a set of lights he turned a very serious face towards me, was about to speak, stopped, and laughed. For the first time I could see how a much younger Sefton had once been in there. I wanted to hug him, though of course I didn't. I asked him what he expected to happen next at the school. I mean, had he, we, conquered not just Michael but what he stood for? Sef's light went out again; he gave me one of those looks I still feared. Like my knowledge of the world was a fleck of spume on the Atlantic Ocean.

"There will be another Michael. Perhaps not as crass or as stupid, nor as gung-ho, but he, or she ..." -.. and he looked at me for a micro-second, he was driving - "...will just be another Michael in a different suit. The old days have gone."

I fixed my gaze on his profile as we crossed the metal bridge over the Whardle, looking for the depth of his regret, but I only saw the ancient stare I now knew so well, out of a head as noble as something in marble in the cool, graceful Louvre.

"What 'old days'?" I said, innocently. I should have known better. He shot me a glance that said I should be trying a lot harder if I really was determined to get him to open up on my favourite theme.

"You don't bloody give up, do you?"

"Nope," I said.

"Listen. I could tell you about how in the past we could come into school, work hard, but have fun – with the kids and our friends. About how I used to walk out of my classroom and drop in on one of Maurice's sixth form lessons and talk to them about Titian for ten minutes, or listen to what they thought of Thatcher; then come back to mine and find Narida in there holding the fort. That essentially we were free because there was no such thing as 'management' or 'the hierarchy.' But it would be pointless – because those days are gone and aren't coming back."

The tone of his voice was flat dead with finality.

"So what is worth telling me, Sef?"

There was a long pause while we drove up the long slope out of Yarrow and over the rise into Measby. Sefton's face remained immobile, like a politician considering the inevitability of a coming war, but when we pulled into the curb outside Barney Plough's, he turned the ignition key and turned to me.

"That teaching is about love. It's what you should have to give those you teach and what you should have for your subject. And what you have for what you do and who you do it with. Will that do?"

There wasn't anything for me to say. Except that I couldn't see where love fitted in with targets, learning outcomes and New Vision committees.

"Look, let's change the subject. That world is gone. We all have to accept that. The question for people like us is how we respond to the way things are right now, in 2002."

As philosophically accepting as he sounded, he grimaced as though drinking bad coffee in august company and having to be polite and say it was good; the sort of thing that broke Sef in half.

"Come off it, Sef; 'respond to?' That's the sort of bland crap Michael would come out with. I know what you're doing – you're trying to stop me following you out of Peggy Lane."

For the first time I saw Sef – not defeated, but surprised – by something I'd said.

"Oh, yes? And how, pray did you get to be so bl-oody clever all of a sudden?"

"I've got a PhD to my name, haven't I - I think I've got it working at last."

"Huh," was Sefton's reply, though it was a shorter and more put upon grunt than that. 'Pitiful,' his face said, which only made me laugh. Then he spoke again.

"If I were you – though thank the Lord I'm not – I'd be shitting myself."

Oh, no, here we go.

"Why?"

"Because if you don't get in there and make me the best cup of steaming café Italiano in the whole of Yorkshire…"

Uh-oh.

"…I'm going to announce to the entire staff room on Monday morning that your prick is the size of a baby acorn. And they'll want to know how I became cognisant of the fact."

I was speechless, as you might expect.

"And I don't know why I ever drink that dog piss of Mrs. Manicure's; it always makes the roof of my mouth taste like the inside lining of a Turkish wrestler's jockstrap."

"A cliché at last, Mr. Demmler! O how are the mighty fallen."

It was high time I dropped the callow acolyte stuff.

"You still get the coffee, though: I guess you've done just about enough to deserve it." I nearly added, 'you big poof,' but thought I'd better not chance it.

"So kind of you, but you still have the test to pass. Then I have to get off: I'm delivering a lecture to the Philosophy department at Leeds University at seven o'clock entitled '*The Mind and the Power of Letting Go.*'"

The neurons fizzed, and in about a second and a half I was staring at him like a crazed junkie, my eyes out on stalks and about to flop on to my cheeks. He gave me a startling look in return, the eyes and mouth full of mischief.

"I'm kidding," he said. "I'm washing my hair."

41
Not So Much Lip
Autumn Term - Week 8, Day 5
Friday, November 1st, 2002
London, West End - Lunchtime

Sometimes you still feel programmed, like life is a conveyor belt you're on having just been coughed up by the big grey production machine. As if there's nothing much you can do to stop what's happening to you. Apart from anything else, every morning you're another day older and soon, enough days will pass for you to realise that actually you're not just a day older, you're "older." Sometimes the situation is so acute you find you've arrived at a place where you have no choice but to move on to a whole new stage in your life. It doesn't happen often but it will sooner or later - you can't fight it. There's school. A bunch of exams, then you have to leave. You pass on to university; more exams. You can put it off, but sooner or later you have to face up it: Manhood. Work. 'It's all right here in the computer, Mr. Weaver. Says here you're 28. You've managed to give us the runaround for quite a time, heh-heh. You've done rather well, you know. But joking aside, we can't delay this any longer: time for you to move on to the next part of your whole life.' One day someone will gently tap me on the shoulder and tell me it's time for the final stage. It's enough to make you want to blow all your wages on hookers. Just kidding. Ah, well, I did give 'em a good run for their money, didn't I. And I'm only 28 - God willing, a long way from the grave.

"You oakair?"

"Mmm? Yeah. I'm fine."

Jez and I were sitting in a little London square. One of those sweet green spaces I believe the city is quite famous for. It was ridiculously warm for the first day in November. And dry enough for us to sit on a bench with our sandwiches and cardboard cartons of hot coffee. Two pieces of cake were waiting at the end of the bench in a brown paper bag. It never seemed to rain any more in London but this was fine by me sitting amid the fallen leaves of the failing autumn. Winter well on the way now. Plunging towards the heart of my first year as a teacher, I was feeling less of an ear-dripping greenhorn even though I still knew nothing really about how to teach. To tell you the truth, as I chewed a sexy little chicken and avocado number, when I could put aside the dark side of the coin, which was often, I was proud just to be picking up the pay cheque. For the first time in my life I felt as if I'd earned every penny of that figure in its little box in the bottom right corner of the slip, the one just down from my National Insurance number - the slice of income tax to help the poor and pay for guns - and another one for something called 'superannuation.' I'd have to ask someone soon what this meant. Numbers to say 'you're a big boy now' - that Timothy Vespasian Weaver (Dr.) is a working man.

"What's 'Superannuation?'"

"'Er, yer pension."

"Oh yeah? That's nice. You know what 'superannuated' actually means?"

"Noah, but I'd have money on the fact that yewer dyin' to tell me. What doos it mean?"

"Too old to be of use."

"Thanks for that English lesson, Doc. Now would you take a look at these varicose veins?"

"You haven't got varicose veins…"

"Noah, 'course ah bloody 'aven't. Not that you'd noah what to do with one if it strangled yer. Doctor Weaver: I ask yer."

"You won't find me arguing with you." Jez had accommodated herself to a situation wherein I wasn't about to sing love songs to her under her window in the middle of the night by giving me a hard time sometimes. It was supposed to be obvious to me that she was joking but underneath, oh, underneath: I'll give you sub-text, my boy. A leaf of rusty brown fluttered down and landed on my left shoe but I was buggered if I was going to go all melancholy on myself today. What was the point? There was no point.

"Great sandwiches."

"Yeah."

Everything had indeed changed. No longer was I the hopeless innocent, the would-be pretender to the throne inhabited by the ghostly Steve. I was now the strong one in the partnership, the one with the whip hand. I sat forward in a position which always makes me feel comfortable: elbows on thighs, hands together in a prayer shape in front of my mouth, observing the day. I ate more sandwich and slurped some more coffee. Feeling good at last. The course is terrible. Some fool about 35 with a hideous goatee, grey cheeks and ridiculous words for us to take to our hearts if he had his way. Prattles on about 'strategies' and 'shared outcomes' and 'the classroom arena.' Where have I heard that before? If this is teaching I don't think I can remain in it long. If this is what it's about now. If this is the way it's going as people like Sef are saying, then I won't be able to stay. Not if they want me to be a slave to the 'fourth week of term so it's a handout about the role of Malvolio in Twelfth Night.'

Filling in grids and doing card-shuffling exercises as if the kids were fit only for jobs tending petrol stations. Not if I'm going to be surrounded, then tied up by the latest trendy jargon. Words almost empty of meaning except for those who wield them like sticks to beat us with. I'm turning into Andy and Colin, but you know what? It feels okay.

"The people who use these words aren't in proper control of their lives, Trap, so they, like, use them to exercise power over those below them in the, er, hierarchical chain of command."

If we aren't going to indulge in flights of fancy and soar in our imaginations over skies and buildings up into the stars then I'd rather go back to America and tend bar. Work in a shop. Shit, anything. Serve a beer and a shot and at least you're doing something honest instead of cheating children out of the chance to sit in warm classrooms expressing something from deep inside themselves; and hear stories from beyond the world they inhabit every day. Being cheated of their academic inheritance, if that isn't too preachy.

"What are you thinking about?" said Jez. "'e-yah, banana or carrot?"

"Giraffe."

"Don't be daft, you. You're turning into Les."

"Oh, can't I? Please," I pleaded, pushing out my bottom lip. If I have to leave teaching it's not the end of the world, is it? But I forgot - I can't go trolling off to the States unless I can take Safeena with me. Which I can't, because she can't leave her family. She told me on Sunday how close she was to her parents, her sister, her grandparents, her aunts and uncles, her cousins, friends of her parents, her mother's hairdresser's gibbon. Knitted together like a nylon spider's web. On and on went the connections torpedoing my hopes. This is a world I might never be able to enter. But she was so real on Sunday, her love burning so incandescently in the evening candlelight I knew for sure I was already inside part of her. Maybe I'll become the first white Muslim in my family. Shake up my mother who will instantly disinherit me.

"What ah you laffin' at? Not me I y'ope."

"No, no. Don't be silly. Would I?"

Jez and I were now forever linked by her afternoon of tears. Like seeing someone naked, making love to them even, once two people cross a dramatic bridge like that they can never go back, neither separately nor together. That event was such a bridge. Maybe I was really now an equal, a partner, a benign brother to her. Really, I didn't want to be her superior. I wanted nothing from her now, so I was free; free to like her, to enjoy her company.

"I'm sorry about Sunday. I really am. I didn't mean to do that to you."

"That's the third time today, unless I can't count. Stop it. You've absolutely noothin' to apologize for." She had her 'posh voice' on, as I liked to call it. I was already teasing her about it in school. I looked at her and felt pulsing warmth leaving me and reaching out across the air towards her.

"It's important to open up and cry, Jez. So few of us can do it, and it's healthy. I can't do it – guys, blokes can't. Be glad that you did. It'll save you."

"I felt like a prize idiot."

"No. You were just being human." I bit into this slab of yellow sponge with soft gunk oozing across the top, courtesy of the Eat It and Weep chain that was farting out branches all over the capital. They weren't around when Janey and I were together, when we used to sit in places like this. It was good cake though.

"Are you and...and Safeena. I don't want to ask."

We'd avoided all this on the train. We left on the 7.47.am and hadn't been awake enough to do anything but grunt at each other until Stevenage burst past the carriage window a couple of hours later. Then we met the frantic hurly-burly of the tube; then it was the course. *New Possibilities For New Teachers: An NQT Top-Up Day.* After being on the receiving end of more bullshit than a vet inspecting a male cow's arse it was unnerving to be required to talk properly to another human being.

"Jez, I don't know. It's early."

"Don't worry. Lewk, I'm going to come clean. I do like you, but ah've no idea about how I feel about anything really, so don't worry. I'm not gonna be phonin' yer in the middle o' the night crayin' or owt daft like that. All I do know is that ah need to ditch Steve. Ah've been with 'im since I was 14, so gettin' over all o' that'll be enough to keep me occupied for a few months. Then, if you're still with Safeena, fair enoof. Good luck to you. You deserve someone nice."

"Jezebel, you really aren't as dumb as you look."

"Uh!" she said in 'how dare you' surprise.

I smiled, still jamming the last piece of Jim Blake into my mouth and reaching for another gulp of strong, sweet coffee.

"And by that time, let's face it, there'll be someone else. You'll never be short of admirers, Jez. You know that."

"I don't noah about that."

"Get out. You're a great looking chick."

"And you're still a pretentious wanker. You and your 'chick' - you're about as American as Kellogg's bloody cornflakes."

"Er, actually..." But I didn't have the heart to tell her. I was a smart enough butt-end as it was.

I realised that this was the first time in my life that I'd told a girl she was good to look at without being drunk, stoned or on the verge of asking them out. What a relief. Always the game-playing with girls – women now; always the measuring out of words like grains of precious mineral. Every syllable calibrated with the precision of a bomb maker. A probing semi-compliment here, a suggestive raise of the eyebrow there, over words whose true meaning was always carefully disguised. It's a wonder we're not all sprouting tumours every fortnight with the stress of it all.

"Hey, look - remember I've got friends who really talk like that."

Getting helplessly plastered, to hungrily mouth-slobber with another human as a prelude to cold fucking, was nothing short of cheating. It was nothing short of disgusting actually. I'd done it, just a little - most of my generation had and as far as I could make out, those coming of age just behind me were screwing like back alley-mongrels the night before the Apocalypse. I couldn't go back in that direction. Jez still looked awfully lovely, but we'd crossed a Rubicon and started to make a 'v' across the landscape. The time I had with Safeena had insulated me from her charms. I'd laid my mat down at someone else's door now, and that was that until further notice. Of course there would be others for Jez. Her big danger was the rebound, not loneliness. She would draw people to her like Third World floods invite cholera. I went 'ouch' with jealousy in a tender spot to think about it, I admit that. My passion for her had still to ebb away completely, but it would, or lay dormant like a volcanic fissure in the igneous rock of my soul.

"What yer laffin' at now?"

"Modern fiction. Hey, we'd better be getting back."

"What's the time?"

"Twenteh-past."

"Right. It's only five minutes walk. We'll be okay."

"God, I y'ate Loond'n."

"Jez, don't be such a woolly back!"

"Don't bloody call me a woolly back, just coz you went to bloody Loond'n Universiteh like the spoiled git that you are."

"You sound like those girls from Byker Grove. 'Fat cow that ch'are!'"

"I'd do some more work on that accent if ah were you...Did you see that programme...The Office when it was on?"

"Of course."

"Doesn't Roger remind you of David Brent?"

"A bit. The girl who introduced him looked like a fat Posh Spice."

"No! She looked like a fat Sandra Bullock...I y'ate all those actresses. Workin' out the 'ole bloody time just to lewk like a lead pencil. Meks me feel like ah've gorran arse like a giant jelly."

"Looks to me more like a vat of thick custard poured into an empty parachute."

"Fook off, you!"

We didn't want to move yet. It was too nice sitting here in the capital sunshine.

"God, I'm way behind wi' me markin'."

"Me too, don't worry."

"I want implants like Trix Trixeter. Do you think they'd suit me?"

"You get lip implants and I'll pull them out again with my bare hands."

"Ooh, he-man."

"You look fine as you are."

"Anyway, I can't have lip implants: it'd interfere with me career plans. I'm going to be a Nedmistress one day. 'Now, girls! Here are the notices.' Tekkin' assembly. Can you imagine it?"

"Yeah. You'll insist on having tripe and onions on the menu for lunch every day."

"Yer not foonny."

"And Tripe burgers. Black pudding and custard."

"Get lost!"

"Ow!"

Chicks. I'm beginning to love 'em.